SKINHEAD

SUBCULTURE CRIME SERIES. BOOK I

SIMON WELLINGTON

SKINHEAD

TABLE OF CONTENTS

Part One..**5**

Chapter 1 7

Chapter 2 28

Chapter 3 45

Chapter 4 61

Chapter 5 78

Chapter 6 89

Chapter 7 111

Chapter 8 138

Part Two **155**

Chapter 9 157

Chapter 10 174

Chapter 11 184

Chapter 12 198

Chapter 13 207

Chapter 14 217

Chapter 15 228

Chapter 16 243

Chapter 17 253

Chapter 18 264

Chapter 19 277

Chapter 20 291

Chapter 21 304

Part Three..**309**

Chapter 22 311

Chapter 23 317

Chapter 24 326

Chapter 25 351

Chapter 26..363
Chapter 27..373
Chapter 28..385
Chapter 29..395

Help Us **425**
Subculture..**427**

PART ONE

CHAPTER 1

"Mark! How are you?"

A sultry voice came from behind him. He turned around to an eyeful of tight sweater and tighter pants.

"Karen! Hi!" He'd had the hots for her all last year and seeing her now, on the first day of school, he decided she'd only become more desirable over the summer.

"Feeling adventurous, Mark?"

"Huh?" He'd fantasized about her a thousand times—him and probably every other guy in grade ten at Gibson High—but she'd never talked to him before, except a few times about homework or something else to do with school.

"I hear you guys started a band." She moved into his personal space and placed her index finger on his chest. "You want to come over tonight and tell me about it?"

The finger began drawing small circles on his shirt, and he could feel the blood pumping into his groin. Karen Hemmingway was a stunner. He let his eyes wander from her short blond hair, down over her large, firm breasts, to the flat belly that merged into wide hips. He could see the bulge of her pubic mound through the skin-tight pants. When he looked back up to her face she was smiling in a way that told him she had welcomed his survey.

But why was she suddenly interested in him? "I don't know if you'd like the kind of stuff that we play to be honest. We play mostly oi, ska, and some reggae stuff too."

"Is that some kind of punk rock?" She asked while her finger traced a line down from his chest almost to the top of his pants. "I've never made it with a musician before."

The blood was still trying to push his dick out of his pants; his facial expression didn't change, but his mind turned off. She didn't give any more of a shit about him now than she had last year. She was just looking to cut another notch in her gun belt.

He looked around. He was standing on the front steps of the high school. It was the first morning of the first day of his junior year. 1998. If someone had told him that he'd be starting grade eleven with a sexual invitation from Karen Hemmingway, he'd have wondered what they were smoking.

"I don't think so, Karen. I'm too busy right now. But thanks for the offer."

He could hardly believe his own words! He'd been dreaming of losing his cherry for as long as he could remember, and most of his fantasies involved the girl who was offering herself to him right now. How could he be turning her down?

She stopped tracing circles on his chest and looked into his eyes. "Nervous, Mark? I'll do things that'll make you forget all about being nervous." She was steadfast in her position and body language.

His mouth was so dry he could hardly speak. "Um, I'm sorry. I just…" He let the words trail off. He was sweating bullets. His body was screaming at him to rip off all her clothes and jump on her right there, on the front steps of the school, but his mind was telling him that all she was interested in was another trophy for her collection.

"Why?" she asked. "What's wrong with the two of us getting it on tonight? You're not gay, are you?" she continued.

"No, I'm not gay." That question angered him—not the gay part, but the part that implied that there must be something wrong with him if he didn't jump when she whistled. "Just because I don't want to jump your bones doesn't make me gay." He took a step upwards, towards the school entrance and away from her. "Maybe I just don't automatically want what you want."

"Bullshit, Mark Heaney! I've seen you drooling over me practically every day for the last two years. What's the matter with you now?"

"Okay, fine." Mark was getting angry. Why couldn't she just take a polite 'No' for an answer? "I don't want to make it with you because you're a society queen. Today you want to screw a musician, but tomorrow, or as soon as your pimple-cream friends get bored with you telling them about it, you'll drop me like a sack of hot potatoes and start jumping on somebody else's pole." He backed away another step. "I don't need that kind of shit."

For a second, she didn't accept what she'd heard. But once it hit her, she went red with furious anger. "Fuck you. You probably *are* gay." She took a step upwards toward him, throwing her shoulders back so that her huge breasts were practically in his face. "And just in case you're not, take a good look at what you could have had, and then go somewhere and jerk yourself off, because you're never going to get another chance, you stuck-up prick!" She poked him hard in the chest and stormed off into the building, giving him the finger as she disappeared through the big doors.

He realized that he was trembling. Part of it was anger at her self-centered assumption that he would jump through whatever hoop she held up, but it was mostly desire. Why had he turned her down? Hadn't he been dreaming for two years about exactly what she had just offered? Hadn't he jerked off about a million times thinking about her?

He snorted aloud with disgust. He should be angry with *himself* for wanting to have anything to do with such a shallow scalp-collector.

But what a body! He couldn't stop thinking about it. He tried to focus on the blue sky. The friends he hadn't seen over the summer. The classes he would be taking this year. The hard martial-arts workouts he'd done with his father. The car he'd been saving up for. But nothing could clear his mind of the thought of running his hand over those gorgeous breasts, and on downward until his fingers found what was waiting below.

Holding his backpack in front of him so no one would notice the wood she'd given him, he tried to look casual as he entered the school and headed for the nearest bathroom. Once the door closed behind him, and he was sure no one else was present, the casual air disappeared and he almost ran to the first stall. He locked himself in the stall and grabbed his dick.

Thirty seconds later, much relieved, but also feeling disgusted with himself for being so turned on by such a trashy slut, he zipped up and went looking for his homeroom.

Grade eleven. Would it be much different from grade ten? How different *could* it be? Same old school—dirty old pile of bricks called Gibson High. Same old useless shit about history and math. Who cared? If only they had courses in music: not choir, or folksongs or some stupid shit like that—but something really different.

He looked at the course list he was carrying. At least automotive shop might be fun. And English wouldn't be *too* bad, with Mrs. Bates as his teacher. He didn't care too much about most of the things that you were supposed to learn in school, but Mrs. Bates made reading and writing interesting. She'd been his English teacher in grade nine, and somehow she'd managed to make him work hard and enjoy it. He wasn't very good at it, but she seemed to appreciate his effort.

Even the social side of school kind of sucked. A lot of kids were really into that. Cheerleaders, he called them, even if they weren't actually on one of the cheerleading squads. Karen Hemmingway was a perfect example. She could be president of the "Cool Fashion of the Month Club", and it pissed him off that he didn't know how to control himself around her. Still, there were a few kids who looked and acted like they actually *were* seriously cool and he hoped that this year he'd be able to hang with them.

And maybe, finally, he could get laid, too. Which made him think that turning Karen down hadn't been the smartest thing he'd done lately.

The first class in his homeroom was social studies. Stupid name. Why didn't they just call it history? And if history wasn't bad enough, the teacher, the one who was going to be his homeroom teacher the whole year, was a total prick. A fat little Nazi called Mr. Barker who obviously got his rocks off by intimidating girls.

Mark had heard rumors about that but figured they were exaggerated like every other rumor that went around the school. Not this time. If anything, the guy was worse than the stories made him sound. Maybe he hated girls because he was so dumpy-looking that no woman would look at him. Or maybe he was some kind of closet transvestite who hated himself. Who knew? What was for sure was that within ten minutes of the start of class, Barker had done his best to make three of the girls feel like shit.

Chalk up another score for good old Gibson High School—armpit of Vancouver's education system. The shithole where all the teachers no other school wanted wound up.

Once textbooks were handed out and Barker had finished establishing the fact that he was far superior to any seventeen-year-old female, he started in on some shit about the Industrial Revolution and how it changed things in England. England? Who gave a fuck what happened in England a hundred years ago? Or two hundred, or whenever the fucking Industrial Revolution was. Why couldn't high school teach less garbage that no one would ever need to know anyway and more stuff that was actually useful?

He tuned it all out and started thinking about the new songs that he and Bruce were working on, tuning back into school only when the bell rang and he could escape to the hallways and go looking for his new locker, and then on to the next class—English with Mrs. Bates. Mrs. "Old School" Bates who was tiny, as well as old, but who could somehow keep even the toughest kids in line in a way that none of the other teachers in this gang-infested school could.

She didn't waste any time. No introductory junk about welcome to grade eleven English, or about rules and regulations, she just ordered everyone to start writing about someone who had influenced them that summer—two pages, double spaced, and thirty minutes to finish.

While they wrote, she handed out textbooks, greeting the students she knew already by name and getting names from those who were new to her. When the half hour was up, she had them pass their papers to their neighbors for grammar and spelling checks, then start on their final copies.

At the end of the class, Mark headed for his locker to put his books away, before joining the herd in the cafeteria. The hallways were full of students. Some had ghetto blasters playing low, some sat in groups on the floors, a few sat on their jackets, reading novels, while others looked like they were in a hurry, pushing through the crowds as if there was something important just waiting for their attention.

Mark wondered what that could be, as he made his own way to lunch. All they could be headed for was the cafeteria or their homes, and neither of those places was worth pushing and shoving to get to.

The cafeteria seemed even less worth hurrying to this year. Especially today, when the first thing that happened when he walked in was Karen Hemmingway, who he hadn't noticed coming up behind him, whispering "Asshole" in his ear as she pushed past.

The cafeteria was huge—seating for four hundred people, easy—but it had to be about the worst place to eat that he could imagine. It was noisy, smelly, and uncomfortable; the lineup moved at a snail's pace. Of course the food sucked, so maybe the overall atmosphere of ugliness was perfectly suitable.

Waiting in the food line, he wondered about the students on the other side of the counter, serving and bringing in more freshly processed slop. They were juniors and seniors who had opted for food services as a prep class. Why would anyone want to take a class in 'How to Work in a Restaurant'? The compulsory classes were pretty much all boring and useless, so why not at least pick something decent for your option? Mark had chosen auto shop as his preparatory class.

After paying for a shrimp salad sandwich and a side of fries, he had enough of the lunch money his mother had given him remaining for a can of Tahiti Treat—his favorite soda. Once that was on his tray with the food, he looked around for a place to sit. The table he and Bruce had sat at most of last year was totally packed with a bunch of dipshits in full grunge: lumberjack shirts, baggy pants, and every one of the guys trying to look like his last shave was exactly three days ago.

They probably all figured Nirvana was the greatest band in the history of the universe, and he was willing to bet his shrimp salad that none of them had even *heard* of 'ska' or 'oi'. But they *would* hear about them both, that was one thing that Mark knew for sure. There was room for a lot of different kinds of music in a person's life, but once you heard the unmistakable ska sound live, there was no way you could not want to hear more of it. It was a great type of music to dance to.

He looked around, trying to find Bruce, and then settled for an empty table near the door when he couldn't see him. Munching on his sandwich, he wondered what the kids in food services would do in a real restaurant, where people who paid them for a shrimp salad sandwich would actually want it to taste like something other than soggy cardboard. Oh well, it was calories, and cheap, so no sense worrying about it. He let his hand and mouth go on autopilot and checked out the girls who were standing in the food line.

A lot of them were in grade eight or nine, but there were plenty that looked to be close to his own age, and even though most of them probably hung out with groups that he wasn't part of, there was still a reasonable selection of good lookers. Maybe this would be the year after all.

He picked out two who looked especially interesting and was starting on a fantasy about both of them at once when his thoughts were invaded by the noise of four guys, seniors by the look of them, pulling up chairs and sitting at the table. He didn't know any of them, and they ignored him completely, talking and joking among themselves as if he didn't exist. They looked like greasers, or maybe gang types; definitely not part of any scene Mark wanted a part of, so he ignored them in return and was about to go back to his sexual fantasy when he heard his name being called.

"Hey, Mark."

"Hey yourself, little brother."

"Bigger than you, dickwad."

It was true. His brother Donny was a little over a year younger, but already taller than Mark and showing no signs of slowing his growth.

"Taller maybe, but too skinny to be worth noticing."

"Yeah? Well, at least I ain't as dumb as you." Donny sat down beside him and started in on his lunch. "Some pretty girls around here, eh?" he said around a mouthful of food.

"Yeah right, like any of them is going to look twice at some human skeleton like you," Mark replied in an authoritative tone.

"Get fucked, baldy! You ain't even got hair on yer head. What the hell would you know about girls?"

"More than you, babyface!" Mark answered.

"Yeah right, get fucked is all I can say," Donny laughed and went back to filling his face and smiling contentedly as he stared into the mass of tight jeans and sweaters.

Mark ran his fingers over his head and felt his short hair. His mother had given him a number-three-guard cut over his entire head. It was easy to manage and he thought it looked good on him. Pretty much the opposite of his younger brother, who wore a thick, wavy, James Dean hairstyle. Opposite in a lot of other ways, too. Donny dressed like the skaters he hung with—loose T-shirt, baggy trousers with a chain wallet, and low-top runners—while Mark went for Fred Perry short-sleeve shirts, Rangers or Doc Marten boots, and Dickey pants with one-inch cuffs; and he hung with the few other skins he knew, plus a few kids who were still into punk.

A lot of them weren't too cool though, and Mark was seriously hoping that with the growth of the skinhead and punk rock movement in Vancouver, there'd be some new friends in the future. Still, there was always Bruce, and nobody could ask for a cooler best friend than Bruce Kellite.

Donny finished his meal, pushed his tray aside, stood up and gave Mark a fast slap on the back of the head, jumping back before Mark could retaliate. "See ya later, baldy."

He might be skinny, but he was fast. Their father trained them both in the martial art of defendo, and Donny knew how to make a slap really sting. Mark knew he could take Donny anytime—he was heavier, stronger, two years more experienced, and just as fast—so he just laughed and said, "Up yours, babyface."

With his brother gone, Mark tuned in to the fact that the four other guys at the table were staring at him and cracking jokes. What was up?

"You got a problem?" Mark blurted out defiantly. "You shouldn't be eating with freshmen."

"Is that right? Is that some new rule around here?"

"A senior who hangs out with freshmen?" The mouthiest of the four laughed out loud. "You some kind of loser that no one else will hang out with or something?"

"Maybe he's got a thing for little boys," hooted one of the others.

"Piss off, greaseball. That freshman is my brother and I'll talk with him any time I fuckin' well please!" Mark backed his chair away from the table to give himself room to move. He didn't think they were looking for anything more than an easy target for some intimidation, but if any of them did want action, Mark was going to be fully ready for it.

One of the first lessons his father had taught him was that the best way to avoid trouble was to make it clear that you weren't going to back down—that anybody looking to lay some hurt on you was going to get himself hurt.

When none of them made any move for him, he stood up, gave them one final stare, and said, "I'll be around if you want to discuss the matter further."

"Count on it!" responded one of them, but Mark could tell by the tone of his voice that it was just talk, that there wasn't going to be any action coming from these wimps; so he walked away.

With time still left in the lunch hour, and no sign of Bruce, he thought he might as well take a walk around the school, see if anything had changed in the old shitpile. Down the long hallways, up the stairs, around the corners, he checked out all four floors, but all he saw was the same old ugly place. There were lockers along both sides of all the halls. The lockers were dull gray, the floors were shiny with wax, and the endless line of fluorescent lights in the ceilings turned the whole place into an institutional hell.

There wasn't much graffiti, but it was only the first day of school, and that would soon change. The gangs would see to that.

Bored and depressed by the endless, ugly hallways, Mark headed for the nearest door. The rear of the school was mostly just paved parking, but he could see who was hanging out, and at least there would be sunshine.

And skaters. There must have been twelve or fifteen of them ripping back and forth across the lot, hopping curbs, some even grinding their boards down handrails. Donny was good at that kind of thing. Thanks to the martial arts training they were both getting from their father, they had great coordination, and, for his age, Donny was a terrific boarder. Mark looked for him, and eventually saw Donny sitting on the grass at the edge of the lot, talking to three girls. 'Nothing changes in our family,' he thought as he moved on, checking out the scene.

Under the trees, between the parking lot and the sports field, was the hangout of the punk rockers and the goths. Some sitting, some standing, and almost all smoking. The music coming from their boomboxes was okay, better than a lot of the stuff he heard around the school, and some of the girls were worth looking at despite the huge amounts of eyeliner they all wore. Still, it would get depressing hanging around with a girl who never wore anything but black, and he kept on moving.

Rounding the corner was like moving to Asia. About a third of the student population at Gibson was Chinese, and this part of the school grounds was their turf. There wasn't much racial violence at the school, and nobody was likely to tell him to fuck off if he stopped or talked to some of the Asian kids, but still, there were a lot of Asians that only hung out with Asians, and this was where they congregated.

There were a lot of East Indians, too. They tended to mix more with the whites, though, so they weren't as noticeable. They also tended to dress more like whatever group they hung out with, whereas the Asians' idea of style was dyed-blond hair and brand-new jeans and puffy jackets in either black or silver. Expensive shit.

'Then there's me.' thought Mark. Lots of whites, lots of Asians, lots of East Indians, even plenty of blacks and Native Indians. But he was one-of-a-kind. How many other kids in the school were descended from Maori head-hunters? Well, Donny, of course, but Donny was tall, skinny, and light-skinned, like their mother; not stocky and dark like Mark and their father.

It had never been much of an issue. There were so many races and ethnic groups at Gibson that nobody made much of a deal of it, but Mark had always been sort of proud of his father's heritage, even if it didn't have much impact on his daily life. Proud too, of his father's career as a soldier in one of the world's elite regiments, the SAS.

As he re-entered the main floor of the school and walked down towards his locker to get his gym clothes, he thought about the fact that most of the kids in the school were a lot more passionate about their subculture allegiance than they were about what race or ethnic group someone was from. And the way they announced their feelings about subculture was through their clothes. High school was a fashion show, and kids spoke through their clothes to anyone who was on the same wavelength as them. Mark himself was no exception. Skinhead fashion was starting to get popular, and Mark did his best not to fall behind.

But right now the clothing that was important was his gym clothing. His P.E. teacher this year was going to be the school's rugby coach, a big, muscular man named Calahan, who looked like a life-size version of G.I. Joe. He had the reputation of being pretty reasonable if you didn't cross him, but tough as nails if he felt you weren't putting out your best effort. Mark didn't want to get off to a bad start by being late for his first class of the year, so he grabbed his gym stuff from his locker and half walked, half ran, for the changing room.

In the locker room, the conversations were all about who had tried to shag what girl over the summer, and who had succeeded. A couple of bigmouth fuckheads that Mark had had run-ins with in the past were loudly claiming that they had scored big time, but he figured that anything that would screw Christian Begotti or Sergio Verras probably had four legs, so technically they were probably both still virgins, just like he was.

He wondered what the response would be if he said something like, "Karen Hemmingway said she wanted me to fuck her, but I told her she wasn't good enough for me." Probably no one would believe him, so he kept his mouth shut, and looked around, wondering who the unlucky one would be, the one Christian and Sergio would try to torment to-day—that's the kind of guys they were, bullies who got their rocks off by finding someone too small or weak to stand up to their hazing.

The class turned out to be co-ed, which was cool. Not only would there be girls to look at, but it also meant that this wouldn't be one of the killer workouts that Calahan was famous for.

Calahan told them that this first class was going to be a run, and started them all off with some serious stretching. Most of the guys, and even some of the girls, had big problems with that. About as flexible as two-by-fours, Mark thought, except that two-by-fours were thin and strong, and most of the lumps in this class were anything but. He relaxed and went into the meditative state his father had taught him to enter when he stretched, and let himself flow into the movements.

After the stretching was over, Calahan gave them the run route and some instructions about technique. As he talked, Mark looked around to see if he could spot Sergio and Christian's likely victims.

It wasn't hard to do. There were girls with braces, there were a couple of really fat kids, but one nerdy-looking kid stood out—a perfect target for the two slimeballs—and Mark decided to hang back a bit and do what he could to protect him.

A few blocks after they left the school grounds, the route took them into a park with a lot of trees, and since that was the only place not out on the streets, in full view of passing traffic and pedestrians, Mark knew that was where the fun would take place. As they approached, he saw Sergio and Christian sprint ahead of everyone, and he knew he was right.

He let them go, and, pretending he had a cramp, slowed to a walk and let everyone else pass him, not starting again until the nerdy kid was about half a block ahead.

It was hard to run as slowly as the nerd, but he forced himself to go slowly, and sure enough, as he turned into the trees, he heard the kid yelling. He sped up and rounded a corner just in time to see the two who thought they were so tough shoving the little guy off the trail and into the creek that ran through the park. They were watching their victim, unaware that Mark was coming up behind them. Without breaking stride, he grabbed them both by the backs of their shirts and heaved as hard as he could, sending them tumbling into the brambles that lined the other side of the trail, then stopped and helped the nerd out of the creek.

"You guys need some help getting out of the old briar patch?" he asked sweetly, as the bullyboys struggled to free themselves from the wickedly sharp blackberry thorns.

They were bleeding and cursing, and the kid that Mark had saved from further torment was obviously scared, but Mark stood his ground, saying nothing, but sucking big breaths in and out, priming his body with oxygen, ready for whatever came his way.

"You guys wanna dance, or are you just going to lay around in the bushes?" It was too much for Sergio Verras. He tore himself free of the brambles, losing skin and blood in the process, and came up swinging. Without even thinking, Mark stepped outside the punch, pushing Sergio's arm, then his shoulder, until he was completely turned around and out of balance. A gentle push in the middle of his back sent him tumbling back into the blackberry brambles, right on top of Christian.

He turned to the smaller boy who had gone into the creek and said, "I don't think they'll bother you anymore, but I..."

"Now just what the hell is going on here?" The interruption was in the gruff voice of the gym teacher. He looked even bigger out of his street clothes, and just as Mark was starting to think he might be in trouble, the nerdy kid spoke up.

"I slipped, sir, and fell in the creek. These guys," he pointed to Christian and Sergio, who were struggling to stand up without tearing themselves up too badly, "they tried to help me, but they slipped themselves." He gestured toward Mark. "He and I were just about to help them up."

Calahan looked at him, standing in his wet shorts and T-shirt, and at Mark, who was doing his best to bottle up a laugh. "Tried to help you, did they?" Calahan knew exactly what had happened, but all he said was, "Well, you can thank them later, but right now I think you should get back to the school for a shower and some dry clothes." He turned to Mark, "You can go along with him and make sure he doesn't catch a cold."

He reached a hand down and pulled first Sergio, then Christian up out of the bushes. "I guess you guys deserve a medal for helping the poor guy up out of the creek. I'll see if I can find one for you after class, but in the meantime," his voice hardened, "get your asses in gear."

The two shot venomous glances over their shoulders at Mark as they headed off, and he knew that he'd bought himself some trouble for the future. Calahan wouldn't be there next time, and he resolved to get even more serious about his defendo training.

"Thanks, man, that was a seriously cool thing to say," Mark said to the smaller boy as they jogged back toward the school.

"It was the least I could do. You saved my ass for sure. They were going to come down and beat me up. They said so, just before you got there. Cheesy fuckers." The swearing sounded weird coming from such an academic-looking kid.

"What's your name?"

"Andrew Kolstrum."

"I'm..."

"You're Mark Heaney, right? I mean, I don't know you or anything, but I heard your name. Somebody said you were in a band. I don't know anything about that, but the way you dress, I could hardly not have seen you around." Andrew looked at Mark more seriously. "I thought that you were a skinhead. How come you helped me out?"

"I can't be a skinhead and a decent human being at the same time?"

"But I thought..."

"That skins were just violent white-power Nazis?"

Andrew Kolstrum stopped and caught his breath. He was too far out of shape to jog and talk at the same time. "Well, yeah, I guess so. Is that wrong?" Mark shook his head in frustration.

"Look at me. The only use the white power groups have for people like me is fuel for bonfires." He put his dark brown arm alongside Andrew's pale white one. "Skinhead has nothing to do with white power. Okay?"

He started jogging again, slowly so that Andrew could keep up. "Some of the white power types have started shaving their heads, but that doesn't make them skinheads. Shit, man, you're wearing running shoes and shorts, does that make you an athlete?" He looked at Andrew, sucking wind just to keep up a slow jog. "I don't fuckin' think so. Skinhead is about a whole lot more than how you wear your hair."

"But…"

"Don't worry about it. Those two slimeballs got what they deserve, and anyway we're back at school, so take your shower and don't worry about it." Since he hadn't worked up a sweat himself, Mark didn't shower, just changed into his street clothes and headed upstairs to his locker. The rest of the afternoon was going to be spent in Automotive shop, but since he was back early from P.E. he grabbed the coveralls his father had given to him, and headed outside to sit by himself and think about what was rapidly turning into the weirdest school day of his life.

First, he'd not only been propositioned by the girl of his dreams, but *he'd turned her down…* The first was almost beyond belief, the second was clear evidence that he was totally insane!

Then there'd been the lunch-hour choirboys. Trying to haze him about sitting with a freshman. What the fuck was *that* about? What was this school coming to that people tried to pick fights with you because you sat with someone in a different grade? And what a bunch of losers— four of them, and he'd backed them down.

And finally, the confrontation with Sergio and Christian. Heaving the two stooges into the blackberry thorns had seemed like the right thing to do at the time, but he knew he'd made a couple of serious enemies. Maybe more than a couple. They had friends, and being cowards, they'd undoubtedly be looking to get Mark in a four-on-one or five-on-one, which was not something he could afford to laugh about. Sergio and Christian and their friends might be cowards at heart, but they were a lot bigger and stronger than the choir-boys he'd faced down at lunch. They'd put a kid in hospital last year, and they wouldn't back off if enough of them caught him alone.

"Not much I can do about it," Mark said to himself as he headed back inside to the last class of the day. "Just watch my back, I guess."

Automotive Shop was going to be doubly good. First, it was something he was really looking forward to. He was more interested in scooters and motorcycles than in cars, but shit, an engine was an engine, and maybe if he learned enough he'd be able to find an old scooter somewhere and fix it up. And second, Bruce Kellite, his best friend, was taking the same class.

After what had happened so far today, time with a friend was definitely needed.

Besides being a friend, Bruce was one talented kid. His father was a studio musician, a session guitarist who had played guitar with the best musicians in the country for years. Bruce was following in his footsteps. Like Mark, he was only seventeen, but he was a wicked guitarist who could already lay down Ventures or Dick Dale riffs better than the originals, and was definitely going to be a legend someday.

On the way to class, Mark reflected on how lucky they were to have fathers like they did. Scott Heaney, Mark's father, was as different from Larry Kellite as coffee was different from tea; but they were definitely the same when it came to how they cared about their families and how they did their best to give their sons all the help in life that they could.

His introduction to Automotive Shop was not what he expected. The teacher, a middle-aged guy named Nickolayison lined them all up against the far wall and said, "I'm gonna consider myself a failure as a teacher if you people don't have fun in my class, but before we even *look* at a car, there is one fundamental rule that every one of you has to get straight right now." He stared at them hard to make sure they were going to commit what he said to memory. "We're gonna be dealing with some heavy pieces of metal, with electricity, and with some dangerous tools and my one rule is that anybody who doesn't take safety seriously is out. Not down to the principal's office for a wrist slap, but out. You all understand that? Not out for the day, not out if you do it again, but O-U-T, right fucking now."

He let it sink in, then went on. "If you screw up because I haven't taught you right, that's my fault, and I'm definitely not expecting the impossible. What I am expecting is that your attitude towards safety is dead serious from day one. You wanna spend your lunch hour smokin weed out in the park, that's fine with me. Just don't even *think* about coming to my shop that day. Same for drinking, same for being sick. I don't care how much you want to be here, if you're sick, then you can't concentrate, and you're a danger to the people you're working with."

Holy shit. No teacher had ever said anything like that before. Mark looked at Bruce and grinned. This guy was straight up and didn't fuck around. It was going to be a good class.

They didn't actually touch a car, or any part of a car, that day. They just got familiar with the tools and the safety procedures, but it was fun, and when the final bell rang it was almost as if no time had passed, and they were both in good humor as they started the walk home.

"You get any homework today?" asked Bruce.

"On the first day of school? I think I'd have killed any teacher that tried to load me with homework on the first day," replied Mark. "Besides, after the day I had today, I'm in no shape to think about homework anyway."

"Why not? What happened today?"

"What fucking *didn't* happen is more like it." With that, Mark launched into the full details, punctuated by comments like, "She said *what!*" or, "Oh, man, they are going to *kill* you for that," from his amazed friend.

"Whoa, man, I was going to suggest that we head over to my place to jam and work on some of the new songs, but maybe I should take you to the psych ward instead. You are in need of *major* mental readjustment. I mean, how many enemies can one guy make in a day?" Bruce scratched his head. "And I'm *still* not sure I can believe you turned down a ride on Karen Hemmingway. I mean, I know she's a slut and all, and just wants to get boned by a musician, but still…"

They walked in silence for a while, until Bruce said, "At least now I know where your brother gets it from."

"Donny? Gets what?"

"No, not Donny. Donny is a fairly together kid. I mean Glen, the eight-year-old madman."

"Oh yeah, well, maybe it does run in the family." Mark laughed. "Did I tell you what he did yesterday?"

"What? Set fire to his school again?" They both roared with laughter as they thought about the day Glen had found a lighter on his way to school and decided to experiment with a garbage can full of paper.

"Nope, this one was just the opposite. He tried to put a fire out."

"Did he get hurt?" There was concern in Bruce's voice, because despite Glen's ability to get himself, and everyone around him, in endless trouble, they both loved the little creep.

"Severely. His ass is so sore he probably still can't sit down." "His ass? He burned his ass?"

"More like my mom burned it for him. Listen to this: You know how my dad likes to sit in front of the fire and unwind with a beer or a glass of wine every night after he comes home from work?"

"If I worked as hard as him I'd do exactly the same."

"Yeah, well, unless it's a really hot summer day, my mom always lights a fire around five-thirty, so that it's burning well when he gets home. So yesterday, she lights the fire and then goes back into the kitchen to work on supper, leaving Glen-the-genius and his little buddy Damon Hasson alone in the living room, playing. And of course, Glen decides that since there's a fire, they should play fireman, so talks Damon into ... "

"Oh, no. Tell me it's not true." Bruce was snorting with laughter. "Tell me you're not going to tell me what I think you're going to tell me."

"Nope. That's exactly what I'm gonna tell you."

"He pissed on it, right?"

"Yup. That's my little brother. Glen the firefighter. The two of them hauled out their little eight-year-old dicks and let 'em rip all over the fire."

"Jeeezuz. We used to piss on campfires at scout camp and that was bad enough. But *inside*?" Bruce was howling. "It must have *stunk*!" Then he got serious. "What did your dad do to him? I'm surprised he's still alive." Scott Heaney may have loved his sons and his daughter, but he was a fierce disciplinarian—something Bruce knew only too well, having been on the receiving end of the Heaney temper more than once.

"Well, that's where he got lucky. My mom smelled it right away and caught them even before they had their flies zipped up. She sent Damon home so his mom could wail on him while she wailed on Glen. Then ... "

"With the wooden spoon?"

"Yup, Glen's ass made repeated contact with the wooden spoon of death. And then she got Damon's mom to send him back and made them haul all the wood and ashes outside, and get to work scrubbing out the fireplace. I walked in about then, and let me tell you, the smell was not pleasant, but it turned out that dad had to work late at the construction site, and didn't get home till almost midnight."

"He didn't find out?"

"Nope. Once the fireplace was clean, we lit another fire, and that pretty much took care of the smell."

"Crazy little bugger. I wonder what he'll do next."

"No way to tell, but it's bound to make the *Guinness Book of Records* in the stupidity category." Mark laughed, "Kinda like me, I guess."

"Yeah, turning down Karen, and then getting Sergio and his gang pissed at you are both *Guinness*-level stupidity."

"Well, it's done now, and other than watching my back there's not a lot I can do about it."

"Except sing." Bruce gave his friend a playful shot on the shoulder. "Wanna come over and work on those songs? If the Juice Monkeys are gonna have a future, we'd better get to work."

"If we want the Juice Monkeys to even be a band, we'd better find us a drummer and a bass player," Mark responded, "to say nothing of a horn section."

"So you coming?"

Mark thought about it. Maybe making some music would be the best way to blow away the memories of the day. "Yeah, sure. Sounds good. Let's just swing by my place first, I've got something to show you."

They headed left, towards the Heaney home, and Bruce said, "What have you got?"

"You'll see for yourself soon enough."

Soon they were turning into the lane that ran behind Mark's house, and then through the gate and up the path that led through his mother's vegetable garden. Instead of going into the house though, Mark steered his friend toward what had once been a two-car garage.

"You're not going into your father's workshop, are you?" Scott Heaney was a plumber by trade, and used the garage as a combination workshop and storage area. Both boys knew it was off-limits unless they were specifically invited in.

"In and out fast, like dad tells me about the missions he used to go on in the SAS. Just a few minutes, and then off to your place. It's not

24

even three-thirty; Dad's not going to be home for a couple of hours." Mark picked up a small flowerpot a meter to the left of the door and retrieved a key from underneath it. "And you really do have to see this."

It was dim in the shop, and Mark immediately closed the door behind them, making it fully dark. "Stay where you are until I turn on the light."

The light went on, illuminating a large room. There was industrial shelving, covered with plumbing paraphernalia, down the full length of one side; a workbench and pegboard tool rack occupying half the other side. Taking up the rest of the space on that wall were a simple desk and chair, and a small shelf unit housing a stereo and a stack of tapes and CDs.

"First things first," said Mark, heading for the stereo. "If we're gonna fly, we gotta have the right soundtrack."

"Fly? What the fuck are you talking about? And what," Bruce pointed to a tarp draped over a bulky object in the center of the workshop, "is that?"

The sound of Credence Clearwater's *Suzy Q* filled the room as Mark grabbed the tarp and lifted it in one smooth motion.

"Holy shit!" Bruce's eyes practically exploded out of his head as he stared at the gleaming chrome, deep black paint, and polished leather of the motorcycle that had been hiding under the sheet. "That is the sweetest thing I've ever laid eyes on. When did you get it, man?"

"Mine? No way. It's my dad's. Now hop on."

"Hop on? Are you fucking insane? What the fuck is wrong with you, Mark? Your dad'll tear us apart piece by piece if we mess with this. Put the cloth back on and let's come back after we ask him if it's okay."

"Ah, quit being such a pussy! There's a couple of World War II leather flying helmets under the workbench. Grab them while I turn up the music. The song's nearly on!"

"Oh, right, the song. Gotta hurry and get the massah his helmet before his precious song starts playing." Bruce didn't move. "Just being in here looking at it is bad enough. But riding it? What if we scratch it? You think he won't notice?"

"He *would* notice."

Mark and Bruce practically jumped out of their boots at the sound of the deep, rough voice.

"Dad!"

"Mr. Heaney!"

Scott Heaney was standing less than a meter behind them.

"You were about to sit on a vintage R50/2 BMW motorcycle. It's a 500cc twin that was built in 1958, that I finished restoring last night." He was not a tall man, but he was built like the trunk of a Douglas fir and radiated an air of controlled violence so powerful that he almost never had to back up his words with action.

"Mark?"

"Yes, Dad?"

"Do you know how lucky you are?"

"Sir?"

"If you weren't lucky enough to have a friend as sensible as Bruce here, you'd probably have already been sitting on the bike when I got here." He moved past them and picked up the sheet, shook the dust off it, and draped it carefully back over the bike. "And if you *had* been on it when I found you, then I *would* have had to tear you apart piece by piece."

"Yes, sir. I'm sorry."

"I doubt that you're sorry for anything besides getting caught, but you are doubly lucky today, because I'm in a good mood. Construction in this city is getting close to an all-time low, but I have somehow managed to score a good two-month contract, so I'm going to take your mother out to dinner instead of ripping you to shreds."

Neither of the boys said anything, and Scott Heaney turned to Bruce. "You were talking sense there, but it sounded like it was more because you were scared of getting caught than because you thought what you were doing was wrong. Is that right?"

Bruce swallowed, but managed to croak, "Yes sir."

"At least you're honest." He looked around the workshop. "Did you mess with anything else?"

"Only the stereo."

"Rewind the tape, put it back in the rack, and shut everything off. When you've done that you can each take an ax and start splitting wood. The woodbox beside the fireplace is empty. When I get home tonight I want to see it full, and I want at least two woodboxes worth of split wood beside the woodpile, plus a basket of kindling. Is that clear?"

"Yes sir," the two boys echoed.

"After that, clean and sharpen the axes and hang them back up, and don't forget to lock the workshop and put the key back under the plant."

"Yes sir," the two boys echoed again.

Scott Heaney stepped out of the workshop, but then stopped and turned to face them. "And one other thing. If you want to break in to other people's property without getting caught, then don't leave shit like this," he bent and grabbed their backpacks from the ground where they'd dropped them, "outside the door."

CHAPTER 2

Swish. Whunk! Swish. Whunk!

Swing after swing, the axes bit into the logs, and gradually the pile of split wood grew.

"Man, you know what I think?" Bruce dropped his ax and wiped the sweat from his eyes.

"What?"

"I think it would have been easier on us if he *had* just killed us."

"He's a Maori, Bruce. He's descended from fucking headhunters. And he was an SAS anti-terrorist. People like that don't kill you unless they can't think of anything worse."

"Well just be thankful that I didn't let you get on the bike right away, or he'd have probably staked you out on an anthill." Bruce picked up his ax and started swinging again. "And how did he get that close to us without us hearing? I mean, he had to open the door, right? How could he do that without us noticing?"

This time it was Mark who put down his ax, and when he spoke there was something in his voice that made Bruce pay strict attention.

"He's the Ghost."

"Ghost?"

"You know Bones?"

"Your dad's friend, the guy that owns the Skavoovee Tavern?"

"Yeah. He's a Brit, and dad's a Kiwi, so they weren't in the same squadron, but they fought together in a lot of places you probably never heard of. He was over for supper one night and dad got called out on an emergency job. Bones stayed to finish eating, and then we got talking after supper and he told me some stuff about dad." Mark's voice trailed off and his eyes turned inward for a moment, then he looked back up at his friend.

"They called my dad the Black Ghost. He'd grown up in the forest. His family didn't move into the city till he was fourteen or something,

28

and he learned to hunt and move silently. And when they moved to the city, there was a lot of prejudice against them—I guess New Zealand's no different than anywhere else that way—and he learned to fight to survive. Add on the training he got in the SAS, and by the time he was twenty-five he was pretty much the deadliest soldier in the regiment. Whenever they needed somebody to do a reconnaissance, or to take a guard out silently, he'd be the one to do it."

"Shit. You never told me any of that."

"I don't think dad wanted me to know. I think he'd have killed Bones if he knew that Bones had told me."

"So why *did* he tell you."

"Sometimes my dad gets pretty intense, and I think Bones wanted me to know that it wasn't me, or the family, that pissed him off; that he was that way because of what had happened to him in the past. Anyway, Bones told me that the first thing you'd know about dad coming up behind you was when he touched you on the shoulder." Mark started chopping again. "Unless you were the guard he was taking out. In which case you never knew anything. You just died."

"The Black Ghost." Bruce sounded awestruck. "Fuck me." Bruce began chopping too, and for a long time neither of them said anything.

When they thought they had chopped enough to fill the woodbox three times over, they carried a load inside.

"Hi Mom."

Jodi Heaney was almost as tall as her husband, but she was as slim as he was stocky and as fair as he was dark. She had been putting plates and cutlery on the table when they walked past her with their armloads of wood.

"Good heavens. Did the sun rise in the west this morning?"

"What?"

"You're bringing in firewood. Normally I have to get down on my knees and beg to get you to chop wood."

"Uh, well…"

"Oh. I see." She laughed. "Your father *suggested* it." She had long hair that was still blonde despite her age, and a trim figure despite bearing four children.

"I thought you were going out for dinner."

"We are."

"So why are you setting the table?" asked Mark.

"For you, silly. Just because your father and I are eating in a restaurant, doesn't mean that you should go hungry." She turned to Bruce: "There's plenty of food if you want to stay, Bruce."

"Thanks Mrs. Heaney, but Mark and I were planning to go to my place to practice, and I think we can both eat there."

"What about the kids?" interjected Mark. "Do I have to baby-sit?"

"No, I've arranged for Sarah and Glen to go over to the Hassons'. I was just planning to set out some food for you and Donny." She picked one of the place settings up. "But I guess Donny will have to eat by himself if you're going to Bruce's."

"As soon as we clean up the axes, we're outta here." Mark dumped his load of wood into the woodbox, hugged his mother, and headed back outside.

"So your dad was a headhunter?" They were on their way to Bruce's.

"No, stupid, but his ancestors were. And probably not even that far back. He doesn't really talk much about that, but I've done some reading in the library. I mean, they're *my* ancestors too, right?"

"Yeah. Shit. And I thought that having a musician for a father was weird."

"Ever hear of the Moko?" Mark asked.

"Moko? Sounds like some kind of new drink at Starbucks. What's that got to do with your ancestors?

"Starbucks?" Mark snorted with disgust. "Moko is Maori tattooing. They did designs on their faces and chests, and they didn't have any yuppie piercing and tattoo parlors on the corner, like around here." They were waiting for a green light, to cross the intersection of Commercial Drive and Broadway; Mark waved his arms at the shops around them. "They used needles made of wood and bone, and you better believe it fucking well hurt. I read that they had to eat a ton before they got it done cuz their faces would swell up so bad afterward that they couldn't eat for weeks." The light changed and they crossed Broadway and continued north down Commercial. "The English that invaded New Zealand thought those facial tattoos were so wild that they used to kill Maori for their heads, to take them back to sell to collectors or museums in England."

"Reverse headhunting." Bruce nodded. "Yeah, I've heard stories about English soldiers and sailors back then. They were just as savage as the 'savages' they were killing."

"Your grandparents were from England, right?"

"My mom's parents were." He was silent a moment. It wasn't that long since his mother had died.

"So you're descended from headhunters just like me."

They both laughed. "Maybe we should change the name of the band from 'The Juice Monkeys' to 'The Headhunters'."

"Yeah, well, first we've got to *have* a band. Maybe your dad…"

Mark had to stop talking and get out of the way as a group of women with brush cuts and army boots stepped from the door of a cafe, taking up most of the sidewalk.

When the path was clear, the teens walked on. "Commercial Drive, man. Ya gotta love it."

"Dyke Road, bro."

"True, but it's definitely the coolest street in this part of the city." Mark eyed the departing lesbians. "Hey man, they wanna lick carpet, that's cool with me. I want the same thing."

"You and me both. But the difference is, they get to actually do it, and all we can do is jerk off and dream about it. Whoa…" Bruce came to a halt and pointed up, and to the north. "Look at that."

The sun, which had been in the clouds, was now low enough to light up the mountains that towered above the city's north shore. The contrast between sunlit peaks and the dark sky behind them was impressive.

"You ever go up there?" Bruce asked.

"A few times. There's trails up to some of the ski areas and Dad sometimes takes the dogs up there for walks. He's taken Donny and me along a few times." Mark absorbed the view. "I'll tell ya though, it looks a lot nicer from here than it does when you're sweating your guts out halfway up. Those trails are *steep*." Once again he waved an arm at the street life around them. "I'd rather be walking around here, than up there, any day. I mean, look around you, man."

Coffeehouses, ethnic restaurants, health food markets, signs in Italian on the windows of shops selling things they could only guess at.

"Yeah, I love it here too. It's a great neighborhood."

"Long as you keep your nose out of gang business."

"Yeah, there is that. But they don't bother you if you don't bother them. And anyway, they're mostly just selling drugs. It's not as if they're robbing banks or doing home invasions or shit like that." He turned right, down a side street. "Speaking of home invasions, let's go invade dad's studio and see if we can talk him into some time down there."

Bruce turned right again, into an alley this time, and then climbed a flight of concrete stairs to a thick metal door set flush into a stucco wall. Beside the door was a small sign reading 'Dead Dog Sound'. "I should tell my dad to get your dad to hang around here. Then he wouldn't need all this security. Nobody's going to break into any place that your dad's guarding."

Inside was totally different to outside. Where the outside had been all concrete and steel, the inside was warm wood, colorful paintings and rugs, music magazines on a low table, and plenty of light flooding in from the big windows on the other wall—windows high enough above the street on that side that no one was going to break and enter through them.

"So how much is the studio worth, that he needs this place to be so burglarproof?"

They'd walked through the reception area and into the living area beyond, and Bruce was rummaging in the refrigerator. He came up with a big plastic milk jug. "He's always adding new stuff, but the last time he said anything about it, it was way over half a mil." He unscrewed the cap, took a long swig, and passed the jug to Mark. "Want some?"

"Half a million dollars. Shit. And all music equipment that you could sell on the black market real easy. No wonder he keeps this place locked up so tight." Mark tipped up the milk jug and let the cold liquid glug down his throat. He wiped his mouth and let out a huge belch. "Excellent. Now, let's see if we can use one of the sound rooms."

Bruce nodded and led his friend back through the reception area and then down a set of inside stairs. At the bottom of the staircase was a solid-looking red door—soundproof, fireproof, and burglarproof.

Bruce dug out his keys, opened the door; the two walked in, re-locking the door behind them.

The room they had entered was a fairly ordinary-looking office. There was a desk, a computer, a fax machine, a printer, a couple of telephones, a couch, and a big wing chair. And a beer fridge, of course; but what was unusual about it was that the wall opposite the entrance had a large Plexiglas window which looked into another room, and that other room had windows looking into half a dozen small sound rooms, and one large band room. Through the window in the office, they could see Bruce's father's sound man: a big black guy named Wilbur Wallace, seated in front of a huge recording and mixing console. They could also hear— actually more feel than hear—the rhythmic pounding of an electric bass and the boom of a bass drum.

Wilbur was wearing headphones, and was concentrating on the console in front of him, but he eventually looked up and waved to the boys to come in—which they did—through yet another heavy, soundproof, metal door.

As soon as they opened the door, they were overwhelmed by the sheer physical wall of sound that had only been hinted at outside. And in addition to the bass line, they could now hear the full power of the rest of the drum set, and the wild, paint-blistering wail of Larry Kellite's guitar.

They knew better than to ask questions or touch anything, and just grabbed a couple of chairs and sat down and listened. They could see Bruce's father in one of the rooms, and the bass player in another. Both were solidly into the music and completely unaware of anything outside the world of the headphones they were wearing. The drummer would be in the same world, in a room of his own, but he was sitting, and invisible to the boys.

Mark pointed to a set of headphones hanging above the console, and when Wilbur nodded an okay, Mark stood and put them on and jacked them into the console. What had been intense before, was now totally mindfucking. Larry Kellite was as good as any guitarist Mark had ever heard, and he loved the music of the sixties—BB King, Townshend, Dick Dale, Clapton before he went soft. Mark truly believed that his friend's father would have been as famous as those great guitarists if he hadn't decided that a home and a family were more important than money and fame.

For his session work, he usually played a custom Gibson that Bruce said was worth more than their car, but today Mark could see he was bending the strings of an old Fender Stratocaster, which meant he was making music, not money. Although, if Wilbur was working the board, that meant that they were at least *thinking* about a project.

Whatever, the music was incredible. Guitar, bass, and drums, doing a sort of psychobilly/Cramps thing that sounded like the best of the '60s combined with the best of the '90s.

The sound wound down. Wilbur gave his console a few final strokes, then hit the switch on the mike that hung in front of him and said, "Finest kind, boys and girls. Finest kind. I think we got it. And we got company, too." Bruce's father came back from wherever it is that musicians go when they're fully into the music, and looked out into the control room. He gave the boys a quick thumbs-up and got down to the business of disconnecting himself from his guitar and headphones.

"How was school?" Wilbur asked them as he took off his headphones and hung them above the console.

"For me, it just sucks, like normal," said Bruce. "For Mark, it's like one adventure after another. Non-stop insanity, but I think you've got the cure for him." He pointed to a silver cigarette case resting on the console.

Wilbur picked up the case and held it up to the window where Larry Kellite could see it, then pointed at the boys. When the guitarist made signs like he was writing, Wilbur turned to them and said, "He wants to know if you've got any homework."

"No." They both spoke at once.

"Okay." The sound man opened his case, took out a fat joint, fired it up, and passed it to Mark.

"Whoa. Thanks, man. This is *exactly* what I need." He sucked down the beautiful smoke, and held it in till he thought his lungs would burst, then exhaled in a gigantic gasp, spluttering, "Fuckin' 'A', man, fuckin' 'A'."

Bruce, in the middle of his own toke, nodded agreement.

His father came out of the sound room. "So, what are you two hotrods doing down here in the dungeon?" He reached for the joint, took a hit, and passed it to the drummer, who was emerging from his own room.

Bruce let out a lung-full of smoke and replied, "We wanted to work on some of our songs. Is it okay if we use the band room?"

"Sure, no problem. We're going to be in here for probably another hour, but you won't bother us as long as you keep the door shut." He turned to Mark. "Staying for supper?"

"If that's okay."

"Yeah, be great. Haven't seen you for, lemme think, almost a day now, so we can catch up." He pointed to the drummer. "You guys know Carl?"

Mark said, "No," as Bruce nodded 'Yes.'

"Carl's the best drummer I've ever worked with. He stops in here whenever he's in town. He's from..." Larry Kellite paused, then turned to the drummer and said, "Where the hell *are* you from?"

"Leeds." The accent was strongly working-class Brit. "But I'm sort of living in L.A. now."

"Okay. Mostly he's from wherever the tour bus is parked. He's touring with the Buzzcocks; they're playing a weekend at Skavoovee, then heading back down the coast to do Seattle and San Francisco."

Mark stuck out his hand. "Skavoovee! No kidding? Do you like it? My dad's best friend owns it."

"Best bloody pub in North America if you ask me. You lads going to come and see us?"

"I wish," Mark replied. "Not for another two years."

The bass player emerged from his cave and soon Wilbur and the three musicians were deep in conversation about the next piece they were going to work on, so Mark and Bruce headed for the door to the band room.

"Bruce, hang on a sec." His father came out after them. "We're just going to do one more. Probably take less than an hour, and Carl's gotta be down-town to meet somebody by seven-thirty anyway, so why don't you guys pull some steaks out of the freezer now, then practice till seven, and then get the barbecue set up on the front balcony."

"How many steaks should we get out? Are Wilbur and Mike staying?" Mike was the bass player, an old friend of Bruce's father, and a frequent guest, just like Wilbur.

"Who knows? Get five out and whatever we don't cook tonight, we'll cook tomorrow."

"Okay. See you in an hour or so." The boys raced off to grab some steaks from the freezer, then back to the dungeon's band room, where they quickly plugged in a guitar and a microphone.

"What do you want to do?"

Mark thought for a moment then said, "How bout something new? You said you were writing a new one about that girl you met, Kelly, the one that works at Safeway."

"Hey, yeah. That'd be good. I've got it written, and I've got a few ideas about the way it should sound, but nothing really firm yet." Bruce put down the guitar he'd been warming up on, and headed for the door again. "It's up in my room. I'll be right back."

For the next half hour they kicked around ideas for melody and chord structure, trying this, trying that, as Mark came to grips with vocal line. The pot had loosened him up, taken the ugliness out of the day, and he was totally into the music.

"You ready to give it a full run-through?" asked Bruce.

"Yeah, I think so. Let's punch up a basic punk rhythm on the Korg and you can just give me chords for now."

Five minutes later they were ready to go and after a simple guitar in-tro, Mark started in, his singing voice powerful and smooth:

"Safeway girl you're really pretty.

Safeway girl you drive me out of my mind. Safeway girl no need to be suspicious

Just looking at you, thinking you're delicious. Here I be, walking down aisle number nine.

I see you stocking those shelves, looking so fine. If I don't eat me some hot humble pie,

Well I think I just may roll over and die.

Safeway girl you're..."

"No, no. It's not..." Mark killed the rhythm section. "That doesn't make sense."

"What?" Bruce flicked out a couple of heavily down-bent notes and waited for an explanation.

"Humble pie. What the fuck is he talking about humble pie." "He wants her, real bad."

"Yeah, so? What's that got to do with being humble?"

"He wants to *eat* her, man! Are you unable to comprehend the concept of horniness?" This time the notes bent upward, a questioning sound.

"Eating humble pie doesn't have anything to do with eating women, you blockhead. It means apologizing. It's what my mom tells me I have to do every time I think I know everything, and then she or dad explains how wrong I was."

"You sure?"

"Of course I'm… Hey… hey, wait a minute, I know what we need…" Mark grabbed the pen and paper that were sitting on one of the amps. "Here, look."

He crossed out 'humble' and wrote in 'honey.' "Gotta eat some hot *honey* pie." He made exaggerated licking motions with his tongue. "I'll do a little tongue waggle after that line, and it'll drive the chicks crazy in the audience."

"Ya know, Mark, it actually would."

"Yeah, right, as if I'm ever going to be in front of an audience."

"You will, man, you will. You're a natural. You've got the voice, and that's not just me talking, my dad says you do, and fuck, he's been working with singers for thirty years so he should know, but you've also got the…" Bruce paused, looking for the right word. "I don't know how to say it, but when you get singing, it's like you somehow take over the room. And not only that, but…"

Both boys turned as they heard the door opening. "Isn't that right, Wilbur?"

The big Jamaican soundman nodded and said, "Whatever you say."

"What I say, is that Mark can sing. I mean *really* sing."

"Course he can sing. All us darkies can sing. What's amazing is that a skinny-ass little white boy like you can actually play a guitar."

Wilbur wandered over behind the drum kit and picked up the sticks that were lying on one of the toms. "What you children working on?"

"New song. Wanna hear it?"

"Lay it on me."

Thirty seconds into it, Wilbur started in on the drums, laying a fast, powerful bass drum underneath, and some delicate cross-rhythms on the cymbal and toms over top of Bruce's guitar. His drumming never got in the way of the song but kept the young singer and guitarist together, and somehow made the whole thing sound like a real song, not like two kids fooling around in a basement.

"Man, Wilbur, you are some drummer!"

Wilbur nodded. "I'm okay. Don't play as much as I used to, but I'm still okay."

Mark and Bruce looked at each other. "Okay? Only okay?" said Mark. "You're so far beyond 'okay' that I can't believe you'd even say that."

"Yeah, compared to you virgins, I'm the intergalactic emperor of music, but compared to someone like Carl..." Wilbur shook his head and laughed. "Hey, lemme go drag your dad in here. You guys have got a good one going and he should hear it. Maybe he'll play bass and then give you some ideas for the guitar part."

"Isn't he playing with Mike and Carl?"

"Nah. They're leaving, so I'll get him in here. Let's have some fun."

For the next two hours, four separate and distinct human beings—two adults and two teens; two whites, a Jamaican black, and a half-breed descendant of Maori headhunters—were fused together by the magic of music into a single entity.

They worked on *Safeway Girl*, then drifted into a jam on the old standby *I Fought the Law and the Law Won*, a song that has survived and flourished in just about every musical style from country to punk rock, and finally, an old sixties surf-rock song called *Surf City*. Mark and Bruce had never heard of it, or of Jan & Dean, the band that originally recorded it, but when Bruce's father dug out an old LP record and put it on, they were instantly hooked on the guitar sound and the super-tight harmonies of the singers.

Larry Kellite finally laid down his bass and said, "Enough. If we keep this up, you guys are going to be better than me by next week, and all us old guys will be out of a job!" He walked around the room, turning off equipment, unplugging cords, putting instruments back where they belonged. "And it'll be you guys playing Skavoovee, instead of Carl." He headed for the door. "Who's hungry?"

Mark suddenly realized that he'd been hungry for quite a while. "The way I feel, we should put that fifth steak on even though there's only four of us." Later, as they were eating, the conversation drifted round to Carl standing in with the Buzzcocks, how their drummer had come down with a fever just as the tour started, and Carl had been available. And to the tavern they were going to play.

"So what's the story on this Skavoovee place anyway?" Bruce wanted to know. "Everybody talks about Skavoovee this, Skavoovee that; as if it were the greatest place any band could ever play." He looked round the table. "What's so great about playing in Vancouver? I mean, wouldn't any band rather play in New York or something?"

Larry Kellite and Wilbur looked at each other for a moment, as if deciding who should answer. Finally Wilbur said, "It all depends. And it changes, you understand. Back in the seventies, the greatest place a big-name rock band could play was a hall in Tokyo called the Budokan. People there didn't even speak English, but they were the best rock audience in the world. Bands *loved* playing there. Then, a few years later, it was just one more hall, one more stop on the road; but for that one period, it was *the* place. And right now, if you're in North America, and you want to play ska, or any other non-mainstream sound, then Skavoovee is *the* place. There's something about it, some combination of the building, the management, the audience, the city..."

He sawed off another piece of steak and shoved it in his mouth, continuing to talk around it. "I don't know how you guys got into ska, but you're ahead of most folks here and in the US. Ska's big in England, kind of the main music, along with Oi, of the skinhead scene, which is big there, right? But here? Well, any big city's going to have a few bars where different subcultures hang, but skinhead—true skinhead, that is—is still just getting established here, and most people haven't even *heard* of ska."

He turned to Mark. "You said something about knowing the guy that owns Skavoovee?"

"Bones. He's my dad's best friend. His real name is Ian, I think. Ian Battle. But dad just calls him Bones."

"Your dad a musician, then?" asked Wilbur.

"A *musician*?" That was so strange that Mark almost sprayed food onto the table. "No way. He's a..." Mark hesitated. His father made a living as a plumber, but to say, "he's a plumber" just didn't sound right. "He and Bones were soldiers. Combat soldiers. And..."

"In 'Nam?"

"What?"

"They fight in Vietnam?

"No, my dad's from New Zealand and Bones is from England. They were in the SAS, and fought in a lot of places in the Middle East and Asia and Africa." He doubted that Wilbur or Bruce's dad knew anything about the SAS, hardly anyone did, and he didn't really want to explain it in detail right then. "The SAS is a sort of super-commando unit." That was about as much as most people could understand about it. "Anyway, Bones was pretty deep into the music scene before he joined up, and when he retired from the army he came here to visit my dad and liked it so much that he stayed. He bought the Skavoovee Tavern, only it wasn't called Skavoovee back then; it was some run-down, dirt-bag place in a junkie zone over in East Vancouver; he fixed it up and started bringing in the kinds of music that he'd liked when he was a crazy kid back in England."

"No shit." Larry Kellite pushed his empty plate away from him and leaned back. "I've never played there, but I've gone there a few times to hear bands. Great crowds, that's for sure. Always wondered about the guy who owned it. It was a biker joint…a major heroin bar, in the old days. I've heard some wild stories about how this new owner had to lay down some heavy lumber on the previous clientele to convince them that they weren't welcome anymore."

"That was mostly him and my dad." Mark had heard the stories, usually by sneaking upstairs from his room and listening to his father and Bones reminiscing over beers.

"Two guys?" Wilbur sounded skeptical. "Cleaning out a biker bar?"

"You don't know his dad," Bruce cut in. "He could probably have done it by himself. If this Bones guy is anything like him, they wouldn't have had any trouble at all."

Mark shot his friend a warning glance. He was proud of his father, but he didn't think Scott Heaney would be very happy about his son spreading the 'Black Ghost' story around town. Bruce got the message and shut up.

"I've met him a few times, Wil." Larry Kellite said, "I've never talked to him about much other than our two idiot sons, but I know when I'm out of my league. He's a big guy. Not that tall, but really powerfully built, and he moves like he's just totally weightless. You're talkin' to him, and you turn your head for half a second, and when you look back, he's gone. Or, one time, we're watching the boys playing baseball with some other kids, and he goes to get some beers for us. He leaves walkin' *that* way..." Bruce's father pointed to his left. "And ten seconds later he taps me on *this* shoulder." He slapped his right shoulder and shook his head in amazement. "What he did wasn't possible. There were fifteen other parents milling around on that side of me, and there's no way he could have got through them all without pushing and shoving."

"But he did?" Wilbur was starting to get the picture.

"Yeah, somehow. And don't ever fuckin' look in his eyes unless you want nightmares for a week. He's real good with his family, and he's been pretty much a second dad to Bruce, but there's something in his eyes that I've never seen anywhere else."

Mark had no idea that Larry Kellite had such an accurate picture of his father. But then Bruce's father was no ordinary man himself. He'd toured with some of the greatest bands in the world, and done studio sessions with most of the rest. Bruce said he'd been heavily into heroin at one time, but had pulled himself free—which took more strength than most people had—and had now built his studio business to the point that it was becoming known internationally. And since his wife had died, he'd raised Bruce on his own and done a fine job.

"So this Bones guy was a bootboy, back in England?" Wilbur was nodding his head, thoughtfully.

"Bootboy? What's that?" Mark wanted to know.

"A skin," Wilbur told him. "You wanna be a skinhead, you should read a little skinhead history mate."

"So how do you know so much about it?"

"Where do think ska music came from? Russia? It was originally Jamaican, kid. There's a big Jamaican community in England, and I lived there for a while before I came here. Back then, skinhead was really hitting it bigtime. They listened to ska and reggae music all the time, and they all wore these big boots, kinda like the ones you guys wear now, and a lot of them were soccer fans. Later on some of them even started riding scooters—Vespa's and Lambetta's as I remember things. Some of them loved to fight at soccer matches—'aggro' they called it—and people took to calling them bootboys. A couple years back they had an awful habit of carrying drywall cutters. Sharp and deadly."

"I don't know if Bones did much fighting back then, but I think he was a rocker. I think it was before there were skinheads. I don't know too much about what he did when he was a kid, but I heard him telling my dad once that he hung out with rockers, and that they liked to fight the mods every now and again."

"Well, whatever he was, he runs a great tavern." Wilbur stood and gathered up the plates. "And one of the things I like most about it is that he doesn't just bring in big-name bands. He's always looking for new bands, new sounds. It's the place where a lot of ska bands really got their start." He left the table and headed for the kitchen. "I'll drop these in the sink, Larry, and then head back down to the dungeon."

Larry Kellite stood as well. "Guess I might as well get back to work myself. Can you guys," he turned to Mark and Bruce, "deal with the dishes for me?"

"Sure, Dad. No problem." Bruce made no move to get up, but looked thoughtful. "There's something I'd like to ask you, if you've got a minute."

His father sat back down. "Sure, what's on your mind?"

"Um, well, it's just that what Wilbur said about Skavoovee got me thinking. You jammed with us today, right?" He looked nervous, but plowed on. "Um, do you think that we'd have a chance of getting a gig at Skavoovee? I mean, Wilbur *did* say that it was a good place for bands to get started."

Larry Kellite thought for a long time before answering. "Okay, first thing is, you guys *are* talented. If you keep at it, you *are* gonna make some great music. The problem with Skavoovee is that it's a high-energy, dancing kind of place just like the Commodore Ballroom downtown, and one singer and one guitar player do not make a dance band."

Bruce started to speak, but his father waved him to silence. "To make the kind of music that gets you booked at a place like Skavoovee, you'd need to find more than just a drummer and a bass player. You'd need horns, and horn players don't grow on trees."

Mark, who had found himself getting increasingly excited about the idea of actually getting onstage and playing, was suddenly despondent.

It must have showed on his face, because Bruce's father continued. "Don't give up the ship just yet. I've got an idea here. But first, are you both certain that you want to do this?" He looked at each of them in turn. "Because if you're not, then there's no point in going any further. You're having fun doing what you're doing, and you've both got potential, but getting a real gig, especially at a place like Skavoovee, means you're going to have to do a ton of hard work, and it's a big commitment because it involves other people."

"You know it's what I want, Dad. It's what I've always wanted."

"What about you, Mark?"

Mark thought hard. "At first I wasn't sure, Mr. Kellite. I sort of started doing this cuz Bruce talked me into it, but every day I enjoy it more and more." He felt a little nervous about what he was going to say next, but he swallowed and went ahead. "The other thing is, it's the first thing I've ever done that I'm good at." He felt himself turning red. "I know I'm not really any good compared to the singers that you play with, but compared to how I do at school, or at sports… Well, I just feel good about myself when Bruce and I play. And today, singing with you and Carl backing me up, it just felt like I was the king of the world."

"Hey, listen. I've played with fuckin' near everybody, and let me tell you, you might not be as good as a lot of guys right now, but you're as good as any of them was at this stage. You're a natural singer. All you need is to keep on singing, preferably with some good musicians behind you, and you can go anywhere you want. The question is: do you want to?"

"Do I *want* to? You bet I do. I just worry that I'm not good enough."

"Hah," snorted the older man. "We *all* worry about that." He drummed his fingers on the table. "Here's the deal. Wilbur's been jonesing to get back to making more music and spending less time at the mixing console. I love playing with him, and I've promised him that I'd keep my eyes open for some kind of semi-regular gig for us. This would fill the bill perfectly."

"Yeeeaaahhhhhh!" Bruce was out of his chair and doing air guitar leaps, Pete Townshend style, around the table. But he stopped, mid-leap and said, "But what about horns? You said we'd need a horn section."

Mark nodded his agreement. He'd been in the dungeon when some really good ska bands were recording, and it was impossible to imagine them without their horn sections.

"For now, we can fake the horns on the synthesizer. It's not the real thing, but it'll get us started. I'll talk to Wil tonight and see if he's interested. If he is, and if we practice regularly for a month or so, then we'll see about finding a gig." He stood and headed for the door to the dungeon, but stopped just before he opened it. "But there's a condition."

The teens stopped trading high fives, and looked up anxiously.

"Even though you're about to become rich and famous ska stars, you still gotta do the dishes."

CHAPTER 3

On his way home, after the dishes were washed and put away, Mark reflected on how different their fathers were, and yet how lucky they both were to have fathers like that. His own father wasn't the kind of guy you could sit around and smoke a joint with, but he had taught Mark so much.

From his father, Mark had learned both self-respect and respect for others. He had learned how to defend himself physically—the defendo training was a perfect balance to his interest in music. And most of all, he'd learned about the importance of family. The world might fuck you over, your country might fuck you over, even people you'd thought of as friends might fuck you over. But as long as you had a loving, supportive family, you'd survive.

Mark smiled at the thought of his little sister, Sarah, a year younger than Glen-the-madman. She'd be in bed now, sleeping the way she always did, with about five pillows piled up all around her, forming what she called her castle. She was happy-go-lucky, cute, and probably brighter than her three brothers put together. Of all of them, she was the one who was probably going to make the most of her education. Mark wouldn't be surprised if one day she was a scientist or a doctor. In fact, the more he thought about it, the more he realized he'd be surprised if she *wasn't*.

"Hi Mom. Hi Dad." His parents were sitting in front of the fire, looking happy and relaxed after their evening out. The family's two dogs, Sassy and Big Dog, were sleeping on the floor in front of them. "How was dinner? Where'd you go?"

"Down to a new seafood place your mom had heard about. On Granville Island."

His father's love of seafood was legendary. Bruce's dad might go for steaks, but Scott Heaney loved fish. He was a typical New Zealander in that respect—either fish or lamb was at the heart of all his favorite meals.

"So it was good?"

"Yes dear, it was wonderful. We had a table by the window, and watched the boats, and the sunset, and your father had some kind of fish that he hasn't had since he left New Zealand." Jodi Heaney had obviously had a glass or two of wine with her dinner. She was stretched out on the couch with her back against the cushions at one end, looking as if she didn't have a care in the world.

Mark was happy for her. The last year had been a difficult one for the construction industry, and both his mother and his father had been worried and tense a lot of the time. The two-month contract his father got was welcome news in the Heaney household.

"I've got some good news myself, if you want to hear it."

"Sure son, pull up a chair."

He sat where he could scratch Big Dog's ears, and told them about Bruce's dad's offer, and about the things he'd said about the boys' potential.

"Oh, Mark, that's wonderful." His mom had sat up and was obviously thrilled by the news.

His father was considerably less thrilled, but since he was never thrilled by *anything*, Mark knew that didn't mean he was upset. What he said was, "I've met Larry Kellite a few times. He's a good man. I don't have a lot of respect for the lifestyle of a lot of musicians, but that man has a good solid grip on reality. Pulled himself out of a hell of a hole, and he takes good care of his boy." He stood up. "I'm going to get myself a beer. Do you want another glass of wine, Jodi?"

"No thanks, hon. But if you wouldn't mind putting the kettle on, I'll fix myself some tea in a little while."

"Mark, anything for you?"

Mark thought about asking for a coke or something but then thought about how happy his parents looked together in front of the fire. With four kids, they didn't get to spend much time alone, and lately, with all the worry about work, life had been tough for them. Why not let them enjoy a quiet evening? "Actually, I'm pretty tired. I think maybe I'll just go down to my room and go to bed."

"Okay. And about this band business: you work hard at it, and when the time comes that Larry thinks you're ready, I'll put in a word with

Bones. I can't get you into his club, and I wouldn't even if I could, but I can at least ask him to come and listen to you or something."

"Wow. Thanks, Dad!"

"No problem. If you're any good, you deserve whatever help I can give you, and if you're not any good, Bones'll tell you straight. But there's a condition."

Mark waited, pretty sure that he knew what the condition would be. "Your schoolwork comes first. As long as you keep up at school, you can play all the music you want. Fall behind at school, and I'll shut you down." Scott Heaney stuck out his hand. "Deal?"

"Deal!" said Mark, sticking out his own hand for the shake, and then finding himself whipped around and levered to the ground with his father's laughing face above him. The man was *fast*.

"How'd you do that?"

"Come down to the club tomorrow night and I'll show you." He helped Mark up. "It's Tuesday tomorrow, remember. Or now that you're a rock star, are you going to give up training and turn into a pussy?"

"Never."

"Good. See you tomorrow night, then. And I'm planning to take the dogs for a hike up one of the North Shore mountains this weekend, so think about making time for that, too."

He'd planned to pull out a notebook and write out some ideas for another verse of *Safeway Girl*, but by the time he'd reached the bottom of the stairs it felt like he was carrying a piano on his back, and it was all he could do to force himself to stop in the bathroom and brush his teeth before flopping onto his bed.

He lay, wondering why he was suddenly so tired, and then realized that he had just been through the wildest day of his life and that it was no wonder at all that he was tired.

Turning down Karen Hemmingway… Facing down the bozos in the lunchroom… Heaving Christian and Sergio into the brambles and then realizing that they were bound to set him up for a beating…

Taking such a stupid risk of pissing off his father, just to show Bruce the motorcycle…

Jamming with Bruce's dad and Wilbur—real musicians…

Being offered a chance to form a real band, with a chance for a real gig, possibly even a gig at the Skavoovee Tavern, the hottest subculture venue in the whole of fucking North America...

Any one of those things would have marked the day as major. To have them *all* happen in one day was fucking insane. He lay, staring up at the ceiling, wondering if it was all real, or if aliens had abducted him on the way to school and taken him to another planet and the whole day was some kind of weird memory implant they'd given him as part of an experiment in over-load psychology.

"Well," he thought to himself as he drifted into sleep, "at least they didn't give me an anal probe."

Sometime later, right in the middle of giving it to Karen Hemmingway, just as he was about to unload his balls into that tight, wet, pussy...

... his alarm sounded.

Seven forty-five. Oh well, another minute and he'd have unloaded all over the sheets. He let his throbbing dick subside, then got up, pulled on some sweatpants, grabbed his ghetto blaster, and stumbled down the hall past Donny's room, to the bathroom.

It wasn't a big house, but his dad had fixed up the basement with a bathroom and two bedrooms so that he and Donny each had some privacy. Glen and Sarah shared a room with bunk beds upstairs, and Mark assumed that by the time Glen needed a room of his own, he himself would have moved out.

Hah. Maybe he'd be touring the world with the Juice Monkeys by then. He parked the ghetto blaster on top of the toilet tank and fired it up. He knew what was in it—a tape of one of his favorite bands, The Who. He turned on the shower, cranked the volume a bit, and got in under the hot water. A minute to shampoo his hair and soap his body, and then, as the sound of *My Generation* filled the room, he grabbed a long back brush and sang into it as if it was a mike.

In his mind he became Roger Daltrey, The Who's lead singer, strutting and dancing across the stage at Woodstock, with three hundred thousand stoned-out fans screaming their joy and adulation.

What a voice that guy had had. And what a band the Who had been—wild boys, whose music crossed all the subcultures.

When the song ended, he turned off the water, grabbed a towel, and started to dry off. The mirror was steamy, but he could catch glimpses of his body, and the thought ran through his mind that it was no wonder Karen Hemmingway had wanted to take him for a ride. Thanks to his father's training, he was in great shape.

Well, if she asked him again, he wouldn't turn her down a second time. "Not that she's likely to ask me again," he said aloud.

He pulled the curtain aside on the small window high on the wall. The basement was mostly underground, but by standing on his toes he could get a look outside. Blue sky. Sunshine. It was going to be a gorgeous late-summer day, and he was looking forward to getting through a day of school without any of the bullshit that had landed on him yesterday.

Wrapping a towel around himself, and grabbing his sweatpants and boombox, he walked out of the bathroom. On the way to his room he banged on the closed door of his brother's room.

"Hey, Donny, your turn for the shower." No answer.

He banged louder and shouted, "You awake, man?"

"Unngh."

"C'mon, asshole. Wake up. You're gonna be late for school."

"Fuck off. Leave me alone," came the muffled response.

"Okay butt-smear, you're on your own." Mark rattled the door one last time and headed for his own room.

As he finished toweling himself off, he looked around. It wasn't a big room, but he'd done his best to make it a place that reflected his personality. The walls were decorated with pictures and posters from the sixties. Rare LP covers were framed and hung on one wall. They featured vintage Motown and rock & roll artists, the kind that he looked to for inspiration in his own music. Chuck Berry, BB King, The Supremes, The Four Tops, the early Elvis Presley, and James Brown. On the opposite wall was a solid collection of Ska band posters. The Specials, Desmond Dekker, Bad Manners, Prince Buster, The Selector, The English Beat, The Business, The Bosstones etc. Even a few punk bands as well like the New York Dolls and the Sex Pistols. His favorite modern bands, the true inheritors of the sixties spirit.

When he was fully dry, he pulled on boxers and socks, then opened his closet and thought about what to wear. He'd managed to score some part-time work over the summer, cleaning up around the construction sites his father worked on, and all the money he'd earned was now either hanging in this closet or sitting in his CD rack. He decided on a blue-checked Ben Sherman shirt. This was followed by fitted Levis with the cuffs turned up, and topped off with a sharp-looking black Harrington jacket. And, of course, his boots but they took so long to do up.

He checked the clock—eight-fifteen—and headed up for breakfast, banging again on Donny's door as he went by.

"Hi, Mom."

"Good morning, dear. Ready for another day?"

"As soon as I eat."

"There's toast fresh out of the toaster, and I've heated up the pan-fried potatoes I made for your supper last night." She filled a plate for him. "They're always better the next day anyway."

Mark filled a big glass with orange juice, grabbed a can of jam from the fridge, and sat down to eat.

"Dad's gone?" he said around a mouthful of potatoes.

"Two hours ago."

"Two hours? Where *is* this new job." Scott Heaney's work took him all the way out to the eastern end of the Fraser Valley, and as far north as the ski resort at Whistler. Although, when he had jobs in those places he usually stayed out there Monday through Friday.

"Chilliwack. It's over an hour's drive each way, but we do need the money, so he's not complaining." She laughed. "Although after a week or two of doing that drive every day he'll definitely start complaining. Especially if there's much overtime."

"It's for two months, right?"

"Yes, and by the end of that time he'll be a real bear. We'll be walking on eggs around here for the last couple of weeks, I imagine." She brought the juice pitcher to the table and refilled his glass. "You're responsible for making sure that he gets plenty of exercise. Even when he's tired from the long days." Mark knew only too well what a difference it made in the house if his dad stopped working out at the club and stopped taking the dogs for long hikes on the weekends. Even though he got plenty of exercise working on big construction sites, he still needed the mental relaxation that came from martial arts and long hikes. Otherwise, everyone in the house suffered.

"Don't worry, Mom. I'll do my best."

"Which is about as good as the average retarded three-year-old," came Donny's voice from the top of the stairs.

"Good to see you, too, asswipe."

"Mark! Donny! Stop that."

"Okay, Ma. No points for picking on somebody as dumb as Mark, anyway." Donny filled a plate and sat down. "Where are Glen and Sarah?"

"Same place they were when you asked that question yesterday morning." Mark laughed. "Don't you have a problem sometimes, living life without a brain?"

"My brain doesn't go into operation till noon, but since it's about ten times as powerful as yours, I don't have any problem catching up to you." He turned to his mother. "So where are they?"

Just as Glen was known for the insane things he did, Donny was known for spending the first hour of every day in a total fog.

"You really don't remember, do you?" She shook her head in amazement. "They don't start school till next week, so they're still asleep. Would you like me to write it down for you?"

"Wouldn't do any good, Mom. At this time of the day, he couldn't read it." Mark stood up, carried his plate and glass to the sink, gave Donny a whack on the back of the head as he passed, and grabbed his school bag off the hook by the back door. "I'm outta here."

"Nope, unless you brush your teeth."

"Oh. Yeah. Right."

Down the stairs. Brush the teeth. Up the stairs. Another smack to the back of Donny's head. Out the door.

No time to walk, so he ran for the bus stop, hoping to make it in time for the eight forty-five bus. It would get him to school just in time, and, better still, Elvis would be driving.

He made it in time, and when the bus doors opened he looked up into thick, jewel-encrusted sunglasses, ducktailed and Brilcreamed hair, and a white suit.

Why anybody would want to impersonate a singer who'd been dead for thirty years was something he didn't understand, but Chase Reed, the bus driver, had been doing it for years. All day, every day. And with constantly good humor. Mark had heard that when he first started doing it the bus company had tried to make him stop, but had got so much flak from passengers who loved the guy that they'd had to give in and let him carry on.

"Hey there, Mark. How's it going?" He even talked like Elvis.

"Not too bad, Chase." Mark replied as he climbed up the bus stairs and showed his pass. He grabbed the front seat, and as usual, Chase slapped a cassette into the small ghetto blaster he kept beside the driver's seat and soon they were both humming along as the real Elvis sang *Jailhouse Rock.*

"So tell me something Chase. You always play the early Elvis tunes right?"

"They were the best, Mark. They were real."

"Yeah, I'm with you on that one, so what I want to know is, if you think Elvis was best in the early days, how come you dress up like he looked when he was doing the lounge-lizard thing in Las Vegas."

"Hang on a minute. Gotta let some folks on." Chase stopped the bus, and greeted an elderly couple as they climbed the stairs. Once he was rolling again, he said, "Thing is, what'd he look like before then? Just like anyone else, that's what he looked like. So how would anyone know who I was impersonating if I looked like that."

The stop buzzer sounded and Chase/Elvis guided the bus into the curb, to let a middle-aged woman off. "Have a good day Mrs. Thompson."

"Thank you, Chase, you too."

He slicked back his hair with one hand and said, "Thangyaveramuch" to her.

Mark giggled.

"So, ya see boy, I don't have any choice. It's your basic existential dilemma. Elvis was spiritually dead before he ever went to Vegas, but now that he's really dead, physically dead, the only way to keep him alive is to be Las Vegas Elvis."

Mark had no idea what an existential dilemma was, and doubted that Chase did either. But it didn't matter, because whatever had happened to Elvis, his music was still alive. Not the later stuff, but the early stuff, when he was just a kid from the hills, singing rockabilly before anyone had ever even heard of rock and roll.

Chase changed the subject. "So how's school goin for ya?"

"One day down, one hundred and ninety-nine to go."

"That bad, eh? So what *does* interest you? You were talking about forming a band last time I saw you."

"Oh, yeah, that's something that *is* going well. It looks like the band is actually gonna happen. One of these days you're going to be hearing a lot about The Juice Monkeys"

"'Juice Monkeys.' Now that's just plain weird, son. What the hell kind of music does a band called The Juice Monkeys play?"

"I dig lots of different kinds of music, Chase. I like music that the major record companies generally stay away from cuz they don't see big dollars. You know, Oi, R&B, Motown, ska, punk, rockabilly. We're going to do covers of some stuff like that, plus we're starting to write our own stuff."

"You ain't gonna drop out of school though, are ya?" Chase sounded concerned.

"No chance, man. Dad would kick my ass into tomorrow at the very thought. Nah, this is just for fun right now. I do it cuz I love it. If we can make some pocket money, and maybe impress a few chicks, well, that's good enough for now."

"Good luck to ya. That's how Elvis started out, ya know. Just singin' cuz he loved to sing." Chase pulled the bus over to the curb. "This is where you get off, Mark. If you and your band ever do play in a club in town here, you let me know. I'll be there to listen."

"I will, Chase. It wouldn't be the same if you weren't there."

Once he was off the bus, Mark took a good look around. Yesterday he hadn't even made it to the front door before the day turned weird. But there was no sign of Karen, or of any of the other problem children, and he walked to his locker, and then to his homeroom, in peace.

Barker started out exactly where he'd left off yesterday. A bunch of useless shit about how the Industrial Revolution affected the economy in England, combined with as much insult as he could lay on any female in the class.

One poor girl took the worst of it. Halfway through the class, a girl called Jasmine Kenner raised her hand. Barker ignored her for a while, even though it was obvious he knew her hand was up. Finally, he stared at her breasts for a while, then looked up to her eye-level and said, in a really snotty tone, "Yes, what is it?"

She ignored his stare and his tone and just said, "Can I go to the washroom please?"

"I don't know dear, can you?" he snickered.

"*May* I go and use the bathroom, please?"

"Why didn't you go before class?"

Mark looked around. Aside from a couple of bozos that he knew were friends of Sergio and Christian, nobody was laughing. Kids were looking at one another and shaking their heads. Sympathizing with poor Jasmine, and wondering what kind of jerkwad got his jollies by pulling shit like this.

"I didn't have to go then, but I do now. If it's that much of a problem for you Mr. Barker, just forget it!" She wasn't a wimp, and was willing to stand up to him.

"Okay, dear. You go ahead. Just be back quickly; we'll all be waiting for you."

The class dragged on for another half hour, and eventually, Mark just gave up and tuned it out. He didn't like spending time studying, but reading from the textbook just had to be better than listening to this prick.

Eventually the torment ended, and Mark strolled the hallways, taking a breather before his English class. He saw some kids that he didn't know, dressed in skinhead gear. They looked to be in either grade eleven or twelve and he was about to go up and introduce himself when he saw something that demanded his attention.

Sergio Verras, and a kid named Rick Warner, who was just as much of an asshole as Christian Begotti, were dealing cigarettes a little ways down the hall. They'd done that last year, too. Mark didn't know if they stole the cigarettes themselves, or got them from some other thief, but they sold them for about half the store price, and they didn't care how young their customers were.

They had their backs to him, and he eased closer, waiting for exactly the right moment. He knew that they carried several brands and that they usually opened their bag and tipped it forward to let the customer take his pick. Or, as was more and more often the case, her pick.

This time was no different. Sergio was selling to some little grade eight greaser wannabe, and as he opened his bag and tipped it forward, Mark made his move, timing it so that he was directly behind Sergio at exactly the point when the bag was tipped as far forward as it was going to get.

He passed by on Sergio's left, but reached around the shithead's back with his right hand, grabbing the bottom of the backpack and up-ending it completely, dumping about a hundred packs of cigarettes all over the floor. Sergio jerked around to see who had done the dirty deed, but of course he turned right, toward the side Mark's hand had reached in from, and by the time he realized what had happened, Mark had disappeared into the crowd ahead, laughing to himself.

Someone had probably seen him do it, and eventually Sergio would find out, but it had just been too good an opportunity to pass up, and what the hell, Sergio hated him already, so it wouldn't make any difference if he did find out.

And, the thought struck Mark out of the blue: wouldn't it just be too cool if one of the teachers happened on the scene as Sergio and Rick were scrambling around, trying to pick up their stash before it got trampled or stolen.

Mrs. Bates started her second class the same way she'd started the first—quickly and efficiently. She handed out the papers they'd written yesterday, handing the right paper to every student even though she'd only heard most of their names once. She smiled at Mark as she placed his paper on the table in front of him. "Good to see you again, Mark," she said as she passed.

How does she do it, he wondered. It had been three years since she taught him, yet she remembered. He checked the top of the paper and saw her neat red '8/10' and also a smiley, drawn beside his score, followed by the words 'It's nice to read that someone is inspired by his parents.' Mark imagined that most of the kids had written about their sports hero or their favorite movie star, and he knew that that wouldn't impress Mrs. Bates very much.

While the students checked their grades and read the individual comments that she had written on each paper, she was busy digging out a big stack of books from the filing cabinet beside her desk. She piled them up on her desk and then asked two of the girls sitting in the front row to help her hand them out.

When Mark got his, he discovered that it was a paperback copy of a novel called *The Outsiders* by someone named S. E. Hinton. He'd never heard of it. "We're going to be reading and discussing this novel for the first part of the year. Have any of you read it?"

Two hands went up. One was Amelia Dorncaster, which didn't surprise Mark, because she got the best grades in the school, in every single subject, and had probably read every book in the universe. The other hand, though, belonged to Jason Doyle, who was a skateboarder, who, as far as Mark knew, didn't have any more brains than Donny. If he'd read it, maybe it would be something interesting.

"Alright, that's good. I'll expect more from the two of you than from the others." Amelia smiled, Jason groaned. He probably regretted putting up his hand.

"Your assignment is to read chapter one for our next class, which is Friday. Does everybody understand that?" She looked around the room. "This is Tuesday. You have tonight, tomorrow night, and Thursday night to read about ten pages. Even the slowest reader in grade eight could manage three pages a night, so I don't want anybody showing up on Friday, telling me they didn't have time."

Mark knew that someone was bound to show up without having read it, and he wondered what punishment she'd have in store for whomever the unlucky one was.

"Now, before we get on with today's work, I'll give you a little background. This is grade eleven, correct? You are all either sixteen, or seventeen years old now. When you read the book, think about the fact that the author was exactly sixteen years old when she wrote this book."

That got everybody's attention.

"She called herself S. E. Hinton because in those days it was difficult for a woman to get a book published. But *The Outsiders* was published, and it became a best seller. She went on to write several more bestsellers, and they've all been made into movies, some of which you have probably seen."

A lot of the guys smiled and looked at one another, as if to say, 'Who would go see a movie made from a book written by some teenage girl?'

She noticed of course. "Kevin," she pointed toward one of the smilers, "What did you think of *Rumblefish?*"

Kevin Bateman answered without thinking much, "Totally cool." And then a funny look crossed his face. "She wrote *that? But how…*"

"How could a *girl…*" her voice was faintly mocking, "write *Rumblefish?*" She had everybody's attention now. "The same way she wrote *That was then—This is now;* the same way she wrote *Tex.*" She held up a copy of *The Outsiders.* "The same way she wrote this."

Most of the kids in the class had seen at least one of those movies, and the thought that a teenage girl was writing books that got turned into movies featuring actors like Mickey Rourke, Patrick Swayze, Matt Dillon, Tom Cruise, and Emilio Estevez clearly had them surprised. Mark reckoned that pretty well everybody would pile into the book as soon as they got home from school.

"There will be a quiz on Friday morning, so don't forget to read it. And, since we're on the subject of quizzes, here's a present for today—a good old fashioned grammar quiz."

As it turned out, the quiz was more like an exam, taking 30 minutes to complete and another 25 minutes to correct. It brought them to the end of the class and lunch.

After grabbing some quick calories in the cafeteria, Mark headed for the back parking lot. In another month or so winter would set in, and there would be five months of dirty skies and pissing rain, so he was determined not to miss a day in the sunshine between now and then.

And it *was* a gorgeous day. The sky was a deep, clear blue, and the few clouds that had been present in the early morning were long gone. Perfect September weather—warm, but not hot, and with a lot less pollution in the air than there was in mid-summer.

He saw an old friend. "Hey Jobbe. How's it going?" Mark asked a boy with a spiked purple Mohawk, and a heavily chained and studded black leather jacket.

"Not bad, not bad. How's it going with you, man? You had a good summer?" Jobbe replied.

"Not bad. Not bad. Dad had me working on his construction sites for most of it, but that was cool. Made some money. And Bruce and I did a lot of jamming. How 'bout you?"

"Oh, you know, hung out mostly."

"Looks like you spent some time in the piercing parlor."

Jobbe Harrington raised a hand to several of the new chunks of metal hanging off his face. "Yeah, did that."

Mark looked at his friend. A lot had changed since they had gone to elementary school together. Jobbe was now a serious punk rocker. The purple, spiked Mohawk marked him off pretty clearly, and he must have had about ten pounds of metal hanging off his flesh and his clothing, but he was still a pleasant guy to talk with.

More and more kids began pouring out of the back doors of the school and soon Mark and Jobbe were joined by a mixed collection of punks. Mark shot the shit with them for a while, then noticed a group of guys in full skinhead gear standing not far away. He didn't recognize them, but with almost two thousand kids at the school, that wasn't unusual. Still, there weren't that many people into skinhead at Gibson, so he was surprised that he hadn't at least noticed them before.

"Anybody know those guys?" he nodded his head in the direction of the skins.

Most of the punks shook their heads, but one girl, who Mark didn't know, said, "I think they used to go to Templeton, but the school district boundaries got changed this summer, so now they're here."

That explained it. "Well, maybe I'll go over and see what they're up to. See you guys."

He walked across the lot to where the skins were standing, and as he approached, their conversation stopped, and five pairs of eyes turned to stare at him, but nobody spoke or did anything to make him welcome. He wondered about their being at a new school; they were maybe just unsure of themselves or something. Still, they were fellow skins, so he might as well make them welcome.

"Hey guys, how's it goin? My name's Mark Heaney. Haven't seen you guys before so I thought I'd come over and introduce myself."

The five guys looked him over, and finally one of them said, "We saw you, but shit, you hang with punks, so we didn't see any point in talkin to you."

Great. Yesterday he wasn't supposed to hang with anybody younger than him, today he was being told that he shouldn't hang with punks even though he liked several punk bands. Mark looked the group over. They all had shaved heads and wore blue jeans with rolled-up cuffs. Three of them wore DMs, the other two had Canadian jump boots. And they split their look between Fred Perry and Ben Sherman shirts. They certainly *dressed* like skins.

"So why the fuck would you want to hang out with punks?" asked one of them. "Punks are welfare, man, totally welfare."

"Yeah, sure, and you guys all have jobs, right?" Mark spat back.

"At least we don't hang out with shit!" The biggest one said, and took a step forward.

"You're an idiot. The scene isn't big enough not to include punk rockers." Mark had had enough of these losers and was about to turn and go back to his friends when the big one took a swing at him.

Mark saw it coming in plenty of time and simply ducked under it, stepped behind the guy and gave him a gentle push in the back, sending him staggering forward, off-balance.

"Listen asshole, I just came over to have a conversation. I didn't come lookin' for this but if you wanna go, then fuck you, I ain't the one backin down! Let's get it on motherfucker! Right fuckin' now!" Mark was shouting, and sucking in huge amounts of oxygen. It was a trick his father had taught him, something that would give him a physical and emotional edge in any confrontation.

"Whoa man, it's cool!" The aggressor held up his hands in a sign of conciliation. "I was just sizing you up. That's all. I wanted to see if you were just a social king, wearing that gear, or if you would actually dance. It's cool man. The name's Greg." He said as he put out his hand.

Mark ignored the hand, keeping his guard up, and watching the other four out of the corner of his eye as he slowly took three steps backwards. "Bunch of losers," he said, half to himself, then turned and walked away, still in the grip of the adrenaline that had flooded his body and brain.

To calm himself, and to give his body a chance to rid itself of the fight-or-flight chemicals, he walked away from the school grounds, and kept on walking, as fast as he could without actually breaking into a run. Gradually he slowed down, and finally, about eight or nine blocks out, he turned around and headed back.

What was with those guys? Didn't they understand *anything* about skinhead beyond the clothes? Mark was no expert, but what he'd heard and read had convinced him that skinhead was about self-respect and doing an honest day's work for an honest day's wage. Nothing in that said that unless you were a skin, you were shit, did it?

Lesson learned, he thought to himself as he approached the school. From now on, he would base his judgments about people on the way they acted, not on the way they dressed.

The rest of the day passed uneventfully. One of the skins who'd been in the parking lot at lunch even apologized, saying that they were all a little nervous, being in the new school. He seemed like a decent guy, and although Mark wasn't about to give any of them a big warm hug, he decided that he'd at least cut them some slack. It had to be weird to get chopped off from all your old friends and thrown into a new school where you don't know anybody other than a couple of other poor sods who got thrown overboard with you.

CHAPTER 4

So it went as September turned into October. He watched his back, and made sure he was never in a position where Sergio and Christian and their friends could find him alone. He watched for the skins that he'd had the early run-in with, but they turned out to be okay guys once they settled into their new school. None of them was ever going to be his best friend, but they were decent company.

Most of the rest of his classes were okay, too. He wasn't really interested in math or science, but as long as he made sure to study regularly he knew he would pass. And if the teachers weren't as great as old Mrs. Bates, at least they were human. His homeroom and history teacher, Barker, on the other hand, was a complete waste of protein—Barker was the most pathetic creature Mark had ever seen walking on two legs. Or four legs, for that matter.

Automotive shop turned out to be even better than he'd imagined, and English was hard but fun. That book, *The Outsiders,* that Mrs. Bates had made them read had to be the best book he'd ever read. She'd even brought in the movie that had been based on it for the class to watch, and pretty much everybody in the class was blown away. Not only was it a great film, but virtually all the unknown actors who were in it had gone on to become a major star. Tom Cruise, Matt Dillon, Patrick Swayze, Rob Lowe, Emilio Estevez. It was like a *Who's Who* of famous actors.

What he was most impressed by in the story was how close the family became after the parents were killed in the train crash. And the description of what it was like to live in the fifties, during a time of gangs based on social class, was really interesting. During those times, the kids weren't scared to rumble.

"I'm in the wrong fuckin' time Bruce."

"Huh? What are you talking about?"

They were walking home from school, and Bruce had been thinking about something else.

"I'm living in the wrong time period. I wish I could go back in time to the '50s. Does that sound weird?"

"Not to me. In fact, I'd give my left nut to time travel to the '50s myself."

"You would?"

"Sure man. Just think, I could meet the young Elvis Presley, the young Little Richard, and the young Chuck Berry. I could meet the founders of Rock and Roll. That would be awesome! Wow, I could even meet Buddy Holly and Fats Domino. Or some of the Motown artists like The Four Tops or The Supremes. Man, wouldn't that just be the shit! Would dad ever be jealous!"

That hadn't been why Mark was thinking about it, but it *was* Tuesday, and they *were* on their way to practice with Wilbur and Bruce's dad, so '50s music was where the conversation stayed.

"We really do have to get a couple of '50s covers together."

"For sure. Something by Elvis, and maybe one by Buddy Holly."

"What about Bill Haley and the Comets?"

"Who?"

"Bill Haley. Hardly anybody remembers him anymore, but dad says he was the first full-on rock'n'roller."

"No way. That was Elvis. What'd this other guy do?"

"*Rock Around the Clock;* you ever hear that?"

"Nope."

"Bet you did. It got used as the theme song to *Happy Days*, on TV. It's killer. Totally killer. And you'd be awesome singing it. I'll get dad to dig out the record and play it for you."

But all thought of Elvis Presley and Bill Haley vanished when they walked down stairs to the dungeon and saw Larry Kellite talking to three guys who were unpacking horns from their cases.

Trumpet. Trombone. Saxophone. Gleaming brass lying in plush velvet beds.

"Got a little surprise for you boys." He introduced the horn players as Kenny, Doug, and Doug. "I'm offering them some studio time for a project they're working on, and in return, they're going to sit in with us a couple of times. If it works for everybody, and we can get a gig, they'll join us for that, too."

Two hours later, Mark was sure he'd died and gone to heaven. Kenny and the two Dougs were great guys, and they'd obviously enjoyed the chance to play some ska. They were experienced musicians, and Mark couldn't believe the difference it made to have real horns behind him, instead of the synthesizer. The increase in the music's energy level was unbelievable, and when Larry Kellite called an end to the session, Mark was so high that he didn't want to stop.

"C'mon Mark, they'll be back, and I did promise them an evening in the studio. And anyway," the guitarist looked at his watch, "it's after six, so you'd better get your ass in gear or you'll be late for your Kung Fu, or whatever you call the fighting you do."

"Defendo."

"Right, well, whatever it is, if you want to go and get pummeled, you'll have to get moving. Do you want some supper first?"

"Maybe just a bit of fruit if you've got some, Mr. Kellite."

"Larry. You want me to play in your band, you call me Larry, like everybody else."

"Um. Yes sir."

Larry Kellite rolled his eyes. "I give up. Yeah, there should be plenty of fruit in the fridge, but don't you want some real calories if you're going to work out?"

"You mean so that I can throw up a nice steak dinner all over the club when somebody starts bouncing me off the mats? No thanks. If I eat some fruit and drink lots of water, I'll be fine."

"What about homework? You guys have homework?"

Mark and Bruce looked at each other, then at the rest of the band. Who wanted to do homework when there was music that needed playing? But they both knew that at the first sign that they weren't doing well at school, their fathers would shut them down in an instant.

"Okay dad, we're on it."

Half an hour later, Larry Kellite found them hard at work in the living room. Mark was doing his final essay on *The Outsiders* for his English class, and Bruce was trying to figure out equations for his algebra class."

"Sorry to interrupt when you're having so much fun, but I thought you'd like to know that I've talked to the guys, and they're happy to go ahead with it."

The teens were off their chairs like a shot. "You mean it? They want to play with us?"

"Yup. They all enjoyed it. They can't practice with us every time, but they will sit in at least once a week, so I figure we'll be ready to audition in about a month."

Mark and Bruce whooped and slapped high-fives.

"Can you ask your father to talk to his friend Bones about that?"

"You bet. I'll ask him tonight, at defendo."

"He takes defendo classes with you?"

"He *teaches* the classes," Mark corrected. "It's not his place, it's actually a hapkido club, but the master there is more concerned about effectiveness than about whether or not you're using some particular style, so he invited dad to come in and teach defendo every Tuesday night."

"Okay then, after the class, or whenever, you can tell him that we'll be ready to audition in a month and that if his friend Bones is willing to give us a listen, we'd sure appreciate it. I'll be going to see the guy myself, but it won't hurt to have your dad put the word in for us first." He poked around amongst the papers and textbooks the boys had been working with. "How's the homework going?"

"Really good Mr. Ke… Larry. I'm doing an essay on how some of the things in this book that was written in the fifties are still the same today." He held up his copy of *The Outsiders.*"

Larry Kellite took the book. "No shit. *The Outsiders*. Does that ever bring back some memories. I think it was my favorite book when I was your age." He flipped through some of the pages. "Amazing to think that she was just a kid when she wrote this. That should inspire you guys with your songwriting. Just because you're only seventeen doesn't mean you don't have anything important to say."

He handed the book back to Mark, and changed the subject. "So what is this defendo shit. Sort of like karate, or kung fu or something?"

"No way! Those styles look great on TV, but when three guys jump you, that fancy shit is about as useful as an extra asshole." Mark was moving, sideways steps, his arms up in a position that would work equally well for parrying a blow or launching his own attack. "Defendo isn't like the Asian styles at all. It's a combination of attack and defense that was developed by a British commando, a guy in the Special Boat Squadron, in World War II." He realized what he was doing and put his fists down. "It's got nothing to do with breaking boards, or putting on shows, it's about making sure that when the fight's over, you're alive and the other guys are dead. The guy that developed it, taught it to other guys in the Squadron, and then it became their official form of hand-to-hand."

"So no flying kicks, or Jackie Chan moves?"

"Whatever works. 'Keep It Savagely Simple' is the defendo motto. If you went airborne against someone like my dad, you'd be dead."

"Sounds heavy. I think I'll stick to music." Larry Kellite laughed. "And maybe the odd Jackie Chan movie."

"Hey there, Shanda, you crazy psycho woman, how's things?" Mark had arrived early at the club, and the only other person out on the mats was Shanda Ellis.

"Not too bad, laddy boy. Ready to get your ass kicked by a lady?"

"Don't see no ladies here..." Mark pretended to look around.

Without warning, she launched a sharp right jab. He knew it was just a teaser, that her real strike would be coming behind it, so he was ready when she tried to take advantage of his block with a fast left. What he wasn't ready for was the way that left disappeared even as he tried to block it. He was left blocking the air and she was inside his guard, unbalancing him with her hip, and landing on top of him as he went down.

He was fast and strong, but no matter what he did, she was one step ahead of him, and before long his elbow was at her mercy, and he was slapping the mat with his free hand.

"Okay! Okay! I'm tapping. You're a lady, okay? Ow! Fuck, that hurts! I'm tapping, for Christ sake. Stop!"

Shanda let go of his arm and stood up, laughing. "Anytime you... Oooofff!"

She landed hard, as Mark swept her feet out from under her, then tried to roll out of the way as he fought for the same armbar that she had used. He thought he had her, but her years of experience won out, and once again he found himself tapping submission.

This time they were both laughing as they stood up, and she slapped him on the back, saying, "You're getting better fast, little boy. You keep training hard and a year from now I'm going to have trouble taking you."

Mark was pleased to hear that. Shanda Ellis was one of the people he respected most. She was a black belt in hapkido, and had been studying defendo with his father for almost five years. If she said he was doing well, it really meant something.

"Assaulting women again, son?"

As usual, he hadn't heard or seen his father approach, but there he was, not a meter away. "Not this woman, Dad. Not unless someone runs her over with a bus first."

They all laughed at that one, and then his father looked around the room. Several more students had arrived and changed, and were starting to warm up.

Scott Heaney went around the room, talking to each in turn, making a joke, or offering an encouraging word. When he had greeted everybody individually, he called them to attention and started the formal class warm-up. Tanjun breathing exercises first, then stretching. After twenty minutes of that, he led them into basic low-level kicks and some basic punches, gradually increasing the speed until everyone was fully warmed up and starting to sweat. From then on, it was individualized training.

He paired the students, usually by similar ability, but sometimes putting a beginner with a more advanced student for special instruction; and set them to work on techniques appropriate to their experience and ability. If there was an odd number, then either he worked with someone himself, or three of the advanced students would work together on dealing with multiple attackers.

Depending on your ability, and on what Scott Heaney felt your weaknesses were, you might work on throws, on boxing, on ground fighting, on blocking, on attack, on defense, on escape, on breathing, on battle psychology... The list was endless, and all the while Scott Heaney observed, not from a distance, but from right up close. Not hesitating to step in and correct, and was always supportive.

Mark was amazed at how he could be so stern and strict, and yet still seem so supportive. Probably, he thought, it was because this class was so tough that people who were not serious about it dropped out after one or two sessions, and the students who stayed were exactly the kind that his father got along with well.

Scott Heaney's mantra was, "If you practice a move once or twice, your enemy will own you when you try it in a confrontation. If you practice a move a thousand times, then you will own your enemy!"

Anybody who felt that he had a move down cold was always welcomed to try it on Scott Heaney. This invariably resulted in the student admitting that maybe more practice wasn't a bad idea after all.

The mats made loud smacking sounds, and the students made loud whoofing noises as they landed. The temperature in the room rose and soon there wasn't a dry body in the class.

"All right folks, water break."

Most of them had large water bottles full of one or another kind of sports drink, and they all guzzled thirstily.

"Questions?" Drink break was always a discussion period, and, as usual, several of the students had questions, either about particular techniques they were having trouble with or about how to deal with particular situations. Everybody was welcome to pitch in with answers, and everybody enjoyed these sessions.

After the break, Mark found himself facing his father. "Punches and parries, Mark!"

"Okay."

Scott Heaney took up a good basic fighting stance, and began throwing medium-speed punches, all the while moving in, forcing Mark to retreat as he parried and blocked.

"You're always better off not to retreat backwards. Nothing wrong with getting away from a fight, but if you're going to stay in the fight, don't ever walk backwards." Even as he spoke, the punches never stopped, and Mark tried to listen as he blocked. "Start walking backwards, you're conceding a psychological advantage. You're telling your opponent that you fear him, and he's going to gain confidence and come after you even harder. Move in a circle. Change directions. Make your opponent think about where you're going to move next, and he won't be able to concentrate as effectively on his attack."

As long as the punches came slowly, Mark was able to tap them away with his leading hand, and his father was complimentary. "You're doing well. See how much harder it is for me to move in on you if you don't back up?"

As the speed of the blows increased though, it got harder and harder. "You're still doing good Mark," his father said, "Just keep it up now. A little faster, and start moving inside or outside of my punches. Try taking the odd shot at me after you parry."

After ten minutes of trying to block the non-stop rain of fists and elbows and forearms that his father was throwing, Mark was so wasted he couldn't decide whether to fall down puking, or just let his father nail him with a really good one and end it all, but he kept on, doing his best, and finally the blows stopped.

"Best I've ever seen you, Mark—you even landed a couple on me. Shanda's right, you're learning fast."

Mark felt like he was dying fast, but he managed to gasp out, "What I've learned is that your fists hurt even when you're operating at slow speed."

"Good. Gives you an incentive to learn to parry and counter at high speed, eh? Grab a drink and then go and sit down for a minute. You've had a pretty good arm and shoulder workout, so I'm going to go pry Shanda off big John and get him to help you with some kicks for a while. Class'll be over in fifteen minutes anyway."

It turned out to be more like half an hour, but eventually, Scott Heaney called an end to the technique session. They all sat for another drink break, another question-and-answer session, and then got back up for twenty minutes of stretching and tanjun breathing for warmdown.

On the way home Mark brought up the subject of an audition for Skavoovee. "I don't want to sound like I'm bragging Dad, but I think Bones is going to like what he hears. I know if it was just Bruce and me, we wouldn't be that good, but with Larry and Wilbur playing with us, and the horn players that Larry got… Well, I think we could bring Glen and Sarah into the band and it would still sound good." He thought over what he'd just said, "Well, if Glen was in it, he'd find a way to make the amplifiers blow up, or have the club burn to the ground, but you know what I mean."

They both laughed at the thought of what Glen could do with fifty or sixty thousand dollars worth of high-tech musical equipment.

"How are things going at school?" his father asked. "Remember our deal."

"I've been keeping up. We're going to be having our mid-term exams next week, and you'll be able to see for yourself when I get the results back."

"Fair enough. Show me decent results on your exams and I'll tell Bones that you deserve a listen."

When they arrived home, Mark went straight downstairs and jumped into a hot shower. Afterwards, dressed in comfortable, baggy sweats, he followed his nose back upstairs and into the kitchen.

"Hi Mom, what's for supper? It smells great." It was well past nine, but on defendo night supper for Mark and his father—and Donny if he went to the club—was always served after the workout.

"How does a pizza feast sound?"

"Fantastic. How many pizzas do I get?"

"As many as you can eat." She was removing two huge ones from the oven as she spoke. "Why don't you slice them. Your father will be here in a minute and you can start."

"Where's Donny? He wasn't at the club."

"There was some kind of skateboarding competition at the park. Your father told him he could skip the workout tonight and go to it as long as he actually entered and didn't just sit and watch."

"Cool. He's probably in the hospital as we speak."

"Shush. He's fine. He phoned just before you got here. There's a big barbecue for all the contestants and he's staying for that. And besides, he..." Jodi Heaney was interrupted by the noise of her husband entering the room with a small child clinging to each leg, each shouting with excitement as he lifted his feet extra high with each step.

"Mark, Mark, will you play tea party with me? Please, please, please!" Sarah let go of her father's leg and raced over to her big brother. "Daddy says he's too tired, but he said it would be okay if I stayed up an extra fifteen minutes if you would play."

Mark hugged her. He knew that his father would be heading straight to bed after supper. He was still working out of town, and had to be out of the house before six. Mark wanted to go to bed himself, but...

"Sure Sarah. I'll come to your tea party." He looked to his mother. "It's pretty late. Are you sure it's okay?"

"Oh, I think it'll be all right. Maybe you should have your tea party before supper, though. I'll keep your pizza warm." She put the pizza back in the oven, and got a pair of Winnie-the-Pooh cups and saucers out of the cupboard and handed them to Sarah.

"Here's your favorite cups, dear. Should I get another one down for Mrs. Bunions, too?"

"Yes please! Mrs. Bunions comes to *all* my tea parties. You know that."

"Well I just thought she might have gone to bed already." She handed down another cup, and then a colorful teapot. "But remember, it is late, so only fifteen minutes, okay?" Sarah pouted hearing that. "Besides dear, if you keep Mark any longer than that he'll faint from hunger." Mrs. Heaney winked at her eldest son as she reached into the fridge and took out the apple juice. She came over to the table and filled all three cups.

For the next fifteen minutes, Mark joined Sarah and her teddy, Mrs. Bunions, on the couch in the living room.

Sarah pretended to be very grown up and interviewed her big brother about high school, and about his band. The important question, of course, was whether any members of Duran Duran were in the band, too, and neither she nor Mrs. Bunions seemed too impressed to find out that they weren't.

"Is this your favorite tea, sis?"

"Yes."

"Where does it come from?"

"The same place as Mrs. Bunions's."

"Where is that exactly?"

"Taibon."

"Taibon, eh? I don't think I've ever been there."

"Of course not. It's much too far away for you to go to, and anyway, there are a lot of tigers there."

"But you've been?"

She gave him a scornful look. "Of course. I had to get the tea, didn't I?"

"Sarah." It was his father. "Sorry to interrupt, but your mom says it's time to end the tea party and get you off to bed."

"Okay." She picked up Mrs. Bunions and jumped into her father's arms. As he carried her down the hall Mark reflected on how peaceful the last month had been at home. Work was going well for their father.

Enough overtime to bring in some extra money, but not enough to fry him. Even Glen-the-madman seemed to have mellowed out. There hadn't been a police car, or an ambulance, or an angry neighbor, or a concerned teacher at the door in almost two weeks. Miraculous.

He picked up the tea things and headed back into the kitchen to do something about his desperate food deficiency.

He was working on his sixth piece of pizza when his father returned. "You're starting exams next week?"

"Yes sir."

"Best prep for exams is to study hard in advance, but then take the last couple of days off completely. Get some exercise on Saturday, and then just totally kick back on Sunday. If the weather holds, would you like to come out with me and the dogs on Saturday?"

Usually, when his father suggested a hike, Mark knew that it was a thinly disguised order, but this time it sounded like a genuine invitation. He'd been hitting the mats pretty hard at the club, but he knew that he could use some full-on cardio. Hiking up a mountain would give him that. "Sure, Dad. That'd be great."

Saturday morning they were up early, and, after a big breakfast, they packed extra sweaters, plus food and water for themselves and the dogs, and headed for the North Shore mountains.

The city of Vancouver is divided into several lobes by inlets of the Pacific Ocean. The northernmost inlet is also the biggest. It is the home of one of the world's major seaports, but civilization ends not too far above its north shore, where broad mountains rise out of the ocean and provide a backdrop to one of the world's most beautiful cities.

They are not huge mountains, but they mark the beginning of two thousand miles of mountain wilderness, for beyond them there is nothing but more mountains. Mountains that rise higher and higher, all the way up the Pacific coast, then up the length of Alaska and the Yukon, not ending until they sink into the sea again at the Arctic coast.

But to say that Grouse Mountain is small relative to the giants to its north is not to imply that it is tiny. Five thousand feet is a significant bump on the earth's surface, and to walk up it, you must be prepared to sweat.

Fortunately, Mark knew that they wouldn't be hiking up the full five thousand feet. They could drive to a parking lot about a thousand feet above the ocean, and their destination was the ski lodge and tourist center at about forty-five hundred feet.

The tourists on this gorgeous autumn day would be taking the Skyride, the giant hundred-passenger gondola that cycled endlessly up and down the mountain. The fitness crowd, dozens of whom were milling around them in the parking lot, would be taking the Grouse Grind, a popular trail that roughly paralleled the path of the gondola. Steep, but so heavily "improved" that there was no longer a single natural hint of the original trail—it had become, literally, a staircase built into the mountain.

Mark and his father, on the other hand, were going to do it the hard way.

They leashed the dogs, walked out of the parking lot, and then entered the main trail system, contouring east above the parking lot like all the other hikers. At the fork where everyone else turned uphill for the Grind, they stayed low, continuing along the old Baden-Powell Trail for another five hundred meters.

Scott Heaney stopped, took off his daypack and got out his water bottle. "Might as well get fully hydrated; we turn uphill here and you'll need all the water your body will hold."

Mark could see a faint trail branching uphill. "Doesn't look like much of a trail."

"It's not. But it's enough, and we're well clear of all the yuppies on the Grind." He took Big Dog off her leash. "Besides, with no people around to disturb, we can let the dogs run free, which is half the point of being out here in the first place." Big Dog trotted off, then disappeared around a bend in the trail.

Mark unclipped Sassy's leash and she was off into the trees like a rocket. Barking, jumping, tearing off in a new direction every five seconds. "Yeah, I guess it wouldn't be too polite to have her tearing around like that in a crowded place."

"All set?"

"In a minute. Just let me get my water bottle and the leash put away."

"Might as well take off your sweater and stuff it in your pack, too."

"It's pretty chilly, Dad. I think I'll leave it on for a while." The sun was up, but in late October it would be another hour before the day warmed up.

"Believe me, Mark, one minute after we start walking uphill you're going to be plenty warm."

"So, I'll take it off then."

"Which wastes time with an unnecessary stop. Take it off now. You'll be fine."

"Okay." Mark didn't see the point of worrying about wasting an extra thirty seconds. Maybe if they were on a commando raid in Borneo, or wherever, it might make a difference, but taking dogs for a walk in the hills? But he also knew when to keep his mouth shut.

He peeled off the sweater, packed it away, and hoisted his daypack. "Okay."

"Sassy! Big Dog! C'mon, let's go. Good girls!" Scott Heaney set off up the trail with the family's two dogs alternately following and leading. Big Dog was a black lab, starting to go gray around the muzzle. She wasn't having any trouble going up the hill, but she wasn't exploding with energy the way Sassy was, and they both knew that she didn't have many more years.

That thought saddened Scott Heaney tremendously. Big Dog loved the kids, but at heart she was his dog. He'd picked her from a friend's dog's litter over ten years ago, and the bond between them was strong.

Sassy was still young, only four, and, with luck, would have many, many years of life ahead of her. She was half Australian Kelpie and half Doberman, which meant that she was a jumper, a climber, and a speed demon. He'd brought her home on Mark's thirteenth birthday, and although she wasn't really a birthday present, she *had* taken to Mark more than to any other family member.

The four of them rambled up through the forest, following something that his father called a trail, but which Mark often couldn't even see. He was in the lead—"You've got to learn to follow a trail someday, son; might as well be today"—but after hearing his father tell him he was off trail for what seemed like the hundredth time, he was ready to give up.

"How can you tell where we are? Half the time I can't even tell we're on a trail; how do you know we're not lost? Shouldn't you be using a compass or something?"

"I can see the trail, Mark, and even if there was no trail we still wouldn't need a compass. Think about it."

Oh, great. Another lesson. "Think about what, Dad?"

"About where we're going, and how we're going to get there." His father took off his pack. "Pull up a stump and take a break. Drink some water."

"I'm not thirsty."

"Drink anyway. By the time you *feel* thirsty, you're way into water deficit. You lose strength, and you lose concentration long before you actually feel the need to drink." Mark drank.

"Now, where are we going?" his father resumed.

"To the lodge at the top of the gondola, right?"

"Right. And where is that?"

Mark was about to point in the direction that he thought they should be going, but he stopped himself. 'Think,' his father had said. Okay, he hadn't been on this particular trail before, but he had been up this mountain a few times, what did he know? "Well, it's obviously up-hill, and since we walked quite a way east of the gondola and the Grouse Grind, we have to be angling back west, right?"

His father smiled. "Right. So which way is west?"

Mark looked at the sun, which he knew would be in the southeast at this time of day.

"C'mon Mark, you don't need the sun for this one. What if it was cloudy?"

"Oh, I get it" What a bozo. They were on the south side of the mountain, so all he had to do was face up hill and point left. "All we have to do is keep traveling slightly left of straight uphill."

"Ta-Da! Shall I give you a medal for getting it almost as fast as the dogs would have?" His father laughed. "And how will you know if you've gone too far left or not far enough?"

"Uh, if we go too much to the left, we'll come to the Grouse Grind." The other one was tougher. What was to their right? He'd been up here before, and he should be able to picture where they'd wind up if they...

"Oh, okay, if we're not far enough left we'll come out on that logging road that they used to haul supplies to the lodge."

"Exactly. Using a map and compass is fine, but using your brain is a lot better. And when you're going up or down a mountain in a thick forest like this, even a map and compass are no good without an altimeter." Scott Heaney dug into his pack and brought out two big bowls and a four-liter jug of water.

While the dogs drank, he continued. "Next summer I'm going to get serious about teaching you how to get around in the wilderness. Maps, compasses, route finding, bad-weather survival, the works; but for now, the biggest lesson I can teach you is to use your head. Stay hydrated, and keep your body well fueled and you'll be able to think more clearly, and if you think clearly you'll stay out of trouble."

When the dogs had finished drinking, he packed up. Mark didn't have to be told that he should get ready, too. He was tired, but he knew that it wasn't just the dogs that needed the exercise. He also knew that they were only about halfway up and that by the time they reached the top, he'd be hurting for real. 'Oh well,' he thought to himself, 'no pain, no gain.'

He concentrated harder on staying on the trail, and found that either the trail was getting better or he was getting better at seeing it. For a while they made good time, but as he began to feel the effects of almost an hour of uphill torture, Mark began to slow down, and although he was trying hard, he found himself having trouble concentrating on the trail.

"Can we take a break, Dad? I'm thrashed."

"Can you handle another five minutes?"

"I guess. Why?"

"You'll see."

About two minutes later, at a spot that didn't look any different than anything else they'd walked through, his father said, "Okay, turn left, off the trail, and contour through the trees."

"Why?"

"You'll see."

Two minutes of bushwhacking, and suddenly the trees ended and Mark found himself facing a small rock wall.

"Climb up it. It's not hard."

Sure enough, there were plenty of hand and footholds, and when Mark pulled himself over the top, about five meters up, he gasped in amazement.

He was standing on a small ledge with an incredible view of the city, the harbor, and the endless ocean.

"Breathtaking, eh?" His father commented as he climbed up to the shelf beside Mark.

"This is beautiful, Dad!"

"Uh-huh. It's pretty much the same view the tourists get from the lodge, but I think you appreciate it a hell of a lot more if you get to it this way, instead of by riding a gondola for fifteen minutes. Basic lesson of life: things you work for are more valuable than things that are handed to you on a plate."

Mark forgot how tired he was as he stared out at the million-dollar view. "We can hang out here for a few minutes if you like. I'm just going to go down and get the dogs. There's an easier way than climbing the cliff just a little further on, and I'll bring them around that way."

The dogs weren't interested in the view, but they both seemed to appreciate a chance to lie down in the sun. Mark and his father talked quietly for a few minutes, then just kicked back themselves. Ten minutes later, as Mark was almost asleep, his father spoke.

"From here, it's only about ten minutes to the top. We can go up there if you want, but the view isn't any better, and you'll be fighting for breathing space with ten thousand tourists, and we'll just be turning around and heading back down anyway. My suggestion is to call this our personal summit and not contaminate our day with a bunch of yuppies milling around the souvenir shop and the bar, but it's your call, I'll go up if you want. I'll even buy you a coke up there if you want that."

"No, I fully agree with you. It's been a great hike even if my legs have turned to jello, and I'll be happy to call this the summit if you want to."

"Good. Pack up your water bottle and let's head down. I'll lead, so you can just concentrate on putting one foot in front of the other and no worrying about staying on the trail."

"Lead the way then. I'll try to keep up."

An hour later, they were back at the car, and forty-five minutes after that they were home. Mark showered, came upstairs for some juice and a sandwich, then went out to the lawn behind the house and fell asleep in the sun, not waking till the yard went into shadow at five-thirty.

Supper that night was a happy occasion. Donny had spent the day at the skate bowl over on Commercial Drive, and felt the same comfortable post-exercise glow as his brother and father. Both boys felt fairly confident that they'd pass all their exams the following week, Glen hadn't been caught at anything lately, mother and daughter had had a great day at the rec center pool, and Scott Heaney topped everything off by announcing that his out-of-town job was ending next week and that he'd already found another contract for the month after that.

"In town, this time. So I'll be able to sleep in till six instead of having to get up at five every morning."

CHAPTER 5

Mark took his father's advice and didn't study on Sunday, either. He slept in, walked over to Bruce's, then took a bus downtown to hang out for the afternoon with his friend. They checked out the scene in the trash district on Granville, bought a couple of CDs of music that Bruce's father had suggested they should listen to, grabbed a meal at Mickey D's, and went to an early movie.

Back in McDonald's after the movie, wolfing down yet more food, Bruce mumbled around his burger, "I sure hope your dad's right about taking the last weekend before exams off from studying. Every other time I've crammed right up till the last minute."

"Yeah, and what did it ever get you?"

"Not much. I always passed everything, but that's about all."

"So? You're going to pass everything this time, right? I sure am. Although," Mark pushed his empty tray away from him, "knowing that unless I studied hard meant we'd lose our shot at Skavoovee had me studying like I was some kind of nerd for the last three weeks."

"Me, too. I actually feel like I'm going to do better this time, but it still feels weird to just goof off for the whole weekend."

"Yeah, but I bet we'll both feel pretty relaxed and focused when we sit down to our first exam." Mark looked around. "Only thing missing today was a couple of chicks to share it with."

"Nerds don't need chicks. If you're gonna adopt the nerd lifestyle, you gotta forget about chicks."

"I don't know, man. Every time I try to forget about women, my dick starts reminding me. I mean, I love music, and I love the martial arts, but it'd be nice to have the time and energy to date an actual girl instead of just my fist."

Bruce took their trays to the tray station. "C'mon, let's head home. It's a nice night, we can walk instead of taking the bus."

"Walk? You crazy?"

"No, it'll be good for you. Exercise takes your mind off sex."

"Nothing takes my mind off sex. Not for very long, anyway." Mark stood up and headed for the door with his friend. "Well, at least it's not uphill…"

"Right, and if we walk, we might see a nice stray dog, or somebody's pet sheep, that you can lure into an alley. Since you can't get a real girl, that is."

"Fuck you. Glen's in charge of bestiality in our family. I'll stick to humans."

"Glen? Glen's been putting it to the neighbor's cat or something?"

"Man, with that kid, it just never ends…but no, I don't think he's been poking the neighbor's cat. I think his first experience probably cured him of even thinking about it again."

"Say what?" Bruce's eyes were practically bugging out of his head. "Glen got it on with an animal?"

"We were visiting my mom's aunt Kate, who had a farm over on Vancouver Island. Glen was about five then, and since he always got his clothes filthy by playing in the mud when we were at the farm, my mom decided that she might as well let him play naked. That way, she could just hose him off a couple of times a day and not worry about washing clothes all the time.

"So, anyway, he's wandering around and decides to climb over the fence into this area where they kept some baby pigs. He…"

"He tried to screw a pig? Five years old and he's getting it on with a pig?"

"Just wait. It's even better than that. What happened was…" Mark started laughing at the memory and had to stop till he got his breath. "Okay, all they had in there at that time was a few little piglets, Glen probably just wanted to play with them, but what happened was that this evil white goose they had was in there too. He'd never have gone in if he'd seen it, shit, it was bigger than him, and even Donny and I were scared of it, it was so vicious.

"So anyway, he sees the piglets and climbs over the fence to play with them in the mud—it's Glen, remember—and meanwhile, Donny and I are about a hundred meters away, exploring a bunch of old cars that they've got dumped there, and we could see it all. This little naked kid climbing the fence and strolling over to play with the piglets and then running back to the fence screaming his head off, with old Gertrude the goose honking and chasing after him full speed!

"He headed for the gate, but he couldn't get it open and the next thing we knew, the goose had him backed up against the fence. We were laughing our asses off, but then the crazy old bird started biting him, so we took off running to help, but before we got there, she'd chomped down on his dick. It looked like she was trying to pull it right off him. No shit. She had it in her beak and was backing away from him, and he was screaming and jumping around like crazy."

Bruce wasn't laughing. "Was he okay?"

"Well by the time we'd have gotten to him, he probably wouldn't have had a dick left, but old aunt Kate had heard him screaming, too, and got there a lot faster than we did. She must have seen the goose from the kitchen window cuz she'd grabbed a broom on the way out, and started wailing on the goose."

"Wailing on it? It didn't run away?"

"You don't know much about geese, do you?"

"No, I guess not."

"Well, they're big, and they're mean as shit if they think you're in their territory. It let go of Glen's willy, alright, but it wasn't backing down one bit, it was just switching its attack to my aunt. Fuck man, it was one of the funniest things I ever saw. Aunt Kate and this goose squared off like something out of WWF, and Glen screaming and holding his dick, and mom kind of running in circles not sure whether to get a band-aid or get the shotgun."

Bruce was laughing now, too. "Oh man, that's too much! The kid's first blowjob was by a goose! And it shreds his dick. So what happened?"

"Donny and I got there about that time, and as soon as we were over the fence, the goose backed off. My mom grabbed Glen, and took him to the house and cleaned him up and then took him to the nearest hospital."

"Jeez. I'd have been worried that they'd call the cops on me if I took a five-year-old to the hospital with a mangled dick. Don't they have to report any kind of possible sexual molestation of a kid?"

"I think the nurses knew Aunt Kate, and besides, who could make up a story like that? Anyway, they put a couple of stitches in, and everything turned out okay—just another day in the life of Glen-the-madman."

"I don't know about that kid, Mark. Sometimes he seems normal enough, but he's gotta be a couple of bricks short of a full load."

"Yeah, maybe. Anyway, you understand why I'm not so keen on animals. I'd rather have a real girl chompin on *my* root."

"You and me both, bro, but it ain't gonna happen for a few weeks. Once we're through with exams we gotta concentrate on getting our act totally together for the audition with Skavoovee."

"*If* we even get an audition. Nobody's guaranteed that Bones is even gonna listen to us."

"He will, man, he will. Stay positive. He's your dad's best bud, and he's gotta know my dad's reputation. He'll give us a chance, but it's up to us to make sure we don't blow that chance."

Five days later, the exam results were in, and a couple of days after that, Ian "Bones" Battle had agreed to give the band an audition.

"Three weeks man, we got three weeks to get *totally* fuckin' honed." Bruce was so excited he could hardly talk. "My dad says that we gotta do four practises a week, minimum, with him and Wilbur, and that the horns have to be there for at least half of them."

"The Dougs still want it? And Kenny?"

"Yeah, my dad says they're hot for it. They wanna play Skavoovee as much as you and me."

Mark and Bruce had finished Automotive Shop, the last class of the day, and were leaving the school when they realized that the kids in the back parking lot weren't acting normal. Instead of moving off toward their homes, they were all standing around expectantly, buzzing with talk, not going anywhere despite the fact that it was starting to rain.

"What's going on?"

"I don't know but there's gotta be at least forty kids out there, just standing around. They're waiting for something."

The two friends looked at one another and spoke simultaneously.

"*Fight?*"

"*Fight!*"

"Who?"

"How should I know? You wanna hang around and see it?"

"For sure."

The kids in the lot were a mixed group. Punks, skaters, jocks, a couple of skins; but no one that Mark could tag as a fighter. Bruce tapped him on the shoulder and pointed to a group that was coming into sight from the other end of the parking area with Sergio and Christian in the lead.

"You think that they're in this?"

"Wouldn't surprise me. I wonder who the lucky victims are? What time is it?"

"Ten after."

"It won't go down here. No way. It'd be stopped before it got started if it did. No, they'll go to the other side of the football field, you know where I mean?"

"That little grassy spot that you can't see from the school? Behind the sheds?"

"Yeah. Has to be. The only other place they could go is the park, and that's too far."

"Shall we, then?"

"Yeah. Let's move before the crowd does." Mark replied, and they drifted slowly toward the likely fight scene, hoping to get a good spot to view the event, but keeping an eye on the main crowd in case the venue was changed. Before they'd gone even halfway, the crowd began to move in the same direction.

"Look who's joined the party."

Mark looked. Leading the parade, along with Christian Begotti and Sergio Verras were three other scumbags: Jeff Anderson, Zoltie Constant, and the guy who had been selling cigarettes with Sergio, Rick Warner. And hanging on to Warner's arm was none other than Karen Hemmingway.

Bruce laughed as Mark sputtered.

"Oh, man, how could she sink that low. Rick Warner is an even bigger asshole than Sergio."

"Guess she was just so brokenhearted when you turned her down that she lost her mind," replied Bruce, trying not to laugh too loudly. When she saw them staring at her, she lifted her nose a little higher in the air, and gave Mark the finger with her free hand.

It was soon obvious that it was Rick Warner who was going to do the fighting. He had taken off his jacket, and was air-punching and making it clear that he was about to "kick the snot out of that stupid jerk."

To Mark's total surprise, the "stupid jerk" turned out to a kid in Mark's English class, George Christiansen. It had to be him, because he, too, was stripping off his jacket, and moving toward the center of the grassy area. But it didn't make sense. Mark didn't know George very well, but he was a quiet kid who mostly talked about computers and physics. Never raised his voice, didn't act like a fighter, and didn't look like he could stand up to a strong wind, let alone a beefy brawler like Rick Warner.

It made no sense; Mark was feeling uncomfortable at the thought of this likable nerd getting shitkicked.

"He hasn't got anyone on his side, Mark," Bruce whispered.

It was true. Warner was surrounded by backup, in the form of his four asshole buddies, but George seemed to be there alone. It was pretty obvious that Warner must have used George as a target for aggression, and that George had had enough teasing and had snapped, and challenged his tormentor to a fight. Now he was going to get punished.

But then Mark noticed something that nobody else in the growing circle would have seen. The kid had adopted a fighting stance like he knew what he was doing. It was pretty common for kids to mimic movie fighters, but Mark knew that what he was seeing was real. Somewhere along the line, this kid had learned how to box. If Rick Warner didn't watch out, the blood on the ground at the end of the fight would be his and not George's.

Or, it might have been if there was any chance of a fair fight, but with Sergio, Zoltie, Christian and Jeff backing him up, there wasn't going to be any kind of fair fight.

"Let's move around to George's side, Bruce. The kid needs some moral support."

"Fuck man, I don't wanna get trashed," Bruce whispered, but he moved into the ring alongside Mark anyway. They both knew what was going to happen if George didn't have backup.

Rick Warner hadn't noticed their arrival any more than he'd noticed George's fighting stance.

"So you wanna lesson in good manners, eh?"

George didn't reply; just stood calmly. Mark could see that George's chest and shoulders were moving with big breaths, though, as he upped his oxygen level. Someone had taught this kid well.

"What's the matter, cocksucker? Afraid to talk?" Warner moved in confidently. "Might as well talk now, asswipe, cuz you won't be talking after I finish with you." And with that, he took a mighty swing.

The crowd gasped collectively, sure that George was going to get creamed, but Mark could read George's reactions almost as if he were the one fighting. Warner had telegraphed the punch long before he even started it, and when he did start it, it was from way back behind his shoulder, and with no thought about defense whatsoever. With ten minutes of training, Mark's seven-year-old sister could have slipped a punch like that, and George had obviously had a lot more than ten minutes of training.

He stepped easily to his left, and as Rick Warner's right arm passed harmlessly by, he hammered the bigger boy's short ribs with two lightning fast right jabs, sinking his shoulder into each one, then letting go a tremendous left hook to Warner's kidney region.

It wasn't pretty, it wasn't something that would be allowed in any fight with rules, but it was tremendously effective. If he'd followed it up with a kick to Warner's unprotected gonads, the fight would have been over right then, but George wasn't the kind of guy who kicked an opponent in the nuts from behind. Instead he stepped around in front of the dazed Rick Warner and said, "Are you willing to apologize?"

The crowd roared with laughter, and Warner stepped back, grabbing as much recovery time as he could before launching another all-out assault. This time George's technique was different—he moved inside the punch instead of outside—but the result was the same: a couple of fast shots to the gut, and then a very carefully aimed right hand that brought blood pouring out of the bigger boy's nose. The kid might not be very big, but he was as fast as anyone Mark had ever seen outside the club.

Again, he could have ended things easily if he were the kind of guy who was willing to hammer a helpless opponent, but as before, he stepped back to give Warner a chance to quit, and that was his undoing.

"Oh fuck!" Mark saw what was coming, but wasn't close enough to stop it. As George stepped backward, Jeff Anderson stuck out a leg, and George landed on his ass. Before he could recover, Anderson had moved in from behind with his boots, and was soon joined by Sergio and Christian.

"Fuck this!" Mark was yelling and sucking in air as fast as he could as he rushed forward and slammed a straight punch into the back lower portion of Jeff Anderson's skull. Anderson fell to the ground like a dead man and didn't move. The four remaining scumbags looked at who had joined the brawl and Sergio's eyes lit up.

"Oh yeah, Heaney, I've been waiting for this. This is going to be a pleasure."

"Yeah, you sons of bitches, let's see if you like five on three as much as five on one! Fuck you all. C'mon, let's get it on!" Mark shouted as he stepped between the gang and George, giving the kid a chance to get up and defend himself. Bruce had moved in on George's other side. He was shaking, but he hated the injustice as much as Mark did.

It came fast and furious after that, but it didn't last long. Rick Warner took one more barrage of punches from the kid he'd expected to have no trouble beating to a pulp, and then collapsed in a heap, blood pouring from his broken nose, and pain radiating through him from a broken rib.

That left the odds at three on three, and George quickly sized up what was going on. Zoltie Constant had thrown Bruce to the ground and was straddling him, throwing punches. Sergio and Christian were two-on-one against Mark and had him on the ground as well. Deciding that both of his saviors needed help equally, George grabbed the back of Christian's shirt and threw him bodily on top of Zoltie and Bruce. That left Mark one-on-one with Sergio Verras, who might have been an asshole, but who was definitely willing to fight. He'd seen what had happened to his buddy Warner, though, and he'd taken a couple of Mark's punches already, so rather than try anything fancy, he just launched himself onto Mark before he could get up.

It was the worst mistake he could have made. If he'd stayed on his feet, he might have had a chance to run away, or even get in a shot with his boot; but going to the ground with somebody who has been trained in defendo is like playing chicken with a semi-trailer—no matter what you do, you're going to lose.

It took Mark no more than five seconds to break Sergio's attempt at a chokehold, and only five more to flip him over and straddle him, giving him a knee in the gut in the process. As Sergio gasped for breath, Mark shoved the first and second fingers of his right hand into Sergio's nostrils, and then yanked skyward with every ounce of his strength, ripping them half off his face.

Those in the crowd who could see what had happened wanted to puke. Sergio just wanted to die. The agony from his torn nose was indescribable and he thrashed around on the ground like a wounded snake, alternately screaming and gasping in pain.

Mark knew that Sergio was finished, and leaped to his feet. George didn't need any help. He was administering the same boxing lesson to Zoltie Constant that he'd administered to Rick Warner. Constant wasn't afraid of pain the way Warner was, and managed to get in a few shots himself, but there was no question about the outcome. George would have a few bruises and a black eye the next day, but Zoltie was going to be in the hurt locker, big time.

Bruce, with no fighting skills, was faring worse. Christian Begotti had thrown him back to the ground and was starting in with the boots. He'd have been better off running, though, because Mark had a clear shot at his back, and the last thing that Christian remembered about that day was the crack of a rib as the top of Mark's foot took him in the side; then the pain of his testicles exploding as the same foot found a new target.

Suddenly aware that the noise of the crowd had dropped to nothing, Mark looked around. Two teachers were running toward them, trying not to slip in the wet grass. Mark desperately wanted to melt into the crowd and disappear, but Bruce looked hurt.

He picked one of George's flying fists out of the air and spun him around. "Get out. Split now and you might get away with it."

George stood his ground. He took one look at Zoltie Constant, who was cowering with his hands covering his bloody face and then turned to Mark.

"Your friend's hurting."

Together they knelt down and helped Bruce sit up. There was blood seeping from the side of his head where his earlobe had been torn by one of Christian's boots, and a gash on the back of his head from where it had hit a rock when he went down, but he was conscious and the adrenaline was still masking the pain. "Showed those fuckers a thing or two, didn't we?"

"Yeah man, but it looks like you're gonna need a stitch or two. Be careful with your ear."

"Ear? What's wrong with my ear?" Bruce felt first one ear and then the other, looking surprised when his hand came away covered in blood. "No shit. How'd that happen?"

The crowd had disappeared, and the fight was obviously finished, but the teachers were all over them like flies on shit, and Mark knew that the real trouble was still to come. He looked at his hands. There were gouges on a couple of his knuckles—courtesy of someone's teeth probably—but other than that, he didn't think he'd taken any serious damage. He ran his hands over his face. No blood, but he could feel swelling around his left eye. And when he bent to help Bruce up, he could feel twinges of pain in his left thigh. One of Sergio's kicks must have landed.

George seemed in about the same condition. He'd taken some good shots, but a split lip, a puffy face, and some bloody knuckles were the extent of the visible damage. He'd taken some boots after Jeff Anderson tripped him, so he was probably going to be stiff and sore from that for a few days, but he was up and walking, which was more than could be said for any of the shitheads who'd attacked him.

The teachers seemed to be leaving Mark and George alone as they helped Bruce to his feet, so Mark took the opportunity to check the carnage.

Jeff was still down. He'd dropped like a bag of sand when Mark nailed him in the back of the head, and hadn't moved since. Rick Warner was sitting up, and not making any noise, but blood was still seeping out between the hands he was holding to his face, and when one of the teachers helped him up, he clutched his ribs and howled.

Sergio had stopped thrashing, but he was making strange mewing noises and the blood was really gushing from his torn-up nostrils. Christian was lying in a fetal position, gasping silently the way a man does after a shot to the gonads. Mark suspected he'd probably be pissing blood for a while, too, from the boot in the back. He was pretty sure he'd hit kidney as well as rib with that shot.

The only one of the five that was standing unassisted was Zoltie Constant. Blood was dripping from a cut over his eye, and his nose was at a different angle than it had been before the fight, but compared to the others he'd gotten off relatively lightly. Which maybe was only just, because he was the only one of the five who hadn't jumped in on George when it looked like George was going to lay a licking on Rick Warner in a fair fight.

"You two!" It was the hard voice of Calahan, the gym teacher. "Yeah, you, Heaney and Christiansen."

"Yes sir?"

"Are either of you seriously hurt?"

"No sir," the two boys echoed.

"What about you, Kellite?"

"I don't think so, sir. I think I cut my ear, though."

"Then get the fuck out of here. Go straight to the school and wait in my office. Do you understand that?"

"Yes sir," they answered simultaneously, but Calahan had already turned from them and was sorting out the rest of the battlefield.

"Sandy." He barked at one of the other teachers, "you get on the phone. Get three ambulances, and make sure one of them's got an Advanced Life Support crew. And tell them to fucking hurry."

He stood up from examining the unconscious Jeff Anderson and shouted at another teacher, "Walt, run to the nurse's office and grab whatever blankets you can find. Bring 'em back out here and let's get these kids covered up and warm." His voice suddenly got louder. "And I mean *run*, you dickhead, not saunter." He paused for a moment, then Mark heard him continue, "And you, yeah you, Constant, can you talk?"

Zoltie must have said 'yes', because Calahan continued, "Then start talking."

Fifteen minutes later Calahan threw open the door to his office and said, "All three of you. In my car. Now." They marched. "We're going to the hospital. Kellite is going to need stitches in his ear, and maybe on his head as well. You two probably don't need anything except a good whipping, but with all the damage that's been done, I'm going to have the docs look both of you over. You can talk while we're driving."

CHAPTER 6

It was past seven when Mark finally got home. The emergency ward at the hospital was busy and they had spent a long time sitting around. Bruce, with his bloody head, had been dealt with fairly quickly, and his father had picked him up, but Mark and George had had to wait. And wait. And wait. George had managed to mutter, "Thanks man, you guys saved my ass," but Calahan shut him up with a glare, and Mark figured he'd better wait till tomorrow at school to talk to this unexpectedly tough kid.

Calahan spent most of the time on the phone. Mark imagined that he was calling parents, and also filling the principal in on what had happened. Great. He'd get shit from his dad tonight, and then from the principal in the morning. Still, how bad could it be? He and Bruce had come to the rescue of a kid who was getting stomped by five guys. If there was any justice in the world, they should get medals, not lectures.

Eventually, a frazzled-looking doctor gave both him and George a quick check, and Calahan drove them home. He dropped George off first, and spent about ten minutes inside his house while Mark waited in the car. Then it was on to the Heaney house.

His father took one look at him, said, "Downstairs," and turned to talk to Calahan.

'It's out of my hands now,' thought Mark, as he descended to his room. Calahan didn't take shit from anybody, and Mark had received an afternoon in detention from him for goofing off in P.E. one time, but the teacher was fair, and all Mark could do was hope that whatever he told his father wasn't too far from the truth.

The fight chemicals were long gone from his body, and he was both exhausted and in pain. He wanted nothing more than to go to sleep, but he knew that he'd better be awake when his father came through the door. When the door opened five minutes later though, it wasn't his father, but his mother.

"Are you alright, Mark?"

"Yeah. A bit sore, but nothing that's going to last."

"And this fight, did you have any part in instigating it?"

"No, Mom. Bruce and I came to the rescue of a kid that was getting beaten up by five guys who were bigger than him."

"Five of them? Attacking one boy?"

"That's right, Mom. There are some real dirt-bags at that school."

"Well, if you were protecting someone who needed help, then I don't have anything more to say. I'll leave it to your father." She put her hand under his chin and lifted his face to the light. "Let me look at you."

She looked him over, and left without saying a word, but was back a minute later with a bag of frozen peas wrapped in a dishtowel. "Put this against your eye. It'll keep it from swelling up any further." And then she was gone again.

It was almost half an hour before his father came to see him, and Mark had begun to worry. What was taking so long? Surely Calahan knew the score? How long could it take him to tell Scott Heaney that his son had stepped into something that most kids would be afraid to step into, and saved another boy from a gang stomping?

When the knock finally came on his door, he didn't know what to expect. Would his dad be pissed at him for getting in a fight? Would he be proud of him for getting into this particular fight?

Mark stood up and opened the door. "Come in."

Scott Heaney entered the room, but his face didn't have any giveaway signs of his mood. "You okay?"

"Yes sir." Well, at least he hadn't started by yelling.

"Really okay, you're sure?"

"Yes, Dad. I took a few shots, but nothing serious. I've been hurt worse at the club."

"Do you understand how lucky you are?"

"Lucky?" Did he mean lucky to get out of a five-on-three without serious damage? Lucky that Calahan had been around to see enough of what had happened to know the score? Mark knew enough not to take anything for granted where his father was concerned, knew enough not to make any smartass remarks about how it was skill, not luck, that had carried him through the fight.

"You have any idea what would happen to a kid like you in jail?"

"*Jail!* Dad, what are you talking about?"

"Jail, Mark, is where you'd have wound up if that Anderson kid had died. And he was this..." Scott Heaney held up a finger and thumb just a hair apart, "...this fucking close to dying. This close, do you understand?"

"Dying?" Mark couldn't believe what he was hearing. He'd toppled Anderson like a tree, but dying?

"Listen to me. You go to jail for killing somebody, you don't wind up in some hoods-in-the-woods camp-out. You wind up in maximum security with a bunch of guys whose idea of what to do with a seventeen-year-old brown-skinned kid is to throw him face down and rape him whenever they feel like. The chances of you getting out of a place like that alive would be just about zero."

Mark was speechless. Literally, speechless. He wanted to talk. He wanted to ask for an explanation, to ask what this was about, but he couldn't make words come out. Sent to jail? Raped? Killed?

"Just answer one question: Did you, or did you not, nail the Anderson boy with a palm strike to the base of the skull?"

Mark didn't remember doing anything potentially lethal, but he knew he'd been totally wired on fight chemicals. He thought back carefully. Decking Jeff Anderson had been the first thing he'd done in the fight. He'd moved in yelling and sucking Oxy, and... Oh, fuck...

"Yes."

"You decided that you wanted to kill him?"

"No."

"That's a kill strike, Mark. It's an executioner's move. You can only do it from behind and there's no defense against it."

"I realize that now."

"So? I'm waiting to hear why you pulled a kill move on a seventeen-year-old kid who was standing with his back to you."

"I'm sorry, Dad, I should never have done it. Is he going to be alright?"

"Answer my question."

"I did it because I lost control."

"That's better. Now, why did you lose control?"

"Because he and four other scumbags were stomping one helpless kid just because he'd had the courage to try to stand up to their hazing. Five-on-one dad. What would you have done?"

"What you should have done... Think. There are ten ways to take out a guy who doesn't see you coming that don't involve killing him. You know that."

"Yes, I do. Is he going to be alright?"

"Of course he's going to fucking be alright. Do you think I'd be standing here jawing with you if you'd killed him?"

Mark didn't say anything.

"I've been training you since you could walk, Mark, and one of the things I've tried to teach you from day one is that along with your power comes responsibility. One of those responsibilities is to protect those who can't protect themselves. You did the right thing jumping into that fight. Facing up to five guys the way you did, to protect some kid you hardly even know, makes me proud. Don't ever doubt it."

Mark stared at his toes, but he could feel himself blushing.

"But you also have the responsibility to use your skills with control. With my training, I can kill anybody who pisses me off, but part of my training is knowing that deadly force is almost never the answer."

"Yes, I understand that now, but in the fight, I guess I lost control."

"Sit down."

"Sit?"

"Sit down, Mark, the lecture's over."

Mark sat on his bed, and his father pulled the chair out from the desk and sat on that. "You pulled that punch."

"I did?"

"I've trained with you for over ten years, Mark; I know how hard you can hit. If you hadn't pulled it, that kid would have been dead before he hit the ground."

Mark thought about that for a while. He didn't remember taking anything off the strike. He remembered zeroing in on the spot at the base of Jeff Anderson's skull, and he remembered seeing him fall, but he had no memory of the actual strike. He knew his father had to be right, though. After ten years of training on heavier and heavier bags, he knew that he had the power to drop an ox with that kind of strike, so he *must* have pulled it.

"Okay, Mark. You stepped in where you didn't have to and saved that kid's ass. Maybe even his life, who knows? If they were putting the boots to him, they could easily have killed him. That's good.

"On the other hand, you came within a hair of killing a kid who didn't deserve to die. You could just as easily have nailed him in the hamstring and he'd have been out for the duration, but you put a kill move on him. That's bad.

"So, here's the deal: I'm not going to reward you or punish you in any way, but you are going to spend the next several workouts practicing the kind of things you could have done instead of going for the base of his skull, and if you ever," Scott Heaney's eyebrows drew together, and the fire burned in his eyes, "*ever* do something like that again, I will personally see that you suffer more than you think it possible for one boy to suffer. Do you understand?"

"Yes, I do. That's fair."

"Yes, it is. Now, tell me about the fight, the whole story, not just the punches and kicks. I want to know everything. Who was this kid you were protecting? Why did the five guys try to stomp him? Who actually started it? Why were you even there when it happened... The whole story."

Half an hour later the older man stood. "You did the right thing Mark, and except for that one punch, I'm proud of you. The Anderson kid is going to be fine—you're lucky on that score—but I expect you're going to pay a price at school. Calahan will speak up for you, and you're not going to get expelled, but he tells me that in a case like this, the principal doesn't have much choice, and you are going to get suspended for a couple of days." He patted his son on the shoulder.

"You did good, boy, you did good. Now go take a shower and then get some sleep."

"A week?" Bruce was not a happy camper.

Mark had gone in first, and when he came out of the principal's office, he told Bruce the news.

"We're out for a week? Oh fuck, why did I get involved in that fight anyway?"

"Because it was the right thing to do. You know that. Now shut up and get in there and take your medicine."

Bruce went in, and Mark sat down beside George Christiansen. The kid's face looked like a child abuse poster, but he was grinning at Mark. Mark grinned back at him and asked, "Where did you learn to fight like that? I don't think there's anybody in this school besides me that could take you."

"Mr. Hufleyn"

"Huh?"

"Mr. Hufleyn. The physics teacher. He could take me anytime he wanted. He's also the one that taught me."

"Hufleyn? That geeky looking guy with the glasses? He taught you to box?"

"You don't have to shave your head and wear big boots to be tough, you know," George said gently.

"Yeah, sorry, you're right. I know that, but still... Hufleyn?"

"That's right. He told me he boxed for Canada in the Olympics when he was young, and he teaches a class down at the Y. Three times a week."

"No shit. I'm gonna have to tell my dad about that. He'll probably invite him to the club."

Now it was George's turn to say "Huh?"

Mark explained a bit about his father, a bit about the club and the hapkido master who ran it, and a bit about defendo. And how his father was always looking for outside teachers to come in and add their knowledge to his.

"I thought all those martial arts styles were really hung up about only doing the moves that had come down with a blessing from some high guru in Asia."

Mark laughed. "Right on. A lot of them are like that. Even hapkido is a bit that way. But the only god that a defendo teacher worships is survival. If Hufleyn has some boxing moves that dad doesn't know, or if he has ideas about training, or fitness, or any of that stuff, my dad'll welcome him."

"Wow. I'll introduce you to him and maybe you can tell him. He's actually a really cool guy." George smiled sheepishly. "Well, maybe in a week I'll introduce you to him. Doesn't sound like we're going to be around here much till then. Oh, shit..."

"What?"

"How are we going to keep up on our schoolwork? We're going to miss a whole week's work." George sounded a lot more broken up about this than Mark felt, but then, a nerd was a nerd, even if he *could* knock the snot out of people like Rick Warner.

"We're covered on that one. The Principal says he's talked to all our teachers and we're supposed to come back tomorrow morning and pick up all of our assignments and study schedules for the week. He'll have them here."

"Oh, good; I sure wouldn't want to miss a whole week."

Right, thought Mark, and I'd sure like to miss a whole year, but I don't always get what I want.

"So what happened to those guys that jumped me? I'm pretty sure that I broke Warner's nose, and I think Zoltie's, too. I wouldn't be surprised if I even managed to break a couple of Warner's ribs, but I didn't really see what happened to the others."

"Jeff Anderson, the guy who tripped you, is going to be alright, he's going to be a bit confused for a few days, but he's not going to have any permanent damage. Sergio and Christian, well, they'd probably be off school for a while even if they weren't suspended."

"What did you do to them?"

"Nothing as pretty as your boxing exhibition, that's for sure. Sergio's going to need some serious surgery to get his nostrils reattached to his face, and Christian, well, I suspect his ribs are a lot more badly broken than Warner's, and God knows what kind of shape his nuts are in." Mark thought about it. "Bottom line is, they're not going to be bothering you, or anybody else, ever again."

"What? You don't think they're going to come for you when they're healed? And for me?"

"George, what you did to Rick Warner, that was sort of humiliating, and I'm sure it was painful, but what I did to those other three guys was something else entirely. I hurt them, George. I hurt them in a way that you can't even begin to understand. Believe me, they are *not* going to be bullying anybody, ever again." He looked up as the door opened. "Hey Bruce. You get the same treatment I got?"

"Yeah. An one-week suspension. And a big fucking lecture about respect for others, and zero tolerance for this kind of behavior, and... well, you probably got it, too. So I guess I don't need to repeat it. He should save it for those jerkwads that jumped George."

"You didn't hear?" George seemed surprised. They both looked at him. "They're out for the semester."

"What? Are you serious?"

"You really didn't hear?"

"No."

"Mr. Calahan told me. Enough kids saw what happened that it's not one of those our-word-against-theirs things. When the principal found out that Anderson, and Verras and Begotti jumped into what was a fair fight and started putting the boots to me when I was down, he tossed them for the rest of the semester."

"Holy shit! Maybe there is some justice in the world. What about that dickhead, Warner?"

"He gets the same as us. One week. Same for Zoltie Constant."

Mark and Bruce looked at each other, and Bruce spoke for both of them. "Yeah, that's fair. Warner's a total butt-smear, but he took you on one-on-one, and got his ass severely whipped. And Zoltie, well, he didn't take any part in it at all until we moved in."

George stood up to take his turn in the principal's office. "What isn't fair is that you guys get suspended. You don't even know me, and you stepped in against five guys to save my butt. You should be getting some kind of an award, not a fucking punishment. I called Warner out, and I've got no complaints, but suspending you guys just isn't right. I'm going to tell the principal that."

"Thanks, man. It won't do one fucking bit of good, but I appreciate it. And you know what?" Mark was trying hard to keep from laughing out loud. "If I thought you were going to get our suspensions reversed, I'd put the boots to you myself. This is actually the best thing that could have happened to us right now."

Bruce was looking at him like he was crazy. George seemed to be willing to give him the benefit of the doubt. He raised his eyebrows in the universal 'Say what?' gesture.

"C'mon Bruce, wake up. This is going to give us forty extra hours to practice. If we use this week properly there's no way Bones is gonna turn us down."

"What are you talking about?" George was clearly confused, but before they could explain, Principal Mayo stepped into the room.

"I'm sure you have an excellent reason for keeping me waiting, Mr. Christiansen. Perhaps you'd like to step into my office and explain it to me."

"I'm sorry, sir." George headed for the inquisition chamber.

"We'll wait for you, man," Mark said to him.

Fifteen minutes later, the three boys collected their jackets and books from their lockers, and headed for the exit. It was break between classes and the buzz that followed them as they worked their way through the crowd made it clear that the word was already out. They had to shake a lot of hands and take a lot of backslaps. Sergio's gang had made just about everybody's life miserable at one time or another, and a lot of people were looking at the threesome in a completely new way. To Mark, it felt good.

The next three weeks were a total blur. He kept up with his schoolwork, even during the suspension, because he knew if he fell behind his father would pull the plug on the band. He worked out at the club twice a week, too. But his mind was on his music. He and Bruce practiced every single day. They worked on covers of old songs, they worked on some new songs of their own, but mostly they worked on the ten songs that they were committed to for the audition.

Larry Kellite had told them that five plus five was the magic number. He said he'd never heard of an audition that required more than five songs. "We have to go in there with five ska songs wired down so tight that we can play them even if the club is burning to the ground around us, but we should also have an extra five available in a variety of styles." He picked up his guitar and laid down a searing blues riff. "Suppose, right in the middle of our killer ska display, this Bones guy says 'Hey, can you guys do punk? The crowds have been calling for punk lately.' Or rock, or blues, or whatever. Then we just launch into whatever it is without even stopping to think about it."

"Disco?" said Bruce. "Should we get a few disco numbers down, too?"

"Yeah, and what about country?" added Mark. "We gotta have a song about our wimmin runnin' off with our best friend."

"Alright. I agree that if he asks us to do disco, we blow the place up and go looking for an audition somewhere else, but you know what I mean."

"Yeah, we do."

So they practiced and practiced and practiced. The horn players showed up at least twice a week, and on those days, they worked on the ska songs—*Drinking and Driving, Sally Brown, Jane Bondage, It's Your Round,* and *It's Not Mine*. On the days when it was just the two of them plus Wilbur and Larry, they'd give the ska tunes a quick run-through and then work on the other five: *In The City* by the Jam; The Who's *My Generation; Jailhouse Rock,* one of Elvis's early greats; *Paint it Black* by the Rolling Stones; and Jimmy Thackery's blues/ rock classic *Trouble Man*.

Finally, on a Thursday night, with just two days to go before the audition, Larry Kellite told them pretty much what Scott Heaney had told Mark before his exams.

"Guys, we're going to go in there on Sunday morning, and get ourselves a job—no question about it; he's gonna love us—and two more days of practising isn't going to do nearly as much good as two days off. So Bruce, your guitar is off limits from now till the audition. And Mark, I'm gonna tell your father that if he hears you singing in the next two days, even in the shower, that he should duct tape your mouth shut."

Saturday night. The movie was over. They'd eaten their fill. They were about to head home.

"It's stopped raining."

"Yeah, so?"

"So you want to go check out Skavoovee?"

"Are you serious? That's the kind of dumb-ola thing your little brother Glen would do."

"What are you talking about? We're going to be going there tomorrow morning with your dad anyway, I just want to go have a look at it. Dad's pointed it out to me when we've driven by in the car, but wouldn't it be cool to go and take a look for ourselves?"

"Well, unless you got two years older in the last couple of days, you're still underage. You get caught trying to sneak in and you'll blow our chances for a gig." Bruce was clearly not pleased with the idea.

"I'm not talking about that, smeghead, I'm talking about just hanging out nearby, checking it out from the outside." Mark looked up at the clock on the wall of the Subway they were sitting in. "It's ten o'clock; there's bound to be some action."

"Hang out on the street around the place?"

"Yeah."

"That is even dumber than trying to get in. Or have you forgotten where it is?"

"What are you talking about? It's in the skids man, a couple of blocks this side of Main and Hastings."

"Yeah, right in the fucking center of the junkie zone. That is *not* a cool place to be at night. You get into a fight there and you could walk away with Hep C or even HIV."

"Oh, come on, the worst thing that's going to happen is that someone will try to sell you some heroin."

"No, the worst thing that's going to happen is that someone is going to knife me so they can steal money from my corpse and go and *buy* some crack."

"Bruce, I'm not as good as my father, or Bones, but I think I can handle any cokehead that gets obnoxious. Besides, look on the bright side: maybe you'll meet a really cute hooker. There's certain areas you can go to down there where there's five dollar specials."

"Eww, no thanks. I'm finally starting to think that maybe Kelly and I are…"

"Kelly? The Safeway Girl? You been seeing a girl while I'm stuck with sheep?"

"Well, I haven't actually been *dating* her. Fuck, when would I have had the time? But we've been, you know, talking a lot, and after the audition's out of the way, I'm gonna ask her out."

"She have a sister?"

"Yeah, two of 'em. One's eleven and one's nine."

"Great."

"You want me to ask if she's got a pet sheep?"

"Much longer without a girlfriend, and I'd say yes. But not tonight. Tonight we're going to Skavoovee."

Vancouver's east side is the heroin capitol of North America. It also has the highest AIDS infection rate in the first world. The two statistics are related—the AIDS is spread primarily through needles—but the streets were thick with wasted-looking, drug-fried hookers, and Mark reckoned that most of them were probably doing their share of disease spreading, too.

They had to fend off half a dozen propositions per block. "Jesus, Bruce, look at them. I wouldn't fuck something like that if *they* paid *me*. They look like soulless zombies."

"No kidding. They make sheep look good."

"I don't get it. I thought hookers were supposed to be good-looking, but these ones look like walking skeletons. Nobody in his right mind would let one of them anywhere near his dick."

"I think it must just be the skids. Uptown hookers must hang out somewhere else."

"And the dealers! Man I wouldn't buy drugs from guys like that no matter how bad I wanted a fix."

"Don't kid yourself, Mark. You get deep enough into drugs and you'll buy anything from anybody. Talk to my dad about that sometime."

Mark tapped his friend's shoulder and pointed down the street. "Hey, look at that lineup. That's gotta be Skavoovee."

Sure enough. As they got closer, they could see the sign: a grinning skull with a cigarette dangling out of its mouth, and the single word 'Skavoovee' underneath it in purple neon.

"Wow! Look how long the lineup is. And check the scooters!"

For half a block, the street in front of Skavoovee was lined with Vespa and Lambretta scooters. Some were chopped up and modified while others appeared in good to mint condition. There were a lot of them, which was a great sign.

"Definitely must be a ska band playing tonight."

The people in the lineup reflected that fact. More skins and scooterboys than Mark had ever seen in one place in his life, as well as a healthy selection of goths, punks, tattoo freaks, and a variety of people who didn't seem to be affiliated with any particular group. "C'mon. Let's cross the street. We'll get a great view if we stand right across from it."

"Okay, but first let's walk right along the line. Maybe we'll get a look inside. I want to know who's playing."

As they got closer, they began to hear blasts of high-energy ska music every time the door opened to let people in or out. There were no signs, though, so Bruce finally got up the nerve to ask one of the mods in the lineup who was playing.

"Mark, you ain't gonna believe this. You know who's in there? Do you have any idea how fast I'd give my left nut for a chance to get through that door?"

"Who, man, who? Tell me."

"It's King Apparatus, man. King fucking Apparatus is the main show. That's a ska band from Toronto called the Blatherskites playing right now and after they finish an oi band called the Subway Thugs goes on. Then King Apparatus will play so we have plenty of time to enjoy ourselves. I don't believe it. We're going to be playing in the same club as King Apparatus!" Bruce was dancing on the street, weaving a line in and out of the scooters. People were staring at him, but he didn't care. "Oh, man, I can't wait to get home and tell dad."

"Keep dancing around like that, and you'll get taken to a detox center. What'll your dad say about that?" Mark grabbed his friend by the arm and led him across the street. "Chill out. Did you see the way that bouncer was looking at you?"

"What bouncer?"

Mark pointed to the doorway, where traffic in and out of the club was controlled by a gigantic bald-headed guy dressed in jeans and a black leather vest. Wild tattoos covered his chest and shoulders and swirled down his arms. "That bouncer. The one who would have bounced your head off the sidewalk if I hadn't dragged you away from the place."

They stayed, glued to the sidewalk, unaware of the junkies and cokeheads who staggered by them, of the hookers and dealers who plied their trades openly, and of the customers who were buying the flesh and drugs. They had eyes only for the three-story brick building across the street, and the colorful, lively, laughing lineup of people waiting to get in and listen to the wonderful music that was spilling through the doors and onto the street.

They would probably have stayed there all night if a gruff voice hadn't brought them back to reality.

"Looking for something, boys?"

It was a cop. One of a pair of cops who had been watching them for who knew how long.

"No sir. Uh, I mean, only Skavoovee, sir."

"Little young for the bar scene, aren't you?"

Bruce was about to speak, and Mark knew what he was going to say. He would start babbling about how they were going to audition there tomorrow, and that would be the end of it. Right there. No way you could play in a bar underage any more than you could drink there underage. And if he told the cops what they were planning for tomorrow, the cops would be on Bones like fleas on a cat.

He cut Bruce off before he could get started. "My dad's best friend owns Skavoovee, sir. We were at a movie and we just walked down here to have a look. We've never seen it before."

"Hmm." The cop looked at him like he was able to see right into his brain. "And who would that be."

"Bones, sir, I mean Ian, Ian Battle."

"Okay, maybe you are telling the truth." The cop looked at his partner, who gave a slight nod, and the two of them walked away, prodding the junkies that were passed out on the sidewalk to make sure they were still breathing, and generally ignoring the street commerce going on all around them.

"Fuck man, can you believe this?" Bruce waved his arms, taking in the entire scene. "This is unreal. This is like ... like ... "

"Like the skids on Saturday night?"

"I don't know, man, but whatever it is, I love it!"

Mark spent the night at his friend's place. At noon on Sunday, they helped Larry and Wilbur pack their gear into Wilbur's van, and headed for Skavoovee.

"Only this time, you won't have to stand out on the street; you'll get to go inside, just like real people."

Wilbur parked in the alley behind the building and said, "You wanna check the door, Larry?"

"Sure." Bruce's father hopped out of the van and rang a bell between a big loading door and a smaller van door. A minute later the small door opened, and the tattooed giant who had been controlling things on the street the previous night stepped out. He spoke to Larry Kellite, then turned around and called to someone inside.

"Pull ahead so the rear of the van is beside the loading door, Wil."

When the van was parked, Mark jumped out and looked around, trying to take in everything at once, but avoiding eye contact with the giant bouncer. Defendo was all well and good, but when you were only seventeen, there were limits to what you could do to a three hundred-pound monster that looked like he would probably consider street-fighting his favorite sport.

But then the loading door started groaning upward, and first the feet, then the body, and finally the head of Bones Battle came into view. He was tall and lean, with broad shoulders and slim hips. Muscles and tendons danced under his skin with every move, and looking into his eyes was like feeling the wind blow out of the Arctic.

"Mark. Good to see you, lad." He had the same working-class British accent that Carl the drummer had had.

"Hi, Mr. Battle."

"Bones. If your music stinks you can go back to calling me Mr. Battle, but if you're any good, then it's Bones from now on." He looked at the other three. "Are you going to introduce me to your mates?"

Mark mumbled his way through some introductions, but all he could think of was getting inside. Music had been his religion for the last two months, and in his mind, Skavoovee was music's holiest temple. Now, finally, he was going to enter the sacred place.

"Right then. Grab your gear, and follow me. Jurgen," he said as he looked at the giant bouncer, "will give you a hand."

Jurgen looked like he'd be quite capable of tucking the entire van under his arm and carrying it upstairs without raising a sweat. But he smiled pleasantly enough and said to Larry Kellite, "I've been setting up for bands for years, so don't worry about me breaking anything."

He had a bit of a German accent, which somehow seemed weird for a guy with so much ink on him. Mark was sure that Germans were just as into tats as anyone else, but it still seemed strange.

Mark picked up one of the guitar cases and followed Bones and Larry. He heard Bones say, "So you're Larry Kellite. Seems like every second

103

musician that plays here has something to say about you. Been wanting to meet you for ages."

Whatever Larry said in reply was lost on Mark, because when Bones led them out of the storage room and into the main club, Mark lost interest in everything except the look of the place. He'd never been in any place like it, and it exceeded even his wildest dream.

It seemed huge. He'd had no idea, looking from the outside last night, that it could be this big. The floor and the walls were all brick. Not the bright orangey-red bricks that he was used to, but bricks that looked like they'd been old when the world itself was still young. And the bar! It went on, and on, and on. It was solid wood that looked as old as the bricks, polished to a deep, dark, cherry black. There was also a gleaming brass foot rail, a long row of high wood and leather barstools, and, on top of the bar, at about two meter intervals, weird looking brass and porcelain things. Beer taps. He'd never seen a beer tap before, but that's what they must be.

Above the bar, reflecting the dim light of the place, was row upon row of glasses, hanging upside down, and, just like in the movies, the wall behind the bar was lined with shelves holding hundreds of bottles.

The room itself was full of tables made of thick, heavy wood, and comfortable-looking chairs with broad arms and padded leather seats. Along the walls, the wood theme continued with partitioned booths that looked both cozy and private. Three women were moving among the tables, laying out clean place settings. Or rather, two women and a girl. She was maybe a year older than Mark, and looked both beautiful, and vaguely familiar. Someone who'd graduated from his school a year before? Someone he'd seen working in a shop somewhere?

Bruce's voice came from just behind him, taking his mind off the girl.

"I don't get it."

"Get what?"

"There's no stage. No dance floor. This is supposed to be a music venue, but there's no place to play or dance. It's just a pub."

Before Mark could answer, Larry Kellite's voice came to them from somewhere above. "Are you two dreamers going to come and help set up, or are you going to just stand there with your mouths hanging open?"

They looked up. Larry was leaning over a railing looking down at them. "Stairs are that way."

They followed his pointing finger and saw that, yes, there were stairs leading to another floor. Mark cast a last, longing look around at the bar—particularly at the young woman—and headed upstairs.

Now *this*, he thought as he looked around from the top of the stairs, is a music club. The back half of the room was tables and chairs, fairly similar to what was on the floor below. Then there was a large clear space, and then the stage. It wasn't too high, so there would be an intimate feel between band and dancers, but it was big enough to hold a large band comfortably. The ceiling was a long way up. Mark thought that this space must have been two floors at some time, with the roof-floor between them knocked out to make a better dance venue.

Wilbur and Jurgen were moving mike stands and keyboards, and a drum kit back out of the way; Larry and Bones were setting up the Juice Monkeys' gear in its place, and talking about people they knew in common.

"Get up here and get to work, you two. Kenny and the Dougs are going to be here in half an hour, and I want everything ready to go when they get here."

Mark and Bruce mostly did what they were told and left the technical end of things to Larry and Wilbur. It took longer than Mark expected. He'd thought that they would come in, set up a couple of amps, and play. But even though they were only setting up for an audition, a one-hour session, Larry wanted everything *exactly* this way or *exactly* that way.

The horn players arrived right on schedule, and once they were unpacked, Larry started a soundcheck. It was a fantasyland for Mark and Bruce, but everybody else seemed to be either busy or bored, so they just hung out, followed instructions, and dug the fact that they were about to play Skavoovee.

Bones had long since gone downstairs, and when the soundcheck was done, Larry Kellite asked Mark to go and find him.

Mark headed downstairs and found him talking to the girl he'd been so attracted to earlier, and looking at the two of them together, he realized who she was. She looked familiar because she was Bones' daughter—

there was a strong family resemblance. He remembered that he'd met her once, probably five years ago, but when he was twelve, girls had been right up there with linoleum on his list of completely uninteresting things, and he'd never really thought about her since.

Terri. That was her name. And she definitely wasn't a skinny four-teen-year-old girl anymore. She was full-figured, and gorgeous. She was also Bones Battle's daughter, he reminded himself, and therefore completely off limits.

"We're ready to play."

"Okay, Mark, I'm ready to listen." He threw an arm across his daughter's shoulder. "Do you remember Mark Heaney? Scott's son? Mark this is my daughter, Terri. She's working here to help put herself through college. She says the boss is an arsehole, but the pay's great, so she sticks with it."

Terri's eyes were full of good humor, and she elbowed her father in the ribs. "Hi, Mark."

"Hi, Terri." He wanted to say something clever, something that would impress her, but his tongue froze, and all he could do was try not to be too obvious about staring.

"Okay, lad, let's hear some joyful noise."

Upstairs, everything was ready. Mark climbed up on the stage, nervous as hell, sure that he'd blow it completely, and at the same time excited in a way he'd never been before. He looked out at the empty room and imagined two hundred and fifty fans, screaming, dancing, and loving every sound the band put out. Larry Kellite must have known what was going on in his mind because he said, "No sweat, Mark, no sweat. Just relax and pretend that we're home in the dungeon and that this is just one more practice."

Mark sucked in air, but it felt like it was leaking out of his ass faster than it came in. "Get over it. Focus. Focus!" He thought to himself, fighting off a feeling of nausea. But then Wilbur was tapping the beginning of the first song, the guitar and bass kicked in, and before he realized what was happening, he was belting out the first verse of *Drinking and Driving*.

After that, it was fun. It was music. And music was something that came naturally to him, carried him along, made him fly. Bones was at a table in the back corner, where it was too dark to see him clearly. It looked like there was someone else with him, but Mark really wasn't noticing. Probably Jurgen. He did notice when Terri and the other two women came up the stairs halfway through the second song, but somehow, when he was on stage, with the mike in his hand, he didn't feel klutzy like he had when he was trying to make conversation.

In fact, it made him feel better that people were there. That there was someone to sing to. He directed his performance toward them, not thinking of them as desirable women, but as music lovers, hungry for the band's energy. They worked their way through the five ska tunes, and then, without anybody really saying anything, Bruce and his father switched instruments and launched spontaneously into Jimmy Thackery's *Trouble Man*. Two months ago, Mark had never heard of Jimmy Thackery; and he'd certainly never thought that blues was something he was interested in. Then one night, Larry had played one of Thackery's CDs for them, and Mark's musical horizon expanded dramatically.

This kind of blues was hard-driving music that would have people out of their chairs and dancing with the same energy that a good ska tune would give them. It also had the advantage of putting Larry upfront for some insane guitar pyrotechnics.

When the last chords of *Trouble Man* faded out like thunder growling in the distance, they segued into the Dead Milkmen's *Punk Rock Girl*, and finally, at Mark's suggestion, Bruce's song *Safeway Girl*. They hadn't planned to use it in this audition, but they had it down as tight as any of the songs they had planned to use, and they all enjoyed playing it. It just flowed naturally. When it was done, they all put down their instruments and looked at each other with the kind of feeling that's impossible for the non-musician to ever really understand.

They'd been tight. They'd been hot. They knew it, and the heat ran through their blood like fire.

As the echoes of the amplifiers stopped ringing in his head, Mark heard Bones's voice from the back of the room. "Jesus, why didn't you tell me they were this good."

"Didn't know, Bones. Never heard them myself."

It was his father's voice! The dark shape in the shadows had been his father.

"Well, you've fucking heard them now, mate," Bones laughed.

"Dad! What are you doing here?" Mark shouted into the darkness.

"The old man isn't allowed to come down to his favorite watering hole and have a beer with a mate?" The two men stood and walked forward. "Thought I'd better be here so I could kick your ass if it turned out you'd been wasting Bones' time." He looked at the table where Terri sat with the other two women, then up to the stage at Mark and Bruce.

"Looks like you've turned this place into a teen club, Bones. Can a man still get a beer, or do I have to go with bubblegum and soft drinks?"

Bones Battle called up to the stage, "You lads thirsty?"

There was a unanimous chorus of 'Oh yeah!' and 'Sure am!' from the band.

"Right, Megan, pints of the special amber all round. You three are welcome to a pint too, as long as you don't forget we've got to be open for business at four."

"Okay, boss." She stood, and said to Terri and the other woman, "C'mon ladies, the menfolk must be served." The three women left the dance floor and disappeared down the stairs.

"You guys pack up your gear and get King Apparatus' stuff back in place, and then we'll sit down and have us a beer and a chat."

The beer was different from the bottled stuff that Larry Kellite occasionally let him have; different even from the microbrews that his father enjoyed.

"Imported from England, lad." Bones told him. "It's the real thing, not the imitation English that you get in most bars. Bloody horsepiss, that is. Now. Business." He turned to Larry Kellite. "How many sets can you do without any repeats?"

"Three right now, four by the end of the month."

"All to that standard?"

"No problem."

"What about weeknights?" Bones tipped his head toward Mark and Bruce. "Their mommies going to let them stay out if they have school the next day?"

"I don't know what Scott will say, but until summer, Bruce is limited to Fridays and Saturdays."

"I don't think it would hurt if they played a weeknight once or twice in the next six months," said Scott Heaney, "but in general I'm in full agreement with Larry. School comes first, and that means that the odd weekend is the limit." He tipped up his glass and looked meaningfully at Bones when it came down empty.

"Right. Mine's getting low, too. Anyone else?"

When everybody nodded or said, "Yes," Bones stood and leaned over the railing. "Another full round, Megan. But this time, two of them are cokes."

Mark and Bruce looked longingly at their empty mugs.

"Bones, it's not just the boys that are part-timers." Larry Kellite tipped up his own beer and finished it. "Wilbur and I are too tied up at the studio to go back to playing full time. We both miss it, but the studio has to come first right now, and I know that if I ever went back on the road, I'd be back in the gutter within a year. No. What we want is what I told you on the phone. Just the odd Friday or Saturday night, and maybe a longer stand over Christmas or in the summer."

"Alright. You've been around long enough that I don't have to tell you how good you are, so I'll have a look at my bookings this afternoon, and give you a call and let you know when. Probably mid-January." He stood and leaned across the table for a handshake. "Deal?"

Larry Kellite took the hand. "Deal."

When the band had packed up and gone, Scott Heaney and his old comrade-in-arms sat down with another pint.

"Thanks, Bones."

"For what mate?"

"For giving the boys a chance. They're good kids, mate. Cheers!" Their mugs clanged together.

"No bother at my end, Scott. I know you can't tell the difference between a good band and a cow with a baseball bat up its ass, which is what that Maori caterwauling you listen to sounds like, but let me tell you, they're tight as a monkey's arsehole."

"That's good?"

"That's good. The boys, and the horn players, too, have the ska sound in their hearts, and Larry, well, Larry Kellite can play anything. He could come in here and play fuckin' Christmas carols and people would dance. And the boys are good, Scotty, they're good. Not as good as they're going to be someday, but with Larry and his friends behind them, they're good enough to play this old barn any day." He held his beer up to the light. "No, they're not going to hurt my beer sales one little bit."

CHAPTER 7

November rolled into December. Bones had called Larry Kellite on the day after the audition and booked the Juice Monkeys for the last weekend in January. With that to keep him focused, Mark found that the hard work of studying, practicing, and martial arts workouts were much less of a burden than he expected. His Christmas exams went reasonably well—he even passed his Social Studies course—and once exams were finally over, he relaxed into two weeks of holidays.

It was a good holiday for the Heaney family. Mark's father wasn't at home for much of it, but he was working when a lot of men in the construction industry weren't, so nobody complained too much.

Going back to school after such a good break was a drag, and the first week crawled by in slow motion. Friday afternoon ended with Automotive Shop, which was better than anything else he'd done that week; but even so, Mark was happy to see it end. He was standing by Bruce's locker with his mind in neutral, waiting for Bruce to sort out his books, when he heard Larry Kellite's familiar voice.

"Bruce. Mark. Jesus. I thought I'd never find you. This place is huge!"

"Dad!" Bruce was so surprised, he banged his head on the top shelf of his locker as he jerked upright. "What are you doing here?"

"Bringing news. Bones called me about half an hour ago. The band he had booked for tonight just canceled—Customs shut them down at the border and they're going to be at least a day late. He wants to know if we'll fill in."

"Tonight? *Tonight*?!" Mark couldn't believe what he'd heard.

"That's right."

"No joke? He really wants us to play Skavoovee tonight?" It was Bruce's turn to question what he'd heard.

"What is it with you two? You suddenly don't understand English? Yes, he *really* wants us to play Skavoovee. Tonight."

"Yeeeeeee Haaaawwwwwwww!" The boys started dancing and playing air guitar in the hall, but suddenly Mark stopped. "I'll have to check with my folks."

"I already did. Your mother gave me a number at the job site that your dad's working on, and I've talked to him. He's cool with it."

"Do you think we're ready? I mean we…"

"You were ready a month ago. We've got enough material for five or six sets, and we only need three good sets for a one-nighter. Now grab your books and let's go. Wilbur's waiting in the van, we've got everything packed and we'll all head down to Skavoovee to set up. After that, I'll take the two of you out for supper."

"But shouldn't we… That is…" Mark wasn't sure what he wanted to say. Half of him was already up on stage, glorying in the adulation of the crowd; but half of him was going into full panic mode. Him? Sing in front of a big crowd at one of the hottest ska clubs?

He looked around. Kids who had been packing books and putting on jackets had stopped what they were doing and were staring openly. He knew that within ten minutes everyone in the school would hear about this.

His stomach started to churn. "Uh… What about clothes? I should go home first and get something to wear for tonight."

"It's already taken care of. You've talked about what you'd wear at your first gig so often that I just stopped by your house and picked it up. Dickeys Pants and a red Fred Perry, right?"

"Yes, but…"

"No more buts. It's time to work."

"What time do we go on?"

"Probably not till around eleven. But don't worry. There'll be so much to do between now and then, that there'll barely be enough time to scratch your ass. Are you nervous?"

"Oh, man, am I ever." Mark looked at Bruce. His friend looked totally in control. "How can you be so calm?"

"I've been dreaming about this day since I was five years old, bro."

Setup and sound checks took forever. Larry Kellite was a perfectionist, and where Mark would have just dragged their gear onto the stage and expected it to work when the show started, Larry tested everything about ten times, adjusting this, moving that, adjusting something else. Never satisfied. Finally, he said, "Okay, that's probably as good as it's going to get. Who's hungry?"

He took them to a steak and pizza place in Gastown, the oldest part of the city. "Don't pig out. You need enough fuel to get through the performance, but if you pig out, you'll regret it."

An hour later Mark understood what he'd meant. The whole band was in the dressing room, working out what they wanted to do in the first set, but all Mark could think of was the knot in his gut.

"Uh, excuse me guys, but I think I'm gonna throw up." He ran for the bathroom, threw open the stall door, and got down on his knees in full porcelain-worship position. Nothing came up, but the churning in his gut was so strong that he didn't dare leave the toilet.

"Mark?"

He knew that voice. His father. 'Great', he thought to himself, 'I wonder what he'll think of this?'

"Where are you, son?" Scott Heaney called out.

"In here."

"Whoa, lad—drunk already?" Bones' voice. Doubly great. They were probably looking at the soles of his feet sticking out under the stall door. Quadruple fucking great.

"You okay in there, son?"

"I wanna puke."

"Nervous?" Scott Heaney said.

"Oh man, am I ever." Then a new thought hit home. "What am I gonna do if I get sick on stage?"

"Don't worry, youth." Bones voice. "Once you're up there, you'll be fine."

"Easy for you to say."

"How long have you been in there?" His father again.

"I don't know. Fuck. Fifteen minutes? Ask Larry."

"Have you puked yet?"

"No."

"Then you ain't gonna. Get up and come out here. I have something for you."

"I don't wanna get too far from the toilet."

"Do you trust me?"

"Of course I do."

"Then believe that you ain't gonna puke and get out here."

Mark stood, and very carefully turned around and opened the door. "What?"

"Time to get dressed. Come on back out to the dressing room."

He followed Bones and his father out of the bathroom. The rest of the band members were in various stages of undress, getting out of their street clothes and into the gear they would wear on stage. Mark still felt shitty, but he reached for the clothes he'd put in one of the lockers.

"Forget that shit. *This* is what you're gonna wear." His father was holding something out to him. It was hanging from a hanger, but wrapped in the kind of plastic bag that comes from a dry cleaner.

All he could tell at first was that it was red. Or mostly red. "What is it?" No, not red, tartan. Royal Stewart tartan. The shape snapped into focus. "It's a fucking kilt."

"Right."

"A kilt? You want me to wear a kilt? Are you crazy? I'll look like a fucking idiot!"

"Whoa there, boy. I wore a kilt when I was in my first territorial regiment, you don't think I look like an idiot, do you?"

"No sir. But you were marching in parades or something, I'm going to be singing in front of three hundred people."

"Ask your friends."

Mark looked around at the band, then back at his father. "You've already talked to them?"

"Ask them."

They all nodded, gave a thumbs-up, and said things like, "It will be totally cool, man."

"Are you guys for real?" He couldn't believe it. "You want me to go up there in a fucking kilt?"

It was Wilbur who spoke for all of them. "It'll be all right, Mark. It'll look cool, and it'll give the band an identity. Ask Bones. He knows the crowd here better than anyone."

"It'll do wonders for the band, lad, it will. No percentage in it for me if you look stupid and everybody walks out." Bones held up the kilt, eyed it, and looked Mark up and down. "You're a big fucker. Your father's training has put some real muscle on you. The lasses'll all be hoping for a look up and under, to see if you've got anything on but the kilt. There won't be a dry panty in the house."

Mark took the kilt and held it out at arm's length. Red, with black and yellow stripes. It could be okay. He had just about bought into the idea when he realized that even if the kilt itself was okay, it would totally suck with the red Fred Perry shirt.

"C'mon man, put it on." Bruce was already dressed. "It'll look fine. And besides, I wanna be able to say that I was the first one ever to look up your kilt."

Mark tried to hand it back to his father. "It's a cool idea, Dad, but it won't work with..." His father was holding something else out to him. A black Ben Sherman.

"Now *that* will work."

Thirty seconds later, he was buttoning the Ben, and less than a minute after that, the kilt was in place, complete with sporran in front.

"Dig yourself in the mirror." It was Wilbur. "You go on stage in that gear, and even the men in the audience are going to get wet."

He turned to the mirror. The red tartan kilt and the black shirt went together like they'd been made for each other. It was a killer outfit, and he knew he'd look great on stage, but then the thought of standing up there in front of three hundred people in a kilt—a fucking *skirt* for God's sake—had him sweating, and thinking maybe he was going to have to puke after all.

Scott Heaney looked at his son, then turned to Bones and said, "Now's the time."

Bones smiled and reached into his jacket pocket. Out came a pint of Crown Royal whiskey. He held it out to Mark.

"The law might say different, lad, but in my club, if you're old enough to sing, you're old enough to drink—under my supervision of course. Take this and take a big gulp. Only one, mind. We don't want you passing out on stage, or barfing on the paying customers."

"But..." The thought of whiskey had his stomach churning even harder.

"One big gulp, son, just like Bones said. Then a big glass of water. It'll calm you."

Mark took the bottle and did as he was told. The whiskey burned his throat, but within a minute the fire in his throat began to change to a gentle warmth throughout his body. He brought the bottle up for another gulp, but Bones took it away from him and handed him a glass of water.

"Uh uh. Just one."

Mark drained the water glass and turned to the band. "Okay, I'm wearing the kilt. I'll feel like an idiot tomorrow, but I'm wearing the damn thing. Let's go."

Nobody moved. They all looked from one to the other as if waiting for somebody to say something. It was his father who finally spoke.

"One more thing, son."

"What's that?" Did they want him to wear a woman's hat, too?

"You go regimental or you don't go at all."

"Regimental?"

"Yup. Get the skivvies off and show those screaming girls what you got!"

"You're joking, right?"

But he could tell from the looks on the faces around him that this, too, had been part of the plan. He thought about telling them to fuck off. He thought about telling them to go up there bare-assed themselves. But to his own surprise, what he heard himself saying was "Sure. What the hell."

Somewhere in the back of his brain he knew that it was the whiskey that was loosening him up, but he didn't care. He could feel the music starting somewhere inside him, and, as he fumbled under the kilt to get his underwear off, he was no longer thinking of anything except the music they were about to play.

Five minutes later, when Jurgen, the big, bald, tattooed bouncer knocked on the door and said, "Time to rock and roll," it was Mark who led the band onstage.

Instruments on, a tap on the mike to make sure it was live, and then, before Mark had time to get nervous, Wilbur's drumsticks came down, and the Juice Monkeys launched into The Who's *My Generation*. It wasn't the ska music that the crowd was expecting, but it had a terrific beat, and by the end of the first chorus, there were people on the dance floor.

With his nervousness gone, Mark checked out the audience. More and more people were heading for the dance floor, and a lot of them were dressed in tight skirts and sweaters. Skirts and sweaters that they filled out a lot better than the girls in his high school.

When the last chords of *My Generation* faded out, they launched straight into ska with The Porkers' *Asleep at the Wheel,* and when the horns cut in, the crowd went nuts. More and more of them poured onto the dance floor, packing it so tightly they could hardly move. Girls in full skinhead gear skanked and danced and smiled up at Mark as he sang; guys hollered and gave the band the thumbs-up. The music cut right to their emotions and it filled Mark with an incredible feeling of both power and joy. A glance at the rest of the band confirmed that they were getting the same rush he was. Bruce looked like he had died and gone to heaven, and even Larry Kellite, who'd played with some of the greatest musicians in the world, was obviously cranked by the audience response.

Downstairs, where the sound of the band didn't drown out conversation, Scott Heaney and his old buddy, Bones, were settling into their second pint.

"You're pretty supportive, Scotty. Letting Mark do this." He waved a hand in the direction of the upstairs. "You even came to his first gig. Not a lot of dads would do that."

Scott drained his mug and smiled. "He's a good kid, Bones. He works hard most of the time; he hasn't fucked up anything too serious, and God knows he loves the music. Besides, when I told him that the only way he was getting up on that stage was if he kept up at school, he buckled right down and his grades have actually gone up." He picked up his empty mug, "And what the hell, if my kid being in a band gets me free beer, I'm all for it."

"Yeah, okay, okay, I'll get you another." Bones took both mugs and came back a minute later with fresh ones.

"You know, Bones, you're pretty supportive yourself, letting them play here."

"Forget it, buddy. My charity extends as far as your beer glass and no farther. If they weren't good enough to play here, they wouldn't be playing here. You can't tell the difference, I know that, but the people who come here to drink and dance would be gone in a minute if I put a bad band on stage." He looked around his club. "See, even some of the folks down here, the ones that just came in for a pint, or a meal, are heading upstairs."

They drank in companionable silence for a few minutes, then Bones said, "Tell the truth mate, when you first asked me if I'd audition them, I was worried, bloody worried." Bones had turned serious. "You saved my life twice, and I didn't reckon I could refuse them even if they weren't up to snuff. But no worries now, let me tell you.

"Listen to that sound, mate. Just listen."

Scott Heaney listened.

"Your boy and his band have got the crowd going nuts, and as long as they make sure the sets aren't too long, and the breaks aren't too short, I'll sell as much beer tonight as I would have if The Pietasters had shown up." He stood, and drained his beer. "On your feet, old man."

Scott Heaney rose. "What's up?"

"See these?" Bones reached into a pocket and pulled out a pair of tickets, holding them so that his friend could see what was printed on them.

"Backstage Pass?" Scott Heaney looked confused. "What do we need backstage passes for? You own the fuckin' place."

"Not for us, mate." Bones stepped to the bar and spoke to the bartender. "We'll be upstairs. Send one of the girls up with beer for us." He turned back to Scott. "Let's go have a look at the crowd up there. Maybe we'll find a pair of likely lasses who've had a look up your boy's kilt and need these passes to get better acquainted with what they saw there."

Mark's father laughed. "You old pimp. What makes you think I'm going to let you drag my son into the gutter?"

"Ha. You think I didn't see you put those rubbers in his clothes locker when we were in the dressing room before the show?"

The two ex-commandos howled with laughter, then headed up the stairs to catch the last songs of the first set.

"Oh, man, would ya look at that…" The set was over and the band was filing into the dressing room, where Bruce had spotted the big tub of beers on ice. "Who wants a beer?" He reached into the tub with both hands and came up with two fistsful of bottles. "Or six?"

Larry Kellite and the horn players looked relaxed and comfortable, but Wilbur, Bruce and Mark were soaked with sweat. Wilbur's was honest sweat from forty-five minutes of drumming, but the two boys had earned their beers partly from the energy they'd put into fronting the band. Guitar playing and singing had only been part of it; the other part had come from the energy they'd thrown into dancing around the stage, energizing the crowd and in turn feeding off the crowd's energy.

Mark slammed his first beer in about thirty seconds and was reaching for another when Larry Kellite intervened. "No way, Mark. You lost about five liters of water up there, and if you replace it with beer you're going to be so fucked up by the end of the night that you won't even be able to go onstage for the last set." The guitarist opened a cooler that he'd brought himself and pulled out a big bottle of Gatorade. "Drink this." He handed it to Mark. "All of it."

"But..."

"No 'buts', just drink it." He turned to his son. "You, too, hotrod. You'll play better, you'll sing better, and you'll feel better."

"And you'll have some energy left for your girlfriends after the show, too." Wilbur put down his own empty beer and reached into the cooler. "You need plenty of those precious bodily fluids to satisfy the ladies, right?" He pointed to Mark's kilt. "All them little girls trying to sneak a peek? You keep drinking beer, little brother, and you won't be able to keep up with them when they come for some of the real thing later."

"Oh, right. As if." But Mark had to admit that the Gatorade was going down without any trouble, and he could feel the energy flowing back into his body. Too bad there *wasn't* someone to share it with after the show.

While the band re-energized and rehydrated, Scott Heaney and Bones Battle got further into their beer and listened to the conversations at the tables around them. Particularly the table right in front of them, where four young women were enthusiastically discussing the new band.

"... and anyway, I think they're *better* than The Pietasters."

"So why haven't we heard of them before. It's not like I'd forget a name like 'The Juice Monkeys'."

"Yeah, like, what CDs have they done? I'd sure buy their stuff, but I've never heard of them, either."

"They don't *have* any CDs."

"And how would you know that? You've never even been to a club before. The only way you got in here was by sticking your tits in the door guy's face so he wouldn't think about checking your ID."

Bones leaned over to his friend and whispered, "She can stick that pair in *my* face anytime she wants to get in here again, too."

"Be quiet you old pervert, lemme hear what they're saying."

"Yeah, yeah, you're drooling in your beer just as much as I am, mate." Bones gave Scott Heaney an elbow in the ribs, but he did shut up.

"I know they don't have any CDs because I know them."

"*What?*"

"You *know* them? You're not even old enough to drink, how the fuck can you know them? I mean, these guys are *hot.*"

"Why do you think I talked Helen into coming here tonight?" said the one who claimed to know them. "Because they go to my school, and I heard them talking about playing here tonight, that's why. The guitar player and the singer are both in half my classes."

The two older girls who had been doing most of the talking looked to the third one. "That right, Helen? Karen actually knows these hotties?"

"That's right." The one called Helen laughed. "She says she's been trying to find out what's under that kilt since the start of the term."

"No shit. I wouldn't mind finding out myself. What a body…"

The two men at the table behind nudged one another and lifted their mugs in a toast. "Looks like we've found a home for those backstage passes, Scotty."

They started the second set with *Bed & Breakfast Man,* and when dancers filled the floor, Mark grabbed a water bottle and hosed down the ones closest to the stage. He was on cloud nine. The feeling—seeing so many people dancing to his voice—was fantastic. They kept the ska music coming right through to the second-to-last song and closed the set with *Brown-eyed Girl.* It wasn't ska, but the crowd loved it and cried out for more.

"You want more?" Mark had them eating out of his hand.

"*Yeah!*" came the response.

"Well hang around for twenty minutes and we'll be back to give you more."

But before he could lead the band off the stage though, Wilbur started banging his drums and called out, "Johnny B. Goode." The band knew what that meant, and soon they were rocking their way through the old Chuck Berry number that let Bruce show off his guitar talent and had the crowd screaming for even more when it ended.

"We'll be back. I promise."

When the band was gone, and the girls at the table in front of his had sat back down, Bones Battle stood and pulled the two passes out of his pocket. The conversation at the girls' table had started back on the subject of what each of them would like to do with what was under the singer's kilt, but they fell silent when Bones approached their table.

"You lasses enjoying the show?"

This was *not* what they wanted to hear. Fifty-year-old men moving in on them was not up there with thinking about getting it on with a guy from a really hot band. But there was something about this particular fifty-year-old guy that kept them from saying anything. It wasn't that he looked mean or anything—they'd have told him to fuck off in about one second if that had been all—but something else, something dark, something that killed any thought of a smartass response.

"Reason I ask, you understand, is that if you *are* enjoying it, I've got something here you might like." He displayed the two passes. "I'm the band's manager, and from what I've heard, it sounds like a couple of you might just like to get to know one or two of the lads a little better. Am I right?"

The one the others had called Helen snatched the tickets out of his hand. "Who? Us?" She burst out laughing. Then, "Wait a minute, there's only two passes."

"True, but then the lad in the kilt's the only one in the band that's single, and, good man though he is, I don't think he could handle all four of you, so you'll just have to fight it out amongst yourselves."

As Bones sat back down, Scott Heaney noticed him adjusting himself. "You gonna take care of that down in the bathroom, or try to get it home to the missus?"

"I'll tell you, mate, with what's sitting at that table, I am sorely tempted to invite one of them down to the back room to deal with it right now." He took a big swallow of beer.

"You can't tell me that you're immune to what's stuffed into all these tight sweaters and skirts."

"No more than you, Bones." Scott Heaney took a long, lustful look around the room. "But I'm no more going to do anything about it than you are."

"Aye, we're a pair of old has-beens. All talk, no tail." He also looked longingly around. "Just be thankful you don't have to look at this every night, like I do."

"Permanent wood?"

"Mahogany, mate, pure mahogany."

"Must be painful." Scott Heaney finished his beer. "I think we ought to get down to the dressing room before they start again. Warn him, right?" He stood and slapped his friend on the shoulder. "What a great fucking dad I am, eh Bones?"

Down in the dressing room the object of their conversation had finished his between-set beer, and was cracking another bottle of Gatorade. As he had left the stage, he felt better than he had ever felt in his life. All the hard work had paid off, and playing a real gig was ten times better than he'd imagined it. A hundred times. A thousand.

Bruce came over and put his arm around his friend. "We're slaying them, man. This is totally fucking awesome. They *love* us. Did you see what some of those chicks out there were doing? They were, I don't know, like *offering* themselves to us. To you and me." Bruce was high on it. "It's like when they listen to us, they forget that they're in public. I bet if you wanted, you could invite one of them up on stage and she'd fuck your brains out, right there, right in front of everybody."

"Maybe I should wear this kilt to school." Mark chugged down his drink. "At least you've got a girlfriend. Well, someone who *might* be your girlfriend. Someday."

"Yeah, well, tonight I'm not so sure that's a good thing." Bruce dug out a Gatorade bottle for himself and drank deeply. "She's coming down here to meet me after the show, which is okay I guess, but if she *wasn't* coming, I bet I could…" He broke off, startled when Scott Heaney materialized beside him.

"Jesus. Mr. Heaney. How do you *do* that?"

"Same way your daddy plays guitar, Bruce. Thirty years of practice." He looked at the sport drink bottles. "You guys aren't hitting the beer?"

"Larry won't let us have more than one."

Scott Heaney thought about it. "Yeah, I never really saw a rock concert before, but you're working out just as hard up there as if you were in the club, aren't you?" He pulled a beer out of the tub and twisted the cap off. Mark and Bruce stared at each other. It wasn't a twist-off cap. "Fortunately, I don't have to work out, or play music, so I can drink all I want to. But I didn't come down here to talk about staying hydrated. No, I came here to warn you both that there might be something special waiting for you after the concert, but from what I just overheard, I guess I only have to warn Mark."

"Sir?"

"Well, if Bruce's sweetie is coming to get him after the show, then you're going to have to do double duty tonight, soldier." He punched his son on the shoulder. "Triple duty if you count the singing."

"Dad, what are you talking about?" His father had obviously had more than just a few beers, and Mark wondered how drunk he really was.

"Look in your jacket pocket." "Dad, I'm not wearing a jacket."

"In your locker, genius boy, in your locker."

What was going on? He'd hung his jacket in a locker before the show and he knew that there was nothing in any of the pockets except his house keys. Still, he knew better than to argue with his father, so he put down his drink, walked over to the locker and checked his jacket pockets.

There. Keys to the house and to the family van. Not that he ever got to drive it. "See, I told…" his hand hit something else. Slick plastic. Some kind of packages. He pulled one out, realizing what it must be even before he saw it.

He turned around. "Dad, how the hell..."

But his father was gone, and he was left standing, holding a package of rubbers in his hand for everyone in the band to see.

Their final set was a triumphant finish to the night. The crowd was loose and joyful. Some of them sang along to the songs they recognized, some stage-dived into the waiting arms of the dancers.

The band gave back as much energy as they received, but eventually, it ended. Mark introduced each of the players one last time, thanked the crowd, and nodded to Wilbur to tap out the intro to the last song.

He didn't want it to end. He held out his arms to the crowd as they cheered and whistled and clapped. He walked over to Bruce and dragged him to the front of the stage to share in the applause. And then, while the cheering was still loud, led the band from the stage.

The crowd wasn't having any of that, though. They wanted the Juice Monkeys back and they began to clap in rhythm, and chant, "One-two, we want you! One-two, we want you..."

They encored with an old Clash song, and as Mark belted out the words 'Breakin' rocks in the hot sun...' the crowd joined in, two-hundred strong, with 'I fought the law and the law won'. It was such a high that Mark and Bruce would have done another complete set, but the older band members put down their instruments and Mark realized that his first gig was now officially over.

"Always leave 'em wanting just a little bit more, Mark. Give them a good show, don't be too stingy, but don't give everything away every time." Larry Kellite was opening beers and passing them to the band members, who were all sitting, leaning back against whatever they could, and gradually coming down from the high they'd been on for the last four hours. "It was a good one, wasn't it?" He raised his own beer in a toast, and the other six raised theirs in response.

It *had* been a good one. With no experience of his own to guide him, Mark might not have been able to judge the quality of a studio session, but playing a club, well, the only measure that counted in a club was what the crowd thought, and tonight's crowd had been wild in their support.

"What about you guys, Larry?"

"What do you mean?"

"Well, Bruce and me, as long as they didn't throw bottles at us, we'd probably think we were the greatest, but you guys," he gestured to include Larry, Wilbur, and the three horn men, "you guys have all done this a million times, right?"

"Listen Mark, I might not have been playing for as long as Larry," it was Kenny, the trumpet player, who hardly ever said anything, "but I know a thing or two about playing clubs, and believe me, tonight was a good one. Right now we might just be a bar band, doing covers of other people's shit, but we're a *good* bar band, and sometimes that's a hell of a lot better than being a big name band."

Mark wasn't sure he bought that. If it felt this good when you were an unknown band filling in for The Pietasters, then wouldn't it be ten times as good to actually *be* The Pietasters?

He was about to ask Wilbur what he thought when the door opened and Bones Battle walked in, followed by his daughter, Terri. He started congratulating the band, going on about how they could play his club any night, but Mark found that his attention was focused on Terri, not on her father.

She was gathering empties and picking up ashtrays, and she looked pretty thrashed from a long night's work. There were beer stains on her clothes and sweat on her forehead. Her hair was a mess, and her makeup needed a complete redo. But for all that, she stood straight, and looked like she wasn't about to take shit from anyone.

As she picked up the empties from the corner where he was sitting, she said, "You were really good, Mark."

"Um, well, Larry and Wil are real pros. It's…"

"No. I mean *you* were really good. Dad told me that this was your first gig and that you never studied music, but I'll bet that no one in the audience would believe that. You sounded great."

"Thanks. Maybe I shouldn't tell you this, but you wouldn't believe how nervous I was before the show." He laughed at the memory. "I actually spent fifteen minutes on my knees in front of the toilet, and the only way they got me to wear this outfit," he touched the kilt, "was to get me, well, not drunk, but…"

"Dad told me." She laughed along with him. "Anyway, you looked good up there, and you sounded great."

She moved off, cleaning the rest of the room and Mark couldn't help comparing her to the girls in his school. She was only a couple of years older then them, but it was like she was from a different planet. They were constantly in your face with how beautiful they were. She didn't stick it in your face at all, and after a full shift at Skavoovee she looked like she'd been run over by a truck, but somehow it didn't matter. It was like her beauty came from inside, whereas the girls at school were just that, schoolgirls who were trying to *look* beautiful.

Not that that was necessarily a bad thing. He thought about what was walking the halls of Gibson High and immediately sprung wood. Yes, he was definitely going to have to do something about…

"Mark?"

He realized that someone was saying his name.

"Wake up, lad, you've got company." It was Bones.

"Huh?" He looked around. The room had filled up since he'd started talking to Terri. Some guy he'd never seen was talking to Kenny, fingering an invisible Saxophone, obviously discussing licks. Wilbur and Larry were talking to three middle-aged black guys, Bruce was deep in conversation with Kelly, and now Bones was saying something about passes.

"What passes?"

"Backstage passes, lad. There's a couple of young ladies with backstage passes, asking to see you."

"Who are they?"

"Only name I know is 'Helen', but the other one says she's a friend of yours."

Mark didn't have very many female friends, and he couldn't imagine any of them coming down to the skids at two in the morning to say hello to him; but then he remembered what his father had said during one of the breaks, and the wood under his kilt grew into a full-on tree.

"Okay."

Bones went over to the door and opened it to let in a woman Mark had never seen before. No teenager, that was for sure, but not that old either. Twenty-three, maybe twenty-four. Medium height, short hair dyed in a mix of blonde and black. She was slim, but not in any way skinny, and her figure was emphasized by a leather vest and skirt so tight

126

that she looked like a dominatrix. She moved into the room like she owned it, and Mark watched her walk toward him. It wasn't until she was almost in front of him that he looked past her to see who his supposed 'friend' was.

Oh, shit.

Karen Hemmingway.

Big, firm tits, and short, tight skirt. She was gorgeous as ever. "Hi, Mark."

Great. Just what he needed. Why had she come here to torment him. His erection disappeared, and he wished he could shoot whoever had given her the backstage pass.

"Are you here to hassle me about that fight with Rick Warner?"

"No. I'm here because I want something from you."

"What?"

"You'll see soon enough."

"What's done is done, okay?" Mark said defensively. "I don't need any more trouble from you."

"Relax. I don't want any either. I picked the wrong side to be on, in that fight business anyway, but you turned me down once, remember? Well tonight I'm not taking no for an answer."

Whoa! That was *not* what he'd expected. He looked her up and down. She was a social tramp, but she was hot! Everything about her reminded him of how much trouble he'd had saying no the first time, and the tent pole came back into position under his kilt. Her friend in the black leather dominatrix gear was incredibly sexy, too. Mark wondered what she was doing here when Karen clearly had nothing but sex on her mind.

"Let's get out of here!" Karen poked him in the chest with her finger, just like she'd done that day last September.

"Where to?" Were her parents away?

"Back to Helen's place."

So that was why she'd brought her friend along. Well, whatever. As long as Helen didn't mind the two of them using her house, Mark was willing. More than willing.

"Mark?" A different voice. He took his eyes and his mind off Karen and looked up. It was Larry Kellite.

"Come on over tomorrow for supper. We can go over the gig and make some plans. Split the money, too."

Right at that moment, Mark couldn't have cared less about money, and as for supper, well, there was only one thing he wanted to eat at the moment, and that sure as hell wasn't steak at the Kellites. He got his mind under control long enough to say, "Okay, see you then," but that was all he could manage before Karen's tight sweater and short skirt grabbed his full attention again.

He was vaguely aware of Larry Kellite laughing as he went back to his conversation with the black guys, but he didn't really care. What he cared about was getting out of the room without having the kilt stick out in front of him, but his dick was showing no signs of lying down. Oddly enough, it was Helen that came to the rescue.

"Why don't you have a shower, soldier boy. If you're staying at my house tonight, you can hose yourself off first. We'll wait for you in the bar."

"But won't the bar be closed?"

"Not for me." She turned to Karen, taking her by the elbow, almost possessively. "C'mon sugar, give the boy a chance to clean up."

Five minutes later he was out of the shower, and five minutes after that, he was in the back seat of Helen's car playing tongue hockey with Karen Hemmingway.

The ride didn't take long, but he had no idea where they were when the car stopped. Some residential district, but he wasn't really paying attention to that kind of thing because Karen's hand was massaging his dick through the fabric of his pants.

Out of the car. Up the walk. Through the door. "Shoes off before you go in." Helen ordered.

He slipped off his shoes.

"Pour yourselves a drink and put on some tunes if you want. I'm going upstairs."

Alright. Mark had been a little worried that Helen would want to hang out for a while, and the thought of trying to make polite conversation when all he wanted to do was dive headfirst into Karen's pussy wasn't working for him. But she obviously understood what Karen wanted, and was getting out of the way. Maybe he'd get to meet her sometime when he wasn't out-of-his-mind horny. But not right now.

Karen had disappeared into the kitchen and returned with a bottle of 7-Up. She opened a liquor cabinet and pulled out glasses and a bottle of Vodka. The drink she handed him was strong. He remembered Wilbur's advice about not getting too drunk if there was sex ahead, and limited himself to a small sip.

Karen seemed to be completely at home. She obviously knew her way around the place. She was loading the stereo, and when the music came on, it was some kind of easy-listening crap, but it killed the lack of sound, so he didn't complain. If she wanted a soundtrack while she fucked him, he could handle it.

He sat down on the sofa as she dimmed the lights, and the next thing he knew she was behind him, with her wet tongue licking his ear. He closed his eyes and let the feeling of pleasure flow through his body.

"Turn around."

He turned, expecting a full-on kiss, but got far more than he bargained for. She'd peeled off her sweater, and those gorgeous, gigantic tits were straining to get out of a red satin bra.

"Oh my God!"

Karen smiled a slow, lust-filled smile and pulled his head into her chest, pressing his face down into that Grand Canyon of cleavage.

"I was hoping I could get your attention."

"You have it!"

"Good," she said as she sat down beside him and took away his glass. She stood up and then suddenly straddled him on the couch as she pushed her breasts into his face. Mark's pecker nearly ripped through his jeans.

Her tongue entered Mark's mouth as he met her lips with his. He put up his hands around her breasts and softly squeezed. His hands couldn't fit all the way around them, and yet they didn't sag. She reached behind his head and sighed as she pushed his head into her cleavage. Mark groaned, then put one hand behind her back, holding her to him as he massaged one of her breasts with his other hand.

She stood, stepped back from him, and said, "Watch."

The light was dim, but not so dim as to obscure the view as she reached behind her, and worked that fastener on the bra, then slowly drew her arms up over her head, taking the bra with them.

The bra dropped to the floor, and she spread her arms wide, emphasizing the thrust of her breasts. "See what you almost missed?"

"Yeah—well..."

She walked away, shut off the stereo, then came back and reached out and took one of his hands. "Come on, let's go upstairs."

He'd have gladly stayed on the couch, or on the living room floor for that matter, but if there was an extra bedroom upstairs, well, that was fine, too.

The hall at the top of the stairs was dark, but she led him confidently toward a doorway through which a faint light spilled, then stepped aside to let him go through first.

On the dresser, a single candle burned. On a stereo, the music of Sting played softly. And on the bed, lay Helen, face down and wearing only semi-transparent panties.

He stood stone still, completely unable to move, as she slowly rolled over, then rose to a kneeling position, cupping her breasts with her hands and rubbing her nipples with her thumbs.

"Hello, soldier boy."

He couldn't speak. Couldn't move.

From behind, Karen reached around and began unbuttoning his shirt. He could feel her fingers on the skin of his chest and belly, but his eyes were on the woman in front of him as she stepped off the bed and walked slowly toward him, timing her steps so that she reached him just as Karen removed his shirt.

She reached out and ran one long red fingernail down his bare chest, hard enough to leave a mark, then stepped back and watched as Karen's hands came from behind him again, working the waist button on his Levis. He could feel her breasts on the skin of his back, feel her nipples, hard against his skin.

He reached behind him, grabbing her ass, trying to pull her closer. "Don't," Helen commanded. "No touching. Not yet."

Obedient, he dropped his hands back to his sides as Karen found his zipper. He looked down to watch as she eased his pants down over his hips, but once again Helen issued a command.

"Keep your eyes on me, toyboy, I'll give you plenty to look at."

Obedient again, he brought his gaze back to the perfect, hard body in front of him, drawing a deep breath as he watched her ease her own hand under the fabric of her panties and move it slowly up and down.

"Want some?"

"Oh, yeah." He was in *way* over his head with this woman, but he knew what he wanted. Or at least what his body wanted.

"Be a good boy, and maybe you'll get some." She pulled her panties down just enough for him to see the top of her bush. It was close-cropped, and trimmed, just like something out of a magazine.

His pants came down and his cock sprang out like a horizontal telephone pole. For a second, he was embarrassed, standing naked in front of this woman, but then Karen's hands came back around him, grasping his shaft, and he forgot everything except his desire.

"No touching from you, either." Helen's command made Karen let go of him instantly. "Now, come around here where he and I can both see you."

Karen moved past him, then into the middle of the room.

Helen's hand was busy in her panties again, as she said, "Remove your skirt."

Keeping her back straight, so that those perfect breasts stayed pointed defiantly outward, Karen undid the waistband of her skirt and let it drop.

No panties. Just beautiful pussy and ass.

Mark looked from gorgeous girl to gorgeous woman, and finally fully understood what was happening. It had been obvious all along, of course, but it was only now hitting his conscious mind. His wildest dream was about to come true. He was about to get it on with not one, but *two* women.

"Get in the chair, music boy."

On the far side of the bed was a simple wooden chair.

"What? What for?" He just wanted to jump on one of them, not sit in some stupid chair.

"You'll get yours, all in good time," said Helen, reading his mind, "but only if you do what you're told." She pointed to the chair again, then turned to Karen. "Secure him."

Mark wasn't sure what was coming, but if these two wanted to play sex games, he was willing to go along. He sat, and Karen approached him, stopping by the dresser to pick up a ball of wool.

She rubbed it against his chest. It was soft and fuzzy, and as she gently rubbed it lower and lower the sensation was unbelievably erotic. Just as he felt that he might explode all over it she pulled it away and moved behind him.

Gently, she tied his hands to the sides of the chair. He might have freaked at ropes or handcuffs, but he knew he could break the wool easily, and was more than willing to play, at least for a while. When she was finished, she stood behind him, first biting the back of his neck, then rubbing her nipples against his shoulders; before returning to stand in front of Helen.

"Kneel," she commanded and Karen knelt obediently. Helen opened one of the dresser drawers and brought out a studded leather dog collar and leash. She fastened the collar around Karen's neck and attached the short leather leash to the collar.

"Now, let's go for a little walk." On her hands and knees, with Helen holding her firmly on the leash, Karen came forward till she was directly in front of Mark. She brought her head between his legs, and, as he watched in astonished pleasure, began licking, then sucking, the head of his dick.

The sensation was incredible, and he wanted to grab the back of her head and pull her all the way forward, burying his shaft in her throat. But he knew that the longer he held out, the longer he played the game, the greater the ultimate reward would be. So he sat, groaning with desire, staring down at the red lips bobbing back and forth along his shaft.

A gentle flick of the leash put a stop to the sensations, and still on her hands and knees, Karen turned toward her Master, then reached up and pulled the flimsy panties down and off.

Helen spread her legs slightly, allowing Karen's probing tongue access to that close-trimmed pussy. "You see what rewards await if you do as you're told, big boy?"

Mark didn't answer. In fact, he wasn't sure he'd be able to speak, but he was pretty sure Helen didn't want him talking anyway, so he just sat back and watched the show.

Another slight flick of the leash and Karen stopped and waited as Helen sat on the edge of the bed, facing Mark. She lay back, spreading her legs wide, giving Mark a full beaver shot, then tugged on the leash again. Karen obediently crawled forward and resumed eating pussy, but this time her butt was pointed straight at Mark, giving him a full beaver *and* ass view.

Helen wriggled and moaned, gradually moving back on the bed, and Karen came up off the floor, moving into full 69 with the older woman. She was soon thrashing out of control, moaning and yelping with ecstasy as she came all over Karen's face.

When the orgasm was over, she pushed Karen away from her pussy and issued another command. "Back on the floor, slave."

Karen, who was breathing in huge gasps, and obviously close to coming herself, tried to pull Helen's face tighter into her own pussy, but when Helen said, "Not yet. It's the boytoy's turn now," she rolled off the bed and put her lips and tongue back to work on Mark's cock.

Helen pulled a vibrator out from under one of the pillows and moved behind Karen, letting the little machine do its job on Karen's clit while Karen's mouth did its own job.

Her hands were around him now, the nails digging into his butt cheeks, and her head slid up and down his dick as she herself started to shake and gasp with pleasure at what Helen was doing with the vibrator.

Just as he felt he was about two seconds from blowing a huge load right down Karen's throat, Helen pulled them apart and said, "Alright, kiddies, let's party."

She jumped back on the bed, spreading for Karen to get back to work. Karen was on the bed in an instant, too, kneeling, her face buried in Helen's soaking wet pussy, her nails digging into her ass just as they had been digging into Mark's a few seconds earlier. Her ass was pointed straight at him again, and this time the invitation was too much to refuse.

He flexed his arms, breaking the thin wool strands that had held him in place, and jumped onto the bed, ramming his shaft right to the hilt in Karen's waiting pussy.

It was hot, wet, and tight in a way he'd never even come close to imagining, even in his most erotic wet dream; and he pounded in and out, feeling the surge begin in his balls, knowing that he was only moments from exploding. He leaned forward, around Karen, gently massaging her clit with one hand, and reaching even further to pinch one of Helen's nipples hard between the thumb and finger of his other hand. It was exactly what both women needed to take them over the edge as well, and the three of them reached a thrashing, groaning, wild, wet climax all at the same time. Mark exploded wave after wave of cum deep into Karen at the same time as every muscle in her body tensed and she emitted a howl of pleasure as best she could with her tongue mashed so hard into Helen's pussy.

For five minutes, they simply lay in a tangled heap, none of them able to move. But gradually Mark became aware of the fact that his face was against one of Helen's perfect little tits. Without really thinking about it, he began massaging the nipple with his tongue, and it was soon huge and hard, and Helen was once again moaning and writhing against him. Her hand sneaked down between their closely pressed bodies and began gently massaging his balls, bringing life back into his soft and shriveled dick until it, too, was huge and hard.

"Roll over on your back."

He did, and she straddled his face then leaned forward and began licking the mixture of his and Karen's juices from his shaft, all the while mashing her pussy against his mouth until both of them were once again in the grip of a completely-out-of-control orgasm. Her delicious juices running over his face, and his cum exploding into her mouth.

Mark had no memory of the next twenty minutes. He lay back, half asleep, as the warm and wonderful feeling of sex with these two desirable creatures flowed through every cell of his body. When he finally came out of his trance, it was to see Helen cinching up a strap-on and mounting Karen from behind, slapping her ass and fucking her doggie style on the floor. Within seconds he was erect again and got off the bed and headed behind Helen.

Two hours, and several orgasms later, Mark was walking home under a starry winter sky. His balls ached, but he was the happiest seventeen-year-old in the universe as he replayed the night's events in his mind. Playing with the Juice Monkeys in the hottest subculture venue in North America, and then losing his cherry to the two hottest chicks in the universe—was it a dream? Had this night been some kind of message from the gods? A message telling him he had been chosen for an experiment in sexual and musical pleasure?

For the rest of January, that did indeed seem to be the case. Helen was seriously into domination and three-ways, and for the moment he and Karen fit perfectly into that scenario. Likewise, things came together musically, and as he looked forward to the weekend gig that Bones had booked them for at the end of the month, Mark was on top of the world.

Word had quickly spread through the school about Mark and Bruce playing underage at Vancouver's alternative hotspot, and rocking the house. That, combined with the stories of the battle in which they'd gone three on five with Sergio's gang and wasted all five of them, made school an entirely different experience for them. Kids wanted to hang with them. Guys and girls wanted to be seen talking to them. Girls wanted to get them into bed.

None of that affected Bruce. He'd never given a shit one way or another what anyone at the school thought of him, and he still didn't. He was polite to people who approached him, and he actually became a fairly good friend of George Christiansen, the kid whose ass they'd saved; but that was it. He'd far rather play music with the Juice Monkeys than go to a party, and Kelly, his Safeway Girl, was all the social life he needed.

For Mark, on the other hand, it was a whole new world. Especially the sex. The threesomes with Helen and Karen were wild, but as word of his exploits spread, he frequently found himself in the saddle with others as well. They were all girls from Karen's social scene, and he didn't have much to talk to them about, but talk wasn't exactly what he wanted from them anyway, so he wasn't complaining.

His schoolwork took a beating, especially the science and math classes, but he figured he'd have plenty of time to study before finals rolled around, so he wasn't too worried about it. The upside to the schoolwork thing was that his dad's job in town had ended and he'd had to take work out at the far end of the Fraser Valley again, so he wasn't around much to get on Mark's case about keeping his grades up.

Mark had overheard a few conversations between his parents on the subject of his dad's work, and things didn't seem great. It sounded like the contractor on the last job had gone broke and no one had been paid for the last month; and the new job was apparently not paying very well, either. Any other time in his life, Mark would have been worried, but with the music, the sex, and his new social status at school, he didn't pay much attention.

Word about the Juice Monkeys had spread, and when Bones' end-of-January gig rolled around, the crowd was huge and insane. There was no nervousness this time, no need to get a little drunk in order to have the courage to wear the kilt, and when Mark hit the stage for the first set, he was totally on fire.

The only downside was that Larry had laid down strict laws about not going out partying till five in the morning after the Friday night gig.

"I don't care what you guys do on Saturday night, but we need you to be in decent shape for the show."

When they left the stage and hit the dressing room after the last encore on Friday, Mark didn't know whether to be happy or pissed that there weren't going to be any groupies getting backstage passes, but it turned out that sitting around the dressing room, sucking back a couple of cold ones with the rest of the band was great.

Bones came down and joined them, and Terri was there, too. She was easy to talk to, and it was nice to have a good-looking girl around without having sex as the only thought in his mind. She was going to university, which he figured probably meant she wouldn't be interested in someone like him anyway, and besides, she was Bones's daughter, and there was no way he was going to try anything with the daughter of a man who was every bit as deadly as his own father. No way at all.

Saturday night, on the other hand, was a total orgy. Helen and Karen picked him up after the show, and the three of them got it on for a seven-hour fuck-and-suck fest that left him walking home at ten in the morning with empty balls, a sore dick, and no energy for anything but twenty-one straight hours of sleep till his alarm woke him on Monday morning.

The next three months were a total haze of music, sex, socializing, and booze. Everyone wanted him at their parties, and it was a rare party that ended with him going home alone. Somebody's parents were always away, and whoever that somebody was either wanted Mark in her bed or was willing to let Mark and whoever he'd picked up use a bed in the house for a few hours. Compared to the Rolling Stones, the Juice Monkeys didn't make a lot of money. But compared to anything Mark had ever seen, it felt like he was rolling in the stuff. Bones Battle booked them for another weekend at Skavoovee in March, and Larry got them three other gigs over the three months at other clubs in Vancouver, which were mostly in the skids. They played one-nighters at The Twilight Zone, the Town Pump, and at Graceland, and just this past weekend, a two-nighter at the Commodore Ballroom—major venues, clubs that were the center of the music scene in the city.

With each gig Mark felt more and more like a god, and less and less like a school kid with final exams approaching. Each night on stage netted him around a hundred dollars, and at first it went out as fast as it came in. He bought clothes. He bought CDs. He bought a portable CD player. He thought about saving so that he could buy a car, or maybe a scooter, but there was always something that caught his eye, and the money would vanish from his pocket.

He didn't really care. There was always another party, always another girl to take his mind off things like planning for the future; and anyway, he reckoned that once the school year was over they'd be playing way more gigs—he could save some money then, and still have plenty to spend.

CHAPTER 8

It was a Tuesday morning in May that the bubble burst. His algebra teacher had had to leave school suddenly—word was he'd started barfing right in the middle of the day's first class—so Mark's algebra class, which would have been the morning's last class, was canceled. For about thirty seconds he thought about staying at school and doing some studying, but since the afternoon started with a spare he decided that he'd head home and grab a couple of hours of much-needed sleep instead.

As he opened the back gate, he heard a sound from the house. It was both strange and familiar at the same time, and he didn't know what to make of it. The closer he got to the house, the louder the sound became, and the weirder he felt.

Moaning? Crying?

It was coming from the open window of his parents' bedroom, but it was way too low-pitched to be his mother's voice. It almost sounded like his father, but he couldn't imagine his father making that kind of sound, and anyway, he'd left for work on Monday morning and wouldn't be back till Friday.

Unsure what to think, he edged closer to the window, and every step brought him closer to the truth. It *was* his father, and he *was* crying.

Scott Heaney was tougher than any man Mark could imagine. He was a street fighter from way back. An SAS anti-terrorist commando. He was the Black Ghost.

And he was *crying*. Low, choking sobs that sounded like they were being wrenched from his chest by demons with red-hot crowbars.

Mark lost all ability to think. He stood there listening to the tears of the man who was more important to him than any other human being in the world, not knowing whether he should sneak away and leave his father alone, or go in and see what was the matter.

The sound of footsteps, and then his mother's voice, brought him out of his trance.

"I've made some tea for us, Scott. Let's have a cup of tea and then maybe we'll be able to figure out what to do."

The sobs stopped and his father said, "There isn't anything we *can* do Jodi, we're going to lose the house."

To Mark, not yet eighteen, losing the house didn't seem like a big deal. Who cared where they lived? But his father, the Maori warrior, wouldn't break down over something unimportant. He stayed still and listened.

"Then we'll lose the house. So what? There are other houses. Maybe we can get something cheaper out of the city. Or we can rent for a while, till things get better."

"It's not that simple, babe. I wish it was, but it's not. We're behind on the mortgage already, and no matter what we do, we're going to get further behind."

"So let's find something cheaper."

"Even out in the valley there's nothing cheap enough."

"Oh, come on, Scott, surely..."

"Listen to what I'm saying Jodi." His father's voice was breaking, and it was all Mark could do not to cover his ears. "There are cheaper houses out there, but it doesn't matter. We could sell this place, sure, but we don't have that much equity in it, and with me only working off and on, who's going to give us a mortgage on something new, even if it is cheap?"

Not working full time? What had happened? Mark thought about the last few weeks. He hadn't been paying much attention to anything except getting laid and having a good time, and from time to time he'd wondered why his father wasn't getting on his case about schoolwork. As he thought about it he realized that his father hadn't been doing much of anything lately. He'd been away most of the time working at whatever job he'd got, out in... With a shock, Mark realized that he didn't even know where his dad had been working for the last while.

How long had it been? A month? No. More than a month. His father had been cheerful and happy for quite a while, working at a job in town, but then, sometime just after the first Skavoovee gig, things had started changing... Mark couldn't really remember exactly when, or why. Something about the job being done earlier than expected and a new job coming up in some town way out at the east end of the Fraser Valley.

That would have been late January and it was now March or something. No. They'd played the Commodore Ballroom in March. He remembered some joke Wilbur had made about the band learning to play marching music because it was March. And he'd written his midterm exams at least three weeks ago, so that made it… May? Could it be May already? Where had the fucking months gone?

With an effort, he jerked himself back to the present and tuned in to the conversation coming out of the window above him.

"… even renting."

"But why, Scott? You're good at what you do. You're honest and you work hard. I know that contractors like to have you on their jobs."

"Right now, Jodi, there just aren't any jobs." His father wasn't crying anymore, but he clearly wasn't happy. "We really don't have much choice. Most guys in the trade haven't got anything. They're screwed, Jodi, totally screwed. This job I'm on now is terrible, but it's the only thing I can get, and if I hadn't found it we'd have been sunk months ago."

"Well we're not sunk yet, and as long as we've got each other and the children, we'll *never* be sunk. If we have to sell this place and rent, then we have to. The house doesn't matter. What matters is the family."

"That's the point, Jodi, I've failed our family. I'm responsible for keeping this family. I've failed." The sobs were coming back and Mark could hardly believe his ears.

"Scott Heaney, you listen to me. You have *not* failed your family. You said it yourself. You're one of the only people in the plumbing trade that's working, which means that you're one of the only ones who *hasn't* failed his family." There was steel in his mother's voice. "We made this choice a long time ago. If money was what we wanted then you could have taken that job running security for those oil barons in Yemen or wherever it was. You'd have made a fortune but you'd have lost your family and you know it. Killing poor people just so some billionaire can get another jet plane is *not* right. You knew that and I knew that. That's why you got out of the Army, and that's why you took up honest work."

"Yeah, and that's why we're starving."

"Stop it!" His mother's voice was harsh. "We aren't starving. We may be poor, and we may have to sell the house and rent some place out in the valley, but we aren't going to starve. We're going to see this through, and when things get better in the construction industry then you'll be doing fine again."

"I don't know, babe. I just don't know. It's easy to talk about how we're going to get through, but I still feel like a loser, and we're still almost two-hundred bucks short of next month's mortgage payment."

There was silence from the bedroom for a few moments, then his father continued. "I'll put an ad in the paper. Maybe I can sell the bike. We'll take a loss, but it'll make up the difference between what I earn and what we need for a few months."

More silence.

"What we'll do after that, I don't know. From everything I've read, construction is going to be down for at least another year, maybe two. I need the van for work, and we don't have anything else left to sell."

"Well, the kids are all in school, so I can try to get work myself."

"And who'll be there for the kids when they get home from school?"

Below the window, Mark slowly reached into his back pocket, and pulled out his wallet. The Juice Monkeys had played Thursday, Friday, and Saturday at the Commodore, and Bruce had brought their share of the take to school that morning. He opened his wallet. It had been a good gig, and his wallet was fat with twenty-dollar bills. Seventeen of them. Plus a ten.

He took out the money and walked slowly around to the front of the house, opened the front door, and walked into the living room. He knew they would have heard him, and, sure enough, his mother came out of the bedroom almost immediately.

"Mark. What on earth are you doing here?"

His father was slower. Probably cleaning the tears from his face, making sure his son wouldn't know that something was wrong.

Mark waited till both of them were in the room. "Take this."

"What?" They both stared at the wad of twenties. "What are you talking about?"

"Take it." He reached out and grabbed his father's hand, stuffing the money into it.

Scott Heaney looked at the money, then at his son, not understanding. "We're going to play Skavoovee again in two weeks. There'll be another couple of hundred then."

Neither of them spoke, but Mark could see the questions in their eyes. "No lies, right? Isn't that what you always taught me? No lies in this family?"

"That's right." He could see the light beginning to dawn in his father's eyes.

"Classes got canceled till two, so I was going to come home and sleep." He waved in the direction of the back yard. "I was coming up the walk. I heard."

They each started to speak, but he cut them off. "No lies. I won't tell Donny and the kids if you don't want me to, but don't try to tell me that I didn't hear what I heard."

Scott Heaney held up the money. "Where did you get this?"

"It's my pay from the nightclub we played at this weekend."

For a long minute nobody spoke. Finally, Mark broke the silence. "I'm sorry. I haven't been paying attention to anybody but me lately… I didn't realize." A tear started down his face, and he turned and moved out from the room, back outside, not stopping till he was in the park across from the school.

"Dad?" Two weeks had gone by since Mark had seen him crying. "You in there?" He was standing outside the garage, knocking on the door, early on Sunday evening.

"No." The voice was from directly behind him, and he was so startled he dropped the key he'd been about to put in the lock.

"How did you *do* that?"

"Approaching you unseen isn't exactly difficult."

"But I thought you were in the garage."

"I was."

"Then how…"

"Number one rule of survival, son. Never assume that what was is what is." He picked up the key and handed it to Mark. "Just because I was in the garage when you looked in the window—yes, I saw you peeking in. Just because I was there then, doesn't mean I'm going to be there five minutes later. Even anti-terrorist commandos have to take out the garbage sometimes."

A pained look replaced the smile that had been on Scott Heaney's face. "Well, former commandos."

"I've got something for you." Mark pulled out his wallet and opened it. "We played a two-nighter at Skavoovee." He handed his father a fifty, a ten, and seven twenties.

"Thank you, son. I guess I don't have to tell you what this means to us."

"Yeah, well, that's okay." Mark was a bit embarrassed. Not for himself, but for his father. He knew that it must hurt this proud warrior to have to depend on money from his son, but he also knew that it wasn't his father's fault that they were in a tight place.

"But we've gotta talk. That's why I looked for you out here."

"Do we need to talk this second, or can it wait ten or fifteen minutes?"

"Yeah, sure. Do you want me to come back in a little while?"

"No, I want you to grab a jacket and a helmet and get on the bike. It's a fine evening; we can talk when we get to White Cliff."

"On the bike?" Mark couldn't believe his ears. His father had never taken any of them on the bike. Not even around the block.

"About the bike. If you weren't giving us your earnings, I wouldn't still have the bike. Where I come from, that means it's as much your bike as mine." He opened the garage and hit the switch for the main door. "You sit there," he pointed to the raised rear portion of the seat, "and put your feet on those pegs." He kicked one of the rear footpegs with his boot. "Keep your arms snug around my waist, and lean with me when I lean, even if it scares the shit out of you." He handed Mark a sheepskin-lined leather jacket from a peg beside the door, and a helmet from the shelf.

"Let's ride."

Fifteen minutes later they dismounted and Mark tried not to show how excited he'd been. "Where are we?"

"White Cliff Park. It's just across a spine of land from the ferry terminal at Horseshoe Bay. It's not unknown, but it's not that crowded."

143

Scott Heaney removed his helmet and undid his jacket. "There are cliffs above the ocean just down at the end of that path." He pointed. "Good place to talk."

They walked a few hundred meters and then cut left along a clifftop till they were out of earshot of the tourists and picnickers.

"What's on your mind?"

"What you said to mom that day when I heard you through the window. About the construction industry not getting any better for a while. Is that pretty much the way it is?"

The older man picked up a pebble and tossed it gently into the sea. "I wish I could say different, but I can't. It'll pick up again someday, and when it does, I'll branch out and start contracting myself instead of just working for other people, but for now… for as long as it takes for the economy to pick up… Well, for now I'm fucked. If you weren't helping, we'd be out of the house." Another pebble went into the ocean.

"I didn't think much of this whole music thing. Larry's a good man, but I never had much respect for entertainers, and it took a lot for me to let you go with it. In fact, if it weren't for Bones, I probably wouldn't have."

He put an arm around his son's shoulders. "I still can't say that your singing in nightclubs makes me happy, but it's a good thing you do, or we'd be living in some trailer park in Cloverdale."

"That's what we've got to talk about. Music is important to me, Dad, and if I thought that I could make the band a full-time thing, I would. But I know that Larry and Wilbur are never going to do any more than a couple of gigs a month—even in summer—and without them, well… Bruce and I are okay, but we're not good enough to make it on our own. Shit, we're not even old enough to play in the clubs."

Now it was Mark's turn to throw stones into the water as he tried to figure out how to say what needed to be said. "The bottom line is that without Larry, the whole thing falls apart. The people in the audience, they see me. They think that the kid in the kilt is the leader of the Juice Monkeys, but I'm not. It's Larry that keeps us together, gets us the gigs, keeps us from making fools of ourselves…"

"And?"

"Dead Dog Sound is doing better all the time, and it's getting harder and harder for him to take the time to practice and play. He loves to play, and he'll always play some, but he's told us that after this summer he may have to cut back."

"What you're trying to tell me is that you can't promise to keep putting four or five hundred a month into the family bank account, right?"

"Not through music."

That wasn't the answer Scott Heaney had expected. "What do you mean, 'not through music'?"

Mark thought hard about what he was going to say next. He'd thought about nothing else for the past week, but confronting his father with it was a lot different than thinking about it.

"I know someone who was in a sort of similar situation once. This was thirty-five years ago or something, but he was my age then, and it's kind of the same as what I'm going through. His family was having trouble, and he didn't really have any way of helping if he stayed where he was so he..."

"... Joined the army and sent some of his pay home every month," finished his father.

Neither one of them knew what to say, and so they sat, side by side, pitching small stones into the huge ocean.

"No lies, right son?"

"That's right."

"Then I'll speak the truth even though it hurts. Dropping out of school and joining the army is the last thing I want for you, but the way things are..." his voice trailed off uncertainly. "No possibilities here in town? No way you can get some other kind of job here that will let you finish school? What about working on the tugs?"

"Grocery stores are about the only places that hire kids with no experience, and I checked every grocery store in the whole goddamn city. Nobody's hiring."

"Shit." Scott Heaney stood up. "Not much we can do about this tonight. Let's go home and sleep on it, maybe think about it for a while, see if we can't find some way around it. Who knows, maybe moving out to one of the small towns wouldn't be such a bad thing, especially if it let you finish school."

They started slowly back toward the bike. "School sucks, Dad. Most of the kids there are just posers who want to look cool. Six months ago, I was Mr. Nobody. Bruce and a couple of the other guys were the only ones who had the time of day for me. Most people thought any guy that shaved his head and wore the kind of clothes I did was some kind of retard. But I go on stage one night at Skavoovee, and suddenly I'm everybody's friend."

He stopped walking and faced his father. "It's just so fucking false. I played the same music before we were in Skavoovee, I'm still wearing the same clothes and haircut I did then." He spat on the ground. "They don't give a shit about me as a person, they just want to hang around whoever is the coolest this week or this month. Having girls dragging me into their beds is alright, but I know that if I stopped singing in clubs, they'd drop me in about ten seconds and go jump on the nearest football player."

Scott Heaney digested this outburst, then replied. "I was wondering when you'd wake up from the rockstar dream. I'm glad to see you've seen through the bullshit, but there's more to school than fashion and coolness, you know. There's something to be said for having an education and being able to problem-solve. That's why I prefer the trades myself."

"If I was getting any kind of education, I'd be looking for a way to stay and finish, but I can't see any use for most of the stuff I take. I mean, what good is biology? I'm not going to be a scientist, so why do I have to study that crap? I'm not headed for university, so what's the point of studying science and math?" He shoved his hands in his pockets and started walking again.

"I'd probably like to make music my career, and if I can't do that, then I'd like to get into a trade, or something technical, and the army is a good place to learn a trade, right? And make an honest paycheck while you're doing it, right?"

"Yes, up to a point, that's right. But there's a lot more to military life than learning a trade and collecting a paycheck. And there's no guaranteed job at the end of it."

"I know that, but…"

"Let's drop it for now, Mark. I understand what you're saying and why you're saying it, but we both need time to think." Scott Heaney looked up at the sky. "There's still an hour-and-a-half of daylight. Let's hit the highway, take the coast road up to Squamish and back. It's a beautiful drive—a twisty road with mountains on one side and the ocean on the other—and maybe the wind will blow some sense into our heads."

They zipped up their jackets and pulled on their helmets. As they mounted the bike, Mark's father turned and said, "One thing you better remember, though. If you want to get into the army, you're going to have to finish this year at school. They may not need Grade Twelve, or even great marks, but they don't want fuckups, so get back to the books."

Before Mark could reply, his father revved the bike and for the next ninety minutes Mark was too busy hanging on for his life to think about their conversation. Ninety minutes later, at the end of the ride, his father stopped the bike about a block from their home. "I'll be heading out of town tomorrow morning, but I'll think about what we've talked about. You do the same, and when I get back, we'll work out what we can. Maybe go for a hike with the dogs so that we'll have a few hours to ourselves. In the meantime, let's keep this joining-the-army business between the two of us, okay?"

"Okay."

"And Mark," Scott Heaney removed his helmet and twisted on his seat so that he could look his son in the eyes, "if you're serious about this, then there's something you need to do."

"School, right?"

"That's right. Buckle down and work your ass off for the rest of the school year. It's only a month till your exams, and I know you've been letting it slide."

"Yeah. I have, but I'll get back on it."

"You'd better."

"Sassy! Big Dog! In you go!" Scott Heaney herded the dogs into the van.

"Where are we going?"

"Reckon you can handle Grouse Mountain?"

Mark hadn't trained for almost two months, and he knew it would be hard. "Can we go slow?"

"Yeah, we'll have to. Neither of us has been getting decent exercise lately, and if we want to have enough breath for talking, then slow is the only way."

"Okay."

It was a beautiful day, but hot, and Mark was soon wondering if agreeing to a mountain hike had been wise. But his father set a slow pace, they took plenty of water breaks, and eventually, they were on the same ledge that he'd been so impressed with the last time they'd climbed this mountain.

For a while, they just kicked back and let the sun work on them, drinking plenty, and dipping into the bag of trail mix that Scott Heaney had produced from his backpack.

The older man spoke first. "So, are you still set on it?" He didn't have to specify what 'it' was.

"I don't want to leave home, but I just don't see any other way." Mark sat up, and shuffled forward so that his legs could dangle off the edge. "I know that Mom will probably want us to move out to the sticks somewhere so that I can finish school, but won't it be harder for you to find work if you don't live here in the city?"

"Probably."

"And I'd never be able to play with Bruce and Larry and Wil, and school would still suck; and how much money would we save by living out there anyway?"

"Some. We'd get by, but you're right, moving out of the city isn't a magical solution to all our problems."

"Then I guess I'm still set on it." In fact, every day that had passed had left Mark not just set on it, but more and more excited about it. The thought of having adventures like the ones he'd heard Bones and his father talking about had him practically coming in his pants, but he knew better than to seem too eager.

"I made some phone calls this week—I know a few guys in the Canadian Army—and it looks like you'd probably be able to enlist…"

"Alright!"

"… as long as you do okay on your final exams."

"Oh."

"Yeah, like I said, you don't need to finish high school, but they don't look too fondly on losers or people who won't work. The other important thing, well, important from my point of view anyway, is that once you're in, the army will encourage you and help you if you want to work on completing your high school education."

"But wouldn't learning a trade be more useful?"

"You'll be better off with both, so I'm going to offer you a deal."

Mark waited. His father's deals were never easy, but they'd always been the right choice in the past.

"As much as I wish there were some other way, I'll help you get into the army, and support your decision all the way."

"And the deal?"

"In return, you promise me that you'll finish your high-school equivalent, GED I think it's called, during your first term of enlistment; and that you don't go in unless you can get into a trade that's going to be useful when you come out."

Mark was less than thrilled at the thought of joining the army just to study more science and math, but he knew his father was making sense.

"Okay. Deal." He stuck out his hand and they shook on it.

The next weeks were a blur of studying and exercise. Larry, who his father had insisted that he talk to, had convinced him that skipping a few practices was not going to hurt the band, and his father convinced him that regular exercise was important.

"You'll study better if you get to the club a couple of times a week, and do a couple of hours of cardio. And the army will look at you a lot more favorably if you're fit than if you're soft and weak."

The morning after his last exam, his father shook him awake at eight. "Nnnnhhh."

"Come on, soldier, time to roll."

"Leave me alone." He and Bruce had partied the night before, and for Mark, the party had ended in a bed somewhere, with a girl whose last name he'd never learned. Lori something or other. He hadn't made it home till after three. "I wanna sleep."

"Tough shit. Get up."

Bleary-eyed, Mark sat up and tried to focus on his clock. "It's eight. What are you…"

"I'm taking half a day off work, but half a day is all I can afford, so get your ass out of bed and get showered and shaved. Clean clothes too, we've got places to go."

"But…"

"No buts. Shake your tail."

Fifteen minutes later, Mark was in the kitchen, sitting down to toast and coffee. "Where's mom?"

"Still in bed. You guys are all out of school, so she gets to sleep in."

"Where are we going?"

"To the recruiting center."

"*What*?" Toast crumbs sprayed the table.

"Relax. I'm not shipping you off to the army today, but if you want to join, you're going to do it right. That means getting started doing some research now. Did you think that you could wait till the band broke up and then just show up at an army base the next day and start collecting paychecks?"

"I…" Mark realized he hadn't actually thought about the process of enlisting at all. "Okay, you win, I'm an airhead."

"No, Donny runs the airhead department in this family, but you aren't used to thinking about the future in a realistic way."

"So I won't be signing up for anything?"

"Not today. And if they can't offer you something decent, then not ever. But there's things you need to know before you make any decisions, and the sooner you know them, the better."

"You mean like what trades are available?"

"Yes, among a lot of other things."

"Like what?"

"Like when they do intakes, where you'd be training, what the pay is, what their requirements are, whether they're even interested in pussy rock singers."

"Okay." Mark finished his toast. "Do we have time for one more cup of coffee?"

"Sure. As long as we don't dawdle over it."

"No problem." Mark poured for both of them. "I just wanted to find out a bit about this trades thing. Did you have a trade? Was it in the army that you got your plumbing training?"

"No, plumbing wasn't something I learned in the army. If I'd had the brains to enlist in a sensible trade, we wouldn't be in the shit we're in now. I'd be a contractor instead of working for a contractor. My trade, if you can call it a trade, was combat field engineering. I learned how to blow things up and kill people, and that's not good for much in the civilian world."

"So what would be good? Do they have mechanics training? Or welding? Or something like that? Automotive shop was the one class I really enjoyed at school, and I wouldn't mind following that up."

"Yeah, there are mechanical opportunities, but remember what I said about talking to some of my old friends who are in the Canadian army?"

"You didn't really say what you'd talked to them about, except that it looked like I could probably get in."

"Well, I talked mostly about what the Canadian military was like these days, and what sort of opportunities there were for somebody who hoped to come out of it with more than a few years of paychecks."

"And?"

"What they told me was that this country's army has gone downhill in the last twenty years. It's not getting the support it needs from the government, and there are a lot of problems with both equipment and morale."

That didn't sound good. Mark wondered if that meant his father was hoping that the visit to the recruiting center would be so negative that Mark would drop the whole idea.

"But," Scott Heaney continued, "there is at least one area that all agreed was worth looking into, and the was the medical corps."

"Medical?" Mark was *not* impressed.

His father laughed. "You want tanks and guns, and blowing things up, right?"

"Or a trade, like mechanics or something."

"Look, Mark, the combat trades, in this country's army anyway, are just not going to give you anything you can take back to civvie street. The infantry is just cannon fodder. Guys who are too stupid to do anything other than follow orders and throw themselves in front of tanks. The armored regiments are the guys that drive the tanks, drive around and crush guys taking shits in the woods. The artillery sit around smoking cigarettes and firing howitzers onto targets so far away they can't even see them. The only combat trade that makes any sense is the engineers, but without finishing high school you're not going to get into that."

Scott Heaney drained the last of his coffee and stood up. "The best trade, by far, in terms of getting something useful that you can take with you when you leave, is medical. Paramedics and ambulance crews make terrific money, and they're in demand just about everywhere." He took their cups and plates to the sink and headed for the door. "There's nothing sissy about military medics, Mark. You'll be shoulder to shoulder with the guys doing the real fighting, and you'll come back home with something more useful than knowing how to fix a broken tank tread."

"I don't know…"

"Don't worry about it. We're just going to do a recce today. Plenty of time to make decisions later."

In the end, it was Bones Battle who helped Mark make his final decision. He'd come over to drop off some books for Mark's father, and found Mark home alone. They'd talked about Mark's decision to enlist, and his unease at the idea of training as a medic.

"Forget it, lad. Real soldiers, and by that I mean soldiers that have actually spent a lot of time in combat, not pouncing around on parade grounds or working in some supply office, will tell you that a good medic is more important to them than God. Praying might make you feel good, but it's the medic that's going to keep you from dying. It doesn't matter whether they're infantrymen or paratroopers or anti-terrorist commandos like your father, if they're real soldiers, they'll respect you. And you know why?"

Mark didn't have a clue.

"Because half the time the medic is right there on the line with them, that's why. You get yourself attached to a combat unit and you're going to be right up there with your nose in the blood and the shit, just like the rest of them, and you're going to be saving their lives into the bargain. It's not like you're living the easy life back in some base hospital at home, like a lot of pussies that call themselves soldiers do. No, lad, you hook yourself up with the right unit and you'll get all the bloody adventure you can handle."

Two months later, the Juice Monkeys played in East Vancouver again at Alexander and Gore. It was a farewell gig at Skavoovee, and two days after that, a month after his eighteenth birthday, Mark was sitting in an airplane, on the runway in Vancouver, ready to begin a flight that would take him five thousand miles across the continent to begin his basic training in Cornwallis, Nova Scotia.

He'd said his goodbyes to family and friends, and now, as he waited for the plane to take off, he opened the envelope his father had slipped him as he gave him a farewell hug. In it was a single piece of paper with these brief words.

"It's not going to be easy, son, but stick with it and you'll be fine. Just remember the six rules of basic training:

"Don't fall in love. At your age, you'll just get burned. Don't ever steal from your buddy. If you're fucking—wrap it. Don't take shit from anyone who's training right beside you. Don't quit on yourself, and don't quit on the people who are relying on you! Don't go through basic alone. If you're having a hard time, call and talk to your father."

PART TWO

CHAPTER 9

All places look the same when you're hungover. Mark Heaney had traveled over five thousand kilometers, from one side of the continent to the other, from the Pacific Ocean to the Atlantic Ocean. But the airport toilet he was throwing up into could just as easily have been back home in Vancouver, or on the other side of the world, in Australia. Porcelain was porcelain, and alcohol brought you to your knees in front of it no matter where you were.

He'd been excited and alert at the beginning of the flight, but three airports, five time zones, and ten complimentary rum and cokes later, he was just one more worshipper in front of the white throne.

He flushed, stood, and turned to the sink to rinse the taste of the barf out of his mouth. The face in the mirror looked a lot better than he felt—although, with his stomach empty, he no longer wished he could just die and be done with it. He stepped back a bit and decided that the body in the mirror looked okay, too. His clothes were wrinkled, but at least he'd managed not to throw up on them, which was more than could be said for the kid stumbling out of the stall beside the one he'd just vacated.

Other than the wrinkles, though, he looked okay. He'd trained hard all summer ("I'm not happy about you going, son, but if you *are* going, then by God, I'm going to make sure you're in shape when you leave") and he looked fit and strong. Maybe tomorrow he'd feel fit and strong, but right now all he wanted to do was lie down somewhere and spend twelve or fourteen hours completely unconscious.

Fat chance. One thing his father had drilled into him over and over was that the instructors were going to find a couple of people to pick on, "...and usually, they're the first people to screw up. You *are* going to screw up, every recruit screws up. Just make sure that you don't do it too soon. Don't try to impress anybody, don't try to be hot shit, and make sure you don't show up late or do anything too stupid until the sergeant has decided who the class goat is going to be."

Scott Heaney had laughed at some memory of his own training days, then continued. "Once they've sorted out who they're going to pick on, they'll cut everybody else plenty of slack. It won't *feel* like they're cutting you any slack; it'll feel like they're ready to grind your ass into hamburger every time you draw breath; but believe me, it's ten thousand times worse if you're the one they've really decided doesn't belong in their army."

So, as hungover as he was, he hauled ass back out into the main terminal and stood beside his bag along with the other couple of dozen young men that were part of this intake. There were two soldiers striding toward them, and he was glad he'd made it back in time not to draw any notice.

"Alright, girls, line up in front of them bags and stand at attention."

A couple of the young men snapped to, like they'd been in cadets or something. Mark and most of the rest faked it—one guy didn't really do anything—and just stood pretty much as they had been.

"You." One of the soldiers stood in front of a kid who hadn't tried hard enough to stand at attention. "Either you stand like you've got a broom handle up your ass, or I'll go get a broom and shove it up there for you." He didn't say it like it was a joke, and when another recruit laughed the soldier was on him instantly. "If I want you to laugh, I'll tell you to fuckin' laugh. Wipe that smile off your stupid face and get it through your head that nothin's going to be funny for any of you pussies for the next three months."

He turned to the other soldier and said, "How many we supposed to have?"

"Twenty-four on this flight. The rest are coming on another flight."

"How many we got?"

"Twenty-two. Want me to go find them?"

The one that seemed to be in charge turned to the line of young men. "Any of you know where the lost sheep are?"

Mark knew, but he kept his mouth shut. One of the others wasn't so smart. "I think they might be in the bathroom."

"Who the fuck are you?"

"Uh, my name's Derek Wilson."

"As far as I'm concerned, your name is shithead, and when you talk to me, you call me Corporal, you got that, shithead?"

The kid was too embarrassed to respond. "I asked you a question, shithead."

"Uh, yes sir... uh... Corporal."

Mark silently thanked his father, and then concentrated on trying not to throw up again as the corporal who had been harassing them herded them onto an old school bus, and told them to sit down and keep their mouths shut.

An hour later, the bus turned onto Canadian Forces Recruit School in Cornwallis, and rolled to a stop in front of an ugly building that didn't look much different from any of the other ugly buildings around them. Out the window, Mark could see another bus pulling in behind them.

"Sit where you are and stay shut up till Master Corporal Marche gets here."

Master Corporal Marche introduced himself by climbing onto the bus and heaving an empty garbage can down the aisle as hard as he could. The thing made a horrible clanging racket, and some kid who had his leg stretched into the aisle yelled in pain when it hit him.

"Off the bus! Get your shit from the cargo compartment and fall in, in one rank. At attention!" he screamed at them.

Still feeling like he might throw up at any moment, Mark scrambled with the others and soon they were all standing in front of their suitcases and duffels, more or less at attention, more or less in a straight line along the side of the bus. Master Corporal Marche walked up and down in front of them, then spat in disgust.

"Look at them." He spoke to one of the soldiers who'd met them at the airport. "Are you sure this is what we were supposed to get? Looks like a bunch of recruits for the faggots and losers club, not for the army." He slapped his forehead in exasperation. "Who the fuck is doing the recruiting these days? Martha Stewart? *You!*" he roared at one of the group, "What's your name?"

"Becker, Corporal."

"You will address me as Master Corporal Marche. You understand?"

"Yes, Master Corporal Marche."

"Well, Pecker, do you think I'm ugly or something?"

Mark, along with probably every other guy in the line, was thinking 'Say, "Yes".'

"No, Master Corporal Marche."

"Well then why the fuck were you staring over there," Marche pointed off to the left, "when I was standing right in front of you?"

"I don't know, Master Corporal."

At least the kid had the brains not to lose his cool or forget to call Marche 'Master Corporal'.

"When you stand at attention your eyes point straight ahead and never, *never*, twitch. You got that?"

"Yes, Master Corporal."

Marche took a couple of steps backwards. "Pecker here is going to show the rest of you asswipes what happens when you screw up. Give me fifty, Pecker, *right now!*"

Becker understood, and got down on the ground and started doing pushups. He wasn't really fat, but he was definitely not thin, and there was no way he was going to get five pushups, let alone fifty. He surprised Mark by making seven before his arms gave out and he sank to the ground, unable to do another. His arms quivered, and his shoulders came up, but his belly stayed where it was.

"Jesus." Marche looked at Becker, struggling on the ground, trying for an eighth. "What a fucking pussy." Then suddenly, "And what the fuck are the rest of you looking at. Didn't I just finish telling Pecker that standing at attention meant eyes front? Are you all fucking deaf or are you just stupid? Pecker here got fifty. Next time he screws up, it'll be a hundred. Same for the rest of you. Fifty, right *now!*"

Mark had been cranking sets of a hundred all summer, and even hung over he knew that a fifty would be no problem, but he could hear his father's voice in his ear as he went down... "Whatever you do, don't show off during basic. If there's one thing that the instructors hate worse than a softie, it's a guy who makes their punishments look easy. Do that, and they'll just keep piling on more punishment."

Mark did a dozen at moderate speed, then slowed down, for a few more, then let his form go—letting his back lose its straightness, and letting his shoulders come up way before his gut—making it look like twenty-five pushups would pretty much kill him. Most of the group didn't make fifteen, so Mark figured that if he faked about twenty he'd be okay. Out of the corner of his eye, he noticed that a couple of the guys, one of the cadet types, and one guy with body-builder muscles, had snapped off the fifty with no problem. The cadet popped back up onto his feet and stood at attention as soon as he was done, the body-builder got up more slowly and stood with a "big deal" smirk on his face.

"You." Marche pointed to the guy with the muscles. "Name?"

"Bill Walsh."

Uh oh. The guy had just given Marche all the excuse he needed. Not that he needed an excuse, Mark reminded himself.

"*What?*" Marche was screaming again, right in Walsh's face. "Around here your name isn't Bill Walsh. Your name is Walsh. And when you talk to me you call me Master Corporal you fucking ignorant ape!" He stepped back so he wasn't spitting right in Walsh's face any-more. "You're dirt, Walsh. You and every one of these pussies are *dirt*. Now, assume the position and start doing more pushups."

"How many?"

This time, Marche didn't yell. Didn't say anything. Just glared.

"Uh, how many, Master Corporal?"

"Until I fucking well tell you to stop, that's how many. Now get down there and start pumping off…" He stopped, and looked up as one of his assistants tapped him on the shoulder.

"There's only twenty-three of them. I put twenty-four on the bus at the airport."

"Well, now. Isn't *that* interesting. Go find out if he's still on the bus, and tell him that if it isn't too much trouble for him, we'd just *love* to have him join us for tea and fucking crumpets." He turned back and looked at Walsh as if discovering some dogshit on his shoe. "Walsh, are you *trying* to piss me off, or are you just naturally an idiot?"

Walsh got the message and hit dirt. He began cranking off pushups as Marche resumed talking.

"I'm probably wasting my time, since none of you looks like you could learn anything, but it's time for your first instruction. I want you all to watch Corporal Laforest." The soldier who hadn't gone back into the bus stepped forward. "Corporal Laforest is going to do his best to look like one of you." Laforest slumped so that his shoulders sagged; his stomach protruded, his legs and arms went slack, and then he started gawking around like a farmboy seeing tall buildings for the first time.

"Ahh-*tennn-shun!*" Mark wasn't sure exactly what Marche had yelled, but he assumed it meant 'Attention', because Laforest snapped ramrod straight, looking like a soldier on a poster.

"Corporal Laforest has his back straight, his heels together, his toes forty-five degrees apart, his gut in, and his thumbs aligned with the seams of his pants. This is not a difficult thing to do, so *do it*."

Mark did his best, but it wasn't good enough. Marche walked down the line and found something wrong with every single one of them, including the two cadet types.

Another set of pushups, and they were on their feet again.

"Walsh, didn't I just tell you that I'd tell you when it was time to stop?" Walsh got the message and went back down. He was covered in sweat, and the pushups weren't coming as fast anymore.

Marche turned to the Corporal who had been standing like a statue. "Corporal Laforest, stand at ease."

Laforest's hands went behind his back, and his feet moved a little ways apart. Other than that, he still looked like he had a broom handle up his ass.

"Platoon! Stand at … *ease!*"

They all tried it, and again they all got it wrong, but at least this time they didn't get any more pushups, because Marche's attention was occupied with the Corporal who had checked out the bus.

"The dickhead on the bus wants to go home. He says enlisting was 'all a mistake'."

"Probably most of these guys wish they could go home, too, but they're not crying on the bus. Tell him to get his pansy ass out here."

Mark didn't hear what the corporal on the bus said, but he must have said something, because Marche replied, "Okay, lock the bus from the outside and we'll deal with him later." He looked down to where Walsh was lying in the dirt. "Okay, Walsh, on your feet and fall in with the rest of them. Any time you think you're tougher than everybody else, you just let me know and we'll talk about it some more."

Marche stepped back a pace and stared at twenty-three remaining young men. "Behind this bus is your barracks, the shack you're gonna call home for the next three months. In two minutes you will pick up your shit and carry it there, along with the recruits from the other bus. Once you are inside, pick a bed and place your gear beside it."

He paused, and when he spoke again, his voice wasn't quite as loud. "Once you are inside and standing in front of a bed, we will give you ten minutes by yourselves. During that time you will have the opportunity to voluntarily place any drugs, alcohol, or weapons you may have mistakenly brought here with you, into the large ammunition container that you will find between every row of beds. No one will be watching you, and there will be no punishment."

His voice suddenly rose again. "Do not, I repeat, *do not* try to hide anything. We *will* find whatever you try to hide, and anyone found in possession of drugs, alcohol, or weapons after this will be punished severely. Possession of drugs will not be tolerated, and the punishment may include time in jail and dishonorable discharge."

He strode down the line, staring each recruit in the face, then stepped back a pace and yelled, "Now, *move it!*"

The next ten minutes was a mad rush. The other bus was bigger and there were close to a hundred young men bumping into each other, dropping their bags, getting lost, asking each other questions, and finally stumbling to a halt in front of the beds.

Some, like Mark, stood waiting, looking around at their new home, and trying to come to terms with what was happening. Others, a surprising number, were madly ripping into their luggage and dropping bottles, baggies, joints, pipes, switchblades, and pills into the ammunition cans. One or two dropped their stashes out a window, presumably thinking that they'd be able to pick it up later.

Mark's father had been pretty clear about that. "The staff have seen it all before, Mark. Anything that you or any other recruit can dream up, they've seen a hundred times already. Don't try to trick them, and don't try to hide anything from them. You can hate them, they won't mind that; but don't suck up to them, and don't try to fool them."

Mark was pretty sure that there would be staff hanging around outside, just waiting to see what was being dropped out of the windows. He wondered whether they'd take whatever they saw, or if they'd wait and bust anybody stupid enough to try to recover it later.

They didn't get to stay by the bed they'd picked, of course. Once the voluntary contraband donations had been removed, the NCOs started yelling at them. Screaming names from lists, assigning people to sections, cursing them for being slow and stupid, demanding pushups, and herding them like sheep from one part of the barracks to another.

At the end of two hours, the one hundred and twenty recruits of 8 Platoon—minus the kid who had refused to get off the bus—had been divided into six sections. The barracks, what the corporals all called "your shack," were H-shaped and two stories high. Each section got a wing, and there were communal bathrooms, showers, and laundry facilities in the middle of each floor. One of the remaining two wings was occupied by the staff offices, and the other was empty.

Each recruit was assigned a bed, a locker, and a cupboard with several drawers; and by the end of the two hours, each recruit understood two things: First, he understood he was free to quit anytime—'Just tell the Platoon Warrant Officer that you want out, and you'll be gone on the next plane'. Second, he understood that if he stayed in, his ass belonged to the army. Corporals were gods, and anything higher than a Corporal was, well… the best that a recruit could hope for was that nobody higher than a Corporal ever noticed him.

The first four weeks of basic training were designed to be a total mindfuck. It started from the moment they stepped off the bus and were punished for not knowing how to stand at attention, even though they'd never been taught, and continued without respite. They were issued a ton of gear and told that everything had to be labeled in a certain way with sewn-in labels, and then stored in a certain way, with punishment worse than death for anyone who failed to comply. But they were never given time for locker layout or sewing. Reveille was at 0530, lights out was at 2200, and since every second of that time was fully occupied, there was no way they could possibly comply.

Nor could they get anywhere close to the seven hours of sleep that a 2200 to 0500 lights out implied. Evenings were supposed to be personal time ('personal administration' the army called it) but since the drill staff always found other things that needed doing—sweeping, cleaning, dusting, floor-waxing—the night was the only time they had to keep up with the stuff they were supposed to get done in the evening.

In fact, they had no time for anything. Even eating was a military ordeal. Stand in line with 120 other poor slobs, get food slopped on your tray by a cook's helper who looked like he hated you, inhale the food in the allotted four minutes, put your tray away, and line up to be marched off to whatever new torture they had waiting for you—usually either Physical Training or some kind of marching, which the army called "drill" but which Mark could never think of it as anything but "more fucking marching."

The physical part of it was no problem. Mark had been working out under his father's instruction all summer, and, once he got the hang of swimming, the army training was easier than his father's. The focus of the first two weeks was swimming, and it took Mark some time to get used to the idea of high-speed laps in a pool at six o'clock in the morning, but he did better than most of the platoon, and the rest of it, the running, the calisthenics, the endless pushups, was easier for him than for just about everybody else.

The mental aspect was something else, though. His father had told him that he'd be expected to do impossible and idiotic things and that the only way to deal with it was just to go along and pretend that it all made sense.

"Don't argue, don't try to figure it out, don't get angry. Just do it as best you can and know in advance that whatever you do, they're going to tell you that you fucked up. It's part of the deal Mark. It's their way of finding out who's going to fold under pressure and getting rid of them before the real pressure hits."

It had all sounded fine when his father was explaining it as they hiked up Grouse Mountain, but here, on the other side of the country, where there was only Master Corporal Marche and his staff of professional assholes, it was definitely not fine.

Each morning, after PT and breakfast, Master Corporal Marche would inspect his Section. Sometimes the Platoon Warrant Officer, a sergeant named Atkins, would walk through with him, but usually, it was just Marche and one or two of his sub-demons.

Uniform, bedspace, floorspace, locker, and personal hygiene. If a recruit's underwear wasn't folded in perfect four-inch by four-inch squares, and lined up exactly as specified, that recruit got pushups. Or, as training wore on, extra miles to run. Clothing and kit was thrown around the room, labels that had taken forever to sew in were ripped out, bedding was pulled off beds and tossed out windows.

It was impossible. It was insane. The first time Mark heard, "Twenty-five, Heaney," because his underwear weren't folded like some kind of Martha Stewart window display, he wanted to boot Marche in the nuts. What kind of asshole thought that folding underwear into little squares was going to make someone a better soldier?

He'd have understood if it was something like letting your rifle get dirty, or not doing your share of the platoon's work, but underwear?

He held his temper and went through the punishment by the book. "Permission to begin, Master Corporal?"

"Yes."

Twenty-five pushups were then pumped off, and then, "Permission to recover, Master Corporal?"

"What else, Heaney?"

"Thank you for improving my slack and idle body. Permission to recover, Master Corporal?"

"Recover."

It was stupid, but he did it. He'd give Marche the twenty-five then stand back to attention while some other helpless slob got tormented for folding his socks the wrong way, or not having his bedcover stretched tight enough to bounce a quarter off.

After the first week, nobody slept on his bed anyway. What was the point? Any wrinkling of the sheets or covers was grounds for punishment, so most of the guys would slide a pillow and a bunched-up overcoat under the top cover so it looked like there was a body there, and then crawl under the bed and sleep on the floor. Of course, sleeping on the floor was also a punishable offence, and once in a while, the duty NCO would pull a surprise middle-of-the-night inspection and bust everybody for a midnight run then make them get into their perfectly made beds just so that they could all be busted again in the morning for wrinkled sheets.

One guy, a kid from Newfoundland named Stephens, was completely incapable of being neat. He got shit every single morning, and Mark didn't know whether to feel sorry for him for the endless pushups and extra laps, or to be thankful that there was someone else too dumb to fold his clothes, thereby keeping the heat off everyone else.

At first, Mark thought that Stephens was going to be the one singled out by the staff as Platoon goat, but somewhere around the tenth time it happened, Walsh, the muscle boy who'd pissed Marche off on day one, snickered and whispered something about 'that brain-dead Newfie' to the guy beside him. His whisper wasn't as quiet as he intended and all of a sudden, there were three drill staff standing in front of him, and Mark knew, from the looks that passed between them, that candidate Walsh had just been elected to a position he didn't even know existed.

"Raise your arms to the sides, Walsh. Shoulder height, palms up." Walsh did as he was told, still with a bit of a smirk on his face.

Marche then picked up the polished parade boots that were standing in front of Walsh's locker and placed one on each of the upturned palms.

"That's where they stay, Walsh. They fall, or your arms drop below shoulder level, and I am not going to be pleased. You got that?"

"Yes, Master Corporal Marsh." The smirk was still in place. Walsh was just too dumb to understand that what the instructors wanted was tough recruits, not recruits with an 'I'm tough' attitude.

Mark could almost read the guy's mind. 'What kind of punishment is holding up a pair of boots? I do lateral raises with eighty-pound dumbbells, and these guys think a pair of boots'll bother me?' Anybody with a brain would have dropped the things after a couple of minutes and taken whatever shit the staff handed him. Not Walsh. Walsh knew that because he could bench press four thirty-five, he was obviously tougher than some skinny corporal who had to be over thirty, anyway, and he wanted to make sure that everybody knew it.

For the remaining ten minutes of the inspection, he held them out, but by the time the staff had finished tormenting everyone in the section, he was starting to sweat.

"Course Senior!"

The recruit whose turn it was to be responsible for the Platoon that day stepped forward. "Yes, Master Corporal?"

"Get your Platoon ready and on the parade ground. You've got two minutes."

"Yes, Master Corporal"

"And make sure everyone understands that if Walsh's arms go below shoulder height, or if he drops a boot, his whole section will share my displeasure."

167

"Yes, Master Corporal."

Two minutes later, they were in formation on the parade ground. Walsh still had his boots out at arms' length, but his face was showing the strain and his arms were starting to tremble. Mark knew that the pain in his shoulders would soon be unbearable.

He actually managed to keep the boots up for the first minute of drill, but they soon fell off and Marche and the instructors made sure that all the sections marched over them at least once.

If it had been anybody else's boots, most of the recruits would have done their best to avoid stepping on them, even at the cost of getting pushups themselves. But Walsh was an obnoxious prick, and at the end of the hour his mirror-polished parade boots looked like they'd been in a cement mixer with a load of sharp bricks.

Mark knew how much effort it took to get even a small nick buffed and shining. Walsh was going to be up all night trying to get the boots back to parade gloss. He'd be more tired the next day, which meant he'd fuck up more, which meant he'd get punished more and get even less sleep… A vicious circle that Mark was glad to be observing from the outside.

It ended as the staff had known it would. Walsh lost his temper one day and took a swing at the corporal who was needling him. The corporal slipped enough of the punch to be sure it wouldn't hurt, but let it land so that there could be no question about 'assaulting an instructor'. Mark was probably the only recruit who knew that the corporal could have ducked it completely if he'd wanted to, but he kept his mouth shut.

The corporal, who was even older and smaller than Marche, gave Walsh a whipping that reminded Mark of George Christiansen's surgical destruction of Rick Warner, then called for the MPs and turned back to the Platoon and said, "Right. Nothing like a bit of exercise in the morning. Makes a man happy to greet the day."

The MPs took the whimpering muscle boy away, and no one ever saw him again, although they heard that he'd had to do time in the military prison before he got his discharge.

After that, it got a bit easier. Not physically of course, but mentally. Most of the candidates who simply couldn't take it had already dropped out, and the ones that were left had figured out that as long as they tried hard, and took the crap that got thrown at them, they'd do okay. That didn't mean it was fun, and as time went on the physical side of things got harder and harder, but they all got tougher, so the added load didn't kill them.

Mark did well enough. There were a couple of nights that he found himself near tears as he lay under his bed, following days when it seemed the staff had singled him out for torment, even though he was giving it his best shot. But most of the time he was okay. He was too tired to worry about the fact that he wasn't making music anymore, and, at least for the first few weeks, also too tired to think much about sex—jerking off a couple of times a week was all he had the energy for.

But as time progressed, he began to feel the need more often. Of the hundred or so recruits left in the course, fifteen were female. The women had one wing on the upper floor, and fraternization was not encouraged. For the first few weeks, it didn't make any difference, but gradually he began to think more and more about the fact that sexual relief was just up the stairs, and eventually the inevitable happened. He'd made eye contact with a few of them, got the contact returned by a couple, struck up a conversation, and one night not long after that, found himself making it in a storage closet with candidate Didi Woodruff.

It wasn't the kind of glorious fuckathon that he was used to with Helen and Karen, or even the kind of fun night he'd gotten used to with the girls that wanted to screw the singer of the Juice Monkeys. It was sex at its most basic and primal. Two healthy, horny animals getting it on fast and furious, with one eye open all the time for the duty NCO.

"Jesus. Did I ever need that," Didi said when they were finished. She was ten years older than Mark, and was not a beauty. Nor did she have any interest in anything other than his cock. She had come just as fast as he had, and when they were done, she didn't want conversation or hugs or anything except a chance to get back to her quarters undetected.

Mark was used to having girls fawn over him, and this was something new. She'd ridden him hard, and enjoyed what he was giving her, but it was clear that anybody with a dick would have suited her just as well.

Still, it had been a lot better than jerking off, and since he wasn't interested in her any more than she was in him, he didn't mind. "You wanna do this again, sometime?" He asked.

"Yeah, sure. You're actually not a bad fuck." She was almost dressed. "I'll let you know."

They made it again two nights later, but then the word got out, and pretty soon everybody else was looking for it, too. With about eighty-five men and fifteen women left in the course, the women obviously had the best of the deal. Most of them claimed to be engaged, and some even said they were married, but every single one of them was doing the dirty with the boys downstairs on a regular basis. In the storage closets, in the shower rooms, sometimes even in the dorms with everyone else listening and jerking off. No fidelity in the army.

Didi must have told her buddies that Mark was worth taking for a ride, because he got the storage closet treatment about once a week, whereas most of the guys were lucky to get laid once a month.

Some of the women were probably decent folks, but the only time he spent with them was twenty minutes in a dark closet, so it was hard to tell. The sex was really nothing more than pressure relief for both the men and the women, and the only people he got to know were the guys in his own section.

No matter where a recruit was from, or where he was headed, he started in the same place: Basic Training at CFRS Cornwallis. Army, Navy or Air Force, ground crew or infantry grunt, medic or artillery; it didn't matter. Likewise, it didn't matter whether he was from the West Coast, the East Coast or somewhere in the middle of the prairies; he did his eleven weeks at Cornwallis, Nova Scotia. So Mark's course included a lot of people that he'd never have met in the part of Vancouver that he'd called home until he flew to Cornwallis.

In any other situation, he'd have made a lot of new friends, learned about new kinds of music, confronted new ideas; but in Basic Training, the pressure was so intense that there just wasn't time to form anything more than casual friendships. When you've been marching for ten kilometers under a full fifty-pound load, there's not much incentive to discuss the meaning of life with the guy who's staggering along beside you.

Most of the guys were okay. The obvious losers had been weeded out by the tough program, and nobody had enough energy left over at the end of the day to be too much of a prick. There were a couple of guys that Mark would rather not have met, but once Walsh was gone, there wasn't any severe friction. Stephens, the Newfie that was always getting in shit for not taking care of his kit, was the one Mark got closest to. Other than being messy, he was actually good at most of the things the staff made them do, so they didn't rag on him too hard, and he was definitely the funniest person Mark had ever met. He could tell stories that had everyone rolling on the floor, and afterward, no one ever knew if they were true.

Even though there wasn't a lot of time for deep friendships, they did learn to look out for one another. The staff had a habit of punishing the whole section for one person's screw-ups, so working as a team, whether it was doing drill, keeping the barracks clean, or taking care of each other in the field exercises, soon became second nature. It seemed natural to share the load—one guy doing the section's ironing for the night; another sewing name labels that the staff had ripped out. Three working together to polish the floors; a couple polishing everyone's boots. Two more inspecting every single drawer and locker, making sure that all clothes and kits were folded and in the exact place and alignment they were required to be in.

It came naturally to Mark. Playing in the band had meant being totally dependent on a small group of others, so he was used to it. Most of the other recruits had no problem, either—they'd played team sports or they were just naturally able to work together—but there were a few guys who just didn't get it. They'd try to dodge responsibility, or they simply didn't care what happened to the section. Every one of those was gone by the halfway point of the course, and the final six weeks were spent in the company of guys that could count on each other.

Because of the edge that his father had given him, Mark came through pretty much at the top of his course. Like Stephens, he got tagged regularly for not having his locker and bedspace in order, but also, like Stephens, he was good at all the physical and military stuff, and he never brown-nosed or complained, so the staff respected him as much as they respected any of the recruits. It was never easy. In fact, physically, it kept getting harder, but they were all tougher, and it *seemed* easier.

The final week was a full-on, six-day, field exercise. Sleeping in tents, eating field rations, humping loads, night navigation exercises, the works. All done in the Nova Scotia winter, with wet snow and freezing rain seeping into their clothes and sleeping bags... mud getting into their equipment, their bodies rebelling at having to survive in extreme conditions... food turning cold before they could get it from their bowls to their mouths, and with the staff riding them unmercifully the whole time. When they staggered home to their barracks on the sixth evening, the ugly shack looked like a castle, and the staff, who had all been professional assholes for almost three months, relaxed enough to almost seem human.

The recruits whooped and hollered in the showers, danced naked in the hallways, and slept in their beds without worrying about wrinkles or midnight inspections.

The graduation party was held in the Junior Ranks Club the following night. It was a no-holds-barred riot, and Mark celebrated by drinking even more than he'd drunk on the plane ride in. The last thing he remembered was crawling over to where Didi Woodruff was sitting barefoot, and trying to suck her toes.

Stephens, who was nowhere near as dumb as he pretended to be, had somehow smuggled in a video camera early in the course and managed to keep it hidden from the staff for the whole time. No one knew about it till the graduation party, when he talked the Sergeant into letting him show some of the stuff he'd shot. He'd set it up in the storage closet that everyone used for sex, and it turned out that some of the closet's visitors liked to do their fucking with the light on, but by the time he was showing those scenes no one was even close to being sober, and everybody had a good laugh.

Mark woke up the next morning to find his toenails painted red, his legs covered with felt marker designs, shaving cream in his crotch, a swastika shaved into his chest hair and his face made up with shoe polish. He also had the mother of all hangovers and spent several hours puking before he could even think about cleaning himself up and starting to prepare for the next phase of his life.

It was a strange two days. No training, no inspections, nobody yelling and screaming. And every couple of hours another group of guys that he'd spent the most intense three months of his life with getting on a bus and disappearing.

Sandy Stephens left early the second morning. Mark was sad to say goodbye to him. Stephens was a strange kid, but Mark had come to like him a lot. He was easily the brightest guy in the section, but he never made any "I'm smarter than you" noise, and he was always ready to help, even when it meant getting his own hands dirty.

Would they ever see each other again? Stephens was headed for battle school in Wainwright, Alberta, to train for the First Battalion of the Princess Patricia's Canadian Light Infantry.

"Yeah, I know," he'd said to Mark, "I'm gonna be a grunt. But it's better than anything I had waiting for me back home. My family have always been fishermen, but now there's no more fish. Nothing but welfare for anybody who hasn't got the money to go to university."

Mark thought about his father's advice to make sure that he would come out of his time in the army with a skill that would get him somewhere in the civilian world. "Why the infantry? Why not the engineers, or the medics, or something?"

"When you're from Buttfuck, Newfoundland, they don't give you those kinds of choices. It was infantry or welfare. But it's okay. The Patricia's a good place to start if you want to get into the Airborne, so I'm gonna be the best fucking soldier in the PPCLI and as soon as they'll let me do it, I'll go for my jump course and then apply to the Airborne."

"Airborne?"

"Closest thing this fucking Mickey-Mouse army has to a real fighting unit."

They were silent for a couple of minutes while Sandy continued packing. "I wonder when we'll see each other again."

"No way to tell, man." Stephens replied. "This country is five thousand miles wide and four thousand miles high. The chance of us being posted anywhere together is pretty much zero. But who knows, maybe if you get bored with listening to fat-asses complaining about their hangnails, you'll wake up and join the Airborne. At least there, you'll get to deal with real casualties."

CHAPTER 10

Canadian Forces Medical Services School, Borden. Somewhere in Ontario. Could have been somewhere in Afghanistan for all Mark knew. He wasn't hungover this time, as he had been on his arrival at CFRS Cornwallis, but it was late afternoon in December. The wind was driving icy, wet sleet into his face and clothing. Soaking and numbing him from the moment he stepped off the plane.

Dark, cold, wet, and miserable. That pretty much summed up his introduction to CFMSS Borden. Weatherwise, the only thing that changed for the next six months was that the sleet turned to snow, and the temperature went from cold, to colder, to *really* fucking cold, before finally starting to warm up in April and May.

But the big difference wasn't the weather; it was the work. Recruit School had been insane—deliberately designed to put the recruits in impossible situations—but medic training was more like something that happened in real life. It was like going to school and playing soldier all at the same time, with the added bonus that what he studied was actually useful and interesting.

There was a lot of basic stuff about health and the human body that wasn't a whole lot of fun, but when they got into the practical aspect of it, things like first aid, setting up intravenous lines, and dealing with fractures, it was better. And when they started learning to apply their knowledge in a military setting—wounds, weapons, mine awareness, helicopter evacuation procedures, setting up field hospitals, first aid in combat situations—Mark was all over it.

There was a downside to it, of course. One of the things that he'd really been looking forward to was the chance to do actual work in the Base hospital, but from the first minute of his first shift of hospital rotation, it was clear that he was just an orderly with a military uniform. Wiping injured soldiers' asses because they couldn't do it themselves, cleaning up floors covered in blood and barf, dealing with the mess after sick guys had shit their beds...

When he'd graduated from Basic, his pay had gone up from a thousand a month to eleven-fifty a month, which he'd figured was pretty cool wages for going to school and getting some good physical training on the side; but after yet another shift of scrubbing human waste off every conceivable surface, the thrill was wearing off fast.

"It's not the medical part." He was on the phone with his father. "I don't mind studying, and I really like the field training. It's this hospital shit. If they want us to learn medical procedures, why do they make us scrub floors and clean up vomit?"

"Because they can." Scott Heaney replied. "Somebody's gotta clean up the puke; you're the low man on the totem pole, so they order you to do it." He paused as if he wasn't happy about what he was going to say next. "Canada's a good country in many ways, Mark, but the government here doesn't give the armed forces the support that it should. Sometimes the military does the best that it can anyway, other times it responds with a sort of 'Fuck you' attitude and does really stupid things. Like a kid that deliberately hurts himself, just to get back at his parents."

Mark didn't have a clue what his father was talking about, and was about to interrupt, but his father carried on.

"Any other country, the military rotates its medics through civilian hospitals, but the Canadian Army brass have decided that their medics will learn better on Base. It's fucked, I know, but you've gotta live with it, even though a month in the emergency ward at a big-city hospital would teach you more about battle casualties than you could learn in ten years in a Base hospital."

"Oh, great. Some General is pissed because the government won't give him more troops or something, so I get to wipe butts and scrub floors. That's really gonna help when I'm trying to deal with some guy who's had his arm blown off."

"Mark, you're in the army now, so you might as well stop worrying about things not making sense. Just keep your head down and your guard up, and you'll do okay... as long as you don't piss your NCOs off too much, that is. You'll be outta there in a few months, and like you said, the rest of the training is good, so enjoy the good and let the bad roll off."

As Mark thought about it in his rack that night, he realized that his father had given him the same advice about getting through Basic—

don't try to make sense of it, just do your best and let the insanity pass you by. Doing the work that an orderly should have been doing was stupid, but he only did a couple of shifts a week in the hospital, so yeah, he could cope with it.

And now that he was out of recruit school, at least there weren't any mind games. Evenings really were personal time, and there was no bullshit about sleeping on the floor and folding underwear into four-inch squares. The non-coms inspected the barracks regularly, but as long as things were moderately tidy, they didn't give a shit. Mostly, they were doing it because someone above them had ordered them to do it, and they didn't treat the trainees like scum. There was a definite line between the trainees and the staff, but they *had* completed recruit school, and they *were* regular members of the armed forces, so the NCOs were mostly willing to cut them a certain amount of slack, even if they hadn't got their first real posting yet.

Another big difference was that Mark, and all the others, were now responsible for their own progress. In Basic, there had always been someone on his case, making him do this, making him do that, supervising every fucking second of his day. Here, he was on his own. There was plenty of physical training, and the NCOs wouldn't put up with any slacking there, but on the medic side, it was up to him. If he didn't study, he wouldn't pass. Simple as that. Nobody stood over his shoulder in the evening making him hit the books. If he didn't do it on his own, he'd fail, get reassigned to some infantry battalion, and spend the next three years digging latrines or something.

Without a trade, digging and scrubbing would be all he could look forward to, so he forced himself to study at least a couple of hours most evenings. Other guys weren't so disciplined, and as the months rolled by, they either dropped out or got booted out after failing exams, or fucking up once too often. They were probably posted to an infantry unit somewhere and were never heard from again.

He stayed in shape, too. The PT was nowhere near as tough as it had been in recruit school, and a lot of the guys let their fitness slide. Some of the medics who were rotating in for advanced courses, guys who'd been in the army for years, were total slobs.

"How the fuck are you gonna feel heading into some battle knowing that your only hope if you take a hit is some fat walrus like that?" Mark pointed to a Corporal a few tables away in the Junior Ranks Club.

"I don't know man. I think if I got wounded, I'd just ask one of my buds to shoot me and put me out of my misery right there." Shane Dargaville was a stocky kid, a couple of years older than Mark. He drained his beer. "I like my beer as much as anybody, but I ain't never gonna let it take me over. I mean, look at him! He's gotta have had seven or eight beers since we've been here, and who knows how long he was here before that?"

Dargaville was tough. He was a farm kid, from somewhere in Saskatchewan, who looked harder than a one-hundred-and-eighty pound roll of barbed wire. He'd done his Med 'A' training a year ahead of Mark and was back at Borden for an upgrade course. It was fitness that had brought them together. Fitness, and, indirectly, Mark's father.

Mark had complained to his father one night on the telephone that the PT at Med training was so bad that he was starting to go soft.

"So do something about it." Trust Scott Heaney to cut through the bullshit.

"Like what? Fifty extra pushups in the barracks before I go to bed?"

"If that was all you could do, then I'd say do it, but why not check out the weight room?"

"Weight room?"

"You're not a recruit anymore, Mark. You're on a big military base that's going to have all the same kinds of facilities as a town. There'll be more than one weight gym, so get off your ass and check it out." Scott Heaney paused, then, "Better still, get into whatever martial arts club they've got."

"Martial arts club? Are you serious?"

"Of course I'm serious."

They'd talked about other things after that. Family, the financial situation, friends; but when they finished their conversation, Mark went looking for the duty NCO and started asking questions. Two days later he showed up for his first martial arts workout in almost five months.

It was strange. Recruit training had taught him that he was a nobody. That his place in the world was to do what he was told and do it fast.

That anyone with rank could, and would, treat him like scum. Here at Borden, he wasn't scum anymore, but his place was still at the bottom of the ladder and fraternization with anybody other than other privates had seemed to be simply out of the question.

But when he showed up at the gym for that first workout, everything was turned upside down. The first clue had come when he'd got lost and couldn't find the gym. It was dark, cold, and snowy, and the base was big. He'd been about ready to give up when he'd seen somebody with a gym bag, trudging toward a building that Mark didn't recognize.

"Hey! Excuse me." The guy had the hood of his parka up to keep out the snow. "Are you headed for the ... "

There was the briefest flash of gold on the man's collar, under the parka, and Mark snapped to attention, saluting and mumbling apologies.

"Easy does it, boy; I'm not going to shoot you."

"I'm sorry, sir. I'm still new here, and I'm a bit lost."

"Well, if you stand at ease and tell me what you're looking for, maybe I can help."

Mark had never spoken one-on-one with an officer before. Corporals were agents of the devil, and a Sergeant was the devil himself. What did that make officers? He forced himself to stand at ease, and said, "Sir, I'm looking for the gym where the martial arts club meets."

"Well, you don't have far to go. That's where I'm heading myself, so come on along." The captain turned back into the wind and began trudging through the snow again, then stopped and said, "Look, we're in the middle of a snowstorm, and you're not on the parade ground, so stop marching and just walk. Like you were doing before you saw me."

"Yes sir. Thank you sir." Mark tried to walk normally, but it was hard. Inside the gym, it was even stranger.

"No saluting, no standing at attention. Once we're on the mats, there's no ranks. You call me Sensei, at least till you've been here a while and everybody else you just call by their first name. Okay?"

The man speaking to him seemed to be the chief instructor, and wore a gi in the kung fu style, with a black belt. He looked like he was about forty, and Mark had no idea if he was a private or a Colonel. He decided the best thing to do was play it cautious, so he bowed and said, "Yes, Sensei."

"You've trained before?"

Mark had changed into his sweats—his gi was four thousand kilometers away—but the bow had probably been a give-away. "Yes, Sensei."

"Where? What style?"

"In Vancouver, Sensei, at a hapkido club. But the master liked to bring in teachers from other styles, and my father taught defendo there."

"We do a bit of everything here ourselves. Mostly kung fu, and Thai kickboxing, but Sergeant Park knows some akido, so if you've done some hapkido, you should be able to roll around on the ground with him and feel right at home." The instructor laughed. "For about thirty seconds, that is, until he puts you into the hurt locker."

The man the instructor was pointing to was no taller than Mark, but he looked like he was close to seventy or eighty pounds heavier, and not much of it was fat. He only wore a green belt, but if he had any speed to go along with his obvious strength, Mark knew he'd be a formidable opponent. His father had often told him that the best way to deal with a good akido fighter was to shoot him before he got close enough to touch you, and this guy looked like bullets would just bounce off him.

"What have you got for me?"

The green belt had seen them looking his way, and was walking toward them. It was weird to hear a Sergeant, especially one that looked this hard, talking politely.

"Not sure yet, but it might be interesting. Kid says he's done hapkido."

"Hapkido, huh? Great. What's your name?"

Mark stiffened to attention automatically. "Heaney, Sergeant."

"Outside this room you can be Heaney, and I'll be Sergeant. In here, you call me Sergeant again, I'll kick your ass up around your ears. What's your name."

"Mark Heaney."

"Good to meet you Mark." The barrel-shaped Sergeant held out his hand. "I'm Walt Park. How long you been doing hapkido?"

"Um, well, mostly we did defendo, but I started when I was pretty young."

The two men laughed. "You're *still* pretty young. You mean since you were fifteen or something?"

"I don't really remember. My dad started me when I was, I don't know, five or something."

That stopped them for a moment. "So, just how far have you come?"

"Um, there's no belts for kids in defendo, but I have my red belt in hapkido."

"No shit." Park was impressed. He turned to the instructor and said, "It's not like your typical belt-of-the-month-club Kung Fu school. Hapkido belts actually *mean* something. And defendo. Well, this just might be interesting."

And so it had gone. On the nights the base martial arts club met, he got to call NCOs, and even a couple of officers, by their first names, and he got to toss them around the mats if he could. It was weird at first, but eventually, he accepted it. It made life in the army seem a bit less surreal, and it was definitely good to be back in training.

Not long after that first night, Shane Dargaville had shown up. He didn't know a thing about martial arts, but he was fit and strong, and eager to learn. Mark had liked him right away, and soon they were spending most of their spare time together.

It was good to be able to talk to somebody who'd been in long enough to have a clue what was going on. Someone who could tell him what parts of his training were actually going to be useful, and what was just for show. Someone who could shed light on what life was actually going to be like in the real army, as opposed to this glorified medical kindergarten.

"It's pretty cool, man. For one thing, there's no more bullshit about what you do when you're off duty. When your shift's over, your life is your own, just like if you were working some job on civvie street. You want to go to the bar? Go to the bar. You want to go to the movies? Go to the movies."

"Actually, what I'd *really* like to do is get laid. And I'd rather not wait four months till I'm out of this place."

"Hmmm." Dargaville got a thoughtful look on his face. "You're still TQ1, so you can't just waltz outta here whenever you feel like it, but you've been here, what, two months now?"

"Almost."

"And you ain't been laid in how long?"

"I did okay at Cornwallis, but as far as I can tell, the women on this base aren't interested in screwing anybody who doesn't have some kind of rank or power."

"Welcome to the army, kid. But just cuz the women here won't screw privates, doesn't mean you have to do without. Let's get you off this base and into town for some shackrat action."

"I can go off the base?"

"Sure. You've been here a couple of months, so as long as you square it with your Section Commander, you can probably get a weekend pass. And on weekdays, well, as long as you ain't on duty, or in shit, you can fuck off to town as long as you don't get back too late."

"No shit? And what's a shackrat?"

"A broad that gets off on screwing guys like you and me. Normally we'd be bringin' them back to the shacks for the night, but you still being a bit of a rookie, the instructors won't let you get away with that, so we'll see what we can find in town."

What they found was not exactly what Mark expected. The town was just as ugly as the base, the bar they went to was even uglier, and the women they picked up and took back to a motel were uglier still. If he hadn't been on his fifth beer when Shane found the women, he probably would have refused, but it *had* been almost two months, and the beer had removed whatever discretion he had left.

They bought a case of beer to take with them, walked two blocks to the room they'd rented, and slammed some tunes into the ghetto blaster Shane had brought along.

Even with the beer he'd drunk, Mark was having a hard time getting into party mode. There was just this one room, so even if the women did want to get it on with soldiers, what were they all going to do? Take turns? One pair waiting outside while the other pair got down? It was winter out there, and the bar would be closed soon. What were the waiting two going to do—run laps around the block to keep from freezing?

But then Shane pulled out a big fat joint, and after it had gone round a couple of time, the less obese of the two shackrats started running her hand along Mark's thigh, and two minutes later, both beds were getting a full work-out.

The women left around four, and Mark and Shane slept till noon, when the motel owner started banging on the door, telling them that if they didn't check out, they'd have to pay for another day.

"What's the deal with the pot?" They were on the bus back to the base.

"The deal is," Shane looked at him like he was retarded, "you smoke enough herb, and even shackrats look fuckable."

"No, I mean, aren't you worried about getting caught? They told us at Cornwallis that getting caught with drugs would get you a dishonorable discharge."

"Yeah, right." Shane snorted. "If they discharged everybody who smoked weed, there'd be no one left in the army below the rank of Colonel."

"Then why…"

"Because you were a fucking recruit, that's why. Who knows, they might even have discharged you if they'd caught you at 'Cornholis', but once you're out of recruit school, they're not going to worry about it."

Mark must have looked confused, because Shane turned in his seat and said, "Okay, time for a little father-to-son talk here. The deal is this: they've got eighty million stupid regs, and technically, if you don't follow them all perfectly, they can feed you to the lions. It's not like civvie street where you get to have a lawyer, and a fair trial. Here, if they want to hand you your head on a plate, they can do it. But the thing is, nobody with any brains is going to join up, so if they bust all the dumb fuckups like you and me, they won't have any fuckin' army left."

"So they don't care about the drugs?"

"Long as you don't do anything stupid, like light up in front them, they'll leave you alone. As long as it's pot, that is. Get caught messing with coke, or heroin, or speed, and you'll get tossed out for sure. And probably get time in Club Ed to boot."

"What's that?"

"What?"

"Club Ed?"

"Military prison. It's in Edmonton, and you do *not* want to go there."

"Bad?"

"Beyond bad. It makes every story you ever heard about Folsom or San Quentin sound like a holiday."

"So I should stay away from getting caught with a roomful of co-caine?" They both laughed.

"Too right. Stick to pot. Better for you, anyway."

"So where do I get some?" Mark had money, and the idea of being able to relax with some good herb now and again was appealing.

"You could probably score some in that bar we were at last night. I didn't see any obvious dealers, but then, I wasn't looking."

"Where'd you get what we smoked in the motel?"

"From a guy on the base where I'm stationed, in Chilliwack. Brought a big bag with me when I came to Borden for the course."

Mark had talked to Shane about his regular posting, at CFB Chilli-wack, just outside of Vancouver, but hearing it again gave Mark a jolt of homesickness. "Man, I wish I was there right now. I haven't heard any decent music since I left home. I'd fucking kill for a night in Skavoovee."

"Well, the bar we were in last night is the best you're going to get till you finish this course and get a real posting."

"Right. And my posting is probably going to be to some armpit base in the middle of nowhere."

"Why don't you try for Chilliwack?"

"How do I do that? I thought they just posted you wherever they felt like posting you."

"Yeah, that's true, but it won't hurt to try. What the hell, talk to your Sergeant and see what he says."

.

CHAPTER 11

Four months later, on a beautiful Saturday afternoon, Private Mark Heaney got off a bus, and reported for his first posting, supporting 1CER—the First Combat Engineers Regiment—at CFB Chilliwack, just an hour outside the city he'd grown up in.

He wasn't sure whether his request for posting there had had any effect or whether he'd just lucked out, but he'd followed the advice his Sergeant had given him, which was, "Work your ass off. The higher in the course you graduate, the more likely somebody'll listen to you."

Mark *had* worked his ass off. He'd studied for at least two hours every night, kept his mouth shut when he was doing shit jobs in the hospital—like putting ointment on the asshole of the guy who'd set his anal hair on fire trying to light a fart—and kept his body in the best shape he could. Since most of the guys on his course spent all their spare time in the Junior Ranks Club, or in town, the competition wasn't too tough, and once again, he graduated almost at the top of his class.

He made sure that he took a day, or a weekend, away from his studies as often as he could. The drinking and fucking he indulged in on those days off was pretty disgusting, but he needed the release; and as Shane had pointed out, if the pot was good, then just about anyone looked fuckable.

Saturday afternoon, on a summer day at CFB Chilliwack, was not what Mark had expected. Canada was hardly a war zone, but Chilliwack was a big base, and he'd expected *something*. What he got was nothing at all. The place seemed dead.

"Where is everybody?" He asked the driver who'd dropped him in front of the Battalion Orderly Sergeant's office.

"In Vancouver for the weekend, if they've got any sense." was the only answer he could get.

The Duty Sergeant didn't act like Mark's arrival was making his day, but at least he wasn't openly hostile.

"Heaney, huh? Hang on while I sort this out. And for God's sake stand at ease, or sit down or something." The Sergeant was overweight, going bald, had a cigarette hanging out of his mouth, and was none too crisp in the uniform department. He dug around on his desk, then in a filing cabinet, finally returning with a folder full of paper. He shuffled through the papers for a while, then said, "Okay. Private Mark Heaney, Medic-A, attached to 1 CER. That you?"

"Yes, Sergeant."

The older man returned to his paper shuffling, then finally said, "Wait here for a minute, okay? I gotta call the Duty Officer and see where he wants me to put you."

He disappeared into a back room, and Mark waited, wondering if he'd been stupid to expect something a bit more exciting than a bored clerk. He looked around the room. It was just one more dilapidated army building, but there was a chromed Bren gun, a souvenir from World War II in one corner, and through the window, he could see a panel from a Bailey bridge on display beside a statue of some soldiers sweeping for landmines with metal detectors.

He turned back and started examining the chromed Bren. "Heaney."

He snapped to attention. "Yes Sergeant."

"We're gonna put you in the Transient Quarters for the weekend. You can clear into base on Monday morning, okay?"

"Yes, Sergeant."

"Jesus. Knock off the 'yes, Sergeant' crap, and get the broomhandle out of your ass. You're not in recruit school anymore."

"No shit" thought Mark, but he kept his mouth shut and stood at ease.

"When you clear in officially, they'll assign quarters, but right now I don't know whether they're gonna want you here on the base, or by the hospital."

"The hospital isn't on the base?"

"It's not far, just across the road from the main entrance to the base, but some of the med staff are quartered over there and some here, and I ain't got a fuckin' clue where they want you. You can go over and check the hospital out if you want, but they'll probably just put you to work, so my advice is just lay low. What's the point of going looking for work, right?"

He wrote something on one of the papers in front of him, stamped it with a big rubber stamp, and put the folder back in the cabinet. "Transient Quarters is the first H-hut you'll see on the right when you walk outta here, so why don't you head over there. Barrack Warden's office is just inside the entrance, by the payphones. Knock on the door and they'll square you away for the weekend, and then on Monday morning you can report for duty at the hospital. 0800, ask for Sergeant Major McArthur. He runs the hospital, and he'll probably have all your paperwork there."

Mark left the slobby, chain-smoking Sergeant, and headed outside. The driver had dumped his bags on the ground and disappeared, so Mark threw the big duffel over his shoulder, picked up the smaller one, and walked the half-block to the first shack on the right. It looked identical to the shacks at Cornwallis and Borden, and Mark could easily picture the inside layout—dorms in each arm of the H, bathrooms, showers, washers and dryers in the middle section. Ugly, but functional.

He left his bags in the entrance, and banged on the door that said, "Warden".

"Come in."

The Corporal that was sitting at the desk, talking on the phone, was less of a slob than the Sergeant, but he still didn't look like Super Soldier. He had the beginning of a spare tire around his waist, and he'd shaved in a hurry that morning, but at least he looked friendly. He said, "Okay, he's here now," into the phone, and then hung up and turned to Mark.

"You Heaney?"

"That's right Corporal."

"And you need a room for the weekend?"

"So I'm told."

"Right." The Corporal laughed. "Nothing like coming to your first posting and finding out that nobody knows what to do with you, huh? Well, don't worry, we'll take care of you. The Sarge ain't too swift, but this one isn't really his fault. It's up to the Med staff to decide where you're gonna go, and they ain't told us yet, so for now, you can put up here. Follow me."

He led Mark to the storeroom and handed him a stack of bed linen, then down the hall and into the first room. "Bring the linen back to the

BW's office, folded, on Monday morning before you leave. If the office is locked, just leave it outside the door. You're the only guy in the building this weekend, so whoever's on duty'll know it's yours. Leave your gear locked in your room till they assign you quarters, but remember to turn your key in before you leave for the last time."

Mark looked around the room. It was a double, identical to the one he'd had at Borden, but the building was so quiet that it seemed strange, instead of familiar.

"What do I do for food?"

"Mess hall's a couple of blocks west. It's pretty obvious. Did the Sergeant give you a meal card?"

"No."

"Well, that's about par for the course with him. I'll phone the BOS and tell them about you, but they probably wouldn't hassle you anyway. They're pretty casual. I'm off at 1600, but I'll tell Milne, the guy who's got the next shift here, about you, and if there's any problem, the mess can just phone him."

"Wouldn't it be easier for me just to go and get a meal card?"

"Not unless you want to wait an hour while Sergeant Hoskins figures it all out. Like I said, he ain't too bright, and it isn't his job. Anyway, he's just filling in there cuz everybody's away."

"Away?"

"Yeah, half the fuckin' base is out on ex, plus a lot of guys are on leave. That's why it's so deserted."

Back in the entrance, Mark picked up his bags, and was about to take them to his room, when he had a sudden thought. He put the bags down and went back to the BW's office.

"I've got a friend stationed here. You know a guy called Shane Dargaville?"

"Never heard of him. What's he do?"

"Same as me. He's a medic. A private."

"Nah, I don't really know many of the wogs, but ask around at the hospital, somebody there'll know him. But there's a good chance he'll be out on ex, so you might not see him for a while."

"Okay, thanks."

"No problem."

He stowed his bags in his room and went for a walk. The base was huge, and he only managed to walk around a small part of it, but what he saw reassured him. The people he saw mostly ignored him, not in a negative way, but more just treating him as part of the operation. It was definitely different from Borden and Cornwallis. No Corporals screaming at recruits, no groups of students running from place to place, no atmosphere of unreality, just people doing their jobs or enjoying a peaceful weekend. This was the real thing, and it felt great to be a part of it.

Monday morning, 0800. After a relaxing weekend of reading in his room, enjoying really good food in the mess, and going for walks in the sunshine, Mark was now standing at attention in front of Sergeant Major McArthur, NCO/IC of the base hospital. He was ready, after nine months of training, to start life as a real soldier.

McArthur was overweight, like every other NCO Mark had seen on the base so far, and had a gigantic handlebar mustache. Handlebar mustaches seemed to be a fashion thing for senior NCOs, but this guy's was the biggest and bushiest Mark had ever seen. It took all his control to keep from staring at it openly.

"At ease, Heaney."

Mark shifted to the at-ease position but didn't relax or let his posture sag. This base seemed pretty casual, but he wasn't going to risk alienating the boss on the first day of his new posting.

"Let's see," McArthur flipped through the paperwork on his desk. "You've come here straight out of Med-A at Borden, is that right?"

"Yes, sir."

"Your first posting, hmmm. Well, I think you've lucked out. With a lot of the Regiment out on exercises, things will be pretty quiet. It'll give you time to break into the job and get used to the way we do things."

He shuffled more paper, then pulled a large card out of the pile. "You'll have to spend most of today completing your in-clearance. I think we'll put you on the base itself, rather than over here by the hospital. That'll give you a chance to fit in with the Regiment better, let you get the feel of things."

He handed Mark the card. "Start by taking your gear from the Transient Quarters to barracks C-11. The Barrack Warden there will assign you a room, and then you can take this card around to all the places listed on it. Quarter-master, paymaster, all the usual things. They'll square you away with everything you need; just make sure you get signatures at every station. Then, tomorrow morning at 0700, you report for duty here at the UMS. Any questions?"

Mark thought about it. He had plenty of questions, but he suspected that the people he'd be seeing in the process of clearing in would have the answers. No point in wasting the boss's time if he didn't have to.

"Should I report to your office, or somewhere else in the hospital?"

"Ah, right. My office. Should have told you, and regular work uniform, not dress."

Back at the Transient Quarters, Mark got directions to C-11, and began the process of becoming a regular soldier. His new digs were a pleasant surprise. From the outside, C-11 was the same as every other H-shack he'd seen, but instead of dorms, or doubles, it was all singles.

A room to himself! Privacy! No more sharing his sex life with everybody on the base. No more snoring roomies. No one to complain if he stayed up late and studied. No one to "borrow" the beer he was saving for the weekend.

The paymaster's office had good news, too. His pay was up. The eleven-fifty a month he'd made during basic trades training was being boosted to eleven-ninety-nine. Not too shabby considering that the army only deducted three hundred for room and board. Throw in the fact that his clothing was paid for, and it was a pretty good deal.

With his pay updated, and an account set up in the base bank, he headed off to complete his in-clearance. New clothes and equipment from the Company Quartermaster, meal card from the BOS, and finally, a visit to the base library for a library card—and a couple of books. He'd read a book about some of the battles of World War II when he was at Borden, and he checked out a couple more here. One about Allied soldiers who became prisoners of the Japanese, and one about the history of his father's regiment, the SAS.

Back in his room, he unpacked, arranged his few personal possessions, and stood back to view his new home.

It was small, barely eight by ten, but compared to what he'd been living in for the last nine months, it felt like the Taj Mahal. And anyway, as long as he had privacy, what more did he need?

He thought about that. With only a couple of exceptions, everything he actually *needed* was issued to him by the army. Clothes, equipment, textbooks, even stuff like soap, towels, and toilet paper were taken care of. Even condoms were free. The only things he needed that weren't issued were personal toiletries like razor blades and toothpaste.

But if this room was going to be home for a couple of years, there were some things that would be nice. Things that weren't absolutely necessary if you were a monk, but that helped make life enjoyable. Like tunes. Now that he was out of recruit school, and basic trades training, the time had come to put music back into his life.

Maybe he wouldn't be doing much singing, but at least he could still listen. He'd seen a mall where he'd turned off the highway on his way to the base with the duty driver. There'd probably be a Radio Shack there, and probably some kind of music store. He doubted there would be any ska in a mall music store, but there'd be something, and as soon as he could get a weekend pass he'd head into Vancouver to see his family, and bring his CD collection back with him.

What next? For the first time in nine months, he didn't have anything to do. It felt weird. He picked up one of the library books, but couldn't even get through the first paragraph. He wished that there was somebody to talk to, but he didn't feel like going around knocking on doors and introducing himself. Friends would be made, he had no doubt, but not that way.

In the end, he went downstairs and asked the Barrack Warden for directions to the Junior Ranks Club. A couple of beers would kill the hour until supper, and he could read there just as well as in his room. He tucked the SAS book under his arm and headed out.

People were coming off shift, and it was good to see some life on the base. The JRs was busy, too. Not packed, but definitely not empty. Mark bought a beer, then found an empty table, sat, and looked around. About half the tables were occupied, mostly with small groups of two or three soldiers, although there was one large group that had pulled a couple of tables together. They were making a fair amount of noise, and from the sound of their laughter, they'd obviously been there most of the afternoon.

The place had all the usual accessories. Pool tables, pinball machines, and right beside the table Mark had chosen, a dartboard. Mark sipped his beer and opened his book, but once again, he couldn't concentrate on what he was reading. He imagined what it would be like in a month or so. He'd be here with friends, shooting the shit, enjoying games of darts and pool, complaining about Sergeants; all the usual things that he imagined a regular soldier did. His daydream was interrupted when a couple of guys from the noisy group decided to play darts. They didn't actually say anything to him as they approached, but their "who the fuck do you think you are?" looks told him all he needed to know. Dickheads who'd be happy to push you around as long as they outnumbered you. Especially the one with Corporal's stripes—he might as well have had a sign reading "Bully" attached to him.

He ignored them, and tried to focus on the book. He'd learned a lot about what it was like to be a soldier in the SAS from his father, and his father's friend, Bones Battle, but this book was a history of the Regiment, and he was looking forward to getting the "official" story. He wondered how that would compare to the real-world version he'd heard from his father and Bones.

But once again, his reading was interrupted. "Get out of the fuckin' way, asshole."

It was the drunken Corporal. He'd lost his balance and bumped into Mark's table. Mark had managed to grab his beer before it went over completely, but some of it had spilled onto the tabletop. He quickly moved the book onto an empty chair before any more beer could spill, and then looked up to see that the drunk was still standing by the table, glaring at him.

"Why don't you find some other table, fuckwad? In fact, why don't you find some other bar. Fuckin' wogs shouldn't be in our bar, anyway."

Mark didn't want trouble. He knew he could take this guy, but maybe it'd be better just to move, and avoid problems. He stood, and was about to walk away when the asshole tried to give him a shove. Mark had seen it coming, of course. The guy was drunk and slow, and it was easy for him to deflect the shove, twist a dart out of the guy's other hand, and plant it firmly in his ass.

He faced the other dart player. "You want some, too?"

When there was no response, he turned, picked up his book, and headed for the door. He was halfway across the room when the pain finally registered in the dickhead he'd darted, and Mark left with a smile on his face as the aggressor pulled the dart out of his butt and started whining.

There'd be no permanent damage, but for a few days he'd get a reminder about how much of an asshole he was every time he sat down. There had been smiles on most of the other faces in the room, and a lot of laughter, so Mark knew that there'd be no official comeback. The corporal had clearly started it and had got what he deserved. Mark laughed all the way to the mess.

"Morning, Heaney." Was there a smile hidden behind McArthur's huge mustache? There was certainly some good humor in his voice.

"Good morning, sir."

"All settled? No problems with your in-clearance?"

"No sir. Everything's fine."

"I hear you even had time for a beer in the JRs." Now the smile was turning to laughter.

"Sir?" What had McArthur found out?

"There were a couple of off-duty medics in the bar yesterday afternoon Heaney, and that bozo you speared showed up here for a tetanus shot last night."

The boss was laughing, but Mark knew better than to join in. He stayed at attention and said only, "Yes, sir."

"At ease, Heaney. You want to tell me about it?"

Mark stood at ease. "Not much to tell, sir. He'd been drinking a lot and wanted to pick a fight. I tried to leave quietly, but he started shoving me around, so I had to deal with it. I didn't want to hurt him, but if I hadn't done something, he'd have kept at me."

"He's six years older than you, and twice your size, Heaney."

"Yes, sir, but he was really drunk. It wasn't a problem." Mark didn't add that it wouldn't have been a problem if the guy had been sober, either.

McArthur stood up from his desk, still smiling. "Using Corporals for dartboards is usually frowned upon in the Canadian army, Heaney, so you're lucky that there were plenty of people in there who saw what happened—who saw that you actually *did* try to leave peacefully—but I do have to ask you if you find yourself involved in fights very often."

Mark thought about his answer. He'd been in a few fights, and he knew that he'd never back down if he was challenged, but he felt he was being honest when he replied, "No sir."

"When was the last time?"

"In high school, sir, about a year ago. A friend and I saw five guys putting the boots to one kid, and we jumped in to save him."

"Okay, Heaney, that's all we'll say about it for now. As far as I'm concerned, seeing my medics stand up for themselves is all to the good. There's a certain amount of prejudice against us wogs on this base, and you've just encountered some of it. You dealt with it, and from what I've heard, you could probably have hurt him a lot worse than you did, so you're not going to get any shit from me."

The smile disappeared, and McArthur's voice got serious. "But understand that I'm not fond of troublemakers. Standing up is one thing. Looking for trouble is another. Likewise, I don't have any use for weaseling or lying. I'd rather hear you tell the truth even if it gets you in shit, than find out that you lied to me. I stand up for my men, but I expect them to treat me with respect. Understood?"

"Yes sir." That was cool with Mark. McArthur might be overweight, and he definitely had a stupid-looking mustache, but it sounded like he'd be a good guy to work for. "Permission to ask a question, sir?"

"Go ahead."

"You said something about 'us wogs.' The guy in the bar called me a wog, and I thought he meant something about me not being white, but then I remembered that someone else had said something about wogs. So does it mean 'medic', or what?"

"It's a derogatory term that people in the combat arms trade use for anybody else—anybody not actually in a combat trade. Mostly it's used against paper pushers, but you'll get it sometimes as a medic, too."

"I see."

"Don't worry about it. Good medics get respect. You'll be out on exercises with the combat arms people, you'll be getting sweaty and dirty and sore, just like them, and as long as you do your share, you'll get respect. Now, let's get to work…"

Work turned out to be not too bad. Sick parade for the regiment was 0800 to 1000, and since the regiment was Combat Engineers, there were always injuries. The engineers built bridges, made roads, laid minefields, cleared enemy minefields and boobytraps, and did a lot of combat driving. They worked with heavy machines, and paid a heavy price if they got careless, so in addition to the usual blistered feet and drippy dicks that an infantry regiment would show up with, Mark was told he could expect to see some serious industrial accidents.

"Bridge sections can weigh several tons. If one of them gets dropped, people get crushed," was how McArthur put it. "And some of their training is with live mines and explosive boobytraps. This might not be a big-city ER, but you're going to see some blood and bone on your tour here."

Mark met the other medics on his shift, and also the duty doctor, a couple of nurses, and some clerical staff. Word about the dart incident had spread, and most of the people he met had a good word for him as a result. Even the doctor, who was a Major, seemed to think that Mark had done the right thing.

That morning, although there were no fractures or traumatic injuries, there was definitely some entertainment. A Private named Morrison had come in with a lower abdominal pain that was probably a hernia. Mark had been instructed to take him to one of the examination rooms, and prep him, which meant telling him to strip and then lie on the examination table. When a nurse came in for a preliminary look, the kid had got a big chubby before she even touched him.

The nurse looked at Mark with one of those "what can you do?" looks, shrugged her shoulders, picked up a ruler from a side table and whacked the guy's boner with it, just as the doctor entered the room.

The erection wilted instantly, and the doctor just rolled his eyes and gloved up for the exam as if nothing had happened. When he approached the table he said to the kid on it, "You're not going to point that thing at me, too, are you?"

"It wasn't loaded, sir. Honest," Was the unexpected answer, and everybody in the room broke up with laughter.

When sick parade was over, Mark took a coffee break with the two other junior medics who were on duty, Privates Vogel and Makarenko.

They seemed like decent guys, and Mark discovered that Makarenko had been in the JRs when the dart incident took place. They were laughing about that, and about Private Morrison's "it wasn't loaded" line, when Vogel suddenly said, "Hey, wait a minute, I bet I know who you are."

That was such a strange thing to hear that Mark didn't know how to respond.

"You did some kind of martial arts move on Corporal Fuckhead, right?"

"Yeah."

"So, are you the guy that Dargaville told us about? He said you were going to get posted here."

"You guys know Shane?"

"For sure."

"Is he..."

"Nah, he's out on ex with Bravo Company, but he'll be back next week. He said you were a good guy."

"How's he doing?"

The two medics looked at one another and laughed. "Same old Shane." said Vogel. "He'd probably live a lot longer if he learned to keep his pecker in his pants; but he's a good guy."

"Yeah. One of these days, he's going to get caught in the wrong bedroom, and that'll be it for his military career."

This led to a general discussion about what the prospects for sex were for a private at CFB Chilliwack, a discussion that lasted until their Corporal banged on the door and shouted, "Tea time's over, girls, back to work."

Work for the rest of the day turned out to be a real mix. Some of it was the same old orderly shit that he'd hated at Borden. Taking temperatures, wiping butts, and cleaning floors. Some of it was clerical. Filing papers, inventorying and stocking incoming supplies. Some of it was driving. Patients needed to be ferried to and from all kinds of places, and the junior medics were the ones who pulled the duty driver assignment. And finally, some of it was medical—prepping patients, giving injections, setting up IVs—but usually it was the nurses or the more experienced medics that did that.

"It's different when you're out on ex," Makarenko had told him at lunch. "When you're in the field, you actually get to do some interesting shit, but here in the hospital, well, what you saw this morning is what you'll mostly get while you're on base."

"Speaking of being on base, how do I get off base? Do I need to apply for leave just to go into town? And is there a regular bus?"

"Nah, once you're off duty, you can pretty much do what you want. You have to apply for leave if you want to be off base after midnight, but as long as you show up for work in the morning, nobody really gives a shit."

"And buses?"

"No prob. You can walk to town in fifteen minutes, or get a cab for a few bucks if you're in a hurry."

"You feel like coming into town with me tonight? Maybe showing me around a bit? I'll buy the beer."

"Wait till Friday and I'll do it. Chilliwack's pretty dead on weeknights. Vogel and me'll probably hit the JRs after supper, though; you can meet us there if you want."

"Cool."

The afternoon shift ended at three PT. Mark had been expecting it to be followed by a run, but what they got was indoor soccer in the base gym. It was co-ed, which was cool, but nobody played very hard, and Mark realized that he'd have to do what he'd done at Borden—manage his own training—if he didn't want to wind up going soft and gaining twenty pounds.

Vogel and Makarenko were good guys, but they were definitely not in great shape, and neither were any of the other med staff that Mark had seen. Well, what the hell. It wouldn't hurt him to enjoy a few days holiday from training, and then when Shane got back he'd get serious.

"Hello?"

"Hi, Dad!"

"Mark! How are you? *Where* are you?"

"Practically next door."

"*What?*"

Mark had decided to keep the news of his posting from his family until he was actually there.

"Yup, just an hour down the highway. I got posted to Chilliwack. I wanted to surprise you by walking up the front steps and knocking on the door, but it looks like I'm pulling duty this weekend, so I decided to phone before you started worrying the army had dropped me into a hole and forgotten me."

"Well, I admit, I was wondering when you'd phone. And don't worry about not being able to get in this weekend. There'll be plenty of weekends, and you won't have to work all of them, so we'll see you soon enough. In fact," Scott Heaney paused, "in fact, it's about time I took the bike out onto the highway, so if having your old man show up won't embarrass you too much, I'll come out and see you."

"Embarrass me? As if."

"So when's a good time? What shift did you pull?"

"Nights. What else? I get off at 1500 on Thursday, and then go back on at 2300 on Friday."

"Welcome to the army."

"It's okay. They're not actually picking on me. Everybody gets weekend graveyards once in a while, and I won't get it again for a month. Anyway, I'll need some sleep when I get off shift, so come on out around three or four in the afternoon. It'll be great to see you."

"Deal. See you at 1600 on Saturday. Now I better let you talk to your mother before she hits me with that frying pan."

He talked to his mother and made a date for the weekend after the coming one, then to Glen and Sarah. When he hung up he felt fully contented for the first time in… He thought back over the years, and realized that he'd never felt like this before. Playing with the Juice Monkeys was a high that he suspected he would never equal, but this was different. This was contentment.

Recruit training had been a three-month exercise in misery, and he'd come through with his head high. Med-A at Borden hadn't been miserable, but it had been kind of like being in limbo, and now, finally, all the hard work and sacrifice were paying off. He had a good job, he was able to help his family, and not only that, he was close to them.

What more could anybody ask for?

CHAPTER 12

"You could ask to get laid once in a while," said Shane Dargaville.

He'd banged on Mark's door at 2200 on Friday night, with a case of beer under his arm and tales of craziness on the field exercise to tell.

"You shoulda been there, man, it was the dumbest thing I ever saw. Fuck, even the cows on my dad's farm are smarter than Lieutenant Jenkins. I mean how the hell do you get to be an officer in a combat arms trade if you don't know which end of a gun the bullets come out of? Anyway, we got him to the field hospital, and he's gonna live, and what the hell, everybody agreed he didn't have any balls before, so it's not like it's gonna be different now. You sure you don't want a beer?"

"Of course I want a beer, but I'm going on duty in an hour, so I can't have one, no matter how much I want to." It was good to see his friend again, and Shane was happy, too.

"None of the medics on this base give a shit about staying in shape, so I've been training with some of the engineers. They're okay. Most of them aren't too bright, though, so it'll be great to have someone I can actually talk to."

"Is there a good weight gym on the base? I looked around the gym where they make us play indoor soccer, but I didn't see any weights. And what about martial arts? Are you still doing that?"

"Oh yeah, for sure. There's even some guys that are pretty good. Better than the pussies at Borden." Shane offered him a beer again, and then continued. "Speaking of pussy, it's great to hear that you're content and fulfilled and all that crap, but what about your balls? Are they content? Mine sure as hell aren't. Four weeks in the field with nothing but chipmunks have left me hornier than a two-peckered billygoat."

Shane looked at his watch. "2230. You better think about hauling your ass over to the hospital. I'm going to catch a ride into town and see if I can do something about my overloaded balls. What are you up to tomorrow? What time did you say your dad was coming out?"

"He'll be here around 1600, and I'll probably want to sleep till close to then, and I go back on duty again at 2300 tomorrow, but why don't we get together when I wake up on Sunday. You can take me into town and..."

"And introduce you to the local ladies."

"Man, you *have* been in the field too long. You've got sex on the brain. You better go out and get thoroughly fucked tonight and tomorrow, or I'll be worried about my own asshole."

"No worries about that. Your asshole is one-hundred-percent safe with me. What I want, you ain't got."

"What's that? Four legs? Is that why you like it here? Cuz there's so many farms close to the base?"

"Well, I *am* a farmboy, right? Now, c'mon, get your uniform on, and let's head out. I'll walk with you as far as the front gate."

Nightshift in the base hospital was strange. Nothing much happened for a couple of hours, then it suddenly went crazy as soldiers who had spent a month in the field followed by six straight hours of drinking were brought in suffering from the usual binge-related problems: broken bones, beatings, alcohol poisoning, minor car accidents.

"It's enough to make a man give up drinking." The shift corporal, like Mark, was cleaning himself off and changing into new clothes after a particularly disgusting encounter with a drunken soldier. "Blood, vomit, and alcohol; what a treat. Makes you wish you had a job fixing cars or something."

"At least he didn't shit himself, like the one before."

The rush eased off at about 0330, and after an hour of paperwork, Mark snagged a couple of hours sleep, then got up to do some mop-and-broom work before the morning shift took over at 0700.

The knock on his door came a couple of minutes early, but he'd been ready for over an hour.

"God damn! I don't believe it," his father released him from a hug and stood back. "I put a kid on a plane last year, and they've sent me back a man."

"You don't look too bad yourself, Dad." It was true. His father had always been strong and fit, but he'd never really looked like superman, but now… "You've been at the gym."

"Your mom got sick of me whining around the house when there was no work. She said I was always complaining about never having enough time to train properly, and that I'd better put my money where my mouth was." Scott Heaney looked down at his body. "It's gonna be tough going back to working full-time."

"You've got work?"

"Starting next month it looks like you will be keeping your whole paycheck." The older man sat down in the room's one chair. "I'm telling you, Mark, this last year hasn't been easy. Taking money from my eighteen-year-old son just to pay rent, was harder on me than anything I ever did in the regiment. If it hadn't been for your mom… Well, there were times when it seemed like there wasn't a whole lot of point in going on if I was just going to be a non-contributing sponge."

"She kicked your ass, did she?"

"Yeah, she sure did. I'm a lucky man to have found someone like her." He looked out the window, and waved an arm to take in the base outside. "You're young, you're in the army, and settling down with a woman is probably the last thing on your mind. It'd be a mistake right now anyway, but someday, when you've blown off the steam that a young guy needs to blow off, I hope you meet a woman who's as good for you as your mom has been for me. God knows, I don't deserve her."

"Ah, knock it off. You've been there for her too, you know."

"Yeah, I suppose you're right. And anyway, we've got better things to do than sit around in this stuffy room listening to me whine. C'mon out and take me on a tour of your base." He stood. "It's getting close to fifteen years since I've been on a military base. Brings back some powerful memories."

"Bet your memories are better than my memories of last night."

"What'd you get into last night?"

"Blood, vomit, and shit right up to here." Mark raised a hand level with his forehead.

His father was laughing as they left the room. "Ha, and to think it was me that steered you into the medic trade. Haha!"

"So what do you think of army life?" They'd finished their walk around the base and were sitting in the JRs, enjoying a beer.

"I've only been here a week, remember, I'm not exactly an old-time soldier." Mark sipped his beer and thought about it. "For me, it's good. I was thinking about it the other night, and I tried to imagine something that would be better for me, and I couldn't. But," he gestured around the bar, "I sure don't want to end up like most of these guys. As far as I can tell, garrison life here is totally about laziness for most of them. They fuck the dog as much as possible when they're on duty, and then either drink or just hang out in their rooms when they're not."

"That's true in the civilian world, too, you know."

"Yeah, but this is the *army*. It shouldn't be that way here."

"Get used to it." Scott Heaney lifted his bottle to his lips, then stared at it in surprise. "This one must have had a hole in the bottom. Guess I'd better get another. You want one?"

"Yeah, sure, but only one more. I gotta go back on duty tonight, remember."

"And I've got to get home on a motorcycle, but one more would be good."

He put a ten on the table. "I've actually had some part-time work lately, so I'm not broke. Let me get this one."

Mark wanted to tell his father to put the money away, to save it for food and rent, but he knew what hearing that would cost the man in terms of pride, so he picked up the ten, said, "Thanks," and went to the bar for the beer. At least beer on the base was cheap, and he'd be able to give his father seven bucks in change.

"So you like it?" his father said once Mark was sitting again. "You're fairly happy with your decision?"

"Yeah, I sure am. But like I said, looking at the way most guys turn into slobs after they've been in a couple of years is pretty scary. You'd think they'd have more pride than that. I mean, what if they actually did have to go and fight somewhere? They'd be hopeless. How could it have changed so much since your time?"

"It hasn't changed."

"What? Think about all the stories you've told me about the stuff you guys did, and then look around this place."

201

"It's always been that way. The SAS was just one regiment, remember. Just because we were hard, doesn't mean that the average soldier was any fitter then than now."

"No shit?"

"No shit. If you were in the Airborne, it'd be a totally different story to what you see here."

"Airborne?" Sandy Stephens, his friend from recruit school, had talked about the Airborne, and Mark had heard it mentioned a couple of other times, but he assumed that it would be pretty much like any other infantry regiment, except with parachutes.

"There's no SAS in Canada, Mark, but that doesn't mean you haven't got a real fighting regiment. The Canadian Airborne Regiment are the guys that get sent out on the peacemaking missions for NATO and the UN. They might not be on the level of the SAS, but they're definitely for real."

"Shit. I wish I'd known about that before I applied for this posting."

"Wouldn't have made any difference. Nobody gets into the Airborne, or any elite regiment anywhere, till they've served for a few years, and until they've completed some training beyond basic." Scott Heaney drained his beer, and put the bottle back on the table. "Finish your beer and let's get out on the bike in the sunshine. There's some back road around here that I've wanted to explore for a long time, you up for that?"

Mark remembered the first time his father had taken him on the bike. It was the day he'd first brought up the subject of joining the army. He'd like nothing better than to get back on the bike. "Sure. But hang on a minute, what courses would I have to take to get into the Airborne?"

"How would I know? I ain't in the army no more. Ask around. Do some research." Mark's father pushed back his chair and stood up. "But one thing I can tell you: you'd better stay in shape. I don't know what courses they'll ask for, but you can bet your ass that nobody gets in unless they're incredibly fit."

So fitness became Mark's religion. It didn't take long for him to realize that life attached to the Combat Engineers at CFB Chilliwack was a dead end. Oh, sure, there were some good guys, and the work wasn't all orderly-level; but for every friend he made, there were a hundred slobs who couldn't see anything in life beyond the next six-pack, and for every broken bone or severed finger he dealt with, there were a thousand floors to clean, a hundred blood- or vomit-stained sheets to haul off to the laundry.

There *were* some interesting times. In the winter of his first year, the whole regiment went north for winter exercises. They trained on the Chilcotin plateau in the northern interior of British Columbia, and it was seriously fucking cold. Working through the night, building a Bailey Bridge when the temperature was twenty below, was way beyond brutal. The guys would come back with lacerations, broken bones, crushed limbs… It was ugly. But worst of all was the frostbite.

To some extent, Mark figured that the injuries were acceptable. If you were stupid, or careless, you got injured. How else was the army supposed to train its men, anyway? And some of these guys really needed the lessons—how dumb do you have to be to get lost between your tent and the shitter in the middle of the night, and practically put an eye out walking into a tree branch?

But frostbite was a different story.

When it came to food and housing, the Canadian Army treated its men well, but when it came to equipment, Mark sometimes figured that a soldier in the Roman Legions was probably better equipped. And that went double for clothing. He'd read in some of his SAS books that in those units, the men were allowed, even expected, to find clothing that worked for them, but in this army, or at least in this regiment, the officers insisted that the men wear the clothing the army issued, and nothing else.

The problem was that the clothing and sleeping gear the army issued was mostly shit when it came to working in subzero temperatures, and the medics wound up treating case after case of frostbite. Which was no joke. If you didn't get at it soon, and deal with it properly, a guy could wind up losing a hand or a foot.

Being one of the most junior men in the med crew, Mark never did get to work much on the interesting stuff, but he got plenty of shit jobs. Jobs like fire picket, gate watch, and endless fucking KP; he was more than happy when the exercise ended and they could return to the base. Winter in Chilliwack might be wet, but at least it didn't freeze very often.

He managed to get into Vancouver at least once a month, and his father visited the base every couple of weeks. It was really cool to see the way his little sister was growing. At her age, a year had made a big difference, and Mark was surprised at how much older she seemed when he first saw her.

He usually paid a visit to Bruce and Larry Kellite when he got to town. Bruce had finished high school and was working hard in his father's studio. "It's okay, but I miss the Juice Monkeys, man. Dad, Wilbur, and I play a gig now and then, but it's just not the same without you."

"There's times when I wish I'd stayed, Bruce. I sometimes dream of being on stage with you at Skavoovee, but I didn't have a lot of choice. I did what I had to do, and it's turned out okay."

"How's your dad?" Bruce wanted to know. "Has he managed to find work?'"

"Yeah, he's back at it. It's going to be a while before things are fully under control, but he says that he thinks the economy has picked up enough that he doesn't have to worry about work for now, anyway."

"Well anytime you wanna quit this soldier thing and come back and make music, you know I'm waiting."

Mark laughed. "You won't be waiting much longer. I've heard you playing and man, you were good back then, but you're ten times as good now. I'll bet that by the time I'm out of the army you'll be touring fucking Europe and selling millions of CDs."

By spring, contentment had changed to disappointment, and life at CFB Chilliwack had pretty much reached a low point for Mark. He'd been assigned to the range when Alpha Company was doing their annual weapons qualification, and he'd been looking forward to finally firing a few rounds, but after sitting in his ambulance for five days, handing out earplugs and bandaging the fingers of guys who'd been careless while working down in the butts, he was ready to grab a weapon and shoot himself.

Even the fitness thing was getting hard to stay motivated for. He trained with Shane Dargaville when their schedules matched, and he usually got to a martial arts workout at least once a week. He hadn't given up, but there were times when he wondered how long he'd be able to hold out, how long before he turned into a beer-guzzling swine, like most of the rest of the base.

Dargaville was a help, but he was also a problem. Mostly, what he wanted to do was fuck. He'd fuck anything that was even vaguely female, and he often managed to drag Mark along on sexual adventures that Mark would wake up regretting.

Like the time in the JRs when Shane had been bragging that medics were sex beasts compared to engineers, and the engineers said, "Prove it!" He came up with the idea of a contest—let the medics and the engineers hit town and bring back the biggest pigs they could find, and then everybody would see who was capable of the greatest sexual feats.

Of course, by "medics", he meant himself and his ace buddy Mark Heaney. "You gotta do it, man. It's a matter of honor. If we let them show us up on this one, they'll never let us hear the end of it. And besides, how can we lose? We're the best lookin, best built, studliest guys on this whole base."

"But…"

"Hey, c'mon. Tell ya what. Not only will I buy whatever alcohol you choose to drink, even expensive whiskey, but I also scored some absolutely killer weed, and there is no way anybody's going to out-fuck us after we get trashed on that stuff. No way."

After a few more beers, Mark had gone for it, as Shane knew he would. Along with the two guys the Engineers had chosen, they hit New York, New York, a bar just off base that catered mostly to soldiers and women who were willing to hang with soldiers. Which, as far as Mark could tell, mostly meant women who were too fat or ugly to get a date in the real world, plus the occasional older woman who just wanted a young stud for a night, and no strings.

In the end, Mark won by unanimous vote. The woman he'd brought back to the shacks had been so enormous that there hadn't been room for them to lie side-by-side on the bed. It had taken him forty-five minutes, and some major fantasizing, to blow his load, but he'd managed to make her come twice in that time, and there were witnesses, guys hanging out on the ledge outside his second-floor window, and even the Engineers didn't argue.

"You were *awesome*, man. Totally fuckin' awesome." Shane had burst into Mark's room the following morning, full of good humor. "Ain't nobody on this base but you or me coulda done that. You made us all proud."

Mark definitely did not feel proud. He felt hungover, and seriously tired. "It was the weed. It *had* to be the weed. No way I could get within ten feet of something like that, let alone get a hard-on, without major chemicals working my brain." He rolled over and looked at his clock. "Seven! Jesus Christ, Dargaville, what are you doing here at seven o'clock on Sunday morning? I've only had three hours sleep. Leave me alone."

"Wake up, bro. You can't have forgotten; we're going stateside to-day."

"Oh, shit." He remembered. Bravo Company was heading to Washington for a joint training ex with the Americans at Fort Lewis. He and Dargaville were attached as part of the medical unit.

"Ahh, fuck. Why did I drink so much?"

"Cuz you're in the fuckin' army. Now let's go."

Fort Lewis was huge, and the exercise was designed and run in a way that made the Canadian Army exercises he'd seen look amateurish. America took better care of its soldiers—gave them better garrison life and better equipment—and the American soldiers seemed full of pride in what they were doing. And talking with some of the American medics, Mark soon realized that his own training, especially the hospital aspect, was even weaker than he'd thought.

The food, on the other hand, sucked. The Canadian army might have its shortcomings, but there wasn't a soldier in Bravo company that wasn't happy to get back to real food at the end of the two weeks.

"And broads, man, don't forget the broads."

Shane and Mark were unpacking, and Shane was on his usual topic.

"You think Canadian girls are better?"

"How would I know, we never got the chance to find out about American babes. That's the problem with being on ex. No sex. No sex on ex." He threw the last of his dirty clothes into his laundry bag. "Hey, we get three days off. Wanna go into Vancouver and show them, city girls, what they've been missing?"

CHAPTER 13

And so it went. He tried not to give in. He did his best to keep focused on the positive aspects of his career, and he knew he had to stay strong, stay on top of his life, if he ever wanted to get into the Airborne. But it got harder and harder. If only life on the base wasn't so fucking *boring*.

The guy that turned it all around for him was actually an older guy, who started off as anything but a friend, a man whose first words to Mark were, "Fuck off, wet-nose."

"C'mon, man, take it easy, you're losing blood, big time. We've gotta get a look at your arm."

"Yeah, who asked you, you shit-eating wog?"

"That's enough, Corporal. Get on the table and let us get that shirt off." The Corporal, a skinny little guy who looked like he had to be almost twice Mark's age, stared drunkenly at the doctor who had spoken to him.

"Who the fuck are you? Fucking doctor wants to take my clothes off? Fucking faggot, probably. Why don't you ask the wet-nose to take *his* clothes off?"

He reached out and grabbed a pair of shears off the side table and turned on the doctor. But Mark stepped in, spun the trouble maker around, slapped him once—hard—across the back of the head, then took his feet out from under him, catching him as he fell; then laid him on the table, gently removing the shears from his hand.

"Sorry, sir, but I think he was going to hurt you."

The doctor looked at Mark like he couldn't decide whether to thank him or place him on charge, but finally said, "Well, since he's on the table, you might as well get his shirt off."

"I think it would be better if I held him while you did that, sir." Mark handed the shears to the doctor. "I know it's my job, but he's kind of violent, and I know how to keep him still."

The doctor looked at the Corporal, who was starting to spout obscenities again. "You can do that without injuring him?"

"Yes sir."

Mark levered the guy's undamaged arm out and around, turning the wrist over so that any more pressure would break it, and then leaned an elbow on that shoulder, with most of his weight on it. "The doctor is going to cut the shirt off your other arm, and you are going to lie absolutely still, and keep your mouth shut while he does, you got that?"

The little Corporal made one attempt to break free, grunted in pain, and laid still. He said, "Fuck you, wet-nose," but didn't make any attempt to move.

"Okay sir, he's going to cooperate now."

"Thanks, Private."

Five minutes later the doctor had pressure dressings on three major stab wounds, one to the bicep, two to the forearm. "Can you hold him still for one more minute, Private? He looks like he's been pretty badly beaten, and I want to examine the rest of him."

Mark eased some of his weight off the wounded man's shoulder. "You hear that?"

"Of course I heard it. I'm not fucking deaf."

"You gonna cooperate?"

"Yeah, yeah, I'll be a little fucking lamb."

"Okay, I'm going to lighten up here. But I'm going to keep hold of your wrist, and if you get stupid, I'll break it, you understand?"

"I said I'm gonna be a lamb, right?" He turned his head so he could look at what the doctor had done to his arm. "Hey, not bad for an army doc. You're gonna have to stitch 'em, though."

The doctor, the same Major that Mark had met on his first day, looked down at the man on the table and said, "Can't proceed, not until I've had a look at the rest of your body, and not until we've got another couple of medics in here to help hold you still." He came around to Mark's side of the table and cut more of the shirt away. "Jesus. What did you do? Try to make love to a freight train?"

There were bruises and abrasions all over his chest.

"Yeah, I think they maybe broke some ribs, but I think what you oughta look at is my gut. And maybe my kidneys. They booted me around pretty good." Minutes later the little Corporal was nodding into Demerol dreamland.

"I think one of the other medics can take over and get him out of here and into the ward. Can I buy you a coffee, Private?" The doctor asked.

Mark was pretty sure he didn't want to go for coffee with a Major, especially one who was about to give him shit for roughing up an injured man, but he was also pretty sure he shouldn't refuse, so he just said, "Thank you, sir."

"That was some slick shit you pulled in there. Some kind of karate?"

"Actually it's hapkido, sir, but there's similar moves in most of the martial arts."

"And that 'thwack' I heard. Did you hit him? It didn't seem to knock him around, but it *sounded* like you hit him."

"Not really a hit, sir. I slapped him. Slap a man hard enough across the back of the head and it disorients him for a few seconds without doing any real damage." Mark sipped his coffee. "I didn't know what to do, sir. I know it's not right to get physical with someone who may be seriously injured, but I didn't want to let him attack you."

"No, you did the right thing, and I'm going to make sure an official commendation goes on your record." The Major laughed. "Never gave anybody a commendation for beating up on a patient before, but there's gotta be a first time for everything."

A commendation. Holy shit! Mark had been expecting a lecture, and he didn't know what to say. "Uh, thank you sir. Thank you very much."

"No problem. You got us both out of a tricky situation, and that bonehead Corporal owes you, too. Stabbing me, and running out of the hospital, which is what I think he was planning to do, would probably have left him bleeding to death somewhere if he didn't die from the ruptured lung first, but I doubt he'll be thanking you."

"Probably not."

They were both wrong. The next evening, when Mark was going through the ward taking pulse and blood pressure readings, the Corporal called him over.

"You're Private Heaney, right?" He didn't sound aggressive, but Mark made sure he stayed out of the man's reach.

"That's right."

"Sorry about last night. Not very smart, picking fights with people when they're trying to save your life."

"Yeah, you were a wild man, alright."

"Doc says I'm gonna be okay. Got a punctured lung, and I'm gonna be pissing blood for a while, but the internal stuff'll heal eventually. Arm too."

"What happened?"

"You don't want to know."

"Try me."

The Corporal closed his eyes and took a couple of deep breaths. "My own fault. Drank too much, got into an argument with a couple of Indians."

"And they went for you with knives?"

"Nah. It was me who pulled the knife. Dumbshit. They took it away from me, which is how my arm got sliced up, and then set to work with the boots. Lucky for me, a couple of the boys heard the racket, or I'd probably be dead."

"They get the guys that did it to you?"

"No way. They buggered off as soon as they saw my friends coming."

"You're lucky they came when they did."

"Lucky? I'm up on charges, and as soon as the doc lets me outta here, I gotta go do the hatless dance in front of the CO. Probably get sent to Club Ed." He started to sit up, but grimaced with the pain and said, "I gotta piss. Can you give me a hand getting off the bed?"

Mark helped him to the bathroom, waited, then helped him back to his bed.

"Thanks, kid. And thanks for dealing with me last night. If I get out of this alive, I'll look you up and buy you a beer, okay?"

"Sure."

"No, kid, I mean it. My name's Walt Jacox. Ask around, the guys'll tell you I'm okay. And just call me Jake, okay?"

"Okay. Good luck."

Over the next few days, Mark got to know and like Jake Jacox. As the man said himself, "I'm not a very good drunk. I get pretty stupid sometimes." But sober, he was good company. He'd been in the army all his life. "Too dumb to do anything else, I guess." And he'd even been a Sergeant for a while. "When something needs doing, I'm pretty good at doing it, but when there's not a lot happening, I sometimes drink, and then, like I said, I get stupid. One time I got stupid enough for the army to bust me back down to Corporal."

"You can't be drinking very much, I've seen you with your shirt off, and you look like you're in really good shape."

"I work at staying in shape, kid. And I probably don't drink more'n a few times a year. It's just that when I do drink, I try to make up for all the months I've been sober, all in one night."

Jacox eventually healed enough to be discharged from the hospital. Mark felt sorry for the guy. He was obviously a good soldier, but he'd fucked up one time too many, and was now probably rotting in a cell in the military prison in Edmonton. Unlike civilian prisons, where the convicts mostly run things, Club Ed was run by the Military Police, whose reputation for sadism was well known.

But three nights later, there was a knock on his door, and a familiar voice said, "Hey kid, you ready for that beer I said I'd buy you?"

"Jake. Hey, I thought you were … "

"Getting abused by the meatheads in Edmonton? Nope. The doc didn't say a word about what I did in the ER, and the CO let me off with a fine and a month's extra duty for the fight. I'm Battalion Duty Driver every weekend for a month, and I gotta do two hours of cleanup on the base every evening. But pickin' up cigarette butts and beer cans beats Club Ed, so I ain't complaining."

Mark got up off the bed where he'd been reading, and turned down the volume on his ghetto blaster. "That's great news, but are you sure you should be drinking?"

"All I'll be drinking is water. I'll probably fall off the wagon again one day, but it won't be for at least a couple of months, so don't worry." Corporal Jacox looked around the room. "What the hell?" he pointed to a poster on the wall, over the desk. "What's a wet-nose like you doin' with a picture of Aretha Franklin?"

"C'mon, Jake; you gotta be old enough to know about her."

"Yeah, *I'm* old enough, but you aren't. How'n hell'd you ever find out about Aretha?"

"I love music. I was in a band before I enlisted."

"You played R&B?"

"No way, we played ska." Mark turned up the sound of King Apparatus, then turned it back down. "Like that. But we listened to all kinds of stuff, and Aretha Franklin fucking rules."

Corporal Jacox shook his head. "Amazing."

At the JRs, Jacox kept his word, and drank only water. "I'm an alcoholic, kid. I used to drink all the time."

"So what made you stop?"

"Haven't stopped. I told ya, I still fall off the wagon now and again, but what got me convinced that I should try to stop was that my best friend damn near got killed cuz I was too drunk to do my job. He survived, but he lost a foot, and when I woke up the next day and realized it was my fault, I swore I'd never take another drink."

He gestured at the scene in the bar. "Come in here some night, and don't drink anything. Spend the whole night in here, and take a real good look at what your buddies are like after they've had a few." He raised his water glass in a mock toast. "You're in the hospital, you see the drunks come in every night. Shit, you saw *me* last week."

Mark had never given a thought about what life would be like without beer. He'd seen how it affected ninety percent of the men on the base, but he'd never seriously thought that he'd wind up like them.

"Yeah, kid, it can get you too." Jacox must have read his mind. "But you look like you haven't given in. You obviously keep yourself in shape."

Most old guys couldn't talk sense for thirty seconds, but this guy reminded Mark of Larry and Wilbur. He didn't pretend Mark was his ace buddy, but he didn't talk down to him, either. He decided to take Jake into his confidence.

"Partly it's that I don't want to wind up like them..." He broke off as he thought about the pig prize he'd won a few weeks ago. No way he'd have gotten involved with that if he'd stayed sober. "But mostly, well, I'm hoping to get into the Airborne, and I hear you've gotta be really fit before they'll even consider you."

Jacox hadn't made fun of his dream at all. "Airborne. No shit. I was attached to the Airborne."

"You were?"

"Yeah, but it was kinda like being a Sergeant. Didn't take the army all that long to realize that they'd made a mistake, and I got punted back into 1 CER."

"So is it worth it? Is it as good as they say?"

"Not for most guys. But for someone like you, yeah, it's probably the *only* regiment that's worth it. But you understand that you can't actually be in the Airborne, right?"

"*What?*" Mark felt like his chair had been jerked out from underneath him.

"Relax, kid, it's just word games. Only infantry can officially be members, but the Airborne needs medics, same as any other regiment." Jake drained his water. "*More* than other regiments, in fact. So don't worry. What you get is to be *attached* to the Airborne. Ya train with 'em, drink with 'em, go into combat with 'em. You want another?" He pointed to Mark's glass.

"Sure, I'll go get…"

"Not when you drink with me you won't. You wanna buy your own beer, you go drink with someone else."

"It's alright, I…"

"You lost the right to buy your own when you saved my fuckin' life the other night."

It was a turning point for Mark. Jake Jacox didn't have much of an education, but he'd learned all he could about training, he had twenty years of experience, and he'd been in the Airborne. He took Mark on the way a coach takes on a young athlete.

"Okay kid, the first thing you gotta do is forget what the army teaches you about fitness, and get back into the kind of training your father taught you, plus some weights. It's a triangle, see. You sit on a three-legged stool no problem, but take away any one of the legs, and you're hosed. You need cardio, like those hikes up Grouse Mountain you told me about. You need speed and power, which is what you got from the hapkido and defendo. And you also need as much overall strength as possible, which is what weights give you. You followin' me so far?"

"Yeah."

"Okay, now think about that stool again. You got your three legs, which is what you need, but unless there's something holding those legs together, they'll just spread apart and break. That's where stretching and warm-up and cool-down comes in. Holds everything together. I know you probably never thought about that, which is okay when you're fifteen, but when..."

"I'm on it, Jake. We *never* started a defendo workout without almost a half-hour of stretching and breathing exercises. Same for cool-down."

Jacox also dragged Mark's ass up mountains. "No, don't worry, we ain't talkin about ropes and glaciers and shit, just gettin five or six thousand vertical feet every weekend. Nothin like it for cardio. And good for your legs, too, specially since there's still a ton of snow up there. Real double whammy."

He cracked the whip over him in the weight room twice a week. "It's about discipline, not how much weight you can pile onto the bar. You'll get ten times the results from doin' it right with lighter weight than you ever will from trying to heave the bars around the way most of these idiots do."

And he insisted that Mark get back into regular attendance at martial arts, and especially boxing workouts. "Yeah, yeah, I know. It ain't defendo, the holiest of holy styles, but it'll do wonders for your speed and endurance. And boxing against guys who are as good as you keeps your head from getting big. Teaches you about pain, and about not giving up."

They were twenty miles southwest of the base and halfway up some mountain trail that was seriously whipping Mark's ass. "Dealing with pain, and not giving up, are the two things that are going to decide whether you make it in the Airborne or not. It ain't easy to get in, but it ain't impossible either. There's plenty of guys can jump out of airplanes, and do thirteen chin-ups, and six laps in seven and a half minutes. But *stayin'* in, now that's a whole other thing. You wanna stay in the Airborne, kid, you better learn how to handle pain."

With Jacox training him, Mark felt his old enthusiasm return, and he submitted his formal, written application for a jump course. He knew he might not get it for a while, but he also knew that he was going to be ready when the time came.

He still went drinking and slutting with Shane Dargaville whenever he could, and he enjoyed friendship with a few other guys on the base, but his focus was on training, and staying off the CO's shit list.

"Be the Gray Ghost, kid." is what Jacox had told him. "Do your job without complaining, and do not, I repeat, *do not*, get yourself in any shit. There's a lot of competition for the jump course, so if you get noticed by the RSM or the CO, you probably ain't gonna get in."

Three months later, it all paid off. He was unpacking cartons of supplies in one of thehospital storerooms when Sergeant Major McArthur walked in.

"Heaney, I've got a question for you."

"Sir?"

"Do you like flying?"

What kind of dumb-ass question was that? "Uh, I guess so, sir. I haven't really done much."

"How'd you like to try it without an airplane?"

It took Mark a few seconds to get it, but when he did, he punched air and whooped, then realized who he was standing in front of. "Sorry, sir. I…"

"It's okay Private. Anybody crazy enough to jump out of an airplane, well, you can't really expect them to maintain proper discipline at all times, can you?"

"Yes, sir. I mean no, sir."

McArthur handed him an envelope. "Your orders to jump school. Report to the gym tomorrow morning at 0900 for the preliminary tests."

"Yes, sir."

"You understand that if you don't pass the prelims, you don't get the course?"

"Yes, sir." Mark wasn't worried about the preliminary tests. Jake had prepared him well, and he knew that forty pushups, forty-five sit-ups, thirteen chin-ups, and six laps in seven-and-a-half minutes were not going to be a problem.

McArthur looked at him. "You've been training hard for this, haven't you?"

"Yes, sir."

"Well, good luck. If you pass the prelims tomorrow, you'll ship out the day after. Report to me once you've finished at the gym and we'll see about giving you the rest of the day off—assuming you pass, of course."

"Thank you, sir."

Two days later, he was standing at attention, along with thirty-five other hopeful young soldiers, in front of an H-shack at CFB Edmonton.

"Welcome to jump school." The Sergeant addressing them wore a British-style camo jump smock and a maroon beret, with the insignia of the Canadian Airborne Regiment. "Your room assignments are posted on the Barrack Warden's door. When I dismiss you, you will take your gear to your rooms, and then pick up your linen."

He sounded almost friendly, but he looked tough enough to wrestle lions. Kind of like Mark imagined his father and Bones would have looked twenty years ago.

"You are not in recruit school here. All of us on the staff wish you well, and unless you force us to do otherwise, we will treat you with respect. But this course will be as physically brutal as we can make it, and whether you succeed or fail is entirely in your own hands. At the end of each day, your free time will be your own." He paused for a moment, then added, "But if you are stupid enough to do anything other than get as much sleep as you can, I guarantee you'll fail."

He let that sink in, then continued with, "I am Sergeant McLeod, and I will be waiting for you here in front of the barracks at 0600 tomorrow morning. You will be in PT gear, and you will be on time. If any of you have arrived without an alarm clock, speak to the Barrack Warden now. Do not try to explain it to me tomorrow."

When he was sure they all understood, he finished with, "At the top of the stairs leading to the second floor of your barracks, you will see, hanging on the wall, a large wood carving of the insignia of the Canadian Airborne Regiment. Pinned to this insignia are thirty-six sets of wings, and on each set of wings is the name of one of you standing in front of me. My goal is to make sure that at the end of this course, every set of wings still pinned up bears the name of somebody who truly deserves to be in my regiment. What you must understand is that I, and all my staff, will not hesitate for one second to remove the name of anybody who does not deserve this honor. Dismissed."

Whoa! What had he gotten himself into? This guy was like nothing Mark had seen so far in the army. He spoke to them respectfully, but he looked like if you pissed him off he'd rip off your head and spit down your neck. Once more, thoughts of Bones and his father came to Mark's mind.

CHAPTER 14

0600. Mark hadn't been sure what to expect, but whatever he'd thought of, it wasn't this.

"Before any of you were accepted into this course, you were given a preliminary fitness test at your home base. This should be an automatic guarantee that you are fit enough to begin training here. Unfortunately, past experience has shown us the necessity of retesting every intake ourselves."

What was this about? How were forty pushups, or six laps in seven-and-a-half minutes in Chilliwack different from forty pushups, or six laps in seven-and-a-half minutes in Edmonton? It was only a quiet, "Oh, shit," from the man beside him that made Mark realize that not everybody took regulations as seriously as the Corporal who'd tested him at CFB Chilliwack.

And sure enough, just over an hour later, thirty-three of them stood on the landing at the top of the stairs and watched as the Sergeant pulled three sets of wings off the big CAR insignia, and dropped them on the floor below it. "You have twenty minutes to shower and shave. Breakfast will be served at 0730 in the mess, and you will be there on time."

The next two weeks were physical hell. Everything was done at a dead run, and every one of the instructors was as hard as a sheet of steel. They could run further, run faster, and do more pushups than anyone he had ever seen, and the only time they weren't pushing the men as hard as they could were during lectures.

Mark soon realized that on this course, he was measuring time not in days left in the course, but by minutes left till the next time he could stop running.

He had expected that his training would let him cruise the physical part of the course, but even for him, it was hard. The instructors assumed that anyone on a jump course was aiming for the Airborne, and they were ruthless in ensuring that no one passed unless they were Airborne material.

Every day, another one or two sets of paper wings joined the pile on the floor below the big wooden insignia, and every day, the remaining men looked at the pile and wondered how long they could keep their own wings on the board.

Some couldn't keep up on the daily runs, or meet other physical performance objectives. They were warned once, and if they fell behind a second time, they were out. Some couldn't handle the material they had to learn in the lectures. One guy couldn't force himself to jump from the practice tower, and another, who was happy enough to jump, couldn't get his mental act together to say the simple phrase 'One, two, three, check parachute' as he descended. The instructors gave him several chances, but he just couldn't do it. He loved the jumping, and he'd shriek like a kid on a waterslide, but he couldn't say, "One, two, three, check parachute."

At the end of the second week, there were sixteen left.

"Next week, in addition to continuing your physical training, you will make six jumps. You are free to use the weekend as you see fit, but once again, I advise you to be judicious. If you are tired, or hungover, your performance will suffer, and we will notice. Dismissed."

Mark knew he needed to blow off some steam, so he went into Edmonton, checked out the newspaper and found that DOA was playing that night. It was a good bar with a good band, and Mark partied his ass off. He woke up Saturday morning in a strange bed, but he'd done that often enough to be used to it, and the woman sleeping beside him didn't actually look half bad. He was tempted to wake her, but he knew it wouldn't take much to wind him up into party mode for the whole weekend, and he was serious about passing this course, so he dressed as quietly as he could, and left.

On the bus back to the base he thought about the previous night. The bar he found wasn't the kind that he'd been going to for the last couple of years. It was not an army bar, nor was it a civilian bar that catered mostly to soldiers. It was an alternative music venue in a city with a population of almost a million. The women there were not shackrats, just ordinary women out for a drink and some music. No doubt some of them were sluts, and probably some of them were angels, but most of them, like the woman he'd gone home with, were just people.

He thought back to the night of the pig party, when he'd won the prize for fucking the biggest and ugliest woman possible. What a difference. Kendra, the woman he'd just spent the night with, might not have been ready for the cover of Penthouse, but she was a decent-looking woman. And what's more, she'd been interested in something more than just finding somebody drunk enough to fuck her.

She'd actually been fun to talk to. She knew something about the kind of music that Mark liked, she'd spent the evening in a bar without getting so drunk that she couldn't stand, and she was clean and well-dressed.

He'd lied to her, of course. He was certain that if he'd told her he was a soldier, she'd have dropped him like a hot rock. He'd said he was training to be a paramedic in the Vancouver area, so it hadn't been a big lie, and she'd seemed interested both in him and his work.

It reminded him of Bones's daughter Terri, and how cool it had been to talk to a woman without having any sex between them. True, by the time they'd had a few dances and drinks, it had been obvious to both him and Kendra that sex was on the evening's program, but somehow it hadn't seemed important—they'd get to it, and they'd probably both enjoy it, but it had somehow seemed secondary to just enjoying the evening together. They'd even gone for a walk after they left the bar.

A *walk*. Unreal.

He spent the rest of the weekend on the base, eating, reading, thinking, and sleeping; but at 0600 on Monday morning, all thoughts about women were driven out of his head with the words, "Congratulations, gentlemen. Today you get your reward for two weeks of pain. Today you jump."

Mark had no fears. He had an image in his mind of floating gently down through the air, of feeling total freedom and total excitement. He was psyched.

Then the jumpmaster hit the switch that opened the rear ramp door of the big Hercules C-130, and Mark just about shit his pants. The noise was horrendous, the drop to the earth looked insane, and jumping out of an airplane was suddenly the absolute last thing he wanted to do.

But there was no longer a choice. He was shoulders-to-chest with 16 other guys clipped to the static line, and when the green light came on and the jumpmaster yelled, "GO!". They went charging one after the other out the back of the plane like turds dropping out of the ass of a gigantic flying dinosaur.

There was a second of eerie, floating silence, and then a huge jerk and an explosion of sound as his chute opened.

"YeeeeeHaaaaa!!!"

"Fuuuuck meeeeeeee!"

"Sheeeeeeeeee-it!"

The yells of the jumpers filled the air, and Mark made noise along with the rest of them.

But not for long. The ground was still a long way below, but it was coming up fast, and he knew that there was only a limited time available to practice what they'd learned in the lectures. He tried some simple steering, and then concentrated on making a landing he could walk away from. No fancy stuff, no hitting the drop-zone bulls-eye—that could come later; all he wanted out of this jump was to make sure he came out of it healthy enough to make the next jump.

"Not bad," he thought to himself as he finally got untangled from the chute that had collapsed around him. "A bit rough, but not bad."

He looked around. Most of the others were down, and most of them, like him, were struggling to their feet, and silently congratulating themselves for surviving. A groan of pain brought him back to reality.

Where was it coming from?

He looked around, and soon spotted a collapsed chute with no one stan ing. Cursing his slowness, he fought to get free of all the buckles and straps, then raced for the unmoving soldier.

Dropping to his knees, he saw that the man, a Corporal named Jenkins from the Royal Canadian Regiment, was alive, and at least not squirting arterial blood.

"Jenkins, it's me, Heaney. I'm a medic. Are you okay?"

"My legs. I can't move my legs, man." The soldier was moaning. "Oh fuck. I can't even feel them." He started to roll toward Mark, who immediately held him still.

"It's gonna be okay. We'll take care of you, but you've gotta lie still. You understand that? It's important for you to just lie still and relax as much as you can so that you don't do any more damage."

"Damage? What's wrong, man? Am I..." The young man broke down sobbing, but at least he was lying still.

"Hey, easy. You're probably gonna be fine. Probably just had a rough landing, but let's not take any chances, okay?" As he spoke, Mark ran a quick check of the man's vitals, and then a fast once-over for bleeding or fractures. There was nothing visible, but if the guy couldn't feel his legs...

Mark waved and called, and finally attracted the attention of a jumper who was bundling his chute about a hundred meters away. When the guy ran over, Mark stood and spoke quietly to him. "Scott, we need a medivac. Jenkins may have broken his spine, and we can't move him. Haul ass over to the truck..." He pointed to the six-wheeler that was coming out to meet them, "...and tell them that we need serious help out here. Then get one of the other guys, maybe Johnson if you can find him, to come over here and stay with me. You got that?"

"Yeah man, I got it. Possible spine injury, full medivac. I'm on it." Scott Walters took off at high speed, waving his arms like a crazy man, and within two minutes, the truck was racing toward the injury site.

At first, Mark couldn't believe that they'd be wasting valuable time. Why hadn't they just blasted off for an ambulance? But then Sergeant McLeod stepped out and knelt down beside him.

"Give me the ten-second version, Heaney."

"No motion or sensation from the waist down. No other obvious trauma. His vitals are steady."

"Okay. There's a radio in the truck, Heaney. You get in there, and my driver will patch you through to the base hospital. I've got enough experience to keep Jenkins here from getting up and going dancing."

Mark didn't rise. He kept his body between Jenkins and the Sergeant. "You understand about not moving him?"

"You'd try to deck me if I moved him, wouldn't you?"

"Yes, Sergeant."

"Don't worry, Heaney, I understand about spinal injuries. Now get on the radio."

Ten minutes later, Jenkins was strapped to a padded spine board in a helicopter that was rapidly disappearing from sight. An hour after that, McLeod was addressing fifteen very subdued jumpers.

"Now you know. You had the blast of your lives coming down, but you also found out that it's not a game. Jenkins was a good man, but he got careless for one second, and now he's on his back in a hospital wondering if he'll ever walk again." He let that sink in. "It's what will happen to you, or to me if we ever let ourselves get careless. It's the risk we take every single time we jump out of an airplane. Do you all understand that?"

They all nodded slowly.

"Good. Because in three hours you'll all be jumping again, and at least five more times before you leave here this weekend. I don't want to see any more of you going out of my course on a spine board. Now," his tone changed, "you have ten minutes to wash up, and at 1200 you will all be in the mess. At 1230, you will all report to the lecture hall, and at 1400 you will be bussed to the airfield, as you were this morning. Dismissed."

Lunch was relatively quiet, but by the time the plane took off, most of them were full of excitement, and this time, when the jumpmaster lowered the ramp, they were eager.

"Hi, Dad."

"Mark. Great to hear your voice. Where are you?"

"Edmonton. I've gotta be on the bus to the airport in fifteen minutes, but I wanted you to be the first to know that your son got his wings."

"Congratulations, soldier. You're making your old man proud."

"Thanks. Say, I don't have to report for duty till Monday, is it okay if I drop by for tonight?"

"Just tell me what time your flight gets in, and I'll meet you at the airport."

"Looks good, Private." Sergeant Major McArthur pointed to the wings that Mark had sewn on to the left breast of his uniform the night before.

"Thank you, sir."

"So, what can I do for you? I assume you didn't ask to see me just to show me your new wings."

"No, sir. I'd like to make an application for transfer."

"Jump medic, I imagine?"

"Yes, sir."

"You understand that not very many get chosen?"

"Yes, sir, but if I don't apply, then for sure I'll never get chosen."

"Well, I'll get the paperwork started, and I'll do whatever I can to help. The big thing for you to remember is that this could take months or even a year, and during that time you're going to have to keep your nose clean."

"Yes, sir."

Autumn turned to winter, and Mark did his best to stay sane. Jacox made him buy a pair of snowshoes and some real outdoor clothing from a mountaineering store in Vancouver.

"You thought just because it was snowy and cold and wet that we were gonna stop exercising? Forget it, kid. You join the Airborne, your training is going to be non-stop misery, so you might as well get used to it now."

Shane Dargaville, however, wasn't having any part of it. "Listen, bro, my body's just as important to me as yours is to you. It's my gift to the women of the world, and I gotta take care of it. But slogging around in the snow while it's half raining, half snowing? Freezing my ass off on some mountain in the middle of winter?"

He shook his head as if he couldn't believe that Mark could be so stupid. "That's what the weight room is for. That's why God invented the StairMaster. I'll be happy to let you kick me around on the mats every once in a while, but no way am I going out into this shit." He pointed out the window at the huge, wet snowflakes that were turning to slush as they hit the glass.

"Ya gotta love it, hey kid?"

Mark wiped the snow off his goggles, and looked around. They were up on a ridge, almost above treeline. Wind was whipping snow crazily in every direction, and the stunted little trees that grew this high were bent into weird, gargoyle shapes by the weight of the snow that stuck to them. Visibility was no more than twenty meters.

"You realize that if you have a heart attack, I'm fucking doomed, right?"

"Huh?"

"I would never, in ten million years, be able to find my way back to your car."

"Didn't you listen to one word I said on the way up?"

They'd grunted and slogged uphill for the last five hours, and Jake had spent a lot of time with a map and a compass.

"Yeah, but in order to use a map, you've got to be able to actually see something. All we can see is half a dozen scabby little trees."

"Ya know, kid, sometimes I swear that you are deliberately making this harder than it is. Now, pay attention..."

That night, sitting in the JRs, they talked about the strange turns that life had taken for both of them. "I dunno. I met you in May, right? And it's what, almost Christmas? Eight months? And I haven't had a drink. Longest I've ever gone." Jacox shook his head in disbelief. "I saw the RSM the other day, and he actually came over and talked to me."

"What had you done?"

"No, he just wanted to bullshit with me. Can you believe that? Said he'd noticed that I'd been keeping out of trouble. The RSM. Fuck me."

Mark thought about his own life over the last eight months. He'd been pretty close to giving in, to shrugging his shoulders and letting himself go, to falling into his beer and never coming back out. He compared that to where he was now.

"So how long do you think it'll take?"

"What?"

"Till I get into the Airborne."

"Strange as this may sound, kid, the Department of National Defense hasn't actually come lookin' for my input."

"Yeah, but..."

"Look, we've talked about this before. Most guys, it's a year or so before they hear anything. You know that, so stop beating on yourself, and relax. Go find your buddy Dargaville, and go do some drinkin' and whorin'."

"I don't know, Jake, I ... "

Jacox held up his hands as if to fend off a blow. "I don't want to hear it. Okay? You've told me about that woman in Edmonton about eight million times. And you know what? I'm with ya on it. I agree. Those ugly whales you drag back from the bars in town here are not exactly what you want to take home to meet your parents. But they're what you need right now. It's great that you aren't falling into it the way Shane is, but that don't mean you should start goin' to church and lookin' for some Sunday-school teacher to ask for a date."

"But it's just not ... "

"Listen Mark, those pigs, as you call 'em, are no different from you guys. They're just a bunch of lonely broads that are lookin for a bit of a good time. You guys think that you're lowering yourselves to go out with em, right? Well, how do you think they feel?"

Mark had never heard Jacox like this.

"They feel exactly the same as you do. That they're demeaning themselves by fucking a bunch of dirty, brainless, ugly grunts that couldn't get laid in the real world in a million years."

"Are you serious?"

"Course I'm serious. No woman with an actual life would go near an enlisted man. All you wanna do is drink and fuck and fight; which is not exactly high on the list of things most women look for."

Jake Jacox stood, and put his jacket on. "I'm headin' back to my shack. I'm cold and tired, and I need my sleep." He put his hand on Mark's shoulder. "I just saw Dargaville come in, he's over at the bar. Go out and get yourself thoroughly shit-faced and thoroughly fucked, and you'll be fine. There'll be plenty of time for meaningful relationships with women when you retire from the Airborne."

As usual, the older man was right. Mark took his advice—concentrated on today and stopped worrying about tomorrow. Life was good. He trained hard, he partied hard, and he worked without complaining. He went out on ex, he took courses. He learned to drive his father's motor-cycle. He mended Engineers who had got broken laying and breaching minefields in frozen ground.

He knew that if the Airborne turned him down, if he had to spend the rest of his days on bases like Chilliwack, with Regiments like 1CER, he'd eventually give in, but for now, he could handle it.

Music helped. Being close to Vancouver meant that he could get to concerts reasonably often. The Who weren't what they'd been in their early days, but they were still one of the all-time great bands and their shows rocked. The Pogues weren't as well known as the Who, but they put on a great show in the Commodore Ballroom, and he managed to see Sting play the Coliseum.

And every trip to Vancouver included visits to the record stores. He'd come back to the garrison with four or five CDs each time. Old R&B, old rock, punk, ska, oi, rockabilly, even some blues. Ninety percent of the guys on the base listened to country, which made Mark want to puke, but he could always throw his headphones on and rock out to musicians like Chuck Berry, the Who, the Ramones, Sting, the Clash, the Sex Pistols, the Buzzcocks, Brian Setzer, Blondie, the Business, Sham 69, the Specials, the Porkers, the Jam, Goldfinger... The list went on and on. Great bands making great music, helping him get through the days until he got the call from the Airborne.

He also visited his family as often as he could, finding himself amazed at what a wonderful little woman Sarah was turning into, and rolling on the floor with laughter at the stories of the trouble Glen-the-madman got into.

His mother told him the latest as he sat in the kitchen with her one day. He'd noticed that there were new plates on the table and asked, "So you finally got rid of the old set with the flowers on them?"

"You can thank Glen for that."

"Glen?"

"Yes, your brainless brother watched something on TV about rockets and decided to build his own launch site. He set a board over a log and put a brick on one end, then climbed onto the fence and jumped onto the other end."

"And the brick landed on your plates?"

"No, it launched almost straight up, and he stood there watching it. He was so fascinated that he forgot that what goes up must come down, and it came down right on his forehead."

"Oh my God, is he alright?"

"He is now, but at the time he sure wasn't. The brick tore a four-inch gash in his forehead, but it stunned him so badly that he didn't know what he was doing. He just walked into the house as if nothing had happened, with blood pouring all over the place and his skull showing through where the skin had torn away. I was carrying a load of plates from the dishwasher, and when I saw him, I was so terrified that I dropped them."

"So Glen gets more stitches and you get new plates."

Finally, in March, he got the news.

"Heaney." McArthur had found him in the storeroom.

"Yes, sir?"

"You got any plans for April tenth?"

"April tenth?" That was a month away. "I'm leaving for Borden, for that burn management course, on Saturday, but it's only for three weeks. I'll be back here by the tenth, I think."

"You better be, because you'll need time to pack for Petawawa." He handed Mark an envelope. "You got your posting, soldier."

Mark knew McArthur well enough now not to apologize when he finished bouncing off the walls.

CFB Petawawa. Home of the Canadian Airborne Regiment. New home of Private Mark Heaney.

Yes!

Jake Jacox said goodbye quietly. "I'm gonna miss ya, kid. You've done me a world of good."

"No way, Jake. It's you who's helped me."

"Yeah, I've helped, I know, but there's things a wet-nose like you ain't capable of understanding. Maybe in twenty years you'll understand, but being as dumb as you are, that ain't too likely, so in the meantime, just trust me on this one, okay?"

Shane Dargaville, on the other hand, said goodbye as noisily as possible. He threw the mother of all parties—kegs of beer, hookers from Vancouver, shackrats from Chilliwack, immense quantities of dope, and then invited everyone he could think of. Mark's only memory of anything after midnight was the weird way the light from the glowsticks on the walls reflected in the mixture of spilled beer and barf on the floor.

CHAPTER 15

It was different from the moment he stepped off the plane. True, he was no longer a recruit, or a junior private reporting to his first posting, and true, his plane had landed right on the base, not a sixty-mile bus ride away; but it went far deeper than that. The men on this base were motivated. There was none of the slack-jawed, slack-bellied indifference that had dominated Borden and Chilliwack. Everywhere he looked were men whose fitness and pride were obvious in their posture.

Most of the men wore the maroon beret, jump boots, and camo-pattern jump smocks of the Airborne. Petawawa also served as the battle school of the Royal Canadian Regiment, and he spotted the odd RCR uniform, but the majority of the men were Airborne.

He reported to the headshed, and began the process of clearing in for his attachment to 2 Commando, Canadian Airborne Regiment. The process was the same as ever—barrack assignment, meal and library cards, Company Quartermaster for uniform and equipment—but the people and the attitude were totally different. No fat slobs, no time wasting, no 'Jeez, I don't know' from anybody. It was the same with the barracks. Same old H-shack, but this one was clean as a new razor blade. The paint wasn't chipped and stained, the floor wasn't covered in trash, the toilets weren't filthy...

Another shock awaited him at 0600 the next morning. No stumbling, bleary-eyed, to work at the last minute in this outfit. The day started with PT, and in the Airborne, they took PT seriously. A ten-kilometer run was standard, and Mark offered a silent thank-you to Jake Jacox for preparing him.

Even so, he almost died. Jacox had taken him on plenty of 10-k runs, but the pace... These guys were insane. Mark collapsed on the ground when they got back to the barracks, only to scramble clumsily to his feet again when the Corporal who'd led the run started shouting at him, "What the fuck are you doing on the ground?"

Mark did his best to come to attention. "Trying not to puke, Corporal."

That seemed to be the right thing to say, because the Corporal laughed and said, "Okay. You actually did pretty good for a rookie, so we'll let it go. Just remember that you're an Airborne candidate now, you wanna lie down on the job, you better be clinically dead." He looked at Mark more closely. "What company you in?"

"None, Corporal. I'm a medic."

"No shit? A medic that can run 10ks on his first day? Tell ya what, you wanna lie down and puke, I give you permission to lie down and puke."

"It's alright, Corporal. I think I'm going to be okay."

They both laughed, and the Corporal turned to the rest of the group. "Okay, ten-minute warm-down, then hit the showers. See you at breakfast."

And so it went, every day. Discipline was strict but reasonable, and the men and the NCOs lived in an atmosphere of mutual respect. As far as Mark could tell, the deal was that as long as you busted your ass to be the best fucking soldier that you could be, everybody was behind you. Hit trouble, and not only did your buddies support you but so did the NCOs.

Slack off, though, and the amount of shit that descended was unbelievable. These guys were serious about training for combat, and most of the NCOs were combat veterans. In combat, anybody who couldn't be counted on, might as well be one of the enemy, and in this Regiment, the penalty for not doing your best was the instant and total hatred of everyone around you.

That attitude was apparent even in the UMS. Sick parade wasn't full of guys looking for an excuse to get out of work. The guys in this regiment practically had to have broken bones sticking out through torn flesh before they'd voluntarily show up on sick parade.

Which was cool, because plenty of them did get broken bones. The field exercises were fierce, and they jumped all the time. And not just out of high-flying airplanes and into soft fields. They jumped from ultra high and ultra low, they jumped winter and summer, they jumped into forests full of deep snow, into marshes, onto bare frozen ground. They jumped carrying heavy equipment, in any weather, and in remote locations.

And Mark jumped right along with them. He got just as wet, just as cold, just as sore, and just as dirty as they did; and he saved their lives while he was doing it.

He was out on a one-week, remote-drop exercise with the whole of Charlie company about two months after he arrived when he got an un-looked-for surprise. The call had come in while he was still in the air. He'd heard it on the jumpmaster's radio.

"Sunray, Sunray, this is Charlie Six."

"Charlie Six, this is Sunray, send your message. Over"

"Sunray, No Duff, No Duff, No Duff. We need a medic, we've got a man down. Wound to the upper arm, and major blood loss. Over."

All other chatter on all the radios went dead with the 'No Duff.' It was the signal for a medical emergency.

"Charlie Six, this is Sunray." The RSM's voice was calm, but effi-cient. "Give us some blue smoke. Over."

There was radio silence for a minute, but Mark knew that the RSM would be on another frequency, calling for the nearest helicopter to pre-pare for a medivac.

"Sunray, this is twenty-three alpha." That was the pilot of the plane Mark was in. "I can see the smoke. I'm thirty seconds out and I've got a medic on board."

"Twenty-three alpha, this is Sunray. Drop your medic. Repeat, drop your medic. Over."

"Sunray, Twenty-three alpha. We're on it. Over."

The jumpmaster bumped Mark to the front of the line while the pi-lot banked in. "Time to earn your paycheck, Heaney. *Go!*"

The smoke was an obvious target, but even so, it was a hard landing. Six Platoon's drop zone was covered with incredibly dense bush, and full of small cliffs and sharp rock outcrops. Even though he nailed the land-ing to within twenty meters, it still took Mark almost five minutes to hump his jump bag to the accident site.

The victim was a young Private who had been hit with a heavy gust of wind just before he landed. The wind had swung him hard against a cliff face, and when Mark saw the vicious-looking blade of rock that stuck out from it halfway up, he understood why the man had an eight-inch rip down the length of his left forearm. He'd somehow kept it together enough to get his chute off, and cut it up to make an emergency dressing, but like the Corporal had said on the radio, there was no shortage of blood.

Mark took one look at the amount of blood, and told the Corporal to hurry the chopper. "And tell them we need it now, not for next fucking Sunday." He did a fast primary check to make sure there wasn't any other life-threatening damage, and then tuned out everything except saving the man's life.

The victim looked vaguely familiar, but he hadn't been out with Charlie Company before, and after only two months on the base, pretty much everybody in 2 Commando looked vaguely familiar. Whoever he was, he was tough. With blood loss like this, Mark hadn't dared shoot him up with Demerol, and the pain must have been incredible when Mark started working. But the guy hadn't complained. He just lay there, white as a corpse, and did what Mark asked him to.

Halfway through, when he was finally sure that the guy wouldn't bleed to death before the chopper arrived, Mark took a better look at him and suddenly realized who he was stitching up.

"You're lucky I got here in time. Not much call for one-armed lobstermen."

"Wha…"

"Of course you could probably still shoot porn videos."

The man was in pain, and drifting in and out of consciousness from the blood loss, but Mark could see him frowning in concentration. "Mark? That you, man?"

"It's me."

"Told ya I'd make the Airborne, didn't I?"

"Yeah, but if you don't stop trying to move, you're not going to be in the Airborne much longer."

"You're the doctor. How bad is it?"

"You sliced an artery, which is where all the blood's coming from, but I don't think there's any real bad tissue or ligament damage. I've got the artery clamped, and I think if we can get you to a hospital fast enough, you'll be jumping again before long."

"Music to my ears, bro."

Just over a week later, Sandy Stephens showed up for Friday morning sick parade, looking a hell of a lot better. "You nailed it Mark." He held out the wounded arm. "They stitched up the artery, and there's no serious soft tissue damage. Soon as it heals up, I'm back to work." He looked Mark up and down. "God damn. You look like the army's treated you okay."

"You look pretty good yourself. Now that you've got some blood in your body, that is."

"What time you off?"

"1500."

"I'll meet you here. We've got some catching up to do."

At 1500, as Mark came off shift, he heard his name being called. "Mark! Mark! Over here."

Sandy was waiting by the hospital's main admitting desk, with another soldier. "Mark, this is Dean Publicover."

Mark shook hands with a tall, dark, solidly built Private.

"Dean was in 2PPCLI with me, and we got into the Airborne together just over a couple of months ago. It's like being transferred from the sewer, to the penthouse."

"Pretty much the same time as me."

"So you wanna hit the JRs with us? Catch up on the last couple of years?"

"Sure. I've got duty tomorrow, so I can't get too loaded, but a couple would sure be good."

Stephens didn't seem to have changed. He was still the same warm, bright, funny Newfie. He could still tell stories like no one Mark had ever heard, and it was good to see him again. His friend Dean was almost his opposite. Quiet, serious, thoughtful, and careful about what he said. At first, Mark wondered if the guy was something of a wet blanket, but he turned out to have a deadly sense of humor, and he didn't mind laughing when the joke was on him.

They all had a good laugh when Mark told the story of Sandy smuggling the video camera into the storage closet in the shack at Cornwallis.

"You shoulda seen the jaws drop at the party when he plugged that tape into the VCR."

"It'd be even better now, man. Do you have any idea what's been happening with low-light video capability in the last couple of years?"

"Oh, great. Another lecture from Inspector Gadget." Publicover rolled his eyes. Then, when he saw Mark's questioning look, he continued. "Stephens has tried to make up for eighteen years of deprived childhood in Armpit Cove, Newfoundland, by buying every electronic gadget that has come on the market in the last three years."

"Easy for you to say, asswipe. The only toys I ever had were busted lobster traps and whatever fish skeletons my mom forgot to put in the soup. And I had to fight the dog for the fish skeletons."

They'd obviously had this argument a hundred times before, and Mark enjoyed the easy, good humor.

"Pubs here grew up with every toy that his wealthy parents could buy, but he was too busy watching cartoons on TV to even learn how to put Lego blocks together. He's lucky he had me to get him through infantry training. He's the first guy I met who has to be reminded which end of his gun to point at the target."

"One of the first casualties I heard about on my first posting was a guy like that." Mark told them the story Shane Dargaville had told him about the Lieutenant who'd shot himself in the balls with his sidearm during a field exercise.

"Well, he *was* an officer. Can't expect too much of them."

"So, you still have a video camera?"

"Oh yeah. Not the one I had back at Cornwallis, but I've still got one."

"Yeah, and one of every other electronic gizmo that's ever been invented. He was the only guy in our Company, probably the only guy in the whole Canadian Army, that owned a cellular phone."

"Cell phone? What the fuck you want with a cellular telephone? You need to keep in touch with your stock broker while you're out on ex?"

"Hey, I got a terrific deal on that phone, and I don't ever recall you," he stuck a finger in Dean Publicover's chest, "being shy about asking to borrow it to call the pizza man."

"I know, I know. But you have to admit that a grunt with a cellular telephone is kind of hilarious. Like a chicken with tits."

"I'll remember that tomorrow night when you decide you need a pizza at 0200." He turned to Mark. "I got the phone for almost nothing.

Some dope dealer in Winnipeg needed money real bad and sold it to me in a bar for fifty bucks. It's worth over…"

"It's hot?"

"No, it actually was his phone. But I think he owed money to some suppliers and he was selling everything he had to keep them from killing him. Coulda bought his BMW if I'd had two grand in my pocket, and the thing was almost new."

They held a moment's silence at the thought of missing out on a deal like that.

"So how does it work? Don't you have to pay a fortune every time you make a call?"

"Not if you're careful. I found a plan where I pay about forty bucks a month, and all my calls on evenings and weekends are free. So as long as I don't use it during the day, it's not bad. But the main thing is," he turned serious, "it does make it a lot easier for me to keep in touch with my parents. They aren't doing real well, and I send them whatever money I can, but to be able to talk to them wherever I am, well, it helps."

Mark understood. "Yeah, I know all about that. I was pretty lucky, getting my first posting so close to my family, but I sure miss them now that I'm out here." He stared down into his beer glass. "Were you close to your parents?"

"Yeah. My dad had a lot of problems, he's had some bad injuries and there's not much work even for healthy guys, and he drank too much, but he did his best. Never beat any of us, and let me tell you, that's pretty rare in a place like that."

Mark tried to imagine growing up in a place where beating your kids was considered normal.

"What about you, Dean?"

"My folks weren't that great. They had a lot of money, but they fought all the time, and they split up when I was only six. My mom's had a lot of boyfriends since then, but they never last very long and I was happy to get out. Recruit school was more fun than living with my mom, and I hardly ever saw my dad, so when you come right down to it, the army is pretty much my family."

They talked a bit about their childhoods, then got back onto the soldier's favorite subject.

"So where's the action around here? What kind of town is Peta-wawa?"

"I don't know for sure, but from what I've heard it's pretty rough. The place has some industry of its own, so it wouldn't totally dry up if the base closed, but the base does provide a lot of income to the town and the citizens resent that. So soldiers aren't always welcome."

"Well, if it's near an army base, there's gotta be *some* places where the army is welcome. Where a guy can grab some shackrat action."

"Yeah, but I've heard there's also places where you better not get caught alone. There's lots of gangs that like to rumble, so until you learn the rules, I've been told it's best to stay with friends and stay in areas where there are plenty of other soldiers."

"So when are we gonna find out for ourselves?"

"How 'bout tomorrow?" Mark was ready for some action. "I have to work till 1500, but I'm not working Sunday."

"Suits me."

"Me, too."

Sandy Stephens and Dean Publicover had been friends for two years, but they welcomed Mark into their friendship, and soon the three of them were just about inseparable. Mark's work as a medic meant that he didn't see much of them during working hours, and he had to work more nights and weekends than they did, but there was still plenty of time for action.

There were some memorable nights. The Airborne's reputation for fitness and hard bodies meant that they were magnets for women, and getting laid was never a problem. Sometimes it would be orgy-style—no modesty in the Airborne—and sometimes private. The best ones for Mark were the older women who'd sometimes turn up looking for a one-nighter with something more exciting than their overweight, busi-ness-executive husbands. They were a lot less obnoxious than the usual shackrats, usually about a hundred pounds lighter, and they didn't get fall-down drunk to the point that they'd turn completely gross.

Like the immense thing that Pubs had brought back to their motel one night. Sandy had pulled weekend duty, so Mark and Dean had gone into town on their own. Mark had almost told Dean to get a separate room if he wanted to bring in something that drunk, but he was horny, and his own woman was hot to go, so he shrugged his shoulders, ditched his clothes and piled onto the bed with her, while Pubs pushed and pulled, tugging the clothes off his baby whale and steering her toward the other bed.

He seemed to be accomplishing his mission, and Mark stopped paying attention, but a couple of minutes later a loud "Jesus Fucking Christ!" stopped him mid-stroke. He looked to see his friend leaping from the slobbering, giggling thing on the bed, and a second later his nose gave him the reason.

"She was so drunk she shit herself, man. Totally lost sphincter control. All over the bed, all over herself, all over Dean," he recounted the tale to Sandy the next day. "It was the grossest thing I've ever seen in my life. This gigantic, ugly walrus of a woman, lying there drooling and laughing, in a pile of shit that's half diarrhea." He shuddered at the memory.

"I wanted out of there *so* bad, but the room was in Pubs' name, and the motel guy'd have been on the phone to the CO if we'd bailed on it, so we had to clean up."

"Gross. Even for you and Pubs, that's gross."

"You have no fucking idea how gross it was. The worst part was dealing with that demented broad. Pubs was freaking out, running for the shower, and I had to somehow get her off the bed before the shit soaked through and we wound up getting stuck paying for a new mattress."

Stephens was laughing so hard he was spilling beer. "So what did you do with her?"

"I hauled Dean out of the shower, like physically *hauled* him, and made him help me drag her in instead. We peeled the bed and threw the sheets in a dumpster, and let the other broad take care of the walrus. Shoulda thrown *her* in the dumpster with the sheets, man, that's where she belongs. I mean, okay, I'm a medic, I've seen lots of guys lose sphincter control, but this was beyond belief. She actually thought it was funny. She started *playing* with it." He guzzled beer, trying to kill the smell that still haunted him. "I'm telling you, Sandy, it was enough to make a maggot puke. Anyway, once we got rid of the sheets, we went to the office and checked out. We had to pay an extra fifty for new sheets, but no way did we want anything coming back to the CO."

"So are you turned off town forever, or are you willing to go in again?"

"Why? I thought you had duty tomorrow."

"I did, but one of the guys wants to trade shifts cuz he needs next Sunday off."

"Okay, but no way am I getting within a thousand meters of any shackrats. You guys want to do the dirty, that's cool. I'm keeping my pecker in my pants tonight."

It turned out that Dean was as grossed out as Mark, so he was happy just to cruise a few bars and sip a few beers, and the evening stayed uneventful until about 2330 when Mark went into the bathroom for a piss and came out to see five greasers, one of them swinging a pool cue, backing Sandy and Dean into a corner behind their now-overturned table.

He was instantly in full combat mode. Sucking huge lungs-full of air and shrieking obscenities as he raced across the room.

The first guy managed to turn part-way around, but he took Mark's fist on the cheekbone before he understood what the noise was about. The second one, the one with the pool cue, started to bring his weapon up, but went down like a sledgehammered steer when Mark booted him between the hipbone and the lowest rib.

Number three managed to get a knife part way out of his pocket, but all that meant was that he had only one hand free to ward off the rain of blows that Mark laid on him. A left jab to the face brought the free hand up in defense and exposed his whole chest, and Mark nailed him in the center of the sternum with a straight right that had his whole weight behind it.

Since Sandy and Dean had stepped up to occupy the other two, Mark was able to take the time to put a boot into the knee of the first one, who was too busy clutching his caved-in cheekbone to pay any attention to defending himself.

With that one on the way down, Mark turned back to the one who'd taken the chest shot. He was still on his feet, and had finally pulled the knife out of his pocket. Mark launched another feint to the face, and when the knife came up, he stepped outside it and broke the man's arm at the elbow and then again at the wrist.

Dean and Sandy were fit and strong, and would probably have been able to deal with their opponents eventually, but Mark was too full of battle chemicals to stop.

He dropped Dean's man with a roundhouse kick to the lower back ribs, then stepped forward and picked Sandy's opponent's punch out of the air. He levered the guy's arm around and bent the elbow just short of the breaking point.

"Do you have any idea how close you are to dying?"

The guy didn't speak. Just grunted a bit as Mark increased the pressure. "If I ever see you within ten fucking miles of another soldier, I'm going to kill you. Do you understand that? I'm going to break every bone in your body, and then I'm going to cut your balls off and shove them down your throat so you choke to death." He switched his grip so that he could control the man's wrist with one hand, and grabbed a handful of greasy hair with the other, and levered the guy's face up so that he could look him in the eye. "I know what you look like, fuckwad, and if I ever see you again, I'm going to take you apart."

He bent the wrist a bit, forcing the man around. "Take his wallet. Take all their wallets."

Sandy and Dean had never seen Mark like this, and they didn't ask questions, they just obeyed.

"Okay shithead, I'm gonna take all the money you guys have and give it to the bar owner. That's for the damage and the spilled beer. Then I'm going to put your wallets in an envelope and mail them to the police. That's for being the kind of fucking spineless cowards that think five-on-two is fair. My advice is, you go in and collect them and apologize for starting a fight. You tell any stories about this, or mention anything about us to the cops, and you'll be eating and shitting through tubes for the rest of your worthless life."

With that, he spun the guy around, threw him down on top of his wounded friends, and took the wallets over to the bar.

"You know those guys?"

"Yeah, a little." The bartender was a middle-aged guy who looked like he'd seen it all a thousand times."

"They pull this kind of shit very often?"

"They used to. I got a feeling they won't be doing it anymore. You kill any of them?"

"No. The only guy that's hurt bad is the one that pulled the knife. This your joint?"

"Me and my brother's."

"How much you reckon this cost you?"

"Fifty bucks in spilled beer and broken glass, maybe five-hundred in lost business."

Mark looked around. The place had emptied. "Well, let's see what they have in their wallets. Mark opened the first one. It was the big rectangular kind that zipped shut, and connected to a belt-loop with a small chain. "Holy shit!"

The wallet was so stuffed with bills that it practically burst open when he undid the zip. Tens, twenties, and even a few hundreds cascaded all over the counter, and onto the floor. He was more careful with the other wallets, cracking them just enough to see that they too were stuffed full. "Looks like you're not going to have to worry about that lost business. Where were they sitting?" The barman pointed, and Mark walked to the table. The jackets that hung on the backs of the chairs were heavy, the pockets loaded with hundreds of flaps of cocaine. He walked over to the pile of moaning bodies. "You got that cell phone, Sandy?"

"Why? You want a pizza?" Sandy Stephens was still half in shock. "Nah, but I think we better call the cops. These guys are carrying more coke than you would believe."

"And you think us telling the cops about fighting a bunch of drug dealers in a bar is going to get us in good with the CO?"

"You didn't start it, did you?"

"Fuck no, man. You know me better than that."

"The bar guy will back us, and *that* freak," Mark toed one of them, "pulled a knife on me." He stared at the ones that were still conscious. "I used to see guys in the UMS at Chilliwack with bad cocaine habits. *Nobody* deserves that. If you don't want to call the cops, then I'll be perfectly happy to slit every one of their throats. Take your pick."

"Okay, man. 9-1-1, coming your way."

It took them till almost 0200 to square everything with the local police, and they knew they'd have to do it all over again the next morning with the RSM.

239

"If I ever start to piss you off, remind me to stop, okay?" They were in a Military Police van on the way back to the base, and Sandy was looking at his friend in a whole new way.

"How'd you *do* that? You took out all five of them, man. Five!" Publicover was still having trouble believing what he'd seen.

"I thought that all three of you were in it." The Meathead in the back of the van with them was friendly enough. The Petawawa cops had made it clear that the soldiers hadn't started it, and that the entire town would be a much better place with those five off the street.

"Not that it made any fucking difference." Sandy drew a deep breath and then continued slowly. "We were just having a quiet beer, and I guess we never noticed that we were the only soldiers in the place. Usually, there's plenty. Anyway, Mark went for a piss, and as soon as he was gone, five guys jumped up from their table and came for us. I think they must have been planning it, waiting for one of us to leave." He paused, thinking back over what had happened. "They threw over our table, but we managed to get our backs against a wall. And then..."

He stopped, unsure of what to say. Dean finished the sentence for him. "And then Mark took them apart. Every single one of them."

The MP looked at Mark. "Don't recognize you. What company you with?"

"He's a medic, man. A fucking medic."

"Look." Mark decided it was time to put a stop to it all. "It wasn't that big a deal. They were a lot drunker than we were, and none of them really knew how to fight. Putting the boots to drunk soldiers when you're five-on-two is different from having somebody who's sober and knows what he's doing to get the drop on you."

"You guys were sober?"

"Oh, we'd had a couple, but we really were just making a quiet night of it."

"Well, I don't see that you're going to get any shit from the RSM. The bartender backs your story, and the local cops are practically ready to give you a medal, and if the guys you tenderized are who I think they are, then the RSM is going to be okay with it, too."

"Why's that?"

"We lost a couple of guys to really bad shit-kickings last year, and these assholes pretty much fit the descriptions we had. No way to prove anything, and he's not going to give you any medals, but since it was pretty clearly self-defense, I don't think you've got any worries."

The Meathead was right. They were called up, but the RSM had already talked to the tavern owner, and to the police, and all he really said was, "Maybe, in the future, you should make sure you're not the only soldiers in whatever tavern you visit."

"Yes, sir," they had replied in unison.

He looked down at the papers in front of him. "Okay. Stephens, Publicover, you're dismissed. Heaney, you stay."

Oh, fuck.

Sandy started to say something, realized who he was in front of, snapped off a "Yes, sir," in unison with Dean, and turned on his heel and marched out.

"So, Private, I've been reading your file. It's interesting. In fact, I don't think I've ever seen anything like it. Major Hendry in the Chilliwack UMS gave you a commendation for beating up an injured soldier. Our own Sergeant McLeod noted that you threatened to deck him when you were in jump school and recommended that we take you if you ever applied to the Airborne. Now I've got the Petawawa Police Department submitting an official commendation for putting five men in hospital."

He looked back down at the sheet. "And that idiot Jacox. Not only did the Major commend you for thrashing him, he actually phoned me himself to tell me that I should take you."

"Jake? Phoned *you*?" Mark blurted out before he could help himself. "Sorry, sir. Apologies for speaking out of turn."

"I wasn't born RSM of the Canadian Airborne, Private. Jake is one of my oldest friends. If it hadn't been for the booze, he'd have this job, not me."

"He'd been sober for eight months when I left Chilliwack, sir."

"And he's been sober since. There's even a chance that he may stay sober this time. But that's not what we're here to talk about. What we're here to talk about is how you laid waste five guys who know a thing or two about bar fighting."

"With all due respect, sir, everyone is making too big a thing of this. They had their backs to me, they didn't see me coming, and..." He stopped as the RSM held up his hand.

"There were five of them, Heaney. Five."

"Yes, sir."

"At 0800 tomorrow, you will report to the unarmed combat room, in Gymnasium B."

"Sir?"

"I've been in a few bar fights, Heaney, but I'm no expert. Sergeant McLeod *is* an expert. He wants to find out if you could have decked him that day back in jump school."

Mark flashed a picture of his jump school Course Sergeant into his mind, and thought about how much that man had reminded him of his father. "I don't think I could have."

"Well, tomorrow morning, you're going to find out, aren't you? Dismissed."

"Yes, sir."

Sandy and Dean were waiting outside the headshed, but all Mark could do was shake his head and say, "You wouldn't believe it if I told you."

CHAPTER 16

As summer, wore on, Mark began thinking about his next step. His first three-year term would be up at the end of August, and the decision about re-enlistment could not be put off much longer. His father had steady work, and was convinced that things would never be bleak again.

"I've changed the way I look at things, Mark. I'm not just going from job to job, congratulating myself about how many dollars an hour I get. I'm gradually doing more contracting, and less hands-on plumbing. I don't make as much as I would as an hourly worker, but I'm building good relationships with some good people, and we've started a spec project of our own."

"Isn't that risky?"

"It can be, but your mom's working with me, and keeping my head out of my ass. We're making sure that even if everything goes south, we'll still be able to keep a roof over our heads. I won't make as much as if I took bigger risks, but if we're careful, we know that we can build up slowly over the next few years, and that we'll be okay for the future."

"Well, I'm going to keep sending a check every month anyway. If you don't use it, just start up a bank account for me, or invest it in your project or something. If I keep it here, I'll just spend it."

So he didn't have to stay in to support his family. And unlike Sandy, who was from a Newfie fishing village where the unemployment rate was pretty much one-hundred percent, Mark could return to Vancouver where the economy was booming again. Finding a job was certain.

But in the end, it was as much of a no-brainer for him as it was for Sandy.

As he told his father. "It's what I've been waiting for all my life. I'm having more fun than I've ever had, and I'm saving guys' lives while I do it."

"You don't miss the band?"

"Of course I miss the band, but not as much as I'd miss this if I quit. I loved the music, and people worshipped me, but what I'm doing now is okay, too. Here, people respect me."

"So what's the problem. Go sign up. Do another three years and enjoy yourself. You'll get some good medic experience that'll help you get work once you're out, and in the meantime, you can be a wildboy. Be a bastard. Get it out of your blood while you're young, and at the end of three years, you can think about it all again."

Mark put in his official application for re-enlistment the next morning.

It wasn't all fun and games. The jumping was great, the field exercises were great, and he even got to do a lot of weapons training. Work in the hospital wasn't great, but at least it wasn't as boring as it had been at Chilliwack. On the other hand, gas training was *so* bad, that it almost made him question his sanity at staying in.

He wasn't alone, of course. *Everybody* hated gas training, but everybody had to do it, and that included the medics. When the Airborne dropped in, the medics dropped in with them, and whatever the combat soldiers had to deal with, the medics had to deal with as well. That included the possibility of being gassed.

Gas mask training was torture of the worst kind. It started in the gas hut, and it involved real CS gas. A Corporal made sure everybody's mask was on correctly, and then activated several pellets. The only reason, other than death, for breaking the seal between the mask and your face, was the sound of "Gas Clear" from the demonic Master Corporal, who would then do his best to force the trainees to screw up.

Screwing up was something they did only once. The gas was vicious, and the instant the mask came off, it began ravaging their mucous membranes. Eyes, nose, mouth, throat. The pain was indescribable, and the Corporal made sure that they all felt it. Even the guys who didn't screw up were forced to go through the speaking and drinking drill— removing the mask, reciting their Social Insurance Number, taking a drink of water, and putting the mask back on.

Bad as that was, it was child's play compared to doing exercises in full gas gear. The worst, by far, was when they had to combine gas training with combat training. PT on those days consisted of showing up in full combat gear, sealing up inside a gas mask, and then running. The mask filled with sweat and snot almost instantly, and the only way to deal with it was to swallow.

"It's what you tell those shackrats all the time, right? Swallow, baby, swallow." The Corporal laughed like he'd just won the lottery. "Well, you're getting it back now. Anybody caught unsealing a mask will be asked to stand by while everybody else in the platoon is punished. That punishment will be long, and unmerciful, and when it is over, every one of them will hate you."

Nobody unsealed. It was the most indescribably ugly training Mark had ever done, but he stuck it out, and so did everybody else. One guy almost died when he threw up inside his mask, but one of the training staff saw it, and pulled the mask off himself. Everybody else kept running. And swallowing.

If gas training was the low-point, jumping was the high point. And the high point of the jumping was getting attached to a Pathfinder training course. If the Airborne was the elite of the army, the Pathfinders were the elite of the Airborne. They were the guys who dropped in behind enemy lines and then scouted and secured drop zones; guys who moved in stealth mode to scope out enemy positions. It was sneak-and-peak all the way, and insertion was critical. No noisy, slow, low-flying troop planes for these guys. Their training required High Altitude, Low Opening drops, and when they dropped, a medic dropped with them.

The HALO drops were unbelievable. The altitude meant freezing temps and no oxygen, so they came out of the plane in winter gear, with full Oxygen rigs. No static lines either. High-speed freefall until the last possible second, then pull it and pray.

The HALO course was the biggest blast, but it was hardly the only course. The Airborne took preparedness seriously, and Mark wound up on course after course. Helicopter medivac, winter survival, winter warfare, vehicle qualification, weapons training, and regular medical upgrades.

In addition to the courses and the regular workload, there was good martial arts as well. The morning Mark had reported to the gym, McLeod had kicked his ass, but it hadn't been easy, and they both knew that if Mark had stayed in regular training over the past two years, it would have been the other way around.

Everyone in the Commando had to learn a bit of basic unarmed combat, but there was also real martial arts for those who wanted it, and

Mark was thrilled to have found somebody with the same attitude as his father. McLeod was nowhere near as good as his father, but he took the same approach—"If you're alive and the other guy's dead, then you've won"—and he was open to learning new techniques.

After seeing Mark in action, Sandy and Dean both wanted to learn, and all three of them showed up at the unarmed combat room three nights a week when they were on base. Both his friends realized that if Mark hadn't saved them that night, they could easily have been killed, so they took the training seriously.

When he returned to Borden for his TQ3 after a year in the Airborne, he couldn't believe his eyes.

There was no discipline, no pride, no sense of camaraderie. Everywhere he looked there were just fat slobs, marking time, and ducking responsibility. He hated it.

He studied hard, and kept his mind off the ugliness around him by training as much as he could, and the happiest moment of the course was when the plane back to CFB Petawawa lifted its wheels from the ground.

Going back to the endless torture of the Airborne was like, what had Sandy said that day they'd gone for their first beer? Like going from the sewer to the penthouse. Maybe not all the regiments of the Canadian Army were as horrible as Sandy and Dean made 2 PPCLI sound, but after serving time in the Airborne, Mark knew that anything else would *seem* like a sewer.

To celebrate his return, he rented a car and drove Sandy and Dean into Ottawa and took them to hear the Specials. "I know you're an ignorant lobsterman, so it's my duty to expose you to the kind of music you missed out on in your youth."

It was an easy two-hour drive, but they rented a motel room as soon as they got to the city. "It's gonna be 0300 when we're done, and we are gonna be drunk and stoned. No way am I driving back. We can sleep in, check out the city when we get up, and have an easy drive back in the afternoon."

That trip started a tradition. Whenever any of them had something special to celebrate, they'd head into the nation's capital and catch a concert or a good band in a bar. The weekend after Dean got promoted to Corporal, they caught the Mighty Mighty Bosstones.

The months passed, and in mid-August, almost five years after his first enlistment, Mark was standing on CO's parade with all of 1, 2, and 3 Commandos, thinking about what excuse he could give Sandy for not going into town tonight. The shackrat scene was starting to get harder and harder to face, and even though they never got laid in Ottawa, going to a concert was starting to sound like a better weekend than… He snapped his mind back to the present when he heard the RSM call his name.

"Private Mark Heaney."

"What?"

"Step forward and face your Commanding Officer." *Holy shit! What was going on?*

He did as ordered. Stepped forward from his position in the Head-quarterss Platoon, left-turned, marched rigidly to a position in front of the CO, slammed to parade halt, saluted, then took one further step forward, so that he was the required foot-and-half from the CO.

Colonel Pritchard made it short and sweet. A few words about Mark's record, and his contribution to the Regiment, and then he reached out and offered Mark a set of Corporal's stripes.

Mark was too surprised to even take them, but then recovered, accepted the stripes, said, "Thank you, sir," and saluted.

He floated through the rest of the day, numb with pleasure, and that night, with his best friends at his side, and half of 2 Commando present, he proudly hit the bell that hung above the bar in the JRs. His round. Drinks for everybody there. And he was happy to pay for it because whatever problems might come with the stripes, it was one of the biggest single pay raises in the military. His pay had jumped about four thousand dollars a year that morning, and beer for his buds was the least he could do.

He was on the piss all night, and showed up late for work the next morning, but the CSM had already told him that would be okay, so he wasn't worried.

"So, what's it like?"

He and Sandy were sitting in Mark's room. "Well, for starters, I still have to smell you stinking, scumbag privates when I breathe in. What

I'm really waiting for is to make Master Corporal so I can move out of this shack."

"Hey, I had a shower two weeks ago, what's the problem?" Sandy sniffed his pits. "I smell like a rose. And what's so special about you? Pubs never complained about it when he made Corporal."

"Yeah, but you gotta remember that Pubs has got about as much class as a five-dollar hooker." They laughed, then Mark continued, "Actually, the best thing is that I'm a medic, so all my old friends won't automatically start hating me just because I'm a Corporal." That much was true. Corporals were the demons of the universe, but since a medic Corporal wasn't dragging people out on runs, or putting them through gas mask drills, he was a lot less likely to be hated.

"You get new duties yet?"

"Some. They're going to put me in charge of stores and supplies, which won't make much difference right away, cuz I was doing most of it already, but if the big shit comes down like they're saying it might, then stores and suppliess is going to go insane."

Sandy didn't have to ask what the "big shit" was. No one on the base had been talking about much else lately. The United Nations was talking about supporting an American-led peacekeeping operation in Africa, and it looked like the Airborne would be going in.

"You know where Somalia is?"

"Are you kidding? I hardly know where England is. All I know about Africa is jungles."

Sandy was patient. "Not much of Africa is jungle, wonderchild, and Somalia sure isn't. It's on the coast, up near Arabia, and it is stinking hot."

"Arabia? I might be a highschool dropout, but even *I* know that Arabia ain't in Africa."

"No, but you can throw stones into Arabia from where we'd be."

"No shit?"

If the CO knew, he wasn't telling, but the orders came down to all the officers and NCOs to tighten up discipline, and to concentrate on desert combat training and peacekeeping theory. For the men, the microscopic amount of slack that the staff had been willing to cut them disappeared entirely, and an air of seriousness settled over the whole base. Word was that the CO had some kind of wild hair up his butt, and had given the order that no infractions of any kind would be tolerated.

"So, what are we supposed to do?" Dean wasn't impressed. "I'm not going to sit in my room every night for the next six months."

"Yeah, but if we pull something stupid in town, we might not get to go in with the first wave."

"Yeah, I know, but that doesn't mean we've got to start going to church; it just means we shouldn't pull anything stupid in town." Dean obviously had a plan. "So let's go do something stupid in Ottawa."

Mark and Sandy nodded. Not doing something major before they left would suck, but cutting loose in Petawawa carried the risk of being reported. Ottawa would be perfect. It wasn't New York, shit it wasn't even Vancouver. But it was the capital of the country, and there were plenty of restaurants, bars, and nightclubs.

"And plenty of classy hookers. Not like the sluts in town here."

"Count me in. But we'd better get on it soon, because the instant the CO gets the word that we're going, he's gonna restrict everybody to base."

"Yeah, Colonel Pritchard's enough of a dork to do that."

"Whoa, you should talk. He promoted you, didn't he?"

After almost eighteen months attached to the Airborne, Mark knew that for all its good points, it did have one flaw. The officers. Not all of them, but enough.

"Get real. He handed me the stripes, but we all know it was the CSM and the RSM that promoted me. You guys have heard the same shit I've heard. Replace about half the officers and this could be one of the best fucking regiments in the world. Up there with the SAS."

Dean nodded. "Yeah, I've heard some of the Sergeants talking when they didn't know I was there, and I'm with you on that one bro. I've also been reading some of those books you've given me, and I think we've got the men, the NCOs, and the training to match anybody. But until they weed out some of the losers we've got for officers, we're always going to be one step behind."

Ottawa turned out to be perfect. They rented a car and drove down in style. "Hey, we might get killed in Somalia; what good will money in the bank be then?" was Dean's justification. Once there, they found a good hotel, and rented a suite that went for almost three hundred bucks a night. It had two separate bedrooms, a lounge area with a TV and a foldout bed, and the biggest mini-fridge Mark had ever seen.

"Look at the booze, man." Mark had opened the fridge door. "This room comes with enough booze to drown the whole Regiment." He pulled out a beer and a little bottle of whiskey and handed them to Sandy.

"Put 'em back." It was Dean, giving orders.

"Why's that?"

"Cuz it doesn't fuckin' 'come with the room' that's why. They count it when you check out, and every one of those little things," he pointed to the tiny whiskey bottle, "costs five-fifty. I don't mind spending for some comfort, but we can walk down the street to the liquor store and get more for a hundred bucks than there is in that whole fridge."

Sandy looked at the miniature bottle. "No shit?"

"No shit. Let's save our hard-earned coin for the ladies."

"Okay, but first let's hit that liquor store, and lay in some beverages, and then I vote we do something about supper."

"Works for me," said Mark. "The restaurant in this joint looks pretty classy. Wanna try that?"

"Why don't we cruise around a bit first. See what we see, and then decide."

"Okay?"

"Okay."

It went perfectly. Perfect meal. Good booze. Incredible hookers. It was the perfect way to send themselves off into harm's way in some god-forsaken hellhole that they might never return from.

And it ended with a crash at exactly 0330 the next morning when a squad of police in full riot gear came through the hotel-room door and busted them all for trafficking in cocaine.

It was bullshit, of course. They were innocent fish caught in the net of a larger operation, but the call girls they'd hired actually *were* part of a cocaine ring and were all carrying way too much for personal use. But by the time it was all sorted out, their pictures were already in all the national newspapers, and the CO wasn't interested in what the Ottawa RCMP were saying, only in damage control.

And in his frightened mind, "damage control" meant dishonorable discharge.

The Petawawa Meatheads came and got them after two days in an Ottawa jail, but all that meant was two more days in cells on the base until the RSM himself came to get them.

He marched them, with a pair of armed MPs, to his office. "I'll deal with them from here on. You two are dismissed."

The Meatheads weren't happy about that, but one glare from the RSM and they were babbling, "Yes, sir" and bailing outta there in about a tenth of a second.

"Sit down."

Mark wouldn't have been more surprised if the man had turned into a turkey and flown out the window. Sit down? He'd expected, "Bend over so I can shove a red-hot poker up your ass."

"Sir?"

"Sit down." Sergeant Major MacGregor waved to the chairs behind them.

His voice was weary. Not knowing what was going on, the three sat.

"I'm about to be sent into a combat zone without three of my best men, because some chickenshit Colonel wants to be a General, and I am *not* a happy man. You guys have some of the best records in the regiment, and every one of your NCOs, *every single fucking one of them*, would cheerfully frag that asshole if they thought they could get away with it."

Mark sucked in his breath. MacGregor was practically talking treason. He'd be the one getting discharged if the Colonel ever heard what he was saying.

He must have read their minds. "I know the three of you well enough to know that you're going to keep your mouths shut, and take what's coming, but I'd never sleep again at night if I missed the chance to tell you that I had nothing to do with this, this… this *crap!*" He hurled a paperweight across the room so hard that it buried itself in the wall.

Holy flying fuck! Mark thought.

Mark risked speaking. "I'm sorry we put you in this position sir, we were…"

"I know exactly what you were doing, and I know that it's exactly what I and just about every other man on this base would have done in your place. Sure, you got caught with your pants down in public, and I'd be quite happy to fine you and confine you to base for a week. But this?"

He squared his shoulders, and spoke directly and quietly to them. "We've convinced the CO not to have you discharged. It took some doing, but not every officer in this regiment has his head up his ass, and we got that much. But that was the limit. You're all going to be punted to 2 PPCLI, and when it happens I expect you to stand straight, salute, and not make one fucking sound. Do I have your word on that?"

"Yes, sir," all three echoed.

"Until then, you're confined to quarters. Walk tall when you leave this room. Dismissed."

CHAPTER 17

"Welcome to the sewer." Kapyong Barracks at CFB Winnipeg South was hot, humid, and mosquito-infested. It was also dirty and old and poorly maintained. "It's where they send people like us."

Sandy and Dean were giving Mark a tour of his new home. "Second Battalion, Princess Patricia's Canadian Light Infantry. Home of the scum of the army."

"Cesspool of the country. In the winter, it's cold enough to freeze the balls off a brass monkey, and in the summer it's like this."

"But it's September, man. Shouldn't we be getting some good fall days?"

"We'll probably get a couple, just before the snow hits."

Mark looked around. This place didn't look much different from Chilliwack or Borden.

"There's gotta be *something* good about it. I mean, being attached to 1CER sucked, but the base was close enough to Vancouver, and there was some pretty cool country around."

Sandy and Dean looked at one another, obviously deciding who would break the bad news.

"The one single good thing about 2PPCLI is that, even though it's horrible, it's an infantry feeder for 2 Commando of the Airborne." Dean put a hand on Mark's shoulder. "But that option ain't exactly open to us three."

"Fuck." Mark could feel depression settling onto him like bags of wet sand. "What about Winnipeg? It's a big city, right? A million people, right? There must be something happening there?"

"What difference does it make, anyway? We could be outside New York City, and we'd still be going to the same bars, screwing the same shackrats and whores."

They cleared in the next morning, and Mark was even further into the dumps when they met at the JRs at the end of the day. The UMS was about what he'd expected, but his CSM was a slob. He assigned Mark the job of running morning sick parade… "It's actually Master Corporal Shumansky's job, but he ain't around much, so you'll wind up doing it most of the time." He waved his hand vaguely and said, "The rest of it you probably know. The usual. Stores, paperwork, that kind of stuff. You'll be fine. Wilkinson's the guy to talk to." Then he waddled back into his office.

Dean and Sandy, on the other hand, were feeling a bit better than they had yesterday. "Because we came out of the Patricia's and cuz we've had all that Airborne training, they put us in a recce platoon, and it looks like Dean is finally going to get his stripes."

"Yeah, well, after seven years it's about time. Anyway, this isn't going to be like the Airborne, but at least we're not going to be slogging around behind tanks. We'll probably be pounding track in those miserable M113s, but recce is a million times better than anything else."

"M113?" Mark hadn't heard of them.

"APCs. But they're from the Vietnam era, they break all the time, and they're slow and noisy."

Mark didn't have to ask why broken down, twenty-year-old equipment was in use. This was the Canadian Army, and even the Airborne didn't get the kind of equipment that he'd read about other Armies using.

He chugged another beer and headed for the bar for a round of refills. While he was waiting, he thought about what his father had told him when they'd spoken on the telephone about the unfairness of what had happened. "There's nothing you can do to change what happened. You got shafted and your dream is down the toilet. But what you do now will affect what's going to happen in the future. Think back five years. I got shafted by forces out of my control, and I was pretty much ready to give up. But my family and my friends wouldn't let me, and I stuck it out."

He paused, but Mark knew there was more to come. "I never told you this, son, but there were nights when I was pretty close to taking the bike out onto the coast highway, winding it up, and then just not bothering to make the next turn. But you, and your mom, and Bones, well, you got me through it, and look where I am now.

"Oh, don't worry, I'm not thinking of killing myself, it's just… well…" He ran out of words.

"Look. You're making good money, and even though you're out of the Airborne, you'll probably still be able to get some good medical experience. You've got less than two years, and when you come right down to it, your life could be a lot worse. You've got your family behind you, and you've got your two best friends to help get you through. You'll make it. And then you'll have your whole life in front of you."

He'd hung up feeling better, but when the reality of working in the UMS in this shithole was staring him in the face, talk about 'good money', and 'only two years', wasn't very comforting.

What he heard when he got back to the table with the new round was a little better.

"There's something different going on here, Mark." Sandy took the beer Mark offered. "There's a new CO, and it sounds like he's trying to shake things up, but the big thing is that there are rumors that the Battalion might be slated for a peacekeeping mission."

"You're kidding, right?" Mark's initial response hadn't been too enthusiastic. "You've seen what this outfit is made of. These guys couldn't fight off a troop of Boy Scouts."

"I don't know, man." Dean sounded thoughtful. "It's definitely different from when we left. I got a look at some of the exercise schedules for the next few months, and something's up. Sandy figures it's gotta be Yugoslavia."

"Where's that? What's happening there?"

Sandy rolled his eyes. "Mr. Geography, aren't you?"

"Hey, I'm a high-school dropout, remember. I don't know much about, well, about anything." He laughed. The beer was starting to hit him, and he could feel his problems fading. "I did my GED when I was at Chilliwack, but I don't remember anything about Yugoslavia. It's in Russia, right?" He vaguely remembered hearing about it on the news. "Serbia, right? The Yugoslavians are fighting the Serbians or something."

"Yugoslavia is a country north of Greece, but the deal is that it's really a bunch of separate small countries that kind of got shoved together and made into one. Which would be okay, except they all hate each other, and the ruler that kept it all together is dead now, and the Russians don't give a shit anymore, so all these factions are gunning for each other.

Trying to declare independence. There's Serbs, Bosnians, Croats, Slovenians, and I think maybe one or two other nationalities, plus some of them are Muslims and some are Christians, and that's not helping, either."

"And they're tossing us into that?"

"We don't know. Nobody knows. But there's definitely a rumor that we're going somewhere, and that's the obvious place."

A week later it was official. The Second Battalion of Princess Patricia's Canadian Light Infantry was scheduled to rotate into Croatia for six months.

"We're gearing up for inoculations at the UMS next month." Mark had been put in charge of receiving supplies. "Not that Porky would know which end of a needle to stick into anybody."

"Porky?"

"Sergeant Major Kent. My CSM. He and the senior Master Corporal have some kind of scam running and they're never around. I'm not sure what it is, but I sure as hell hope they get their shit together before we get sent to any combat zone."

"Well, there's plenty of time to sort things out. We're not going till next spring."

If the deployment to Croatia had taken place later that month, Mark would have been okay. The disappointment at being punted from the Airborne would have been balanced by the excitement of being posted to another peacekeeping mission. But the transfer date was 15 June, eight months away, and it might as well have been some time in the next century. His work in the UMS was mind-numbingly boring; exercises were both less frequent and less exciting than they had been in the Airborne, and seeing a line-up of slackers and whiners on sick parade got every day off to an ugly start. Before long, the focus of his days became 1500, when he could hit the JRs for a beer.

PT was a joke. Dean and Sandy had it better in the Recce platoon, and the grunts got put through their daily run, but Porky couldn't have cared less about fitness. When Mark had asked about PT, the man had been surprised. "PT? You're not in the fuckin' Airborne anymore, so don't worry about it."

No wonder a lot of soldiers had no respect for wogs.

Winter made everything worse. When the temperature reached twenty below, it was hard to convince himself that it was worth the effort to go out, and when he did go out, it seemed pointless. If he came home alone, he felt lonely and frustrated, but if he did get laid, it would be by some drunken, ugly slut of a shackrat, and the way he felt after that was even worse—unclean and full of disgust with himself.

But what was the alternative? Pretend that working in the Winnipeg UMS was useful work that he should be proud of? Most of the guys that came in were just slackers, looking for a way out of work, and his boss and his supervisor were more concerned with selling cigarettes and booze on the black market than they were with the health of the base.

"Black Market? Are you serious?" Dean was in Mark's room, waiting for Sandy so the three of them could hit town.

"Yeah. They've got something going with a couple of guys over at the CQ and somebody from the JRs has got to be involved, too."

"But how?"

"This is the army, right? It's the shits, but at least we get cheap booze and cigarettes, right?"

"Yeah, so?"

"So the army is bringing in enough beer and booze and cigarettes to poison half the world, and it's all tax-free, because it's government, and Porky and Shumansky and whoever they're working with, are taking it, and selling it somewhere in Winnipeg. Probably to bars or restaurants."

"How do you know that?"

"Cuz they're fucking stupid. If it was you and me planning something illegal, we'd be talking here, in a private room, where no one could possibly hear us, but these guys... Well, they're stupid, and a couple of times I've overheard them talking when they didn't know I was there."

"Overheard whom?" Sandy came in without knocking.

"Mark's CSM, and that dickhead Shumansky, are running some kind of booze and cigarette thing. Stealing from the army and selling it in town."

"That figures." Sandy didn't seem too surprised. "Remember Klophaus?" Dean nodded.

"Who's Klophaus?" Mark asked.

"A Sergeant that was here when Dean and I were. He was doing the same thing with weapons and ammo."

"And?"

"And he's in Club Ed."

"Which is where Kent and Shumansky are going to wind up," added Dean.

"I don't know. It sounds like they've been doing this for years."

"Colonel Jeffries hasn't been the CO for years. He's turning this Battalion around, Mark. If you weren't stuck in the UMS with those asswipes, you'd see."

Sandy and Dean got into a conversation about how the Colonel was changing things both from the top down and from the bottom up, but Mark tuned it out.

Who gave a fuck? Even if Colonel Jeffries turned out to be Julius Caesar and Abraham Lincoln all rolled into one, what could he do? Change 2 PPCLI from being the sewer of the Canadian army to being the toilet seat? Even if he turned out to be God, he'd still have trouble. This was *never* going to be the Airborne, and if it wasn't the Airborne, Mark wasn't interested.

Maybe Porky had the right idea. Take what you can get, and to hell with everything else. The army hadn't exactly treated him well, so why should he care about the army? Come right down to it, the army had fucked him over royally.

" ...what do you say?" Sandy was asking him a question.

"Say about what?"

"The movie."

"What movie?"

"You haven't heard a word, have you?"

"Sorry, I guess I was thinking about something else."

"We were thinking of catching *Lethal Weapon 3*. What were you thinking of?"

"Asking Shumansky if he needs help with the next delivery," Mark blurted out without thinking.

Dead silence. Then, "Are you out of your fucking mind?"

"Whadaya mean? Anyway, who gives a fuck?"

Sandy and Dean looked at each other, then Sandy started to speak, "Mark, you've got to ... "

But Dean interrupted. "Okay, bro, change of plans. We are taking you to the movie we saw last weekend."

Mark saw Sandy nodding his head in agreement. "What movie?"

"We are taking you to see something you've never heard of, something that just came out, called *Reservoir Dogs*. You watch that with us, and then we'll talk about your fucking plan to be a fucking criminal."

"Whatever. Let's hit the JRs for a couple first, though."

"No way, asshole. You are going to be cold sober when you see this. And you're gonna be sober when we talk about it afterward."

"Oh, get real. A couple of beers aren't going to make…" Mark looked at his friends' faces and realized that the only way he was getting a beer was by knocking them both unconscious. "Awright. Awright. Let's go watch the fucking movie. What's it about? Jesus Christ comes back and preaches about the sin of the black market?"

"You wanna be an asshole, be an asshole after the movie, okay?"

They rode the bus from their frozen base into the frozen city of Winnipeg. Mark was silent most of the way. He was torn, thinking of the pride he'd felt during every day of suffering in the Airborne, and of the bullshit existence he was putting up with now. No more excruciating training, no more hardship on ex, no more Sergeant McLeod beating the shit out of him and then saying, "God damn, Heaney, you are *really* good. Another couple of weeks and you're going to be able to do that to me. Won't that feel good?"

Life was easy here, so why didn't he like it?

"So?" They were sitting in the Grant, Winnipeg's home away from home for the soldiers of 2PPCLI—otherwise known as "Shackrat City", or "Drug Central Station"—and Sandy was waiting for an answer.

"Huh?"

"The film, Mark, the film."

"Awesome."

Silence.

"Why are you staring at me?"

"Because we can't believe you're acting this dumb." Dean took over. "Just cuz you don't have an education doesn't mean you're stupid, so start thinking about what you just saw. Think about what happened to all those guys who thought they were so fucking smart. Think about what's going to happen to you if you get involved with people like Kent and Shumansky."

Mark thought about the way everything had gone wrong for the guys in the film, and how they'd all turned on each other. No friendship. No respect. No honor. No mercy.

Sandy brought him back to reality. "Colonel Jeffries is a real soldier, Mark. He's been in combat. I've even heard that he was a merc before he joined up. He's not going to take this Battalion into combat with a bunch of fuckups like Kent. They're going to go down, and if you get involved with them, you're going to go down, too." He made signals at the waitress. "You saved my fucking life, man, no way I'm going to let you throw yours away. Understand?"

The waitress arrived before Mark could answer, and slammed a pitcher and three glasses onto the table. While Dean poured, Mark thought back to what Jake Jacox had once told him. They'd been sitting in the JRs at CFB Chilliwack—it seemed like a hundred years ago—and Jake, alcoholic old Jake, had said, "Come in here some night, and don't drink anything. Spend the whole night in here, and take a real good look at what your buddies are like after they've had a few." Even back then, Mark had known that Jacox had really meant, "take a good look at what you could become" and now it hit home.

He took the glass that Dean offered him, but he didn't drink anything right away. He looked around the bar. It was the same as it always was. Soldiers and shackrats in various stages of drunkenness. But instead of seeing a bunch of guys having fun, Mark saw table after table of young men who hadn't grown up, and older guys who would never grow up. He saw women with no self-respect using soldiers who hated them just so they could pretend they weren't lonely and ugly. He tried to tune in to some of the shouted conversations.

"... so I sent Willis outside to make sure no one came in, then I jerked off in Degator's canteen..."

"... no, cocaine's great. Don't believe what they say about problems, dude, that's just propaganda. It makes you feel great, and..."

"... we had her totally airtight, man. She was blowing Paul, Steve was up her ass, and I was fucking her from underneath..."

He wanted to vomit.

"Hey, look who's here." Sandy's voice brought him back. He followed the pointing arm to the huge figure of Shackrat Sheila.

She was a legend on the base. Ready and willing to fuck anything that owned a uniform. Some of the NCOs used her for initiations. At the end of a battleschool course they'd bring her back to the shacks to take on their entire platoon of newbies. Twenty guys in a row. And she ate it up.

They watched as she hit on guys at various tables, not seeming to worry as she got turned down time after time.

"I bet that O'Connor'll take her."

"Who's O'Connor?" Mark wanted to know.

"He's in our recce platoon. He's got about as much class as she does. Watch."

Sheila had waddled to another table, and one of the guys there was actually talking to her. He reached up and squeezed one of her gigantic tits, then said something in her ear. She giggled and shook her head, but O'Connor, if that's who it was, slid his chair back and rubbed his crotch. She shook her head "no" again, but pointed to the half-full pitcher on the table. Whatever O'Connor said must have satisfied her, because she lifted the pitcher and started chugging.

Only about half the beer went down her throat—the rest spilled down into the grand canyon of her cleavage—but she just laughed and set the empty pitcher down, and then crawled under the table to where O'Connor was unzipping himself.

"I don't believe this. She's gonna blow him, right here."

Mark was sickened. He felt his guts starting to churn, and he ran for the back door, barely making it before spewing his supper into the snow in the alley.

"You okay, man?" Sandy was behind him, patting him on the shoulder.

"Yeah, I think so." But then the image of Shackrat Sheila going down on the soldier in the bar merged in his mind with an image of the night a few weeks ago when her bloated, stinking body had been bucking up and down underneath him, and he turned away from his friend and sank to his knees as his stomach started spasming again.

And again, and again, and again, till nothing was coming up but tiny drools of acidic bile.

"I'm fucked up, Sandy." He stood up. "I'm going home."

"Okay, I'll go get Pubs."

"No, I think I need to be alone for a while."

"You sure you'll be okay?"

"No, I'm not going to be okay, but I still need to be alone."

"Your call, bro. If you change your mind and want someone to talk to, just call me on my cell phone." Sandy pulled out the phone that Mark and Dean made so much fun of, and hit the "On" switch.

Mark was about to speak sarcastically, "Sandy Stephens's crisis center hotline, huh?" But the fact that he had friends who cared was the one thing he had to cling to at that moment, so he just said, "Thanks," then went inside, put on his coat, and headed out into the Winnipeg winter, wondering if the cold wind would blow the foulness out of his mind.

He didn't remember much more from that night. He'd walked around till he got too cold, and then hopped a bus back to the base, where he spent the next day in a fog, unsure of anything.

Work, on Monday morning, was the usual bullshit sick parade, although partway through it, he started thinking back over the last month, and realized that there were fewer and fewer whiners and deadbeats showing up lately. Maybe Dean was right about the Old Man cleaning the regiment up.

He was on coffee at 1400 when Sergeant Major Kent called for him. "Just got some new orders for you, Heaney." The fat man tossed a paper to where Mark could reach it. "You're out on ex with Charlie Company as of tomorrow."

What? One day's notice? "What's going on, Sir? I thought they were taking Thorpe and Dosanjh."

"They were. But this morning they decided to take you instead of Thorpe. So fuck off and go pack or something."

Porky clearly wasn't interested, and Mark knew that asking anything more would be a waste of breath, so he took the orders back to his room, and read them over. Winter combat exercise, one month duration, Wainwright Alberta, supporting Charlie Company, 2PPCLI.

That was Dean and Sandy's company. He'd known they were headed out, and if he hadn't been so messed up mentally on the weekend, he'd have been out partying with them to say goodbye. Weird that he'd get posted to the same ex at the last minute like this, but… and then it hit him.

They'd done this. Sandy and Pubs had gone to their Sergeant and asked him to see if he could get Mark assigned instead of Thorpe. The Sergeant would have told them to fuck off, but they would have explained that… Mark wasn't sure what they would have used for an explanation. Whether they'd have cooked up some story about how much winter medic experience Mark had from his Airborne days, or if they'd just told the truth. "We think our buddy is cracking up and we're scared to leave him on his own."

However they'd done it, Mark realized he was thankful. He desperately needed a kick in the ass, and this would give it to him. A month of combat exercises in the frozen wastes of Alberta would definitely take his mind off the boredom of garrison life at Kapyong Barracks.

CHAPTER 18

And so it did. It was one of the coldest winters on record, and the Wainwright area was known for cold winters. The temps were regularly down around thirty below, and medic duty was for real. The Battalion was way under strength, and a lot of guys had been called up from the reserves to bring it up to the required manpower for the Croatia mission. The regular soldiers were careless and stupid enough, but the reserves...

"I'm tellin' ya, Pubs, the best thing we could do with the reserves would be to paint targets on 'em and turn 'em loose on the range. The regulars need the practice, and it would put the reserves out of their misery quick, instead of having them freeze to death, or get crushed under the APCs."

Dean had brought in a reservist that he'd found wandering around lost, and starting to suffer from exposure. The kid turned out not to have reached the stage of real frostbite, but he was disoriented, and his core temp had dropped far enough that Mark ordered him to spend the night in the heated hospital tent, with several hot water bottles packed into his sleeping bag.

"They might be inexperienced, Mark, but did you hear him complain?"

Mark thought back. "No, not a peep out of him."

"They're almost all like that. Dead fuckin' keen to learn as much as they can, as fast as they can. And you know what?"

"This the sixty-four thousand dollar question or something?"

"Well, you probably don't notice, being stuck here in the field hospital, but the regulars are eating it up. They're so anxious to show what great soldiers they are, that they're actually putting out the effort to do things right so that they don't look like klutzes in front of the reserves."

"You serious?" The scorn that regular soldiers had for the weekend warriors was legendary.

"Yup. We're actually gonna have a decent crew on the ground over there."

"You, maybe. Not me. Not unless Kent and Shumansky have fatal accidents."

"I wouldn't worry. Everybody on the base is pissed about the UMS, so I bet the CO has 'em punted before we go over."

"That would be seriously cool. I think I'd…"

"*Medic.* We need a medic. Help," the radio blared and Mark grabbed it. "Hospital. Heaney here, go."

"We need help real bad."

Great. Serious medical emergency, and they give the radio to some kid who's never used a radio before.

"Okay, calm down; can you tell me where you are, and what your situation is? Over."

"We're out in the field, the others are hurt real bad."

"Take it easy. I need to know your actual location. Something more specific than 'out in the field'. Over."

"Yes, sir. I think we're on a tank range."

Mark wanted to shriek at the kid, but he knew he had to keep talking calmly. He was about to ask again when Dean said, "Ask him if there's a lot of hills around, or if it's really flat."

Mark echoed his friend.

"It's really hilly."

"Okay, that's the weapons range in the southwest corner of the area. I know where it is."

Mark nodded. "Tell me your name, and what's happened. Over."

"I'm Bill Payton, sir. Our APC flipped over. The other four guys are in bad shape. I think one of them might be dead."

"Okay. I want you to stay off the air for a minute while I get a search party out looking for you, then I'll come back on and you can tell me more. Do you understand? Over."

"Yes, sir. I understand. I'll wait till you call me."

Mark knew that the conversation would have been overheard by everyone with a live radio, so he just hit the transmit button and said, "Who's close to the weapons range in the southwest corner? Over."

"UMS, this is Private Lyell, 4 Platoon. We're probably within fifteen hundred meters, but it's hilly. Could take us a while to locate, but we're moving on it."

"You know the area, Pubs?"

"Yeah. Real well."

"Okay, deal with the radio while I grab my jump bag, and then you can drive me."

"I'm on it."

It took Lyell almost fifteen minutes to find the accident site, and by that time, Mark and Dean weren't far. They homed in on the flare Lyell had fired, and Dean skidded the M113 Ambulance to a stop five meters from the wreckage.

"Jesus H. Christ, Pubs, they must have been going two hundred klicks an hour!"

They were looking at a smashed-up mess that had once been a Canadian Army Iltis Jeep. It was crumpled up at the end of a short skid track, but the skid track started in the middle of nowhere, and it was obvious they'd come over a hill at a speed high enough to have them airborne for fifteen meters. Mark grabbed his jump bag and hit the ground running. All soldiers in the Airborne got good first-aid training, and he knew that Dean would be right behind him, ready to help out as much as possible.

Which was a good thing, because there wasn't going to be anybody else he could count on for a while. The kid on the radio had sounded pretty dazed, and Lyell, or his partner, was on his knees puking his guts out. The other one was coming toward him, but Mark could tell from the glazed look in his eyes, that until the chopper got there, he and Dean would be on their own.

He grabbed a quick look at his watch. 1140. The Captain had called for a chopper at 1118, but in this weather, it would take them almost half an hour just to get the machine warmed up enough to fly, and another twenty minutes to get here.

He passed a leg, lying in the snow. The hip end had done some bleeding, but not much. In temperatures like this, with no heart pumping hot blood through them, the severed veins and arteries would have frozen in seconds. He had no doubt that this was what had made Lyell puke, but what it meant to Mark was that there were now only four casualties to worry about, not five. Whoever had once been attached to this leg would have been dead within a minute.

He saved three of them.

He'd done a fast triage. The kid who'd radioed had a broken arm, and was in mild shock. Easy to deal with. The guy without the leg was as dead as Mark knew he'd be. Also easy to deal with. The other three were bad. Compound fractures, head trauma, internal injuries for sure. Not much blood visible, but one of them was obviously bleeding out internally, and Mark made the difficult decision to forget him and do what he could for the others. At least with the inhumanly cold temperature, the dying guy wouldn't feel much pain.

They worked their asses off until the medivac chopper arrived. Dean was good. He'd taken his first-aid training seriously, and he was smart. Without him, Mark felt sure there would have been at least one less live body going out on the chopper.

"Buy ya a drink, bro?" Dean had said in the end.

Mark looked around at the scene. Corpses, blood, medical garbage, and the wreckage that had once been an Iltis. A drink would be a blessing. "You know about some bar just over one of these hills?"

"I threw my pack in your ambulance. Brought my own bar." Dean held up a silver thermos bottle.

"You're the man, Pubs. Get the lid off. God knows I... Oh, shit!"

"What."

"You heard what the chopper pilot said. Captain's gonna be here any minute. If we smell of booze..." He pointed to the bodies.

"Yeah. I guess you're right. The way things work in this army, we'd probably get court-martialed for murdering them."

They retreated to the warm ambulance and put the thermos away. "Fuck, am I ever cold." Dean was shivering.

"Yeah, you get working on dying people and you forget your own body." Mark realized how cold he was himself.

"Heaney?"

"That's me, sir." Mark vaguely recognized Captain Ogilvie's face through the fur-trimmed hood of his parka.

The Captain didn't say anything more or ask for a report. He just stared around at the site. Finally, he turned to Mark. "Three of them walked away?" He sounded surprised. "They must have logged almost fifteen meters of air-time."

"Nobody walked away, sir." Mark shrugged his shoulders. "There was a young reservist who got thrown clear and landed in that big snow-drift." Mark pointed. "Broke an arm pretty badly, but managed to get to the vehicle and get the radio working. Tough kid. If he hadn't kept his shit together they'd all be dead now. The others were, well, one was dead when we got here, one was dying, and I'm not sure that either of the other two are gonna be alive tomorrow."

The Captain took another walk around the scene, pausing to look down at the leg. When he got back to where Mark was waiting he said, "You enjoy paperwork, Heaney?"

"No, sir."

"Well you better develop a positive attitude toward it, because it's what you're going to be doing for the next week. Paperwork, and more interviews and debriefings than one man ever ought to have to go through."

"Sir?"

"We've got two dead, two who may be dying, and nobody was sup-posed to be in this area today. We can't keep this a secret, and the media's going to be all over us." He shook his head. "Did you smell booze on any of them."

"Yes, sir. All of them."

"Great. Just fucking great."

Mark suspected that however much paperwork and debriefing were in store for him, there'd be ten times that much for the Captain.

"Okay, Heaney. Head back to the main compound, and report to my office. You'll probably get there before me, but I won't be too far be-hind you. Who's with you in the ambulance?"

"Corporal Publicover, from the Recce Platoon."

"Not a medic? Well, he'll have to come with you, and you can tell me all about why you brought one of my soldiers instead of another medic. Who's minding the field hospital?"

"Private Dosanjh, sir."

"Is he competent to handle it by himself for the rest of the shift?"

"Yes, sir." Dosanjh was young, but Mark trusted him more than he trusted most of the older medics. "The only casualty there now is a guy that Private Publicover brought in this morning. Mild exposure. He just needs to stay warm and get plenty of hot drinks. If anything comes up, Dosanjh knows enough to hit the radio for help."

"Okay, Heaney. See you in about an hour." The Captain pulled a camera from under his parka. "I'll take pictures of the scene, and be about ten minutes behind you."

The first interview was in Ogilvie's office, but it wasn't just him and Dean and the Captain. Colonel Barnes, the CO of CFB Wainwright was there, as well as the base's senior Medical officer, a Major named Pertis.

Mark told his story. Dean told his story. Then came the questions. They were questioned separately, then together, then separately again. Tape recorders were running the whole time, but Mark knew that he and Pubs were on solid ground. He'd handled it well. Pubs had handled it well, and Pertis, the surgeon, had been on the phone with the hospital in Calgary where the victims had been taken, and was backing them all the way.

"Listen, Bob," he was addressing the Colonel. "I've just talked to the Chief of the ER in Calgary, and he says that the docs that did the work on those two clowns both agree that the care they got in the field was first class. These two," he pointed to Mark and Dean, "did a goddam good job, so back off."

Mark hadn't been comfortable about the tape recorders at first, but he was glad they were running now. Whatever happened, he and Dean were going to come out of this okay. The two guys in the Calgary ER, on the other hand, were probably going to wish they'd died in the crash. Drunk on ex was bad. Stealing a vehicle was real bad, but killing two people? Yeah, they'll wish they'd died.

It didn't take a whole week, as the Captain had said it might, but it was four days before Mark was back on his regular shift again, and he never wanted to fill out another report, or talk to another officer, as long as he lived.

"Reckon it's safe for me to buy ya that drink now?"

They were leaving the last meeting, on the last day of the inquiry, and the Colonel had thanked them for their cooperation and told them that they could return to duty. "You may get called to testify before a Board of Inquiry, sometime in the future, but for now, it's over for you two."

Mark thought about a drink. He and Dean had decided that as long as they were in the spotlight, they wouldn't risk having alcohol on their breaths, even in the middle of the night. Theoretically, exercises like this one were dry. And while like most people, they had their stash of booze, they knew that it would be military suicide to get caught drinking while the inquest was going on.

"Yes, my man, you can buy me that drink now."

Sandy was with them, and Dean filled three glasses from a bottle of whiskey he'd brought over under his parka. They toasted, and Mark tossed his straight back, then waited for the fire to start warming him from the inside. He accepted a refill but sipped it slowly. The first glass was doing its work, and he was in no hurry to get drunk. "Oh, man, does that ever feel good. This is the first time I've relaxed in almost five days."

Dean was obviously in tune with him, leaning back in his chair, with his eyes closed.

"You know what's weird about this?" Sandy had had to put in a couple of extra shifts while Dean was away from duty, so he was happy to mellow out as well. "What's weird is when you think about this from a non-military perspective."

"Huh?"

"No, seriously. Haven't you seen it on the news a hundred times? A bunch of kids tie one on and then get killed in a car crash?"

"I guess."

"Do you think that the ambulance guys have to spend four fucking days getting interviewed by whoever runs the ambulance service? Or by the mayor of whatever city they're in? No fucking way. It's 'Two die in alcohol-related crash, three survive' in a headline for one day, and then everybody's forgotten about it. The cops charge whoever was driving, and no one cares. Right?"

Mark and Dean were both paying attention now.

"It's exactly the same as what happened to us in Ottawa. If we'd been civilians, just three horny guys who picked up the wrong hookers, everybody'd have forgotten us in a couple of days. Would we have lost our jobs?" He didn't wait for an answer. "Of course not. But the army is so fucked up that they get everything backwards. All the senior officers care about is covering their asses."

"Ogilvie's not like that."

"No, he's a stand-up guy, and so is Jeffries. But from what you've told me about this guy, Barnes, the only thing he cared about was how this was going to affect his record. Reminds me of that bastard Pritchard."

Mark thought it over. "Yeah, you're right about a lot of the officers not caring about anything other than their careers, but I've talked to my dad about that a lot, and he says that a lot of the blame has to go to the government. They want to talk about what a great army they have, about peacekeeping with NATO and all that shit, but they won't give us any money or support. Most officers with half a brain figure that out and quit. The ones that stay are losers to start with."

Sandy and Dean had often been on leave in Vancouver with Mark, and they both knew and respected Scott Heaney. "No argument there, but it still leaves us working for a bunch of losers and cowards. I sure wish we were still in the Airborne."

"I don't know man, have you been following the rumors out of Somalia lately?" When the other two looked at him like he was crazy, Sandy continued, "Yeah, okay, you've been kinda busy lately. But word is that the Airborne is not exactly doing a great job."

"What?" they both echoed.

"I got a call from Hugh the other day. You remember Hugh Campbell?"

"Sure, we know Hugh," Dean said, "but how'd he call you? He's in some fucking desert in Somalia, and you're in the middle of the frozen prairie."

"He's not in Somalia. He got malaria and got a medical discharge. He's back in Toronto now and he called to say hi."

"And you just happened to magically have your cell phone turned on at that moment?"

"Of course not. The only time it's on is when I call my folks on Saturday nights, but he left a message on my voicemail, and…"

"Voicemail?" Dean was incredulous. "What the hell are you doing with voicemail?"

Mark took up the teasing. "You afraid you'll miss a call from your agent? Sharon Stone wants you to co-star in her next movie?"

"Back off." Sandy's voice had an edge. "It costs me less than three bucks a month, and with my dad sick, I'd pay ten times that."

"Sorry, man, it's just, well, it does sound weird to hear a grunt talking about his voicemail. But yeah, if my mom or dad was really sick, I'd do the same," Mark said.

"Okay, anyway, Hugh had left me a message, so I called him a couple of nights ago, and he says that he figures the guys that are getting the med discharges are the lucky ones. Morale is the shits, and stuff is happening that's gonna hit the newspapers before long. He says we should be thankful we got punted."

"No way. What's he talking about?"

"He says it's complete anarchy, and that some of the officers are starting to encourage the men to take the law into their own hands. Punish looters. Intimidate people."

"Seriously?"

"Seriously. Hugh was hard. You guys knew him. He was like us. Going on a peacekeeping mission was the biggest thing that could ever have happened to him. If he says he's glad he got malaria and got out, then you'd better believe that it's fucked."

Mark hadn't known Hugh Campbell as well as Sandy and Dean had, but the guy had seemed tough as nails, and every bit as dedicated as they were.

"So what you're saying is that maybe we should be thankful that they tossed us into the sewer just at the time when some real officers started to clean it up?"

"That's right. I was no happier to get punted than you were, but we just might have lucked out. We complained about the officers in the Airborne often enough, and it looks like we were right."

Mark poured them all another round from Dean's bottle. There was a time, not long ago, when he would have been on his fifth or sixth drink by now, but he didn't feel that need anymore. The inquiry had been frustrating and tiring, but the accident had pushed him to his limit, and he was proud of the job he'd done. He felt better about his posting, better about his work, and better about himself. There was only one serious problem still hanging over him.

"We may have some good officers, and most of the NCOs are okay, too. But I'm stuck with the kind of guys that gave the PPCLI the sewer reputation."

Sandy and Dean looked at one another in a way that Mark knew too well. They knew something he didn't.

"I don't think you're gonna have to worry about Porky and his band of thieves."

He didn't say anything and just waited for the explanation.

"We got talking to as many people as we knew we could trust, and everybody agreed."

"Agreed about what? C'mon, guys, spill it."

"Agreed that they were not willing to go into a combat zone with wogs like that. It's okay when you're only an hour from a real hospital in Canada, but none of us wants to take the chance of getting wounded in a place where Sergeant Major Kent is running the UMS."

"He's a hazard to everybody's life bro, and you're not the only medic who's overheard things. Wilkinson helped us, and so did that kid you like, Dosanjh. That guy's got a real brain under his turban."

"Helped you with what?"

"We did some detective work, bro, and then wrote the CO an anonymous letter with all the details of Kent and Shumansky's black market deal. Turns out it wasn't just booze, but prescription drugs too. Even food from the mess was winding up in restaurants in the city."

"So you're going to have a new boss when you get back."

The new boss didn't fuck around. He had Mark in his office on Mark's first day back, and there was no bullshit about.

"How was the exercise? I'm sure we'll enjoy working together." Company Sergeant Major Montaigne got right to it with no wasted words. "I've studied the records, Heaney, and it's clear that you weren't involved in what happened. It's also clear that you hate paperwork, but you're the one who knows more about the stores here than anyone else, so until I find a replacement for Master Corporal Shumansky, you will be taking over his job.

"You will work with Corporal Wilkinson, who understands record-keeping but doesn't know anything about stores, and when we board that plane for Croatia in ten weeks, you will have ensured that 2 PPCLI will be taking with it the best-equipped field hospital in the history of the Canadian army."

This guy didn't fuck around.

"You will have access to me twenty-four seven, and you will use that access wisely. I do not want to run out of penicillin half-way through the op, just because you didn't want to bother me. Is that clear?"

"Yes, sir." Where had they found this guy?

He passed Mark a slim folder. Inside was an outline of what looked like a basic first aid course. Plus a lot of stuff about general health in third-world countries.

"You want to give courses to all the men."

"That's right. Croatia has a civilization that goes back thousands of years, but it's been a combat zone for long enough now that conditions may be as unsanitary as any third-world location. I do not want our men getting sick because they think that they're on holiday in North Dakota. I also want them all to get a basic review of combat first aid. We don't need anybody dying because the guy next to him didn't know how to put a pressure dressing on a wound."

That made sense.

"Now, look at the last page."

Mark looked. It was a partial list of the UMS staff. His own name was at the top.

"These are the people that you want to teach it?"

"That's right. But I've only been here two weeks, so I'd appreciate your comments."

Mark looked over the list. It was almost exactly the names he'd have picked himself. "I'd replace Walters with Dosanjh, but otherwise it looks fine, sir."

"Dosanjh. The young guy that was out on ex with you and Charlie Company? You sure about that? He's not even a year out of Med-A. Only nineteen years old, right? How are the guys going to react to instruction from a wet-nose?"

"He handled some tough situations out on the ex, sir. The guys in Charlie Company'll pass the word that he's okay. The thing is, he's really smart, but he seems to be able to explain things to guys without pissing them off. I heard him telling guys how to take care of their frostbite, and they seemed to understand him better than anyone else. The guys he treated didn't come back with infections."

"Okay. You know them all and I don't, so write him in." Montaigne picked up another paper from his desk. "This is a revised schedule. The CO wants the men to get these courses, and I agree. Wilkinson will deal with the paperwork side of it, but I want you to sort it all out with the instructors. Make it clear to them that their teaching has to be as simple as possible. Seriously, Heaney, most of the soldiers in 2PPCLI aren't exactly Nobel prize winners. If you can teach them to boil water before they drink it, keep their dicks wrapped when they poke the local broads, and get a pressure dressing on a bleeding buddy, you'll have done better than I expect." Montaigne stood, indicating that the meeting was over.

"Can I make a suggestion, sir?"

"Of course."

"The med staff needs to get some PT. Sergeant Kent didn't…"

Montaigne cut him off. "Already done. They all bitched, but they've all been doing it for two weeks."

For the next month, Mark didn't have time to scratch his ass. Montaigne hadn't said anything about working overtime, but the workload was enormous. The store's situation was insane. Shumansky had been keeping two sets of books, and in addition to figuring out what wasn't there that should be, Mark had to deal with a steady stream of shipments of supplies and equipment for Croatia.

The First Battalion of the PPCLI was over there now, so he'd be arriving at an existing hospital, but when he'd mentioned that to Staff Sergeant Montaigne, all he got was a look that could have blistered paint, and a curt "Expect nothing."

So he dug in and did his best. Wilkinson worked with the Battalion RSM to schedule the health and first aid classes, and Mark worked with the instructors to make sure that the classes actually had some value. He knew they'd still have guys coming in with drippy dicks, and with water-borne diseases, but he hoped it wouldn't be as many as if they hadn't done the courses. He gradually got control of the supply situation, and finally, the day came when the last group of grunts got their lecture on STDs, and the last box was labeled and ready to go on the planes. He slept for eighteen hours, partied with Sandy and Dean for about eighteen more to celebrate Sandy's promotion to Corporal, then slept for twenty-four.

Two days later, on the 14th of June, they flew out of the sweltering, mosquito-infested Winnipeg summer. The talk on the plane was subdued. Rumors about the situation in Somalia had been getting stronger and stronger, but a few days ago, every newspaper and TV station in the country had gone berserk with stories of the Airborne beating, torturing, and executing civilians.

The emotional pain of getting booted from the country's elite regiment had never really healed for Mark or his two friends. But when Sandy showed them the cover of a newsmagazine he'd bought at the airport newsstand, with a photo of a soldier gloating as he held up the beaten and bloodied face of a teenage kid toward the camera, Dean summed it up for all of them.

"Looks like we're the lucky ones after all."

CHAPTER 19

A week later, they weren't so sure. They'd been cooped up on the plane for eighteen hours—even when it had been on the ground for refueling—and when they'd finally staggered off, they had to start unloading the aircraft, and reloading everything onto trucks. Personal kit and barrack boxes went onto one set of trucks. Food and mess supplies went onto another. Combat equipment had its own set of trucks. And of course, Mark had to make sure that medical supplies went where they needed to go.

A few of the officers, plus some senior NCOs had flown in several days earlier, but even with them directing things, the scene was a nightmare. Most of the men had been awake for over twenty-four hours, some had been airsick, they were jet-lagged, and the realization that they were a long way from home, in a place where many of the locals would as soon kill them as look at them had finally set in.

But they did the job, and eventually, the last box had been loaded onto the last truck, and the grunts piled onto the wagon train themselves and most were unconscious before they left the Zagreb airfield.

They'd been posted to Sector West, supposedly a fairly peaceful area, and the first they saw of it, after a night on the road, sleeping as well as they could in the convoy, was sunrise on a city of tents.

No three thousand years of Croatian civilization, no ancient cathedrals in towns with narrow, twisting streets. Just acres and acres of fucking tents. "Brilliant." Mark overheard someone say. "We coulda taken the bus to Shilo and it woulda looked just the same."

Shilo was a training area a little ways south of Winnipeg, and Mark had to agree that the tent city he was looking at here wasn't much different than the tent city at Shilo. Or at any of a dozen other training areas.

He looked around. The camp was on flat ground that had probably once been farmland, but there were mountains visible in most directions, and he'd read that the country was pretty rugged.

Other differences gradually became obvious. All the vehicles were painted white, with the letters "UN" in blue on the sides, and most of the soldiers he could see were in some uniform he didn't recognize.

"French," said somebody. "There's a few troops from some different third-world countries, but mostly it's us and the French."

Great. Word was that the French troops would run away at the first sign of aggression, and the Canadians had all been hoping that they'd be posted to someplace on their own. No such luck.

In-clearing, which was called AAG for reasons Mark never did learn, wasn't too bad. The officers and NCOs that had come over in the advance party had obviously worked hard to make sure it went smoothly, and that paid off. There were a few fuck-ups, but no more than he'd seen on bases back home. Score another one for Colonel Jeffries.

Like everybody else, Mark got a UN ID, and a cheesy-looking blue baseball cap with the UN logo on it. "This'll really scare the shit out of the Serbs and Croatians, won't it?" he said to the soldier behind him in the line.

Once AAG was completed, nobody had anything on his mind except finding the tent he'd been assigned, and hitting the cot for some serious rack time. "Let the Frogs handle things till tomorrow morning."

The next day was duty assignment and endless lectures. As a medic, Mark didn't have to attend the lectures, but Dean found him that evening and started complaining even before he was fully inside Mark's tent.

"Do you have any idea how fucked this is?"

From Mark's point of view, things weren't bad at all. Montaigne had run a combat/peacekeeping med unit before, and he'd made sure that the UMS was in good shape, but Mark was pretty sure Dean didn't want to hear about that, so he just said, "Bad?"

"Bad? *Bad*? This is so fucked that it makes 'bad' look good." He flopped onto the webbing chair beside Mark's cot. "I won't go through the whole sad four hours of lectures bro, but the bottom line is we might as well have left our weapons back in Canada." He jumped up in anger, then sat right back down again in frustration. "We can take 'em on patrol, but we can't load them."

Mark couldn't believe what he was hearing. "You carry unloaded weapons? What are you supposed to do in the face of hostility? Club your attacker unconscious?"

"I guess. We all get issued one magazine, but it has to be carried in a pocket. Get caught with a magazine in your weapon and you can get fuckin' charged by the RSM."

Mark had never heard that much disgust in Dean's voice.

"They might as well just ask us to paint targets on our chests and backs."

The weeks that followed proved Dean right. The UN soldiers' reputation for cowardice, combined with the fact that the combatants knew the Peacekeepers were under strict orders not to engage in any confrontational behavior, made the whole operation a joke.

They were in Croatia, a long way from any official battle zone, but enough of the local population was of Serbian descent that tensions were high, and "incidents" were common. Mark had to laugh at that word. It sounded like somebody bumping into somebody else by accident in a crowded bar, and maybe exchanging a couple of punches. What it actually meant, was "atrocities". Armed gangs, sometimes soldiers, sometimes civilians, from one side or the other would go on a killing spree, and whatever the reason, the result was the same—more corpses.

The killers were usually efficient, but sometimes there were survivors, and the survivors would wind up in the UMS.

It didn't take the men of 2 PPCLI long to realize that any vehicle containing young men probably contained weapons and explosives as well. In a sane world, the Peacekeepers would have been allowed to keep the peace, by stopping, searching, and detaining; but in the bizarre world of the UN's Operation Harmony, the stopping and searching could only take place with the suspects' permission, and the usual response to a request to search was, "Fuck off!" And often, search requests were accompanied by an AK47 pointed at the Peacekeeper's face.

Morale went straight into the tank, and the only thing that made it tolerable was that it seemed there was no innocence. If they'd had to stand by while a group of vicious killers assaulted a peace-loving community, it would have been different, but here, as far as the Canadians on patrol could tell, everybody was just as vicious as everybody else, and the soldiers' attitude quickly became, "Who gives a shit. The sooner they kill each other, the better."

"We're just babysitters, Mark." It was Sandy Stephens in his tent this time. "Babysitters with our hands tied. There's hundreds of years of recycled hatred at work out there, and none of them are innocent."

Sandy had bought a bottle of slivovitz from some farmer and was well into it. Drinking was strictly forbidden, but what was the choice? Mark had heard that real slivovitz was brandy made from plums, but what the locals had was homebrew made from whatever fruit or vegetables they could get their hands on. It was pure moonshine, about as smooth as a mouthful of fishhooks, but it was what was available, and with enough Coke to drown the flavor it was drinkable.

"Canada's multicultural, right?" Sandy waved the bottle at him. "We got every race and ethnic group and religion you can think of, all living together. We get along, right? I mean, do you give a shit that my skin's a different color than yours? And what about your CSM, Montaigne. He's a Frog, right? Do we care about that?"

He'd reached the stage where the slivovitz was going straight from the bottle down his throat, and he answered his own question. "We do not care. His great-granddaddy and our great granddaddies did their best to kill each other, and his home province is even trying to secede from the fucking country, and we don't care."

Mark took the bottle from Sandy's hand, and set it on the floor, on the far side of his cot.

"I know what you're saying, but I don't have the answer any more than you do. In Vancouver, in the area I lived anyway, half the population was Chinese, half was white, and the other half was from India. We all got along." There was really nothing more to say. Every soldier in the Canadian Peacekeeping force had this conversation ten times every day, and none of them had an answer.

A few minutes later, Dean entered the tent. "Well, what a lively fucking party this is."

Mark picked up Sandy's bottle and passed it to Dean. "Here. Drink enough of this and you'll be miserable, too. There's some Coke under my cot if you want it."

Dean took a long swallow straight from the bottle, gagged, but kept it down. "Fuck, that's awful."

"Go grab a chair from the UMS. If anybody says anything, tell 'em I said it was okay."

Dean was back a minute later with a folding chair. "So, did Sandy tell you the news?"

"What news? That this situation is seriously fucked?"

"We're moving out tomorrow."

"Where to?"

"Coupla Charlie Company platoons got a five-day patrol into the hills north of here. Me and Super Newfie here," he nodded to Sandy who was now snoring gently, "are going to be running recce for them."

"They gonna let you carry loaded weapons?"

"We're each running a three-man patrol. I don't know about him, but any patrol I run is not going to be carrying their magazines in their fucking pockets."

"You need a medic?"

"Each platoon'll probably have a medic, but we don't get to bring one along on sneak-and-peek. I asked."

All long-range patrols took a medic, but Montaigne had made it clear to Mark that he wouldn't be going out any time soon. "I need you here. I promise that you'll get out, but not till after the first month," he had said.

It was a compliment about his ability, Mark knew that, but it still hurt. Running sick parade. Organizing stores. Organizing a health lecture series for the Engineering Company that had rotated in three weeks after them.

Boring.

He did the work, and he drank. It might have been tolerable if there was something to do evenings and weekends, but there wasn't. Every soldier would get a couple of seventy-two hour passes, and one big seventeen-day leave during the tour, but that was it, and Mark knew that his first seventy-two wasn't going to be coming up anytime soon.

When he wasn't actually on duty, he could walk, or try to catch a ride to the village a couple of miles away, but the village was even more depressing than the camp, and the only reason to go there was to try to buy booze.

There was no nightlife in the village. Fuck, there was barely any life during the day. Half the houses were burned-out shells. The people were mostly empty-eyed and miserable looking, clinging desperately to life in their village for the simple reason that there was nowhere else for them to go.

Somewhere in the country, there were cities and towns and villages where people lived normal lives, but Mark knew he wasn't likely to see those areas. There wasn't much point in basing a Peacekeeping force in an area that was already peaceful, and he knew that as long as he was in Croatia, he'd be stationed in areas that were devastated by ethnic violence, areas where the Croatian majority was attacking the Serbian minority, but the Serbian minority was large enough to fight back.

He treated the wounded as well as he could and medivacked out those he couldn't treat. Montaigne had shown him some official UN booklet on field hospitals. It went into great detail about "medical support infrastructure", based on the concept of the "golden hour", which assured that no casualty brought to a field hospital would ever be more than an hour away from lifesaving surgery.

They'd had a good laugh about that. The theory was great. Ninety-something percent of casualties could be saved if they got the right treatment within an hour. The problem wasn't with the theory. The problem was with the reality of watching people die because the golden hour routinely dragged out to two or three or four hours. Mark was pretty sure that if some visiting UN bureaucrat stubbed his toe, there'd be a chopper on the site in five minutes, but if it was just some farmer who'd had his leg blown off by a landmine or a grunt who'd been run over by a jeep, forget it.

When Dean and Sandy had come back, their story wasn't much different. "What a waste. Two platoons, two recce parties, and they could have sent a pair of boy scouts in and accomplished the same job."

"Yeah, they'd have seen exactly what we saw. A pretty mountain valley full of peace-loving Croatian farmers, not one of whom had a clue about what happened to the three farms that were burned to the ground."

"Oh, I think they are hit by lightning," said Dean in his best mock-Croatian accent. "Three families vanished, three farms with nothing left but ashes, and nobody has a clue."

"There's a bunch of dead Serbs buried up there somewhere, but nobody saw anything, nobody did anything, and nobody knows anything."

Sandy pulled a jar out of his pack, opened it, took a big swallow, and passed it around. "At least they make better booze than the bozos around here."

"So these people got together one night and murdered their neighbors?"

"Actually, I don't think they did. I think it was probably a Croatian Army unit, or maybe one of the militias." Dean took his turn on the jar. "But none of the people we saw seemed very upset about it, so as far as I'm concerned they might as well have done it themselves."

"These people really don't care, Mark. You shoulda seen them. The only thing they were really worried about was how to divide up the land they'd liberated. Pubs and I were talking about it on the way back yesterday and we both have the same feeling—the best thing to do would be to cull the whole herd and give the place to somebody who really needs it. Like those poor starving fuckers in Somalia that haven't got anything at all. This place is a paradise compared to somewhere like Somalia, and all the stupid bastards here can think about is killing each other."

"We've been out on a lot of patrols since we got here, and this is great country. Farms, mountains, beautiful rivers. It's not as if there isn't enough to go around, so why can't they get along?"

Same old question. And as usual, they had no answer. The only answer they could find was to get drunk and not think about it.

"You know what I wish?"

Mark and Sandy looked at one another, and Mark spoke for both of them. "Same thing we wish, but you're just gonna have to fantasize and jerk off, cuz you ain't gonna get it."

"No. Well, yeah, but right now I wish I'd gone into the Engineers when I joined up." He drained the last swallow from the jar and reached into his pack for another. "You know some of 'em from when you were at Chilliwack, right?"

Mark nodded. Delta Company of 1 CER was camped practically next door.

"You talk to 'em some, right?"

"Sure. None of my close friends from those days are here, but I know some of the guys."

"They're not as fucked up as us grunts, are they?"

Mark was about to say that 1CER was far more fucked up than 2PPCLI, but he kept his mouth shut and thought about it. "You know, Pubs, you're right. I can't say that I've seen any of them dancing in the streets, but they do seem to be doing okay."

"Ya know why? I'll tell ya why. It's cuz they're actually doing something useful. They got sent over here to clear minefields and build roads and bridges, and that's what they're doing. And look at us. We're sent over to keep Croats and Serbs from killing each other, but the instant we got here, we got told we can't actually *do* anything. We roar around in our APCs with our cute fuckin' blue baseball caps, but God help any of us if we actually try to do some peacekeeping."

"You're right about that," Sandy was nodding. "Remember Harrison?" They all remembered Harrison. He'd stepped in and clobbered a couple of Croats who were kicking a Serb to death, and practically been cashiered for it. "I think you're right," Sandy continued. "The Engineers are doing okay. Sure, the bridges they fix get blown up again the next day, and these assholes lay more mines as fast as our guys clean up the old ones, but at least they get to do what they came here to do. And the same goes for you wogs, too."

Mark started to protest, but Sandy held up a hand and stopped him. "Think about it, dude. I know you've been complaining about the lack of support in medivac situations, but mostly you get to do your job, right? I mean, sure, sick parade is the same bunch of whiners and guys with drippy dicks, but I've seen you roaring around in that Unimog, hauling guys to the hospital and saving their asses. The reason you're pissed…" Sandy stopped and thought about it. "No, the two reasons you're pissed, is first, you're not getting any party time, and second, cuz you think you're missing out on all the glorious fun and excitement that us Peacekeepers are getting."

Alcohol was obviously starting to take over Sandy's brain, but Mark had to admit that, drunk or not, his friend had nailed it. Montaigne ran a good operation, there were real casualties to treat, and compared to a typical day in the UMS back home, his days here were okay. Driving the Unimog, a German-made ambulance that growled like a monster truck, was a blast. So what was he complaining about?

No party time, and no patrol time.

"Morning, Sergeant."

"Heaney."

"It's been over a month."

"I knew you'd be reminding me of that one of these days."

"In fact it's been over two months."

"I know, I know."

"So unless you want to have to medivac me out to a psychiatric facility, you're gonna have to let me out of here."

"I'd love to, but you have to understand that we've got a resupply truck coming in on Friday and I need you to ... "

"Dosanjh can handle that as well as I can, and you know it. C'mon Claude," it was the first time that Mark had called Montaigne by his first name, but he wasn't even aware of having done it, "either you cut me a seventy-two, and some patrol time, or I am gonna go so bat-shit weird that you'll come in here one morning and find me eating the fucking tent canvas."

Montaigne thought about it for a while, and finally said, "Yeah, you're right. And I probably need it as badly as you, don't I?"

Mark nodded. "Yup."

"Okay, go run sick parade, and check back with me when it's over. I'll try to find a patrol to send you out on for a couple of days, and if you kind of supervise Dosanjh for the first day of the resupply, I'll do what I can about a pass. Might not be till sometime next week, but I'll get it for you as soon as possible."

"Thanks, Sarge. And don't forget about getting out of here yourself once I'm back."

"Tuesday?"

"Too fuckin' right, Pubs. Tuesday it is."

"So where you gonna go?"

"I ... " That stopped Mark in his tracks. "Shit, I hadn't even thought about that."

"Well, maybe you oughta think about it. Truck is going to leave here on Tuesday for Zagreb whether you're on it or not, and you have to report back for duty on Friday whether you actually went anywhere or not."

"Yeah, man, you're right, but..." Mark realized he didn't have a clue. "Where do most guys go?"

"Most guys get off the truck in Zagreb, spend three days totally shit-faced, and come back with their wallets gone, and their dicks hurting whenever they piss. A few guys fly to Paris or Rome because those are the only places in Europe they've heard of, but they can't afford anything, so they hang out in some rat-bag hotel and come back broke, too. You and I, on the other hand, will go to Budapest and live like kings."

"Budapest? Where the..." and then the full meaning of what Dean had said sunk in. "You and me?"

"Can't let a little lost lamb like you go wandering around Europe alone, can I? If Sandy or me wasn't there to hold your hand, you'd spend three days drunk in Zagreb where everybody hates us, and you'd come back wondering why you bothered to go in the first place."

"But how do you know you can get your seventy-two at the same time?"

"I already got it. I'm scheduled for Sunday-Monday-Tuesday, but nobody else in my unit is off that week, so the Sergeant won't care if I push it back a couple of days."

"But I don't know anything about Budapest. In fact, I don't think I've ever *heard* of Budapest. Where..."

"Trust me."

"Okay, bro, I'm in your hands."

"Not fucking likely."

The patrol was as boring as Sandy and Dean had told him it would be. But cruising around the countryside and sitting up on top of the APC in gorgeous summer weather was about fifty times more enjoyable than what he'd been doing for the last two months, so he wasn't complaining, even if the flak jacket he had to wear was so stiff that he couldn't bend. They stopped at a couple of villages so that Mark could tend to some sick and wounded locals who were afraid to come to the UN compound, and then spent the next three days occupying a UN-designated check-point.

In theory, this meant that they would stop and search every vehicle that passed through in either direction. In practice, it meant that they searched a couple of horse-drawn farm wagons, and listened to carload after carload of young men tell them to go fuck themselves.

The powerful Browning 50-calibre machine guns mounted under armored cupolas on their M113s, and the Canadians' reputation for not running away like the French did, meant that nobody tried to kill them, but it was obvious to Mark that he'd be wise not to go wandering around the countryside by himself.

"Jimmy?"

"Yeah?"

Mark was trying to stay out of Dosanjh's hair while Dosanjh inventoried and stored the boxes that were coming off the truck.

"You know anything about Budapest?"

"Sure. Capital of Hungary. Amazing city."

"You've been there?"

"Me? You think that if my family could have afforded trips to Europe, I'd be in the Army? My parents came over from India when I was four, man, and they aren't doctors or scientists."

"So how do you know about Budapest, then?"

"Just because we were poor doesn't mean we were ignorant."

"Hey, keep your shirt on. I'm asking cuz I want to know the answer. *I* never heard of Budapest."

"Seriously?"

"Yeah."

Jimmy Dosanjh looked at him as if seeing some kind of strange alien. "You didn't take geography? Or European history? It's part of grade ten and eleven Socials, right?"

"I guess. I didn't really pay attention to that kind of stuff."

"The Austro-Hungarian Empire was one of the main powers in Europe right up to the end of the First World War. Budapest was pretty much the center of that. It's been a center of civilization for a thousand years or something. I'd kill to go there, even if the Russians did do their best to destroy it." Dosanjh put his clipboard down and stood up from the box he'd been kneeling beside. "So, if you've never heard of it, why are you asking?"

"I'm supposed to be going there in a couple of days, and I thought I'd better learn something."

Dosanjh shook his head in amazement, then got back to work.

It turned out to be everything Dosanjh had said and a thousand times more. They stayed in a hotel that looked like a castle, they ate strange but delicious food, they bought gorgeous whores, they visited real castles that made their hotel look small and cheap. And they came back with money in their pockets.

Fifty years of Russian domination had left the country's economy in ruins, but with the Russians gone, the Hungarians were working their butts off to get things back on track. Once they did, the hotels and the food wouldn't be cheap anymore, and the Hungarian women wouldn't be selling themselves to ignorant Canadian soldiers, but right now, in August 1993, they were still clawing their way back from the Russian darkness, and Mark was only too happy to have made his small financial contribution.

Sandy was waiting for them when they got off the truck. "So, what'd you bring me?"

"Real booze." Mark shook his duffel so that Sandy could hear the bottles clinking. "Man, you are not going to believe what you're about to hear."

"Neither are you."

"Huh?"

"We're outta here as of two weeks yesterday."

"What?" Mark really couldn't believe it.

"They declare peace while we were gone?" asked Dean.

"Peace? Get real. We're going to a real war zone."

"*What*?" This time Mark and Dean spoke simultaneously.

"We've got a new commander, and he's turning us loose."

Dean practically dropped his bag. "They ditched Colonel Jeffries? But I thought he'd be trying to get us more authority all along."

"No, not Jeffries. The whole operation's got a new commander. Some Frog General that ain't a pussy like most of his soldiers. He wants us down in Sector South because it's turning really ugly there, and he says we're the only people that he trusts.

"Holy shit!" Mark was amazed. "What did all the Frogs say when they heard that?"

"You would not believe how pissed they are. But who gives a fuck? If they'd stood up when the Croatians took over that dam and reservoir, maybe I'd care. It's because they've been such fucking cowards that we've had so much trouble, so fuck 'em."

They'd all heard about Sector South. Where Sector West had a relatively small Serb population, Sector South was home to a huge group of ethnic Serbs, and the fighting had been hot and heavy since the beginning of the war.

"So we're going in alone?"

"No. He's bringing in some Frogs, but we're the ones who are going to be on the front line. And if he's a real soldier, like he seems, then whatever French unit he brings in ain't gonna be pussies like the ones here."

That was true. The French military, in general, was known worldwide for retreating at the first opportunity, but Mark had read that some of their special forces units were really hardcore.

Sandy had more news. "And he wants us to start getting serious. Now."

"Here?"

"You bet, bro. I shot the tires out from under a carload of lippy militia fucks yesterday, and man, you shoulda seen them shit their pants when I opened up with the fifty. We had an interpreter along with us at that road-block so that he could make sure they passed the message along to all their people that our orders are changed and from now on if they fuck with us, they're going to get killed."

Mark thought about that. 2PPCLI was by far the most heavily armed force in the area. They'd brought over a full compliment of war-fighting equipment, including a heavy-weapons Support Company with 81mm mortars and TOW anti-armor guided missiles to back up the M113-based grunts. All the warring parties knew that, but they'd been able to get away with thumbing their noses at the boys in the M113s till now because they knew that the UN High Command had forbidden any engagement.

With that order ripped up, things were definitely going to change.

And change they did. There were two more confrontations where locals tried to bluff their way through checkpoints and both of those ended with a few rounds from the Brownings.

But Mark didn't have time to worry about that. Montaigne had gone into high gear, and when the order came to roll, Mark passed out in the back of a truck and didn't wake up for ten hours.

CHAPTER 20

The line between the Serb and Croat forces in Sector South was fairly straight except for one long bulge of Serb villages, called the Medak Salient, that stuck deeply into Croatian territory. A lot of formerly Serb-held positions had been wiped out in January when a French force had run away, but this one area remained. Colonel Jeffries had told them in a meeting before they left that the Croatians were known to be planning a massive attack and that they were not going to be impressed by white vehicles with "UN" printed on them.

"They believe that all they have to do is fire a few rounds at us and we'll run and let them get on with their butchery. You will teach them that this is no longer the case. You have General Cot's permission to return fire, and to use deadly force as you feel appropriate. And more than General Cot's permission, you have my *orders* to do so. I did not bring you over here to serve as babysitters, or as targets. I brought you over here to impose peace, and that is what you are now going to do."

The men had cheered, and the Colonel had sent them to their respective units for fuller briefing.

Montaigne had told his Med unit about the Medak Salient, and that the UMS was going to be practically on the battlefield. "Nothing we can do about it. It's where our soldiers are going to be, and we have to be where they are."

Sector South headquarters for 2PPCLI was the town of Medak, and the shit was already hitting the fan when they arrived. A Croatian Guards Brigade—real soldiers, not the half-witted farm boys they'd had to deal with in Sector West—commenced the assault on the Medak Salient at almost the exact moment the lead Canadian platoon was moving into the village of Medak.

Shells were coming down everywhere, but it sounded to Mark, who was monitoring radio communication, that 9 Platoon, and the other platoons that had followed it in, had managed to find shelter in abandoned buildings and were doing everything they could to sandbag their positions, and were maintaining discipline.

The first 'man down' came in just before 1600, but there was no request for a medic. "He's okay. Nothing broken, and we've got the bleeding stopped. We'll bring him out when things quiet down."

The next one was more urgent. "We're sending Knight out with a 113 to bring a medic in. We can't risk moving him." But before the 113 roared into the area where the convoy was parked, the next call came in. "Better send two medics."

Mark looked at Montaigne for permission, then turned to Dosanjh and said, "You up for it, kid?"

The M113 took some small arms fire, and there was a fourth casualty by the time they got there, but they pulled it off. Nobody died. The grunts gave them plenty of covering fire when they moved from building to building, and besides, once he went into medic mode, Mark didn't really notice what was going on around him anyway.

Darkness brought an end to the shelling, and when a recce platoon reported that the Croatian unit had pulled back, the main Canadian column rolled in and life returned to semi-normal.

The grunts and the heavy-weapons boys worked through the night constructing fortifications and setting up defensive positions, while Montaigne and his med unit searched for, and found a secure position for the UMS. It was one of the few buildings in town with a real basement. "We'll set up on the main floor, but if things get ugly, we can move downstairs. It ain't pretty down there; it stinks, and it's dark. But they can blow the building into the next world, and we'll live through it," was how Montaigne put it.

If the Croatians had pressed their attack through the night, they might have succeeded. But Serb reinforcements rolled in from all over Yugoslavia and in two days, they managed to fight the Croatians to a standstill. They'd lost ground, though. The Medak Salient had been pinched off, and all that remained was an isolated group of villages occupied by Serbs, plus 2PPCLI dug in Medak itself.

It might have gotten worse. The Croatians had the manpower and the firepower to finish the job, but the main Serbian army began shelling the Croatian city of Karlovac, and then dropped a couple of long-range missiles right into Zagreb, and finally the two governments, under pressure from the international community, agreed to yet another cease-fire.

"The governments of Serbia and Croatia have signed a treaty called 'The Medak Pocket Agreement'," said the Colonel. "Under the terms of this agreement, Croatian forces will withdraw back to their positions preceding 9 September—the day we got here—and we are charged with the responsibility of making sure that the agreement is implemented and adhered to."

Once the briefings got down to the Company and Platoon level, it was a different story.

"The deal is," Sandy was back from a day of sneak-and-peak, "not only do a lot of the local Croatian commanders not know about this agreement, they probably wouldn't follow it even if they did. They've got some Serb villages under their guns, and nobody is going to stop them other than by force."

"So, what are we supposed to be doing?"

"The plan is that tomorrow morning, Charlie Company plus some of the Frogs, take over the Serbian front line. Then, in the late afternoon, once the heavy-weapons guys have their anti-tank shit in place, Charlie Company moves out and secures a crossing on the main road that separates the Serbs and Croats."

Mark dug into his barrack box and pulled out a bottle of brandy that he'd brought back from Hungary. "Want some?"

"Yeah, but not too much. I've gotta be crisp tomorrow."

Mark poured a couple of small shots and put the bottle away. "So they've gone and put themselves out in the middle of a road, right under the guns of both armies. Then what?"

"Yeah, they'll be exposed alright, but they've got all the anti-tank shit covering them, so anyone who attacks is going to take serious casualties. Anyway, the next morning, Delta Company, plus a French Company, will cross through and occupy the Croatian front line. Once that's secure, Battalion tactical headquarters move in, set up shop, oversee the Croatian withdrawal, and enforce a demilitarized zone."

"How do you know all this?"

"Cuz I'm supposed to be leading the recce platoon that goes in ahead of Battalion HQ and reports on what the Croatians are actually doing, as opposed to what they say they're doing."

"And you say that the Croatian commanders in the field haven't actually received orders from Zagreb to cooperate?"

"Not as far as we know. And they probably wouldn't cooperate even if they had received orders. That's why the heavy-weapons unit is going to be there."

"This is not going to work."

"You know it, and I know it. And I think General Cot knows it too, but he doesn't have any choice. Unless we go in there with a major show of firepower, we might as well go home. He's come down here himself to run the show."

"What does the CO think about that?"

"Word is that he's cool with it. Apparently, he knows Cot from somewhere before, and they're on the same wavelength about peacekeeping, which means your UMS is going to be busy."

Mark didn't see all of what happened the next day, but he followed it on the radio, and it was obvious that Sandy had been right. The Croatians had no intention of moving back, and as soon as Charlie Company moved out of town, they came under small-arms fire. Since they were still in the trees it was possible the Croats thought they were a Serb force, so they were ordered to move into the open, where the white paint and UN logos would be clearly visible. All this accomplished was to make them the target of a barrage of heavier fire. Not just machine guns, but rocket-propelled grenades, and 20mm anti-aircraft guns.

They hauled ass back into the trees and got busy proving that things had changed in the world of peacekeeping. For the next fifteen hours they shot it out with the Croatians.

Three hours into it, the call came in from 7 Platoon. "We need a medic." 7 Platoon had bunkered down in the village of Licki Citluck, and were in the middle of the heaviest fighting of all.

"No way." Montaigne had seen Mark moving to get his jump bag. "That's less than 150 meters from the Croatian line, and you can't get in there. No one can get in there."

"I can." Dean Publicover had brought over coffee and a meal for Mark at the UMS, and had been sitting listening to the radio along with the med staff. "I've been in and out of there, and I can get Mark in."

Montaigne looked at the two of them. "Fuckin' Airborne rejects," he said, half to himself. Then to Mark, "How good is he?"

"He's *real* good, Claude."

"And I'm also smart enough to know it's not worth risking a medic unless there's a good chance of pulling it off," Dean added.

Montaigne got on the radio. "Zero seven Alpha, this is eight-three Alpha. Give me your sit-rep. Over."

"Eight-three Alpha, this is Zero seven Alpha. Private Dubois has taken an AK-47 round in the gut. We've got the bleeding stopped, but we need him taken out on a number-one priority."

"No shit," Mark thought to himself. A bullet in the gut was guaranteed death unless you could get to a real hospital. Even if there wasn't enough internal bleeding to kill you right away, peritonitis would kill you within a day or two. And it was a painful way to die.

"Roger Zero seven Alpha. I'll send a starlight in with a man from the Romeo platoon on the understanding that you will provide whatever covering fire or assistance they require. Over."

"Understood eight-three Alpha, over."

It was an epic that Mark would never forget. They did the first two klicks in a 113, with Dean driving like a madman through the open spots, dodging and swerving, trying not to give the Croatian gunners a target they could track; and finished by fishtailing into a hollow after a narrow miss sent dirt and trees flying not five meters from their vehicle.

"The easy part's over, bro. From here on, we earn our pay." Dean shut off the engine and pulled out the key. "Key's on the floor in front of the gas pedal."

Mark didn't have to ask why Dean wasn't taking it with him. If Mark was the only one who got back, he'd need the key.

"We're safe in this hollow. Grab your jump bag and come on out so I can give you the lay of the land." Dean led him to the far edge of their sheltered area and got down on his belly. "Follow me."

Mark took a good look. What seemed like open ground actually had an old streambed running through it, and there was enough cover to make it to the next forested hill. He dropped down and spent fifteen minutes getting intimate with the dirt. Dragging and pushing the jump bag made it a lot harder than it would have been otherwise, and knowing that if his head or his ass lifted more than a few inches it'd get blown off was terrifying, but he'd done it on ex, so he kept his mouth shut and kept moving.

"Village is down there."

They were standing behind the hill and temporarily safe from Croatian fire. The village was maybe two hundred meters away, but Mark didn't like what he saw. The streambed they'd been following would give them cover most of the way, but the last fifty meters...

"Pubs, it's a plowed fucking field after the streambed turns. There is *no* cover."

"You're thinking like a grunt."

Mark took a long look. The streambed didn't just stop in the middle of the field, of course. "You *can't* be serious."

"I've done it, bro. Trust me."

Where the streambed turned, it ran straight toward the forest where the Croatians were throwing steady fire into the village. "It goes straight into the fucking Croatian Army."

"Nope." He handed Mark a pair of binoculars.

"Jesus, Pubs, you're insane." The stream did run into the forest, but a shallow ditch, running from the village, joined it just before it entered the trees. "So we are going to go over and have a smoke with the Croatians and tell them to pretend they don't see us while we crawl along a ditch that can't be more than a foot deep, not five meters from where they are machine-gunning our buddies?"

"You knew I was crazy before you volunteered for this one. But I'm not stupid. That ditch is never shallower than eighteen inches. I've crawled in it. I know. And after twenty meters we're behind a stone wall."

"It could be eighteen *feet* deep, Pubs. They don't have to see us. We're gonna be five meters from them. I make *noise* when I drag this thing." He kicked the jump bag.

"They're firing machine guns and artillery, remember? Nobody in that forest could hear you if you dragged your fucking ghetto blaster. Now, shut up and let me talk on this radio."

"Zero seven Alpha, this is Romeo. I'm about to bring your starlight in. Over."

"Zero seven Alpha here. Where are you Romeo? Over"

"About ten minutes out, and we're going to need a little help for the last two minutes. Over."

"What do you need, Romeo? Over."

"Zero seven Alpha, when I call for it, I need you to put some hurt on the machine gun emplacement at GR 654357. Over."

Silence. Mark could imagine the Lieutenant checking the map, hunting down grid reference 654357.

"Romeo, this is Zero seven Alpha. We are pinned down here, there is no way we can take that emplacement out. Over."

"I'm not asking you to take the fucking thing out, just to lay some lead on it." Dean temporarily lost his cool and abandoned standard radio procedure. Mark knew that the RSM would roast his bones for that, but at least he'd made his point clear. "Can you do that when I call it in? Over."

There was a brief silence, then, "I can put some fire on it, Romeo, but only for a minute. They've got a clear shot at any position we can fire on them from. Over."

"A minute is plenty, Zero seven Alpha. I will not be able to talk, but when I want you to open up, I'll just start clicking, like this." He hit the push-to-talk switch six or eight times. "You okay with that? Over."

"I copy that, Romeo. I will put my radio on squelch when you give me the word and then wait for your clicks. You'll know I've got your message when the rounds start coming in. Over."

"Good. Just tell whoever is doing the shooting that they'd better not fire short. You understand? You put short rounds in there and you are going to be kissing your medic goodbye. Over."

"Sure. I…" Silence. Then, "You *can't* be coming in that way." The voice was aghast.

"No other way, Zero seven Alpha. You want Dubois stitched up, then Florence Nightingale is going to need your covering fire. We are heading out now, so turn to squelch and wait for my signal. Out."

"Roger Romeo, and good luck. Zero seven Alpha out."

Dean shut off his radio, put it back in its holster, and dropped down to the dirt. "Time to go."

The first hundred and fifty meters were easy. The stream was actually deeper here than it had been in the last section, and they made good time. Dean had stopped just short of the turn and stuck a small mirror out so that he could see around the bend. "We're clear. I'm going to go a little faster than you, and I'll set up shop right where the ditch comes in. There's a bit of an overhang there, and if anything goes wrong I should be able to give you some covering fire while you hightail it back to the trees. When you arrive, I'll signal for the Lieutenant to open fire. When the firing starts, you forget about noise and make speed."

A lot of responses went through Mark's mind, but he just said, "Let's motor."

Dean was gone like a worm with a rocket pack, and Mark followed, making the best speed he could, not looking up, until he bumped into Dean's foot. For the last few meters, the gunfire seemed to be coming from right above them, and the noise was deafening. Even when it stopped his ears were ringing so badly that he couldn't hear anything. At least Dean had been right about that part of it.

Dean must have been busy clicking because gunfire erupted from the village, and he could see tracer rounds from two positions converging just over his head. Dean was gone with the first round, and Mark humped along behind as fast as he could, no longer worrying about silence, just trying to keep his ass and his jump bag from showing above the top of the ditch.

Eighteen meters. Fifteen. Twelve. The gun behind him opened up, and he knew that was the end of their help from the village. Eight meters. Five. Four. It was like crawling through molasses, dragging a piano. The harder he struggled, the slower he seemed to go.

And the jump bag. He knew that if he tried for speed, it would catch on something and tip up enough to show. He took a deep breath, thought of what his father would do, and forced himself to slow down. The gunners behind him had stopped firing, and he knew they'd be taking a good look around. This was *not* the time for haste.

Dean took the bag from him when he got to the wall, and on hands and knees they made good time the last thirty meters. The Lieutenant was waiting for them where the wall joined the first building, and motioned them through the open doorway. "I'm Lieutenant Vickers. We can talk about how fucking crazy you are later, right now, Dubois needs you pretty bad."

That was the understatement of the year, but an hour later, Mark was pretty sure he'd live, at least for twenty-four more hours. "You understand about gut shots, right?" he said to the Lieutenant.

"Yeah. Peritonitis and one-hundred percent mortality if he doesn't get to a real hospital."

"That's right. I've cleaned him up, stitched up what I can, and I've got an antibiotic drip running into the IV, but it won't mean shit if he's not out of here tomorrow."

"That's out of your hands and mine, Corporal. At least you've given him a chance. Why don't you get some rest? I'll put one of my men in here in case he takes a turn for the worse, and you get some sleep."

"I'm not sleepy right now. Corporal Publicover lugged an extra weapon in; maybe I could put it to use."

"Well, I ... "

"You bet, bro. I got just the job for you."

"I believe I'm still in charge of assigning jobs here, Corporal Publicover."

"For sure, sir, but I've been thinking about your position, and, well it's that gun we crawled under that's causing most of your problems, isn't it?"

"God damn right." Vickers was angry.

"If it wasn't there, you could set up one of your 113s just to the west of the church and raise some real shit with the fifty. Clear out that forest in about two minutes."

Mark didn't have a clear enough picture of the village and the forest in his mind to know what Dean was talking about, but Vickers obviously did. "You got that pretty fast."

"For a grunt, you mean?"

"Sorry. What did you have in mind? Crawling back out in the ditch and taking it out single-handed?"

"Why not? I've got a couple of grenades, you give me some HE, or nape, or plastic; whatever you've got, and I won't even have to be accurate."

"I can't order you to do that."

"Nobody fucking *asked* you to order me. What I'm *asking* for is something that will explode."

Vickers didn't budge. "And you're going to drag Heaney along with you?"

"No fucking way. I wouldn't drag his wog ass within a hundred meters of anything that could explode, but he's ex-airborne, and a better shot than anyone in your platoon is going to be. I want him set up with my rifle and binoculars, in a position where he can start killing Croatians if I goof."

"You saw how fast they lined up on us when we gave you your covering fire."

"So he only gets two or three. Maybe that'll be enough. And besides, my weapon has a flash adapter, and if he's firing single shot, and no tracers, they're going to have a hell of a time finding him. Think about where the sun goes down."

"Heaney?"

"Works for me, sir. But before I get into position, I want my jump bag out at the end of the wall in case I have to run out and put a Band-Aid on John Wayne here."

"You guys *are* crazy, aren't you?"

"Yup, and we're also braver and smarter than anyone you've worked with before. Now show me what you've got that'll go boom."

Half an hour later, Mark was in the tower of a small church, with the sun starting to set behind him. Dean's rifle was up on a sandbag rest, and he knew that with a setup like that he could shoot two-centimeter groups at the hundred and fifty-meter range he was looking at. With the sun in their eyes, it would take them forever to locate him.

It almost went the way they planned it. Almost.

Dean crawled out, hunkered down under the slight overhang, primed his homemade atomic bomb, leaped to his feet, hurled it straight over the armored shield the gun was poking through and dropped back down. Two seconds later, there was a blinding supernova of light, and then an explosion that hurt Mark's ears.

Everyone at the gun position would have died instantly, and the gun itself would be scrap metal.

The problem was that not everyone had been at the gun position. Ten seconds after the explosion, with Dean just standing up to start his sprint back to the village, somebody opened up from the forest and cut him down. Mark wanted to sprint himself. Down the stairs, out along the wall, grab his bag and out to his friend, but he forced himself to hold steady.

There. Movement in the trees. He lined up on the vague shape and waited. The man stepped quickly from the edge of the trees, already in the motion of throwing a grenade, but Mark was ready and dropped him in his tracks.

Now he had to sprint.

Down the stairs. Yelling at Vickers, "Get that 113 in position, right fucking now!" as he raced through the command post.

He dove out the final doorway and hit the ground in a long roll, then did a racing crab-walk to his jump bag.

Into the ditch, and into slo-mo. Bullets were slamming into the dirt above him and whining over his head, but he knew that they couldn't see him. They'd have figured out that someone had been in the ditch, and would just be throwing as much lead at it as they could until they could get a mortar hauled around into position.

"Dumb fucker must have been out having a shit, huh?" Dean was breathing heavily and had his hands clamped to his side. "You know it's only a question of time before they start shelling us, right? Maybe you should go back while you still can."

"Fuck off. Let me look." He scrunched around, flipped the bag open, and hauled out a bag of saline and one of the big sterile pads. "Let go of yourself, asshole. I can't fix you if I can't see what's broken."

Dean forced himself to relax, and Mark ripped his shirt open.

Ugly. Big fucking mess of hamburger between his hip and his short rib, but right along the side, so maybe, just maybe, no internal organs were trashed.

"How's it look."

"Looks like you ain't dead yet." Mark pulled another dressing from the bag and stuck it in Dean's mouth. "Bite down on that, hard. Forecast calls for pain."

Kerwhump!

The first shell was twenty meters long and way back toward the village, but Mark knew they'd find their range with a couple more shots, and then they'd walk shells all along the ditch.

He ripped open the bag of saline and rinsed away the blood and dirt. Dean writhed in pain but kept control.

"As long as you don't get killed, it looks like you're gonna live." He dropped the dirty dressing, pulled another one from the bag, opened the package and slapped it over the exit wound. "Hold that in place."

Dean did as he was told and Mark threw a smaller pad over the entrance hole, then did his best to tape the dressings in place without exposing any of his or Dean's body parts to the rifle fire that was still pouring in.

Kerwhump!

Short this time, but not by much. The next one would be right in the ditch, and after that, they had very little time. The Croatians would drop mortar rounds into the ditch every ten meters, and keep on doing it till they were sure there was nothing left alive.

Or until Vickers got the fucking fifty going, and sent the mortar crew to hell.

"Can you crawl?"

"Not fast enough to get back before they mortar every inch of this ditch."

"Now who's thinking like a grunt? We're going the other way. Back along the streambed. Now, can you crawl, or do I have to drag you?"

"Guess we'll find out."

Dean started moving. He was obviously way into the hurt locker, but he bore down and moved. Too slow...

Kerwhump!

That one was right in the ditch. Twenty seconds to load and fire, so forty more seconds if they put them in at ten-meter intervals.

"Hold still." Mark crawled right over his friend, knowing that his ass would be showing, but knowing that it was their only chance. "Okay, you crawl, I'll pull. Go!"

Kerwhump!

They were at the corner, but Dean was losing it, and Mark had to risk showing himself to get enough leverage to pull. He was around the corner, into the main streambed, and with a huge pull, he dragged Dean behind him.

Kerwhump!

The earth shook, and dirt and stones, and something else, spattered all around them.

"You owe me a new jump bag," said Mark, pulling shreds of bandage out of his hair. "Now, c'mon, let's keep..."

That was as far as he got. The roar of the Browning cut him off mid-sentence, and after that he just stayed hunkered down and tried to make sure Dean didn't bleed to death. Vickers would either waste the mortar team or he wouldn't. Nothing Mark could do about that. In half an hour it'd be full dark and he'd probably be able to walk back standing up, but for now, best to keep his head down.

CHAPTER 21

"Heaney! Hey, Heaney! You out there?"

The firing had lasted only about ten minutes, and now someone was calling his name. He was about to answer when Dean grabbed his shirt.

"Stay down. Wait and see if this idiot draws any fire."

Mark waited, but there was no shooting, and soon he could hear another voice calling.

"You reckon it's okay?"

"Yeah, that last one was Vickers. If the Croats had left a sniper behind, he wouldn't pass up a shot at an officer."

Mark slowly got to his feet and said, "Over here, sir. We're okay, but we're going to need a stretcher."

They got Dean back to the village, and Mark washed his wounds properly and put on clean dressings he'd robbed from the platoon's first aid kit.

"You'll be okay, Pubs. But the forecast calls for more pain, and Dubois over there needs the painkillers more than you do. You gonna be able to handle it?"

"Guess we'll find out about that, too."

The firefight ended all along the line that night. The Croatians had taken a shitkicking, and were ready to talk when General Cot came down the road the next morning.

Mark only heard about that later, though, because he'd spent almost the whole day sleeping. He'd stayed up through the night tending Dubois, and talking to Pubs, who was in too much pain to sleep. The medivac chopper had come in at first light and Mark had ridden it as far as the UMS. He'd volunteered to walk but Vickers put him under direct orders.

"Two extra minutes isn't going to kill Dubois, and you know it. So, either you get on the chopper, or I'll shoot you fucking dead. You understand?"

"Yeah, if you put it that way, sir; I guess I understand."

Mark rejoined the world the day after, just in time to find out that the Croatians had done it again. They'd guaranteed safe passage for the UN force into the Serbian zone, but when the Canadian column rounded a corner at the narrowest part of the valley, they found themselves staring into the face of the Croatian army, blocking the road, and ranged along both sides of the hill above them.

If it had been the forces they'd gone up against previously, they'd have just fought their way through, but this time the Croatians had a T-72 Main Battle Tank, a gift from Germany, and there was no choice but to sit.

They could see the smoke from the villages in the distance, and they understood now why the Croatians had fought so hard to delay them.

The whole world had heard about the Serbian policy of ethnic cleansing by that time, and Mark, along with everyone else, had expected to be protecting Croatia from a Serbian invasion. After four months, he understood that both sides were capable of murder, but now, with smoke rising from the whole countryside, it was clear that the Croatians were busy covering up some major ethnic cleansing of their own.

Ethnic cleansing. That was another typical piece of UN doubletalk. "Ethnic cleansing" was what UN bureaucrats wrote in their reports when they couldn't bring themselves to say "genocide".

"Ethnic cleansing" was fifty or a hundred soldiers with armor and machine guns massacring a village full of civilians. Raping the women, torturing the men, and then butchering everybody from the youngest baby to the oldest grandmother. And because they knew that someday a son or a brother might return from the war, they'd slaughter all the livestock, burn the houses and crops, and throw a corpse or two down the wells.

It was Colonel Jeffries that came up with the solution. There were about twenty reporters at the back of the convoy, and he brought them up to the front and held a press conference. He explained what he was sure was going on in the villages down the road, and he made sure the cameras got plenty of coverage of the way the Croatians were interfering with the UN mission.

What guns couldn't accomplish, the cameras could, and the Croatian Commander backed down and let them through.

It was too late to save any lives, of course. But not too late to gather clear evidence of what had happened. Truckloads of firewood had been hauled in to speed the incineration of every wooden building in the towns, and the stone buildings had been blown up with explosives. Wells had been poisoned with oil or had the corpses of livestock thrown in. Not a single body was visible anywhere in the open, but once the soldiers started exploring the basements, they found bodies of women and children, tied, shot, doused with gasoline, and lit on fire.

Mark and Montaigne had to view every body, and after a while, it was more than Mark could handle. He would rather crawl back into the ditch in Licki Citluck and face the mortar fire, than look at one more victim of this genocide.

"You don't get a choice, Mark. You don't get to be half a soldier. Not here. Not with me. You can have ten minutes to go and puke, and then you're coming back to help me write up the report on the next one."

It ended, eventually. But Mark was not the same man he had been when it started.

"I never want to see a Croatian again, unless it's over the sights of a rifle." He was in his trailer, back at Medak, venting his rage and frustration to Sandy Stephens.

"What about Serbs?"

"What about 'em? Helpless women and girls, and old people. They butchered them, Sandy. Just like fucking Hitler and the Jews."

"That's true, but why do you think you didn't find any bodies of men?"

"Huh?"

"You didn't find the bodies of the men because all the men were off somewhere, raping and torturing and killing Croatian or Bosnian civilians in some other village. They're all innocent, and they're all guilty, Mark. You and I have no more of a chance of understanding what is going on here than we have of winning the Nobel Prize for literature."

Sandy sounded serious and Mark started paying attention. "Do you think we'd be different if we'd grown up here? They're human, same as you and me. Whatever's done this to them, it would have done it to us. Don't try to understand it. We've done a hell of job stopping it from going further, and we can be proud of that. It looks like the Croatians aren't going to be willing to fight us again, so we're all probably going to get home alive, and we should be thankful for that. So let's put in the last two months doing the best job we can, and settle for that."

"Yeah, I suppose you're right. But you didn't have to look at all those bodies."

"Who do you think *found* most of those bodies?"

"You?"

"That's one of the things that recce platoon leaders get to do."

"So you saw…"

"Yeah, I didn't have to do cause-of-death reports on 'em like you and Montaigne, but I saw."

"And you can accept it?"

"No, but I can't change it, and neither can you, so I'm gonna do what you should do. I'm gonna soldier on and do my best to keep it from happening again."

"Maybe someday I'll be able to think that way, but right now, every time I close my eyes, I see another corpse."

"Yeah, well, like I said, I didn't have to examine 'em." Sandy dug around in the cupboards in the trailer. "At least here we get class accommodations. Ah, here we go, I knew you'd have a bottle or two somewhere."

He held up his find. "More of that Hungarian brandy. Perfect." He unscrewed the cap and passed the bottle to Mark. "Get drunk. It won't fix anything, but right now, you mostly need to do some serious forgetting.

"Yeah, you're right. As usual." He took a long, long, swallow. "You want some?"

"Yeah, there's some things I'd like to forget, too."

Mark was on his second long hit, when someone pounded at the door.

"Fuck off. I'm off duty." The door opened, and a Corporal that Mark didn't recognize came in. "You deaf? You gonna get out or am I gonna throw you out?"

"Throw me out and the RSM will just send somebody else, so you might as well come with me."

"The RSM?" Mark looked at the bottle. He wanted another hit but gave it back to Sandy. "Guess I don't get to get drunk just yet. Hang on till I get back."

He found a clean shirt and put it on, then turned to the nameless Corporal. "You going to tell me what he wants me for?"

"He didn't tell me. Just said to get you and bring you to see him."

"Probably wants to recommend you for a medal. Vickers has been spreading the word about what you and Pubs pulled off."

"What Pubs pulled off, you mean. That guy is crazier than a shithouse rat."

"Yeah, and you saved his crazy ass."

"I suppose. Anyway, wait here, I'll be back."

Twenty minutes later, he came back through the door, but he didn't speak, just sat on his bed with his fists clenched.

"What is it, Mark? You okay, man?"

With supreme effort, Mark pulled himself together. "They're sending me home, Sandy. It's my father." His voice was so quiet Sandy could hardly hear him. "He's been in an accident." He started to shake. "Something collapsed at a construction site he was working on. He's in hospital, in a coma." Now his words were mixed with sobs. "They don't know if he's gonna live."

PART THREE

CHAPTER 22

"Shit, that's your daughter, isn't it, Bones?"

"You remember her, Mark?"

"Yeah, she was working here that last year I was in town, right? Going to university, I think. What's she doing back here now?" It was eleven o'clock on a Tuesday morning. Skavoovee had just opened its doors and the first of the lunch crowd was drifting in.

"Same as she was doing then. Helping her old man and getting paid for it into the bargain." Bones Battle hadn't changed at all as far as Mark could tell. Tall, lean, still the owner of a full head of hair. Maybe more gray in the hair, but if anything, he looked fitter and more muscular than Mark remembered. "She did a nursing degree and she's working full time in the ER at St. Paul's, but she still does a couple of days a week here when she can."

"Hell of a good-looking woman she's turned into. And nursing isn't the cakewalk it used to be. You must be proud."

"Same as your old man, Mark. We both lucked out in the kid department."

At the mention of Mark's father, they both fell silent. They'd come to Skavoovee from the hospital, where Scott Heaney lay in a coma, unmoving and unresponsive.

"Your mother's having a hard go of it, Mark. I'm glad you're back."

"Yeah." The sight of his mother's gaunt and tear-stained face had almost been harder to take than looking at his father. "Well, the CO gave me extended leave, so I can stay for a while, but with dad out of action, and Donny maxed out just supporting his own family, I'm going to have to get back to drawing a paycheck pretty soon."

"Your father was my best friend. Saved my life and fucking near bought the farm doing it. So if your mom needs help, you let me know. I've done okay with this tavern, lad, and I know Scotty'd do the same for my family if it was me on that hospital bed."

Bones turned away, speaking over his shoulder: "You want me to pull you a pint?"

"Thanks, Bones. A pint would be appreciated." And drawing it'll give you a chance to hide your tears, you dirty dog. Mark didn't say the words but kept his back to the bar till he heard the pint hit the counter behind him. He was having a little trouble in the eye department, himself.

"So, if you don't mind me asking, what is the situation for your mom? Finance-wise, I mean."

They were now both standing with their backs to the bar, pints in hand, surveying the scene in the restaurant. "Not bad, Bones. Not great, but not too bad. He was working for a legit contractor when the accident happened, and Workman's Comp is covering the family up to a point. My mom's been in no condition to deal with that sort of thing, but I talked to them and got things organized. They'll cover mortgage and food, but that's about it. Things won't be too good if I don't get back to work before too long."

"Donny?"

"I'm sure he'd help if he could, but they've got another kid on the way, and he says he's pretty much maxed out just covering his own mortgage." Mark looked down into the dark surface of the beer in his mug. Donny had changed in the last few years, and not for the better. He wasn't coming to the hospital much, and as far as Mark could tell, he hadn't offered much sympathy or support to their mother.

"I've got some savings. I always sent home a few hundred a month, even after they didn't need it anymore, and dad invested it for me, but that's only going to last so long, and then I'm going to have start pulling a paycheck again."

"I understand. Sometimes you have to soldier on whether you want to or not."

"But it's not money that's the problem, though. If I re-enlist next fall when my hitch is up, I'll be making decent money. After what happened in Croatia, they'll probably make me a Master Corporal before long, and I'll have plenty to send back." He tipped the mug up and drained it. "No, it's not the money. It's mom. I've talked to the docs and none of them is willing to give dad much of a chance."

Bones looked at him sharply.

"No. They're not saying he's gonna die, but he's almost guaranteed to be a quadriplegic and with a shot to the head like that, who knows what kind of mental function he'll have."

This time it was Mark who walked behind the bar and filled the pints, while Bones pretended to be interested in the empty room in front of him.

"It's a rock and a hard place that I'm stuck between, Bones. She needs the money I'll earn by going back to the army, but she needs me here, too."

"She's tougher than you think, Mark. She'll pull through."

"Eventually, yeah. But not for a while, and the CO's going to have to pull my chain in a few weeks. Who's going to take care of Glen and Sarah when I..."

He broke off as Terri Battle approached.

"Mark?" She sounded unsure.

"Hello, Terri."

"You've changed. If dad hadn't said he was going to meet you this morning, I wouldn't have recognized you." She was tall, like her father. And like him, there was an aloofness about her; a sense that she'd seen things that most people would never see. *Well, working in the ER at St. Paul's—the Vancouver Knife and Gun Club, as it was known — would put that look in one's eyes pretty quickly*, Mark reflected.

"You've changed, too, but I did recognize you." She was less pretty but much more beautiful. Slim, straight-backed, dark-eyed, hips and breasts not sticking out, but very obviously there.

"I'm sorry about your father. Dad's told me a lot about him."

"Thanks."

She touched his arm briefly, then moved off to deal with a pair of suits that had come in the door.

"Guess she didn't remember me."

"Don't kid yourself, she remembers you very well. But she's right about you having changed. You were only seventeen when she saw you last, remember; and prancing around in that fuckin' kilt the way you did, thinking mostly with your number-two head, the impression was a bit different than what's standing beside me this morning."

"Just an underage skinhead wannabe with a hard-on? That what I was?"

"No, you were always more than a wannabe. Can't say that you were a true skin, but you were on the way, and shit, prancing around on stage is what singers do, so there's no disrespect when I say that."

"I never gave up on being a skin, you know. I've given up on most of the skinheads I've met, but the philosophy… Well, I guess I'm still a believer." Mark ran a hand over his close-cropped skull, and looked down at the clothes he was wearing.

"Not so different from me, lad. In my heart I'm still a rocker just like I was when I was sixteen, but we're both older, and we've both been through the mill, and we've left the bullshit part of it behind. A lot of blokes never do, you know. They go on acting like they were still kids with no responsibilities even though they're thirty, forty, even fifty years old." He gestured to where Terri was seating the two businessmen. "Not much different than those assholes. Get up in the morning, put on the uniform, but never think about what it means. They're so wrapped up in the day-to-day insanity of their business that they never stop to think about whether they'd be better off or happier doing something different."

He leaned back with his elbows on the bar and looked around. "Same with a lot of the skins that come in here. They put on the gear, but never think about what it means. Or about what they're doing with their lives. Too wrapped up in the bloody 'scene' to ever wonder about anything beyond where the next beer is coming from."

"Who's to say that you and I wouldn't have ended up the same if the army hadn't kicked our asses into reality, Bones?"

"Dunno, lad. Anyway, that's enough philosophizing for a Tuesday morning." He finished his beer and put the empty on the counter. "Enough beer, too, or I'll not get any bloody work done this afternoon. I'm trying to get Skankin Pickle here for the long weekend, so I'd better get back to work."

Mark put his own empty mug beside Bones's. "Yeah, me too. I should get back to the hospital for a bit, and then I have to be home by three so that I can make sure that Glen and Sarah get some kind of snack and get started on their homework."

He pulled out his wallet and started to lay a ten on the bar but Bones stopped him. "The day you pay for a beer in here is the day after my funeral."

"But…"

"No buts."

There was steel in the older man's voice, and Mark knew better than to argue. "Thanks Bones."

"Least I can fuckin' well do. Now, before you go, can you make it back here on Thursday night?"

"What time?"

"Late. After your mom's home from the hospital and your brother and sister are in bed."

"Sure. What's up?"

"Band you might like to hear. Call themselves The Planet Smashers, and they're only playing one night."

"Never heard of them. What do they play?"

"Anything that'll get the crowd off their asses. Probably more ska than anything else, but plenty of variety. Same approach that you took with the Juice Monkeys."

Hearing his old band's name spoken aloud, here in Skavoovee, the tavern where it had all started, brought wave after wave of memories crashing over him. Bruce, the songs, Larry and Wil, the crowds, the sex, the kilt… He could see his father standing in front of him before the very first show, with the kilt in his hand…

"I'm surprised you even remember the band's name."

"*Everyone* remembers. You guys are a legend on the local scene now. Appearing out of nowhere, playing some of the best gigs anyone can remember, then disappearing without a trace."

"Long time ago, Bones."

Back at the hospital, Mark sat silent watch over his father. His mother was in the room, but she had fallen asleep in her chair and he didn't wake her. He knew that she was so distraught that she wasn't sleeping at night; that the only sleep she'd had for the last few days was a few uncomfortable hours in the chair by her husband's bed.

Glen and Sarah had gone back to school. Glen seemed thankful for that. He'd been uncomfortable in the hospital, and uncomfortable with his mother and sister's grief. Denial. Pretend the bad thing hasn't happened, and maybe, when you wake up in the morning, it won't have happened.

Sarah, on the other hand, was completely miserable. Neither of them had been told the full extent of their father's injuries, but he'd been unconsciouss for five days and she could read the truth in her mother's face and posture. Mark wasn't sure that she was ready for school, but she was an enthusiastic student and he hoped that once she was in class, her mind would be occupied by her schoolwork.

Sound from the bed startled Mark. "Nnnn..."

His father was making noise. His eyes weren't open, and his body was as still as ever, but his mouth was trembling. There was sound coming from around the tubes that were running into his nose and throat.

Mark's hand was reaching for the call button, but he stopped himself.

What was a nurse going to do if he did call? Come bustling in, making noise, waking his mother, raising her hopes. He did a quick check himself. Breathing and pulse were regular; he decided to wait. If his father regained consciousness, he'd wake his mother, but not yet.

He waited and watched and listened, tracking the rhythm of his father's breathing, and taking a pulse every couple of minutes. After twenty minutes he went back to the book he'd been reading, but no sooner had he picked it up, then more groaning made him drop it again. This time there was an increase in heart rate and even as he was pushing the nurse call, his father's eyes opened...

CHAPTER 23

"It's no good hoping or pretending, Bones." It was Thursday night and Mark had shown up at Skavoovee. "The only way he's ever getting out of that bed is if he gets lifted."

"They're sure?" Bones had taken Mark downstairs, to his office in the basement of the building. "A mate of ours who'd been shot was told he'd never walk again and he…"

"Bones, his spinal cord is completely severed, nothing below his chin is ever going to move again." Mark put his hand on Bones Battle's shoulder. "Not ever."

"Shit."

"Not even that, Bones. Not even his shit. He's going to be getting his food through a tube, and dumping his shit through a tube, for as long as he lives."

Neither of them spoke for a long time after that. Scott Heaney hadn't been a thinker, or a reader; his life had been a physical one, and losing his body…

"What about his mind?"

"Too early to tell, but it looks good. He took a shot to the head when that wall collapsed, probably a brick, and he's still not making complete sense, but he's a hell of a lot better than when he first woke up. The doctors won't say anything one way or the other, but my guess is that there won't be any permanent brain damage."

More silence. "Your mom?"

"She's okay right now, but it's not going to last. With dad conscious and talking a bit, she thinks everything's going to be okay soon, but eventually, she's going to have to face the fact that he's never going to get out of bed again, and it's going to hit her pretty hard. Same for the kids. Glen's been acting numb ever since I got home, and Sarah's a basket-case."

"What about you?"

"He's my father. I love the man, I don't just respect him. How do you think I feel seeing him lying there?"

"Same as I would in your place I expect, but that's not what I meant."

"Yeah, I know." Mark took a deep breath. "I'll handle it. It's not going to be much fun being stationed in some shithole on the other side of the country, knowing that my family is going through this, but there's nothing I can do about it, so I'm going to have to do what he always told me to do when things got tough—soldier on."

"How do you feel about the medic end of it?"

"It's good when there's something to do, but after Croatia, well, putting bandaids on guys with cut fingers doesn't really offer much of a challenge."

"Reason I ask is that I reckon you could probably get into the ambulance service here if you wanted to. Pay'd be better, you'd be around your family, and it'd be the real thing, not taping up sprained ankles and handing out aspirins."

"I'd jump on it Bones, you know that. But it's a union gig. It could be a year or more before I get in, and God knows how long before I made full time. What am I going to do for money in the meantime?"

"You keep up your martial arts training?"

"Huh?" Where was Bones heading? Men like him didn't blow smoke for no reason, but Mark couldn't figure out why he was asking about training. "I haven't been able to do defendo the way my dad taught it, but wherever I've been stationed I've found some kind of training. Hapkido, Thai kickboxing, kendo, boxing, whatever I could do. Why?"

Bones Battle stood and stretched the kinks out of his tall frame. "I've got a mate who's in the Ambulance Service. I talked to him, and he told me pretty much what you already know; that getting in ain't easy. But he's senior enough to have some influence, if you go out with him a few times and show him that you've got what it takes, you'll probably be in, a hell of a lot sooner than a year…"

"But…"

"And in the meantime, if you're willing to do some clean-up and learn how to pull beer, you've got a job here."

"Bones, I…"

"It ain't charity, lad. We're busier than ever here, and I actually need the help. I know that anybody can push a mop, and working the bar isn't too hard either, but there just aren't that many people that I'd trust to work security in here. Jurgen is great. He's so big and mean-looking that no one wants to tangle with him, but he can't be here all the time, and on some nights he needs backup. Right now I'm the only backup there is, and it's just not enough."

"I don't know what to say."

"Don't say anything. The band'll be on in a few minutes. Go upstairs and enjoy yourself tonight, and think about this over the next few days."

"It's not entirely my choice. The army owns my ass for another ten months, and even if I apply for a year's compassionate leave, I..."

"I already talked to your CO. He'll back you all the way, whatever you decide to do."

"Colonel Jeffries said that?" Jeffries was a good leader, and took care of his men, so Mark wasn't too surprised that he'd given him a long compassionate leave, but what was Bones talking about?

"Yeah."

"But why would he..."

"He's run into your dad and me a time or two."

"What? How did he..."

"Fuck off. Go upstairs and have a night off. We'll talk in a few days."

The band had already started their first set; Mark could hear them as he came up from the basement. Whoever they were, they sounded pretty good. Maybe Bones was right. Maybe he should take the night off from worrying and thinking, and just do some dancing and drinking. He'd have to be up at seven to get the house going, so he couldn't get shit-faced, but a few beers and a couple of hours on the dance floor...

"Pint of Boddington." The barman pulled the pint, but he wouldn't take Mark's money.

When Mark tried to insist, the barman said, "You want to get me fired?" He rolled the first taste of the beer around on his tongue and offered a silent toast to his father's best friend; then started paying attention to the music. Designator. Cool name. He'd never heard of them, but if the song he was listening to now was any indication, they could sure as hell play.

He started up the stairs, looking forward to hitting the dance floor, then stopped as the guitarist cut loose on a solo. The guy had fire in his fingertips, for sure, and it made Mark think of the old days, when he had been on fire in front of the crowds himself. He started back up the stairs and reached the top in time to see four horn players step forward to take over. Two guys with trumpets started tossing riffs back and forth—the crowd was going nuts!

It was early, but the place was crowded and Mark couldn't find a table without at least a few drinks on it. Well, sitting could wait. He drained the beer, put the empty mug on a table with some other empties, and hit the floor. He raised an eyebrow at a group of three women who were dancing together, and when they gave him the nod, he joined in and got serious about shaking his problems loose.

The thought ran through his mind that this was the first time he'd ever been on this side of the stage. Every other time he'd been here, he'd been *on* the stage, with girls like the ones he was dancing with ogling *him*. He looked at the crowd, and sure enough, a lot of them were focused on the band. He could see the longing in the eyes of the women, and the envy in the eyes of the guys. He checked the stage, and sure enough, the singer was playing to the crowd just like he himself had done so many years before. This guy was skinny and white, and wore a white T -shirt and weird shorts that came down past his knees, but he was putting on the same show that Mark had once done.

A better singer than Mark had been, but then this guy wasn't a seventeen-year-old.

Three of the horn players had stepped back, leaving the saxophonist out front with the singer. When the saxophonist finally stepped back, Mark was able to get a look at the guitarist. He was turned away, laying on a couple of final chords as the song ended, and saying something to the bass player. But when he turned around, Mark's jaw dropped open and he stopped dead on the dance floor.

Without thinking about how uncool it might seem, he shouldered forward, vaulted onto the stage, and yelled, "Bruce! Jesus Christ! Bruce!"

The entire band turned toward him, wondering who the fuck was messing with them, and then they, too, dropped their jaws as the guitarist ran forward and hugged the muscular-looking skinhead that had invaded their stage.

Bruce Kellite kept an arm draped around Mark's shoulder and dragged him over to one of the mikes. "Do any of you out there remember the Juice Monkeys?" he shouted to the crowd. There was a low buzz, then isolated shouts of, "Yeah, man," then cheering.

"You remember Mark Heaney? The maniac in the kilt?"

More cheers. Then from somewhere in the thick of the crowd a bra came flying toward the stage.

"Whoa. Someone sure remembers." He turned to Mark and said, off-mike, "You wanna sing with us?"

"Fuck, no. I've hardly sung in six years, man. I just saw you up here and kinda forgot my manners."

"Well, if I'd seen you I'd have dragged you up here anyway, so don't worry. Come backstage at the break, we've got some catching up to do." He pulled a mike close. "C'mon, give it up for the guy who started me off in music." He grabbed Mark's hand and raised it in the air, leaning in close as he did, saying, "Bones told me about your dad, Mark. I'm sorry."

"Thanks, bro." Mark looked out at a sea of faces and bodies. "He helped us get our first gig here, didn't he?" He waved to the crowd, slapped Bruce on the shoulder and said, "See ya downstairs," and jumped off the stage.

"C'mon, little sister. Get your skinny butt outta bed."

Sarah's eyes popped open. There was a moment of disorientation. Then she sat up and threw her arms around Mark.

"Whoa. Ease off or you'll break ribs." He stepped back and looked at her. "It's good to see you smiling again."

"Why shouldn't I be smiling? Daddy's pulling through, and you're home for a visit. We should *all* be smiling."

Mark smiled, despite their trials. Sarah was a great kid. He'd only seen her a few times since he left Chilliwack, but each time he'd been amazed at how much she'd grown up, and yet still managed to keep the energy and excitement at life that she'd had as a little kid.

"Well, your teachers won't be smiling if their best student doesn't get to school on time, so get moving. I'll head downstairs and wake Glen, then start working on breakfast for all of us."

"Hmmph. I'll get up…" She pulled the covers up around her in a sudden surge of modesty, "… *after* you leave, but you'll have fun waking Glen up."

"Why is that? He get up to something crazy last night?"

"Um, no, not really. Well, he *did* stay out pretty late, but that's normal."

"Hanging out at the 7-11?" He laughed at the thought of Glen-the-Madman, fourteen years old, hanging at the corner store, practicing to be fifteen.

Probably set the gas pumps on fire some night.

"I don't know where he hangs." Something in her voice told him that she was trying to send a message, but didn't want to talk about it.

"Okay, I'll go shake him and see if he's any worse in the morning than Donny was at his age."

He was, and he wasn't. Donny had been downright surly in the mornings, always willing to make it clear to anyone who would listen, that anything that happened before noon was of zero interest to him. But that had simply been the way he was, not a sign of any deeper problem.

Glen, on the other hand, wasn't surly at all. It had been hard to wake him. Repeated shaking and prodding had produced little response beyond a few mumbles.

"Jesus. I know some corporals who would just love to have you in their platoons. Wake up, bonehead, or I'll go get a bucket of cold water."

Eventually, Glen responded, but he certainly wasn't Glen-the-madman of six years ago.

"Ow. That hurts, man." He rolled away from Mark's prodding hand.

"Well, get up then, and I'll stop doing it."

"Do I have to?"

What the fuck kind of response was that? "Yes, you have to. It's time to get ready for school."

"Okay."

And that was that. Glen hauled himself slowly out of bed and started to dress, not really paying any attention to Mark.

"See you upstairs, then."

"Whatever."

Mark spent most of the next two days at the hospital. His father could talk for short periods. He didn't have much energy though, and would often drift into sleep in the middle of a sentence.

He had one fairly long lucid period on the second evening. It was late, his mother and the kids were home in bed, and Mark had gone back to the hospital to sit by the side of this man who meant so much to him.

"That you, Mark?" There wasn't much light in the room, and it was amazing that Scott Heaney had recognized the shape coming through the door.

"Yeah, it's me." Mark moved to where his father could see him better. "How are you feeling?"

"Dumb question, troop. You probably know that I'm not feeling anything. Leastwise, not from the neck down."

Mark didn't say anything.

"It's my spine, isn't it?"

"The doctors haven't really … "

"No lies, Mark. Not between you and me. Not ever."

Tears filled Mark's eyes. "Yeah, it's your spine. Final report's not in, but the docs aren't giving you much of chance of getting out of bed again."

"How'd it happen?"

"You really don't remember?"

"Last I remember is walking along a sidehill on the site. It had been pissing rain for a few days and the ground was really soft. I remember the earth giving way beneath me, but I'm fucked if I know how sliding down a mudbank could break my back."

"When the embankment gave way, most of the wall above it fell on you."

"Does your mother know?" Scott Heaney suddenly stopped. "Wait a minute. What are you doing here? I thought you were in Croatia."

"I was. The CO gave me compassionate leave when they sent the news. And mom was pretty messed up for a few days, but since you woke up she's a lot better."

"Days? What the fuck are you talking about?"

"You've been in here over a week now. You were unconscious till a couple of days ago, and this is the first time you've really had your shit together."

Scott Heaney digested this news. He moved his head from side to side, looking at the room he was in. "So this is it, huh? This is what I get to do for the rest of my life. Move my head a few inches each way, and talk to whoever comes to visit me?" His voice shook as he tried to control his emotions. When he was calmer, he said: "Well, fifty-four years is more than a lot of guys get, so I suppose I shouldn't complain."

He faded into sleep after that, but later, as Mark was about to leave, he woke again, and spoke without any preamble, "Is the family going to be okay for money?"

"Don't worry. Workman's comp is going to carry most of the load, and I'm making enough to fill in the gaps."

That seemed to satisfy the older man, and once Mark was sure he'd fallen asleep, he headed for the door.

"Mark."

"Yes."

"Don't let my bike get rusty."

"I won't, Dad."

The neurosurgeon who was in charge of the case made it official early on the morning of the third day.

"I'm not going to bullshit you, Mark. What you see is what you're going to get for as long as he lives. I'm sorry. I understand that he was quite a man, and if there was anything, anything at all, that I could do, I'd do it."

"Surgery?"

"I wish. But he had two vertebrae completely crushed. I mean they are blown to powder, and there's just nothing left of his spinal cord in there." The doctor looked at something on his desk. "You're a paramedic?"

"Yeah. Military though, not ambulance."

"So you understand about spinal injuries?"

"Yes."

"Well, the bottom line here is that about four centimeters of your father's spinal cord is gone. Crushed to pulp. For all practical purposes, it simply doesn't exist. He'll be able to move his head, and he can breathe. That's it, and that's all there's ever going to be."

"I understand." He thought about his mother. She was *not* going to understand. She was forever hopeful—an optimist. She'd have trouble accepting that there was no hope for improvement. "Have you talked to my mom?"

"Not yet. I wanted to talk to you first. Sorry to put more load on your shoulders, but I suspect your mom is not going to take this news very well, and I wanted to make sure that someone was going to be there to help her get through the coming year. It's not going to be easy for her."

Year? What was going on here?

"We're going to be keeping your father here for a bit longer, but that's more a precaution than anything else. There's really nothing that we can do for him, and you'll be looking at bringing him home in three to four weeks. Caring for him is going to be a huge emotional and physical load for your mother, and I understand that she still has a couple of young ones at home..."

CHAPTER 24

"Hi Terri, is your dad around?" He'd come to Skavoovee, not knowing whether it would be open at this time on Sunday morning or not. The front had been locked, so he went into the alley and rang the bell at the loading door.

"Mark. What are you doing here on a Sunday morning. Shouldn't you be in church or something?"

"Huh?" Preoccupied as he was, it took him a while to realize that she was joking. "Oh. Skavoovee *is* my church."

"And you wish to see the High Priest. Do you have an appointment?"

Any other time he would have laughed at her jokes, but this morning his mind was in a turmoil. He loved army life and he hated it. He wanted to go back to it and he wanted to stay here. He wanted to take care of his family and he dreaded the thought of taking care of his family.

"I need to talk to your dad. Is he here?"

A slight frown crossed her face, but she stood aside and motioned him in. "He's in his office, doing the books."

He walked past her, and headed for the office. To his back she said, "You're welcome," but he didn't hear her.

"I don't know what to do, Bones, I just don't know anymore." He had barged into Bones Battle's downstairs office without knocking, and was now sitting slumped forward with his head resting in his hands.

"Welcome to the club."

"No, Bones, I mean it."

"So do I, lad."

Bones' voice was serious and Mark looked up, not sure what to think. "The only people who think they know for sure what to do at all times are people with no brains. People who never think." This was not what Mark had expected to hear.

"You think I know what I'm doing? No way." Bones pulled a package of cigarettes out of his desk and lit one. Mark had never seen him smoke before.

Bones noticed the stare and said, "Yeah, I light up once in a while. Not too often, although I suppose that anytime is too often." He leaned back in his chair and blew smoke at the ceiling. "Look. If you do the same kinds of things over and over, then you usually know what to do when there's some little change. Like the Club here. I audition some band and they play something a bit different than what I put on most of the time. Do I agonize over whether I should book them or not?"

He paused, but Mark didn't say anything.

"Of course I don't. I may not know for sure how the crowd'll react, but I can usually guess, and even if I'm wrong, it's no big deal. But when it comes to something out of the normal line, I'm as much in the dark as you. Look at this shit." He pointed to the ledgers and stacks of paper on his desk. "I'm getting busier all the time and I've got a chance to buy a warehouse a couple of blocks from here. Should I go for it? Move the club into bigger digs? It'll give me a chance to do some things I can't do here; it'll mean that I actually own my own premises; it'll mean a chance to make a shitload more money than I can make here."

He stared at his cigarette as if he might find an answer in the smoke that was curling up from it. "But it'll also mean mortgaging myself to the hilt, and if I'm wrong, if the crowd don't follow me to the new place, then I'm fifty-six years old and broke. I really don't have a fucking clue what to do."

He took a last drag off the cigarette and stubbed it out.

"When I was your age, I had a Sergeant that I figured knew everything. Any kind of combat situation, he'd lead us through it. He seemed tougher than Superman and twice as smart. One afternoon in his tent, he blew his brains out." Bones shrugged, stood up and walked around the desk to where Mark was sitting and rested a hand on his shoulder. "I can't tell you what's the right thing to do. Nobody can. That's the way life is, Mark, and you have to accept it. In the end, you just make the best decisions you can, and then live with it. If you do your best, you'll be okay and so will your family."

Mark felt as if the weight of the whole universe was on him. If someone as wise and as experienced as Bones Battle didn't know what to do, what hope was there for someone as young and foolish as himself?

"Tell ya one thing, though."

"What?"

"You should go into it with as much information as you can. I talked to my mate that's in the Ambulance Service, and he'd be happy to take you out for a ride-along. It won't commit you to anything, and at least then you'll have some idea of what you'd be getting into if you decide to stay."

Mark lifted his head. That made sense. "Should I phone him or something? Make an appointment?"

"I already did. You show up at Station 248, over on Powell Street, at seven o'clock on Wednesday, and ask for Ed Cody. Bring a white shirt, dark pants, and expect to be on duty all night."

"You old bastard. You know more than you let on."

"Wrong." Bones was serious. "I *don't* know the answers. I *don't* know whether you should stay here or go back to the army. That's gonna be your decision, and I don't envy you. Checking things out in the Ambulance service is just common sense, not a final answer."

The next two days were increasingly bleak. Scott Heaney was now in full possession of his mind, but if anything, that made things worse, not better. He tried to appear happy when his family was there, but Mark could see through the act easily, and he expected that his mother could, too. Even Sarah had become gloomy.

On Wednesday morning, the neurosurgeon took Mark and his mother into an office in the hospital. Gently, he informed Jodi Heaney that her husband was never going to get better.

"He may live for many years, Mrs. Heaney, and it looks like there is no brain damage at all, but he will be paralysed from the neck down."

She had cried at first, then went numb. The doctor went on to explain that sometime in the next two or three weeks the family would have to either take him home or arrange for care in another institution.

"This is not something that you're going to want to think about today, I understand that. But it's a decision that you're going to have to make relatively soon."

He spoke to Mark. "I'll give you the name of a home-care consultant, and once your mother is able to deal with it, you can make an appointment. She'll go through what's required for care of someone in your father's condition, and then you can decide if you want to do it at home or not. It's a major commitment—I won't lie to you about that—and many families are simply not equipped to cope. If you are, and if it's a responsibility that you think you want to take on, then fine, but if not…"

"Scott is *not* going into some… institution." She spat the word out with disgust. "How dare you suggest that we dump him off like some bag of garbage?" She burst into tears.

"He's not suggesting that, Mom. He's saying what has to be said. What we do about it is our choice." Mark helped his mother out of the chair and led her to the door. "I'll talk to you tomorrow, Dr. Brinkman."

"Okay, Mark." The doctor reached for a pad on his desk and scribbled something. "And may I have a quick word with you before you go? There's a chair just outside the door for your mother."

A moment later, Mark was back. Dr. Brinkman handed him a sheet from the pad he'd been writing on. "I may be wrong, but I suspect that things are going to get a lot worse for your mother before they get better. Get this prescription filled—it's a mild tranquilizer called Halcyon—and have it on hand if she needs it. It'll help her sleep, and unless she really abuses it, it's not going to cause any dependency problems."

He held the door open for Mark and said quietly, "You've got a tough haul ahead of you, and your mom is going to need a lot of help." He handed Mark a card. "This is the woman I mentioned. She's on staff here at the hospital to advise families in your situation. Make an appointment to see her with your mom, but also think about getting in to see her on your own first."

Mark understood. He wasn't happy, but he understood.

Donny was waiting in their father's room when Mark got there. He'd got a job at a plywood mill soon after leaving high school, and married not long after that, with a baby following the marriage by five months. The lippy skateboard punk was long gone, and the man who had taken his place was someone that Mark didn't really know. He rarely came to the hospital, and never to the house. He had put on at least forty pounds in the last couple of years, and the odor of tobacco smoke polluted the air around him.

"Hi Mark."

"Donny." He led his mother to the chair beside the bed and leaned over her shoulder. "Hi Dad."

Scott Heaney didn't answer.

"I've gotta go get some supper together for Glen and Sarah," he said to his brother. "And then I've gotta be down at the ambulance station by seven. Will you give mom a ride home so that she's there by nine?"

Donny looked at his watch. "I don't know. I told a friend that I'd meet him at six and I…" He shut his mouth when he saw the look on Mark's face.

"She'll want to stay here as long as she can, but she needs to be home for the kids by nine. And she's pretty miserable, so she needs someone here with her. If I find out that you hustled her out of here early so that you could go and hang with your buds, or that you took off early and then came back after a few beers…" he let the words hang, but Donny got the message clearly enough.

"Okay, keep yer fuckin' shirt on."

Provincial Ambulance Station 248 was deep in the skids, not all that far from Skavoovee. When he walked in the front door, Mark found himself in an empty waiting room. Through a door on his right, he could see into what was obviously an office, but at seven in the evening it was empty, too. A hallway led off ahead of him, but he could hear some noise to his left, so he pushed open a door and found himself in the main garage.

It was obviously built for two vehicles, but there was only one there at the moment. A big white and red Dodge that looked a hell of a lot different from the modified APCs he was used to.

The ambulance's back doors were wide open, but he couldn't see anybody.

"Excuse me, I'm looking for Ed Cody," he said to the room in general.

"That'd be me," a British voice said from inside a storeroom. "Give me two seconds."

The man that emerged a minute later, with his arms full of medical supplies, was short and stocky, maybe fifty or so.

"I'm Mark Heaney."

That got him a blank look. "The guy that Bones... Ian Battle spoke to you about."

"Oh, right." He set his load down on a cart and stuck out a hand. "Good to meet you." He turned and called over his shoulder, "Wes, c'mon out here."

Another man walked out of the supply room, also carrying a box. "This is Mark, the ride-along I was telling you about."

The new guy was taller, thinner and younger, but he had the same look of competence. He stuck out a hand.

"Wes Patterson."

"Mark Heaney, Wes. Thanks for doing this."

"No problem. Ed said you've got some experience?" He made it a question.

"Six years as a medic in the army. I know it's not up to the standard that you guys have to perform to, but I just got back from a tour in Croatia, and that was pretty real."

"Combat?" That was Bones's friend, Ed.

Mark thought about what he'd seen and done there. "Yeah. And things that were a lot worse than combat." Was war on civilians 'combat'?

"Sorry."

"It's okay. I understand why you asked."

"Good. Bones told me you'd been around the block, but you wouldn't believe some of the people that think they're up for it and then blow their lunch when they see what's actually out there."

"Makes it tough for us when our ride-along turns out to be another casualty for us to handle," added Wes. "So you're thinking about joining the Ambulance service?"

"Yeah, but I hear that it's pretty tough to get in."

The two civilian paramedics looked at each other. Ed finally answered. "It's fucked, is what it is. What we've got is a province-wide service, but each station does its own hiring, and there's no fixed standard. The station director can hire whoever he likes, and then train them once they're in."

His partner took over. "They shouldn't even look at hiring someone till he's qualified, but guys with no qualification but an industrial first aid ticket get hired all the time. They get hired, they go for their EMA-1, they flunk out. All that time they're getting paid, and some guy who's already got his ticket is out in the cold cuz he didn't suck up to the right people."

This was not sounding good. "So is there even any point in me coming out with you guys or am I just wasting your time as well as mine?"

"Well, it depends." Ed was speaking over his shoulder as he went into the supply cupboard. "Our director, here in 248, actually has his shit together and hires good people. He also listens to his staff." He came out with another box. "But this station isn't high on most people's list of places they want to work."

"Why is that?" Mark looked around. It had the feel of a good regimental command post. It was clean and well organized without looking like they made a fetish out of it. And the two guys in front of him looked like the kind of guys you hoped would be backing you up when the shit hit the fan. Who wouldn't want to work here?

"It's the middle of the skids, Mark. It's a fucking combat zone out there just as much as it was where you were. We don't have tanks and artillery, but we've got drugs and guns like you wouldn't believe. This city is the heroin capital of North America and the murder capital of Canada. Probably half of our patients have AIDS, and probably three-quarters of them are drunk or drugged when we deal with them. It ain't pretty."

"If I wanted it soft I'd re-enlist."

They looked at him like he was crazy.

"Croatia was the real thing, but I might never get to a combat zone again, I'll spend most of my life on army bases where all I'll get is guys with hangnails, complaining that they need medical leave."

"Well kid, it's going to be real enough tonight. It's welfare Wednesday and the streets are going to be flowing with blood and vomit." Ed Cody looked at his watch. "We've got about fifteen minutes. Did you bring a white shirt and dark pants?"

Mark lifted the small duffel he was carrying. "Right here."

"Change room is over there." The older man pointed. "Get dressed and you can help us restock the truck."

Twenty minutes later, just five minutes after they'd finished getting their vehicle ready for their shift, Ed and Wes got their first call.

"We squared away in the back, Wes?"

"Good to go!" Wes closed the door, pointed Mark to a seat positioned at the head of the stretcher, and moved up to the front passenger seat.

Mark clicked on his seat belt as the big bay doors opened and the ambulance rolled out into the night.

Ed hit the lights and siren, as Wes looked out the window and called, "Clear on the right." They accelerated smoothly through the intersection and Wes leaned back toward Mark.

"There's a box of gloves just above you, you might as well glove up now, and you can hand me two pairs as well."

Mark gloved up. "What have we got?"

Wes was back at the window. "Clear on the right." He turned again, took the gloves Mark was holding out to him and said, "Thanks. Two-car MVA at Main and Hastings. And I've gotta watch the traffic till we get there."

"Going left-lane," Ed called, and cranked the Ambulance onto the wrong side of the road. Over his shoulder he called out to Mark, "When we get there, you grab the jump kit, the O-2 bottle, and the collars." He swerved right, then back left. "Collars are under the bench. When I stop, you go out the rear with that shit, then tuck in behind me and stay behind me so I know where you are. Got it?"

"Got it."

Mark checked the locations of the gear Ed wanted him to haul, and got ready to roll.

Thirty seconds later, Ed hit the brakes. Mark ditched his seat belt, and unbuckled the belt that had been holding the Jump Kit and the O-2 bottle, grabbed them and the box of collars, and hit the pavement as soon as Wes yanked open the rear door.

Lights were flashing everywhere. The cops were already there, a rescue truck from the fire department was rolling to a stop, another ambulance was coming up behind them, crowds of people were milling around, but Mark didn't notice. He'd automatically gone into full emergency-response mode the second his feet had hit the ground, and other than a quick scan to make sure that there were no hostiles among the spectators, his attention was totally focused on the wreckage in front of him.

A big Ford pickup had T-boned a mini-van, and from the way both vehicles had ridden right up onto the sidewalk, he didn't expect that anybody would be leaving this scene on their feet.

Ed had bee-lined straight for the minivan, with Mark two steps behind him. Wes had headed for the truck but veered off and joined them at the van when he saw the crew piling out of the second ambulance.

The impact had been in the middle of the van, and after a quick look for leaking oil and gas, Ed managed to yank the driver's door open. Mark saw the spider-web of cracks in the window and knew that the woman draped over the steering wheel would probably have head trauma.

"Hello dear, I'm Ed, I'm with the Ambulance Service. Can you hear me?" he said. The woman moaned in response.

Wes ran to the back, where the doors had blown open on impact, and made sure there was no one else in the van, then headed for the ambulance, as a pair of firefighters from the rescue truck laid blocks behind the van's tires.

"Can you take a deep breath for me, Ma'am?" Ed Cody asked as he took C-spine control and gently attempted to lean her toward the back of the seat.

"Get a tall collar, Mark, one of the green ones."

Mark put the Jump Kit and O2 bottle down, opened the bag of cervical collars and pulled out a green, then climbed in through the back and helped get the collar around the woman's neck.

Ed kept up a gentle stream of questions as they worked. "What's your name, dear?" It was Theresa.

"Do you know what day it is, Theresa?" She wasn't sure.

"Do you know where you are?" She said Vancouver, but it sounded like she wouldn't have been surprised if they'd told her she was really in Rome.

"Can you wiggle your toes for me, Theresa?" She said she could, but her toes didn't move.

"Were you on your way somewhere when this happened, dear?" She wasn't sure.

Wes had returned, lugging the stretcher and a green case. "Got the K.E.D. boss."

"Good, we'll need it in a minute. Hand Mark some gauze and Hibitane." Mark took the gauze and the bottle of Hibitane solution, and without being told, carefully swabbed the blood away from the large open gash that had been torn across the woman's forehead. He knew that it wasn't medically necessary, but he understood why Ed had had him do it. There was an extra set of hands, so might as well put them to use. If nothing else, it would make the woman feel like she was being well taken care of.

With his primary survey finished, Ed said, "Okay, we're gonna extricate. Mark, you okay to take C-spine control from me?"

"Yes."

"Okay, move into the passenger seat and then take over."

With Mark holding the woman's head still, Ed and Wes maneuvered the Kendrich Extraction Device behind her back and underneath her. When they started to do up the chest straps and leg straps, she cried out in terror.

"It's okay, dear. This is just a special jacket with metal supports. It'll let us move you to the stretcher without hurting you, okay?"

"Okay."

"Thatta girl. You're really brave, you know? And we'll have you out of here in no time. Now, can you wiggle your toes for me again? Great, and a deep breath, okay?"

With the buckles all done up, the woman couldn't move even if she wanted to. Wes wedged the spine board between her hip and the seat.

"Wes, you take C-spine control from Mark."

"Ready Mark?"

"Ready, take control."

"I have control."

"Mark, you bring her legs up and toward you as I rotate her."

"Ready when you are."

"Ready for a move, Theresa?"

"Uh huh."

"Okay sweetie, we're going to move on three. Wes, Mark, ready?"

"Ready," they echoed.

"One. Two. Three."

They rotated her so her back was toward the door, then tipped her onto the spine board with Wes never losing C-spine control.

Faster and more smoothly than Mark believed possible, the two paramedics unfastened the buckles which had kept her legs in a firm sitting position, and eased them down onto the board, then strapped the board securely onto the stretcher.

Ed pointed Mark toward the foot end of the stretcher, put a mask on the woman, started Oxygen, and said, "Roll it."

They wheeled her quickly into their unit, and as Wes locked the stretcher in place, one of the firefighters brought the jump bag in and secured it with the air of someone who had done it a thousand times.

Ed did a fast check, said, "Thanks Marty" as the firefighter exited, then shut the rear doors and headed for the driver's side, motioning Mark toward the passenger side.

"Everybody strapped in?"

"Yup."

"Yes."

"Okay, we're outta here."

Mark took a quick look at Wes Patterson, who was switching the Oxygen flow from the portable bottle to their humidified on-board tank, and starting a secondary survey, then turned back to Ed Cody.

"You want me to call the intersections?"

"I'd be much obliged. Just give me a minute to get on the blower." He pulled the mic off the dash. "48 Alpha."

"Go ahead 48 Alpha."

"We're 10-8 scene, five minutes to St. Paul's. Over."

"Copy that 48 Alpha. Out."

The siren cut in, and they were rolling.

"Okay Mark, time to make some speed. Call the intersections with either 'Clear on the right' or 'Oncoming'."

With possible spinal and neural damage on board, they didn't high-ball the way they had on the way to the scene, but Ed Cody could drive like no one Mark had ever met, and they were rolling into the emergency bay at St. Paul's within minutes.

"Follow us in, but stay out of the way and don't talk, okay?"

"Okay."

They wheeled Theresa into Emergency. There were a lot of people sitting and standing around, some bloody, some obviously in pain, but the head and spine trauma got priority and the admitting nurse directed them straight to an examining room.

Another nurse met them, took a report from Wes, and immediately got out her flashlight and flashed it into Theresa's eyes. Mark couldn't see what the nurse saw, but he could tell from her body language that pupil reaction was slowing. She left the room in a hurry and brought back a doctor who immediately began his own surveys.

"Unbuckle her and get her onto the gurney."

The paramedics unstrapped the spine board from the stretcher and eased her onto the gurney the doc had indicated, still in the K.E.D., and still lashed to the spine board.

"You done with us?"

"Yeah, thanks guys."

"What about the spine board and the K.E.D.?" Mark wanted to know. "Do we just leave them here?"

"For now. They'll put them in the Ambulance Service room when they're done." Wes pulled open a door. "See?"

There was a variety of Ambulance Service equipment neatly leaning against the walls, and stacked on shelves.

"Grab a board and a K.E.D. and let's hit the road."

With the pressure off, Mark relaxed and helped the paramedics load the stretcher, a spine board, and a K.E.D. back into place in the unit. He made sure everything was secure, and then sat while Wes wrote a brief report of the call on a clipboard that lived in a door pocket.

When he finished the report, Ed turned to Mark. "Good work. I wouldn't let most of the people that ride along get out of the unit, let alone come anywhere near a casualty, but you've obviously been around the block a couple of times."

"Yeah, I suppose I have. Most of what I've seen outside of that one tour in Croatia was nowhere near this severe, but no, this isn't my first MVA."

"Severe?" Wes laughed out loud. "That one barely registered on the severe meter. You just wait."

He didn't have to wait long. Wes called in and notified dispatch that they were clear and headed back toward the station, but they'd only made a couple of blocks when the next call came in. It was a request that they check-in by telephone.

"They don't like to broadcast the heavy stuff over the airwaves," said Wes as he grabbed a cell phone off the dash and dialed. He listened for a minute, said, "Burrard and Davie," to Ed, then went back to the phone.

"Okay, we got a robbery at the Texaco on the north-west corner. Police are there, they collared the perp, but he's apparently stabbed the attendant with a syringe. He managed to inject the entire contents and the attendant's freaking all over the place. He says the guy told him it was car gas mixed with LSD."

"*Jeesuz!*" He hadn't seen shit like *that* in the army.

"Yeah, fuck knows what kinda shape the guy'll be in when we get there, but we better be ready for violence."

"Well, if there's one thing I'm probably better at than you guys, it's dealing with violence. If the guy really is violent, let me go in first. I can put him down without hurting him."

"Martial arts?" Ed didn't sound thrilled.

"Yeah, but probably different from what you're familiar with."

"Well, there'll be cops there, so it's probably not gonna be a problem."

Mark passed two fresh pairs of gloves forward, and by the time he'd gloved himself, the unit was pulling to a stop in the bright light of a gas station.

This one turned out to be easy. The young gas-station attendant was scared shitless, but not violent at all. One of the cops led him out even before they pulled to a stop, and within thirty seconds they were on their way back to the hospital again, with Mark holding the ziplock the cop had given him with the syringe in it.

"What do you make of it?" Ed wanted to know.

Mark found the overhead light and flicked it on, held the bag up in front of it. "Can't tell much. Looks like traces of a blue liquid." He killed the light and got back to calling the intersections.

Wes did primary and secondary surveys as they rolled, but other than elevated heart rate and some sweating, the kid seemed fine. Frightened half to death, but not exhibiting any signs of poisoning. Maybe it was just water and food coloring.

They turned him over to the emergency staff at St. Paul's and this time managed to get half a coffee at the station before the next call.

It was a guy bleeding to death in front of a bar where he'd picked a fight with someone who carried a knife. He died halfway to the hospital.

"Write it off, Mark. We'd all like to save all of them, but we just can't." And so it went. MVAs, overdoses, fights, overdoses, heart attacks, overdoses... until about 0400 when it finally wound down.

"Most days we don't get so many ODs, but Welfare day is overdose day. They get money, they go out and get high, and the shit that's available in this town is the purest you'll find in North America. China White. A little too much of that, and they're not breathing anymore and their buddies call 911." Wes was kicked back on a couch in the station lounge. "Course half the time their buddies are just as out of it as they are, and don't notice, so it's the morning crew that gets the call when someone finds the body."

"So most nights aren't this wild?"

Ed took over. "The calls we got tonight weren't any different than normal." He'd returned from the kitchen with a tray of sandwiches and coffees and offered them around. "It's just that on Welfare day we get more of them. This was just business as usual at 248, Mark. You work West Van, and it's mostly taxi service for elderly patients going in for checkups, but down here, well..." He chowed down on a sandwich. "Down here, this is what you get. How'd you like it? Wanna come back for more?"

"You'd take me?"

"No problem. I'd take you any damn day."

"Take you before I'd take some of the guys that are actually in the service." Wes was talking with his mouth full, but his words were music to Mark's ears. "There's lots of stuff you still need to learn, but you'll pick it up fast enough, and you know when to stay out of the way."

"You guys tell me a day and time, and I'll be here."

They got a couple of hours of sleep after that, Ed and Wes in rooms with beds, Mark on the couch in the lounge; but with dawn starting to show in the east they hit the road for another one. Heart attack this time.

"It's heart hour," said Ed. "Happens all the time. Early morning, guy tries to get out of bed, and wham!"

This one turned out to be non-fatal, but it took a fair bit of time, and when they returned to the station at 0740 the day crew was waiting to restock the unit for the next shift.

"So you wanna do this again?"

"Oh yeah."

"Same time on Sunday then."

"I'll be here."

Riding home on his father's old BMW, he felt like he was flying, but once he had the machine parked, twenty-four hours with only a brief nap hit him like a truck, and it was all he could do to open the house door.

When he did, he was face-to-face with Glen, who was just leaving for school. He was tucking a pack of cigarettes into his jacket pocket, but Mark didn't have the energy to comment. "If the kid gets lung cancer today, it's his problem," he thought to himself, heading downstairs for the bed in Donny's old room.

Noon. The alarm woke him and he stumbled into the shower. Hot first, then cold. He stayed under the freezing spray as long as he could, then toweled off, feeling at least partly rested and revived.

What a night.

He headed upstairs and rooted around the kitchen, looking for something to make for lunch. The fridge was almost empty, and what was in it was nothing that he was prepared to eat. A half-bowl of soup, a couple of pieces of left-over pizza from… He couldn't remember when they'd had the pizza. Two days ago? Three?

The cupboards were the same. Hardly anything left. Definitely nothing worth eating.

His mother was spending twelve hours a day sitting by his father's bedside, not eating, not thinking about her children. It was understandable in a way, but it definitely wasn't healthy for her. Probably not for his father, either. Nothing to reinforce his misery like having her there crying about the horrible condition he was in.

Mark had no idea how to get her to reconnect with day-to-day life. He assumed that it would happen in its own time, but until then, it looked like he'd be doing the shopping.

Not the cooking, though. Instant coffee was the limit of his kitchen ability. But maybe if he brought home a few bags of the kinds of things he remembered her always cooking, she'd at least take some time away from the hospital to prepare decent meals for Glen and Sarah. Something better than the peanut butter sandwiches and left-over pizza they'd get with Mark in charge.

And then there was the problem of bringing his dad home. Caring for him properly was going to be hard work, and Mark wasn't sure his mom was up to it. Certainly not in her present state. And if all her energy was focused on her husband, what was going to happen to Glen and Sarah? Who was going to kick Glen's ass about smoking? Tell Sarah how to deal with the boys that were going to be all over her before long?

A lot of it was stuff that his mom had been doing all her life, but what if she didn't get her shit together? Donny sure as hell wasn't going to be any help. And what if…

"Fuck this."

He gave up trying to find anything to eat, and he gave up thinking about all the what ifs. He didn't know the answers to the home-front questions, but after last night, he knew where he wanted to work. He headed out the door and fired up the bike.

"So, if I can't pay for a beer, can I pay for a burger?"

"Sure. And you can pay for beer, too. Just not in *my* tavern."

"Okay, how 'bout if I come and work here, pay off my bar tab pushing broom."

Bones motioned to one of the waitresses that was working the lunch crowd. "Can you bring us a couple of meals, Kyla? I'll have the usual." He turned to Mark, "Know what you want?"

"Doesn't matter a whole lot. A good big burger with everything, a side of fries, and a pint of something not too dark."

"I'll pull the pint for him myself and then we'll be upstairs. Bring the food up there, whenever it's ready."

"Okay boss."

"So you've decided to stay?" The upstairs was roped off, and they had the entire floor to themselves.

"What I did last night was what I thought I'd be doing when I joined the army. It's real, Bones."

"Soldiering can be pretty real."

"Not in this country. Two three-year hitches and the only time I got near the kind of thing I saw last night was that one week in Croatia—and even that was mostly bagging bodies. I could spend the rest of my life in the army and not get anything like that again."

"Aye, in the Canadian Army, anyway."

"On the bases here we got training casualties occasionally, but most of the time it was just dealing with wankers on the MIR, and it was really getting to me. I'd pretty much stopped training, I was partying every night, drinking way too much... I was turning into something you and dad wouldn't have liked very much. Something *I* didn't like very much, either."

Bones nodded. "We didn't have that problem in the SAS, but I saw a lot of it in the ordinary regiments. The peacetime military can be a pretty dead-end place."

"Well, Canada's pretty much always at peace, and we haven't got anything even remotely like the SAS." Mark tasted his beer. "Closest thing we've got is the Airborne, and with what happened in Somalia, there's talk that it might even get disbanded."

"Ah, but the Ambulance Service has Station 248, and Ed tells me that you were on it like a dog on a sirloin."

Mark held off replying while Kyla put their food on the table. "The usual" that Bones had ordered turned out to be a glass of water, a very small roast beef sandwich, and a side of raw vegetables.

"Giving up on food?"

"Trying to stay in shape. If I ate and drank what my customers ate and drank I'd soon be in the same kind of shape they are."

"Are you training anywhere?" Mark had always assumed that Bones, like his own father, kept up his fighting skills. But he'd never heard the man talk about it.

"Yeah, that's something I've never dropped. I usually go to a kick-boxing school down in Chinatown, three or four nights a week. Your dad was always on about defendo, but I'm breaking up fights in a bar, not taking out sentries in the bloody jungle somewhere, so I'll stick with what I enjoy."

They worked on their food for a while. Bones finished first. "So what did you think of riding shotgun with Ed?"

"Like I said, it was real. I think I'd probably want to go for it even if dad wasn't paralyzed."

"And you want to scrub my floors while you're waiting in line?"

"Gotta pay for my beer, somehow." Mark lifted his mug in a mock toast. "And hearing some good music while I work isn't going to hurt, either." He ate the last forkful of his fries. "What about the last of my hitch? You said something about the Colonel being willing to..." He tried to remember just what Bones *had* said, "To back me up in my decision, or something. Just what does that actually mean."

"You mean, was he just blowing smoke out his ass, or will he actually help get you out?"

"Yeah."

"He'll help. You'll get an honorable discharge, you're going to get a commendation for what happened at Medak, and Ed and his partner are going to go to bat for you with their Station Chief, so it should work out okay."

Mark could hardly believe what he'd heard. "How do you know all this? I don't mean about Ed, but about Colonel Jeffries. Why would he do something like that for me? And what's he doing even *talking* to you?"

"He wasn't always in the Canadian Army. I told you he'd run into your dad before, and that's all I'm going to tell you."

"But he..."

"Drop it, Corporal."

Mark took a deep breath. "Okay Sarge, it's dropped, but I owe you, big time."

"Wrong again, Mark. I didn't call in any favors, and I didn't do any begging. I just explained the situation, and the rest came from him."

Mark tried to make sense of it. Jeffries had a reputation for taking care of his soldiers, but what was this about knowing his father? He thought back to the rumors that Sandy had heard, about Jeffries having once been a merc. But he was a full Colonel in the Canadian Army, so what was he doing talking to Bones?

Mark had heard, and overheard, countless bull sessions between Bones and his father, and he knew that Bones had been the ultimate don't-give-a-shit enlisted man. He'd been so good at what he did that he'd get promoted to Corporal after almost every mission, and he'd been so bad at all the rest of it that he'd get busted back to private every time. His idea of what to do with officers mostly involved using them to scout the locations of land mines.

He shook his head. There were mysteries in the universe that were never going to be solved, and this was obviously one of them.

"Okay boss, I give up. But I do thank you. Is that okay?"

"Yeah, that's okay. You're a good kid, and your father's a good man. He'd have done the same for Terri, if it was me lying in that bed. Just remember one thing…"

"What's that?"

"If you screw up here at Skavoovee, it's no big deal. I hired you, and I can fire you again. But if you screw Ed around, I'll kick your arse into the next world."

Mark knew that he would. "Don't worry. And by the way, is it okay to ask how you know Ed? Or is that a sacred mystery, too?"

"No mystery there lad, he's Carole's brother. My brother-in-law."

Friday and Saturday were painful. His father continued to retreat inside himself, and his mother became more and more depressed and miserable. Mark had bought groceries, but the one meal she'd tried to cook had been a disaster. She was haggard from lack of sleep and distraught with the thought that she was failing her husband by not being at his bedside.

"Mom, he knows you want to be with him, but he also needs you to take care of his children."

"You're right, Mark." She'd replied, but two minutes later she was looking at her watch and saying, "I really should be at the hospital you know."

In the end he'd bullied her into taking two of the Halcyon tablets that the doctor had prescribed, and twenty minutes later he carried her up and tucked her into bed. She'd always been slim, but when he picked her up he realized that she had lost a huge amount of weight.

As for his father, the only time he had shown any spark of interest was when Mark told him of his plan to move home to Vancouver.

"You're sure about this, Mark?"

"Yes sir."

"Bones told me that your Colonel's going to recommend you for a medal."

"A commendation."

"Commendation, medal, doesn't matter. With six years, and with what you did in Croatia, they'll probably bump you to Master Corporal if you stay in. You sure you want to give that up?"

"Sure, I'll probably get promoted to Master Corporal, but it'll be Master Corporal in charge of hangnails and constipation. So yeah, I think I can give that up."

Mark told him about the night ride with Ed Cody and Wes Patterson in 48 Alpha. "Remember what you told me before I signed up, about getting a trade that'd be of some use when I got out?"

"I remember. Looks like I was right, eh?"

"As usual."

They both laughed. Then his father grew serious. "Your mother has always been strong, Mark, but she's not handling this very well. I think maybe she's just run out of strength." He went silent for a moment, then, "You'll take care of her?"

"Always."

And that was it. Scott Heaney drew the invisible curtain that cut him off from the world, and Mark couldn't get anything more out of him.

With Sarah's help, he fixed meals for them, and did what he could to make sure that homework got done, and that Glen made it to school on time. Sarah was still miserable, but not as much as before, and bossing her big brother around in the kitchen seemed to cheer her up.

"Maybe I should show you how the vacuum cleaner works. I know you're just a dumb-ola soldier, but you might be able to learn how to vacuum."

"Sounds too high-tech for me. They made us lick the floors clean in the army. None of this modern stuff with vacuums."

Glen stayed withdrawn. He didn't seem miserable or depressed, but he was quiet, and uninterested in anything much beyond sleeping. On Friday afternoon, though, he'd phoned home from a friend's place asking if he could sleepover.

"Sure, no problem. Who's the friend?"

"Nobody you'd know, just a guy at school."

"Well at least give me a name and a phone number in case I need to reach you."

"Um, just a sec." There'd been a pause, some muffled conversation, then, "It's 344-8680, his name is Bill."

"Okay, have fun. See ya tomorrow."

"Sure."

The kid still didn't sound like Glen-the-Madman of old, but at least he was coming out of his shell enough to hang with his friends again, and that was a start.

Sunday night in 48 Alpha was a yawn. Half a dozen med calls, and only one trauma call. Even the trauma call—the lights and sirens kind of call—hadn't been that serious. The elderly man who'd slipped on his front steps and broken a hip was in a lot of pain, but no serious danger.

They'd had a fair bit of downtime, and Mark took advantage of it by asking the two paramedics what he could do to help himself get in.

"Well, to start with, you can study these." Wes dug into his briefcase and dropped a couple of thick books on the table in the station lounge. "Texts for the EMA-1 course, and for the Industrial First Aid Course."

Mark leafed through the books. The Industrial First Aid was pretty basic. Mostly the kind of stuff he'd done in his first medic course at CFB Borden. The other one looked way more serious.

"You're already way beyond the First Aid Course, but if you spend an evening or two going over the book, you'll be able to walk into Workman's Comp and ace the exam without taking the course."

From what he'd seen of the book, Mark felt that he'd probably be able to ace the exam right now, but he'd promised Bones that he wouldn't screw this one up, and being cocky was the surest way to guarantee a screw-up. And what the hell… It wasn't like he was going to be pressed for study time. He was at the hospital most days from about ten until two, and then again for a couple of hours in the evening, and he might as well study, cuz his father hardly ever talked.

"The EMA-1 is a different story." It was Ed talking now. "It's a tough course. You might get a probationary hire on the basis of your military training, or because you've got an industrial ticket, but you're not going to stay in if you don't pass the EMA-1. You've dealt with some of it in the army, but not all, and some of the things you've learned, you're going to have to unlearn."

At the end of the shift, they made a date for the next Wednesday and Saturday. "Wednesday won't be like Welfare Wednesday, but it'll be more exciting than tonight. And Saturday, well, Saturday's always busy. We earn our pay on Saturdays."

Monday afternoon he started at Skavoovee.

"No, you're *not* going to work behind the bar. You'll be helping unload trucks in the alley. If I wanted to go out of business I'd put you behind the bar, but until Terri's rich enough to support me, I have to keep turning a profit."

Bones laughed at Mark's expression. "You think that because you've had a few beers here, and once mixed rum and cokes at a party, that you can tend bar in one of the busiest taverns in this city?"

"You and my little sister have such overwhelming confidence in me. Still, maybe I shouldn't complain about you, *she* doesn't even think I'm capable of sweeping the floors."

"Smart kid. I always knew she was the one that got the brains in your family. Maybe I should have hired her."

That afternoon he unloaded beer, wine, liquor, food, and cooking supplies from a seemingly endless stream of trucks; and in the evening he monitored the keg room, hooking up fresh kegs to the lines as needed, and ferrying about four million cases of beer up from the storeroom to the bar. He was amazed at the quantity of booze that was being sold on a Monday night. If it was like this on Monday, what must it be like on Friday and Saturday?

Seeing the operation of a place like Skavoovee from the other side of the counter was a revelation. To Mark, a bar had always been a place to order a beer, and maybe get a burger. Maybe listen to a band sometimes.

Big deal. Keep the beer cold, fry up some hamburgers, and let the band worry about the music.

How wrong can you be?

The one thing he'd been right about was having music to work to. Bones had booked the well-known English ska band The Selector for the coming weekend, with a local skaband, Skaboom, opening for them followed by an new oi band called Emergency. The Selector would be playing Thursday through Saturday, but Skaboom started up on Tuesday, Mark's second night. They were still relatively new, but they had a lot of energy, and more than once, he wished he could be up there on stage with them. Or, if not on stage, at least skanking away and having a beer or two.

Bones was strict about that, though. Staff were welcome to drink and dance themselves into oblivion on their own time, but not while they were working at Skavoovee. Mark understood that, but the pull of the music was strong.

When his shift ended at eleven, he did go upstairs, planning to get a bit of a buzz going, then hit the dance floor. But the band took their break just as he got there, and his good mood deserted him before he'd even tasted his beer. The thought of dealing with tomorrow was interfering with enjoying tonight.

His mother was a basket case. She'd finally recovered enough that she'd be able to get out milk and cereal for the kids, but she was still a haunted, red-eyed wreck, and Mark felt that it was important for him to be present at breakfast so that her misery didn't infect them too much.

He'd drive her to the hospital, but with an all-nighter coming up with the Ambulance Service, he knew that he'd have to get as much sleep as he could during the day. Plus study. Plus get in at least a couple of hours with his father. Plus be there for the kids at supper. Plus pick up his mom at the hospital and drive her home before his shift at Station 248.

He'd be lucky to get two hours of sleep during the day; if he partied tonight, he'd be so tired tomorrow night that he'd probably fall asleep, or do something stupid, while he was out with Ed and his partner.

"You're not the happiest customer in this tavern, are you?"

"Huh?" He was startled by the voice. He hadn't noticed Bones approaching. "No, I guess you should be happy that the rest of them aren't like me."

"Usually the miserable ones sit downstairs at the bar, not up here with the music."

"I'm not miserable, just not in party mode, I guess. How's dad?" Bones took a couple of hours off every evening to visit his old friend.

"Piss poor. Maybe there's people that could accept what happened to him, but he's not one of them."

"The doctors say that it's pretty normal for him to be depressed at this stage, that a lot of people do eventually accept it."

"He was a morose old bastard when he was up and running, and now he's just totally crawled inside himself." Bones picked up the beer that Mark had hardly tasted. "You mind? Doesn't look like you're going to drink it."

"No, go ahead."

"He's given up Mark. He's hiding back in there somewhere, but I don't know if he's ever going to come out again." Now it was Bones's turn to put the beer down untasted. "I'm sorry, lad. I wish I could tell you that his old mate went in and cheered him up, but ... "

They sat silent, staring at the pint mug, while conversation buzzed at the tables around them between sets. Middle of the week or not, the scooter crowd was out to drink and dance and impress each other with their clothes, hair, and attitude.

Shallow people, Mark thought; social butterflies. The weekend crowd would be better. The Selector would bring out a lot of the skinhead scene, people who were less concerned with how cool they looked and more concerned with just having a good night out after the week's work.

"Look at all these fucking posers. I look at them, and then I think about my dad. I just can't get it out of my mind, Bones. What it must be like for him, lying there, knowing he's never going to move again. It would have been better if it had killed him." He stood up. "Ah, shit. I better get outta here before my gloom affects everybody."

Bones stood and the two men walked downstairs, and through to the back where the BMW was parked just inside the loading door. The door rose, and Mark pulled on the sheepskin-lined leather jacket that had once been his father's.

"Get some sleep, lad. I'll see you on Thursday."

"Thanks. And thanks for not giving up visiting my dad."

"Part of the deal, Mark, it's part of the deal."

"What do you mean?"

"That guy, Publicover, the one whose life you saved at the Medak Pocket. What would he do for you?"

Mark thought about that. "Probably anything. Whatever I needed. Whatever I asked."

"And if he'd saved your life?"

"The same. Whatever he asked."

"That's the deal."

CHAPTER 25

The first call on his shift with 48 Alpha was a drunk who'd tried to cross a street mid-block without checking oncoming traffic. They got him to the ER with head trauma and two broken legs. As Mark was getting ready to leave a familiar voice from behind him said, "Quite the job, isn't it?"

It took him a minute to realize that the nurse who had spoken was Terri Battle. She was gloved, gowned, masked, and covered in blood. "Sorry I can't stop and talk—I've got to get this gear off and I'm too bloody to touch anything myself." She held up her hands to show just how bloody they were.

"Yeah, I can see. Well, we'll probably be in a few more times tonight, I'll talk to you when you aren't quite so scary."

"And how's my favorite uncle?"

It took Mark a moment to remember that she was Ed Cody's niece. "He's fine. He's just out at the unit writing this one up."

"Say hi to him for me, and tell him that if you guys get the chance we could all go for a coffee later. Maybe at three or so, when things are quiet."

"Sure. That'd be great. I'll tell him."

The next one was an addict who had OD'd in the skids. Wes gave him a shot of Narcan that got him breathing again. It also killed his high, and the three of them had to listen to a lot of abuse on the way to the hospital. Mark wondered whether it would ever register on the guy that they'd saved his life.

The one after that was a young couple who had gotten carried away with a vibrator. It had gone so far up the woman's rectum that they couldn't get it out. She'd been in a lot of pain, but Mark was willing to bet that her careless husband was going to suffer worse once she got home.

He'd seen Terri again, briefly, but she was on the run, and had only been able to wave to him when he called, "See you at three."

He would have seen her at three if the fourth call had been something different.

"48 Alpha."

"48 Alpha, go."

Mark was used to the dispatch procedure and could follow it now without paying any attention.

"Call in on the phone, over."

"Will do."

Wes picked up the cell from its holster on the dash and dialed. "48 Alpha, whatcha got?"

He listened for moment, said, "Yes, that's right," then listened some more. "Okay. I copy, We'll deal with it and get back to you later."

He put the phone back but didn't say anything at first. Ed gave him a 'What's going on' look, and finally he said, "Better pull over."

When the unit had rolled to a stop by the curb, he turned in his seat. "It's your dad, Mark. They lost him."

"Aaahhhhh." It was half groan, half wail.

"I'm sorry, Mark." Ed reached back and put a hand on his shoulder. "Bones told me about him. He was one of the good ones."

Mark clamped his eyes shut as hard as he could, but he could feel the tears leaking out anyway. He put his hand on Ed's and hung on, taking strength from the contact.

Finally, he looked up, wiped his eyes, and said, "I'm okay. I know I'm going to lose it at some point, but for now I'm okay. Thanks." He grabbed Kleenex from the box above the stretcher and blew his nose. "Have they told my mother?"

"No. They wanted to let you know first so that there'd be someone to support her when she learned."

"How'd they find me?"

"His friend—Ed's brother-in-law—was there when it happened."

Thank God for that. If Bones hadn't been there... If they'd called his mother first... It was going to be bad enough with him there to support her.

"We'll drive you wherever you want to go. Or if you just need a bit of time we can park this bus and go for a walk or just sit here and talk."

"I guess I'd better..." He stopped. He didn't really have to do anything in a panic. It was too late to say anything more to his father and waking his mother up in the middle of the night to give her this news wasn't doing her any favors. "I think the best thing would be to take me back to the station. My bike… my dad's bike, is there. I'll ride it to the hospital and do whatever they need me to do."

"We're cleared to drive you, Mark. You don't need to worry about the bike tonight."

"Thanks Wes, but I think getting on the bike would do me good. It's the best way I know to say good-bye to him."

"You're sure?"

"I'm sure. And that way I can pretend it's the wind that's making me cry."

They took him to the station.

"You sure you're okay to hit the road on this thing?"

"Yeah, I'm not going to get drunk and kill myself or anybody else, if that's what you mean."

"That's what I mean. And Mark," Ed held up a hand to stop him from firing up the BMW, "you call me when you're ready to come out on the road with us. Don't worry about this Saturday. Take care of your family."

"I'll be here at eight on Saturday. It's what he'd want."

He kicked down hard and rode the soft thunder of his father's old iron into the empty night.

"What are we gonna do without him, Bones?" The old soldier and the young soldier were standing side by side, looking down at the flesh that had once been Scott Heaney.

Bones Battle was grim-faced and red-eyed. He'd obviously been doing some serious crying himself. His arm was around Mark's shoulder, half to reassure Mark, half to support himself. "We'll do what he'd tell us to do…"

"Soldier on."

"That's right, lad. First time he told me that was when he was carrying me out of the hills in Oman. We knew we weren't going to make it. The bullet had broken my femur, and I was bleeding like crazy. He'd got the sniper that got me, but there was another one in the rocks somewhere and we had hardly any cover. I wanted him to drop me and let me die, but he wouldn't. I still remember what he said: 'It's a tough game, Ian. You can't win, you can't break even, and you can't even choose not to play. You know you're going to lose eventually, but until that happens, you soldier on. It's part of the deal.'"

Bones turned away and Mark could see his shoulders shaking as he tried to control the sobbing. Finally, he straightened up. "It's a rotten fuckin' life sometimes, Mark."

They stopped talking when a doctor entered the room. It was a young guy that had been on most nights.

"I'm sorry, Mark. Sorry about your father."

"It's okay, doc. We're going to miss him, but it wouldn't have been much of a life for him. Do you know what happened?"

"Hard to say. He took quite a beating in that cave-in, and he's been lying motionless for almost three weeks. Could have been a blood clot in his leg or abdomen that picked this moment to break loose, that often happens. Could just as easily have been a brain aneurysm. He took a real shot to the head, and even though he had full brain function…" He held up his hands in a gesture of defeat. "Bottom line is, we don't know, and probably never will. You've seen enough trauma yourself to know that this kind of thing is pretty common."

He turned to Bones. "I've got to talk to Mark about arrangements for the body, but if you want to stay here for a few more minutes, you're welcome to."

"No, I reckon I've said all I need to say to the cantankerous old bastard. If Mark wants me to wait for him, I'll wait; if not, I'll just go somewhere quiet and crawl into a bottle."

"You want to do that alone, or will there be room in it for me, too?"

"I reckon so." He looked at his watch. "The tavern'll be closing in about fifteen minutes." He pulled out his key ring and levered a key off. "This'll get you in the back. The main door beside the loading bay. I'll be at the bar."

Dealing with the doctor kept his mind off his loss. And riding to Skavoovee, his mind was mostly on how to deal with telling his mother. He knew that he would need some time to himself soon, some time to let the tears flow and to howl his grief to the night, but right now he needed to spend some time with the man who had been his father's best friend.

He thought about the obligations of friendship. Most guys that called themselves friends felt some obligation to each other. When a friend needed help, you did what you could. But the bond between Scott Heaney and Bones Battle had been far deeper than that. It wasn't something that Mark would have understood before his experience in the army, but now... Dean and Sandy both owed their lives to him.

And in a way he owed his life to Dean and Sandy. He'd saved them from quick death, but they'd saved him from slow death at his own hands, and he knew that if someday one of them needed him, he would be there; just as they'd be there for him if the need was his.

No questions asked, no sacrifice too great. His life was theirs now, and their lives were his. And he knew that Bones had been in the same position with his father. Still, the price that his father had finally collected from Bones had been extreme, and Mark didn't want Bones carrying that load alone.

They needed to talk.

When he arrived, Bones was sitting at the bar, with all the lights out except a single dim one above the bar itself. He was not alone.

"I told her not to come, but she's got a key." He shrugged. "She never listened to me before, though, so I guess I'm not surprised."

She took his hand, said, "I'm so sorry, Mark," then wrapped him in her arms and held him the way a mother holds a hurt child.

She wasn't his mother, but he needed the warmth and he let himself go and accepted what she gave. When he felt some of his strength return, he stepped back. "Thanks, Terri."

"I called her to ask if she'd be willing to help with your mom." Mark must have looked blank.

"Dad told me about the way she's broken down since the accident, and I saw for myself when we visited a few days ago."

Mark hadn't been aware that Terri had visited, but he knew that Bones and his wife occasionally came by in the evening.

"He asked if I'd be willing to be there when you told her the news in the morning. Mom will come, too. You're a good son to her, but I think that she's going to need some things that you can't give her."

Mark was stunned. She hardly knew him, hardly knew his family. "I don't know what to say... how to thank you. I was dreading having to tell her."

"There *is* no good way to do it. I've seen a lot of families go through this at the hospital in the last few years, and, well, it *always* hurts. For someone who's already been suffering like your mom though, it could be a lot worse than usual. I know it'll help if my mom is there, and maybe me, too." She squeezed his hand again. "Right now, though, you probably need a drink."

She moved behind the bar, got two shot glasses and poured generous drinks from the bottle her father had started.

Bones raised his own glass. "He was a good man, Mark."

They touched glasses and drank. Terri, who had not known Scott Heaney well, stayed out of the glass clinking part of the toast but drank with them.

"You going to have a funeral?"

"I don't know. That was something the doctor wanted to know, about what to do with the body. They asked me about organ donation and I said yes. But once they've taken whatever they need, they have to send the body to a funeral home." He ran his hand through the stubble on his head. "I don't know. I mean he wasn't religious or anything, so I thought maybe there'd be some kind of place where... I don't know... some sort of non-religious funeral for us and whatever friends wanted to come."

"You don't need to decide tonight, Mark." That was Terri. "The hospital can store his body for a couple of days, and I think you should talk to your mom about what she wants, and let her decide."

"Yeah, I thought about that, but I don't know if she's going to be capable of making any decisions."

"Terri and Carole will be with her tomorrow," Bones replied. "I'll make sure that Carole talks to her about that. And there's some other things you'll have to do, like calling your grandparents, dealing with your dad's will, maybe getting a lawyer if the Workman's Compensation Board doesn't make satisfactory arrangements to take care of your mom and the kids." He poured them all another drink. "It won't be easy for you to think about the practical side of it, but I'll help where I can."

"What time does your mom get up, Mark?"

"Usually around seven."

"There's no chance that she'd just head into the hospital early, is there?"

"No, I drive her. And I can't do that till the kids are on the way to school."

"Okay, Mom and I will be there a little before seven." She looked at her watch. "Which is in five hours. We should all go get some sleep."

"You two go ahead. I think I'll stay here for a bit and have a couple more in his memory."

"My car's out front, I'll lock up behind myself." Terri gave Mark another hug and headed for the front door.

Mark pulled the key Bones had given him and handed it back. "Guess you can come down and lock up behind me."

They went downstairs without speaking, and Mark pulled on his jacket, opened the door and maneuvered the bike through it into the alley behind the Tavern. "Thanks for thinking of all those things. Having Terri and Carole there tomorrow is going to make a world of difference."

"You're welcome. Least I could do."

Mark straddled the bike. "And Bones, about my dad's death…"

"Aye?"

"He called in his IOU, didn't he."

"What are you on about?"

"No lies, Bones. That's part of the deal, too. He never lied to me and I never lied to him. He wouldn't want any lies between you and me either, and you know it."

"No, he wouldn't."

"Yesterday night when you asked what I'd do for the guy that saved my life, and I said I'd do *anything*, you told me that was the way it was between you and dad. You were trying to tell me then, weren't you."

"You sure you want to get into this, lad?"

"It's okay. I don't need to talk about it, I just want you to know that you don't have to carry it alone. You did what you had to do… what he asked you to do. If you hadn't done it, then eventually I would have had to, and… well, I'm not sure I could have."

He kicked the starter down and over the low rumble of the engine, said, "You did the right thing, Bones."

The roar of the departing bike echoed off the walls of the alley, then faded, leaving Bones Battle alone with the memory of what his comrade in arms had asked of him to settle the old debt.

"Bones." It was Tuesday night, about ten o'clock, and the two were alone, with the room in darkness except for what little light came in from the hallway.

"Right here, mate."

"I've seen better days."

"No argument there, you look like a bag of shit." Bones laughed. "Course, you *always* looked like a bag of shit."

Scott Heaney hadn't given him the smartass answer he expected. For a while he just lay there, staring at the ceiling, then finally said, "I don't feel like a bag of shit, Bones, and that's the trouble. I don't feel *anything*. My body's gone, and my mind was never good for much anyway." Bones had had no answer. "What kind of life is that?"

He hadn't had any answer for that, either.

"If being in this bed could somehow help Jodi or the kids, then I'd lie here no matter how much I hated it. But it doesn't, does it? It doesn't do them a fuckin' bit of good. They'd be better off emotionally and financially if I kicked it. And for me, it's torture. I can't face the thought of being like this for another week, let alone another five or ten years.

By that time Bones knew what was coming. "I can't, Scott."

"I ain't giving you the choice, Bones."

So, the next night, he'd returned, but this time with a syringe full of China White that he'd taken from the body of a dealer who'd never seen him coming.

"You sure about this, Scotty?"

"If you've got some clever fuckin' idea that'll make me enjoy living like this, I'm all over it, otherwise, yeah, I'm sure."

"You realize that this is going to make us even, right? If I kill you then you got no right to ever ask another favor of me."

Scott Heaney laughed. "Yeah, after thirty years we'll finally be even, so get on with it and don't look back."

Bones pulled the rig out of his pocket, pulled the cap off, and poised it over a syringe-entry point on the IV line that ran to the vein in his friend's forearm.

"Last chance mate."

"I ain't changing my mind any more than you would. Get on with it and then leave. Just remember that I didn't give you a choice, so there's nothing to be on your conscience. You're doing the right thing."

Bones pressed the plunger all the way down. "Good-bye Scotty. I love you man …"

He pulled out the empty syringe from the tubing, recapped the needle and replaced the rig in his pocket, then bent down, whispered, "You were the best," and walked out of the room.

The next two days were an emotional blur for Mark. His mother was a wreck, alternately shaking with sobs, and then retreating into herself. Sarah was grief-stricken. Glen seemed to have completely isolated himself from the whole affair, spending most of his time in his room, and saying nothing unless spoken to directly.

Terri's mother took over the house—making sure that food was prepared and served, comforting Mark's mother, taking Sarah's mind off the loss of her father by having her help in the kitchen.

Terri helped too, mostly by adopting Sarah as a little sister. Taking her and Sassy for walks, helping her re-organize bedrooms for the visiting grandparents, and reassuring her that life could, and would, continue despite the tragedy.

For Mark, Saturday night in 48 Alpha was both a welcome relief from the turmoil at home and a vital reaffirmation of his place in the world. Saving lives, in a place where life was cheap, gave him a sense that his own life was meaningful and worthwhile.

Just after midnight, they got a Code 3 for the Cobalt Bar. A man was down on the sidewalk in front, and two guys were laying the boots to him. The cops weren't there yet, and a small crowd had formed, people who thought watching a helpless man get kicked to death was great entertainment.

Ed and Wes would have waited for the police, but Mark just said, "I'll deal with the rough boys, you come in behind me." He bailed out of the unit and bellowed, "That's enough. Back off and let us get to work."

"Fuck you, asshole," said the bigger of the two, the one who'd been doing the actual kicking, and lined up for another shot.

It never landed. As he drew his foot back, Mark was on him, intercepting the kick, levering the leg up, and spinning the man into his partner, causing both of them to topple to the ground.

The two paramedics were on the victim immediately, checking vitals and then intubating and starting chest compressions.

The first of the attackers staggered to his feet. He was obviously drunk, and Mark wasn't too worried about him, but the second guy came up fast, hand reaching for his pocket, coming out with a knife that flicked open and slashed wildly for Mark's chest.

Mark had no conscious thoughts, but his instincts were operating in overdrive. The guy was cold sober, he'd come up off the ground and got the knife out with blinding speed, and held it like he understood how to fight with it. Mark's subconscious had taken that in, and he knew, without even knowing that he knew, that the seemingly wild thrust was deliberate, a fake to draw the usual martial arts block.

So he threw the block a little more slowly than he could have, letting the guy think that he'd been fooled, and when the knife changed direction to sever his bicep, his blocking arm dropped away and his other hand came in from below, grabbing the knife-wrist, bending it down, then bringing it around so that the attacker had no choice but to follow it or have it broken.

The knife clattered onto the sidewalk and Mark kicked it under the ambulance as he followed the man down, planting him face-first on the ground with his wrist still under control and Mark's knee in the center of his back.

Wes was hustling from the ambulance, carrying the defib unit, but Mark could sense a change of mood in the crowd and yelled, "Get him in the fucking truck *right now*."

The paramedics understood, and lifted the casualty straight in through the back door as the first beer bottle smashed against the side of the ambulance.

Knowing what was about to happen, Mark fell flat on top of the knifeman, rolled so that the guy was half on top of him, then rose, dragging the guy up in front as a shield, smiling grimly to himself as a bottle bounced off the guy's head.

He backed into the unit, hauling the guy behind him and yelling, "Get the fuck out of here."

With the back doors still open, and no one strapped down, Ed couldn't floor it, but he got out as fast as possible, and once they were a couple of blocks away, he stopped, got the back door closed, and helped Wes get the casualty up onto the stretcher and strapped down.

All the while, Mark kept the attacker in full submission. "If you so much as twitch, I'll break your elbow. You got that, fuckstick?" He drove the point home by levering the guy's elbow to within a millimeter of the breaking point. "Answer me, fuckwad, or I'll break it just for fun."

"Arrggghh," was all the guy could manage through the pain.

Wes was doing his best to keep the victim alive, Ed was driving under full lights and sirens, as fast as he could with Mark and the attacker not strapped in, and simultaneously calling in on the radio, alerting dispatch to have cops waiting for them at St. Paul's.

When it was all over, when the cops had taken the knife artist away in handcuffs, and the doctors had taken over his victim, Ed drove the unit to the nearest 24-hour restaurant and called in to tell the station that it was break time for 48 Alpha.

"They'll call us if it's life or death, and if there's absolutely no other unit available," he said as he holstered a radio, "but otherwise, they'll leave us alone long enough for me to buy you supper."

"He'll have to fight me for the check," said Wes. "You saved our asses out there, Mark."

Mark shrugged. "You guys put your lives on the line for other people all the time. I'm glad I could help."

The fight chemicals were mostly gone from his body, and his mind was going over what had happened. "You know, I think I should talk to the police some more." They'd all given brief statements to the cops that had been waiting for them at the Emergency Ward. "That was more than a bar fight we stepped into. The big guy, the one that was doing the kicking, was drunk enough, but the other guy, the one we gave to the cops... Y'know, I think he might be a pro."

"A pro? What do you mean?"

"Let's go inside and eat, I'll tell you there."

They all ordered, and Mark explained. "I think he was a killer. A professional. He would have killed almost anybody else. No shit. He was faster than anyone I've ever seen on the street, and that move he pulled on me, well, it took him years to learn that. Nobody who spends his time hanging around in bars could have done that."

"And you're even better?" Wes turned a bit red. "Uh, sorry man, you save my life and now I'm calling you a braggart."

"It's alright. You've got no way to judge, but yeah, I am better." In his mind he watched the man coming up off the ground again, and the knife coming toward him. "Not by much, though." He shivered, despite the heat in the restaurant. "Anyway, what I'm trying to say is that he wasn't some guy who lost his temper in a bar fight. He was hanging back, letting the other guy do the kicking, and he was totally sober."

He leaned back as the waitress set their plates down, then continued when she was gone. "I don't know what the guy on the ground did that earned him a death sentence, but I think you should get on the radio when we're done, and ask dispatch to get one of those cops to meet me somewhere."

They all chowed down, but when the food was done and they were working on their coffees, Ed said, "We don't normally have hired killers trying to knife us, but working out of 248 *is* dangerous. It's dirty, it's hard, and it's dangerous. Guys have been beaten up, and one paramedic was killed a couple of years ago. Are you sure this is what you want?"

"Well, I…"

"No, hear me out." Ed wagged a finger at him. "This is going to sound harsh, Mark, but now that your dad's dead, you don't need to stay here. With him a quad, your mom would have needed you here full time. But since he's gone, well, she'll be messed up for a bit, but she'll get over it, and be able to cope a lot better before long."

Wes nodded agreement and said, "You're good, and you'd be a great guy to have in the service, but for most people, it's not much of a life, so think it through carefully."

"If you're wanting to stay, we'll go to bat for you with the Station Chief. But if you want to go back to the army, or do something sane, then we'll understand."

Mark didn't have to think about his answer. "This is where I belong, so pay for my dinner and let's get back out there."

CHAPTER 26

Over time, life returned to normal. His mother didn't really recover; his little sister was still shaken, Glen was still withdrawn and unusually quiet, but they settled into a pattern that they could all live with. Mark worked three fourteen-hour shifts a week at Skavoovee—Thursday, Friday, and Saturday—rode along with Ed and Wes whenever he could, and studied hard.

He challenged the Industrial First Aid Course exam, and aced it, to get his Double-A ticket. Two weeks later, the Station Chief at 248 called him in and asked if he was ready to go full-time.

"Officially, you'll be listed as 'Part-time', but that's just a union definition. You don't get an official shift, but if you're willing to work, you'll get as many hours as anyone else. You up for it?"

"Yes sir."

The man smiled a little, said, "Welcome to Hell," and then got down to explaining all the bureaucratic bullshit that went along with getting hired into the Ambulance Service.

"The first thing I've got to do, is study my ass off." He had gone straight to Skavoovee to celebrate, and to thank the man who'd put him on this road. "I've gotta do an EMA-1 course. It's the shit, Bones, the real shit. I've got six years field experience, but I was never any good at school, and this course has a written exam that's ten times harder than anything I did in high school."

"You'll do fine, lad. You might not be headed for a Nobel Prize in brain surgery, but you're no dummy, and you know how to work hard."

"Well, I don't know about the not being a dummy part, but I'm smart enough to appreciate what you've done for me. So thanks."

"I got you your first ride, that's all. Wasn't me who impressed Ed, it was you. If you've got to thank somebody, thank him."

"I already did. He and his partner went to bat for me with the Station Chief, and I appreciate that. I'd expected to have to wait six months or a year."

"He told me the police put in a word for you, too."

"The cops?" Mark was surprised.

"You didn't know?"

"Know what? What are you talking about?"

"That guy that pulled the knife on you, didn't anybody tell you about that?"

"No, but then I haven't been out with Ed and Wes for over a week, so…"

"The guy is wanted just about everywhere you can think of in the US and Canada. He's an enforcer for one of the big Russian drug organizations, and he's killed more people than you'd believe. Including a couple of cops. They can't believe you took him down unarmed."

"He was good, Bones. If he hadn't been looking at me as an ambulance attendant maybe he'd have been able to take me. I don't know."

"Well, whether you were good, or just lucky, you are definitely flavor-of-the-month with the coppers, and they put in a commendation to your Station Chief."

"No shit?"

"Not a trace."

"Fuck me." Mark thought about it for a minute and then said, "Remember the night my dad died, and we were in here drinking with Terri?"

"Not likely to forget that, now am I?"

"What were we drinking?"

"Remy Martin, XSOP"

"What?"

"Cognac. What you'd probably call brandy."

"You got any left? I think we should do some celebrating tonight."

Bones pointed to the clock at the end of the bar. "Four-thirty in the afternoon isn't exactly night."

"Getting into the Ambulance Service is the best thing that's ever happened to me, Bones. It's like, after wandering around in the dark for all my life, never knowing what the fuck I was doing, I finally found out where I belong."

He looked around the bar. There were a couple of suits in a booth, looking at the screen of a laptop, and arguing heatedly.

"Look at them, Bones. They're staring at some fucking computer, and getting all pissy about who sold the most fucking widgets this month. Something that doesn't make any fucking difference to anyone who hasn't got his head totally up his asshole. Well, today, I got given a shot at doing something that actually *matters*, and I want to celebrate. I want to get a load on, I want to eat good food, I want to go upstairs tonight and dance, and..." He slapped the older man on the shoulder. "And who knows, maybe I'll even get lucky." Mark shook his head in wonder. "Although it's been so long that I probably won't even remember how."

"You'll figure it out. But before you get too far into my liquor supply, we have to talk about a couple of things."

"You're the boss, boss. I'm listening."

"You're not on a regular shift at the station yet, are you?"

"Not officially. I get plenty of shifts, but until I've got my EMA-2 qualification, I'm not officially full-time."

"So what are you going to do about working here? You still have time for that, or should I start looking for somebody else?"

"I'd like to keep it up for now. I think I can manage it, and still get enough work in on the course."

"You actually *want* to keep working here, or you need the money?"

"Well, I'm going to be getting a moderate paycheck from the Ambulance Service. How much depends on how many shifts I work, so some extra money would be useful but it also happens that I *like* working here. Besides, I know you've got Lets Go Bowling scheduled in a couple of weeks, and the Toasters for next month. If I quit, I'd miss all that great music."

"Okay." Bones was thoughtful. "But you're underestimating the work it's going to take to get through the course. I talked to Ed about that, and I've got a deal for you."

Mark didn't say anything, just waited to hear the offer. "Your mom's parents are still at your place, right?"

"Yes."

"With them, plus your mom, plus your brother and sister, you're not going to get the time and privacy you need to study at home, so here's what I suggest. You keep coming in the same three days—Thursday,

Friday, Saturday—but you only work from nine or ten till closing. I'll clear some space for you in my office downstairs, and you use the first half of your shift for studying."

Mark thought about it. "Okay, on one condition."

"Which is?"

"You don't pay me."

Now it was Bones' turn to think. "How about I pay you only for the hours you work?"

Mark wanted to say that the older man had already done enough for him, that it was his turn to give, but he'd had to pay his father's parents' airfare from New Zealand, and part of his mother's parents' from Scotland, and even the simple funeral they'd had had cost more than he expected. The money would help.

"Okay. Deal."

"Good. And now that that's out of the way," Bones went round behind the bar and pulled a bottle off one of the liquor shelves, "I guess I have to pour you a drink. You being such a shit-hot bounty hunter and all."

"Say what?"

"Taking out that killer, remember?"

"Oh, right." Mark accepted the drink and sipped it slowly. "This is even better than I remember." He raised his glass. "Here's to my dad, and to the future."

Bones wasn't drinking, but he nodded. "You'll make him proud of you, lad."

Customers were starting to fill the tavern. Mostly people off work and stopping for an end-of-the-day pint. "Funny, isn't it," said Mark, looking at the people sitting at the tables and in the booths. "It's like this city is really two separate cities. These people, where do they fit in with that guy that pulled the knife on me? With what I see every night, I go out in the ambulance in the skids?"

"Same thing in the military. Most of 'em are just pencil pushers and warehouse workers. People like your dad and I, we might as well have been from another planet."

"There's some people out on the streets that act like they're from another planet, that's for sure." Mark took another small sip of the cognac and rolled it around on his tongue. "Did Ed tell you about the home invasions we've been getting called to?"

"No."

"Last couple of weeks we've had four or five. Always the same. Some old woman gets a knock on the door in the middle of the afternoon. It's a guy saying he's from the Salvation Army, that he's come to pick up the stuff she said she'd donate. She opens the door to explain that she didn't call for a pickup, and the guy and his buddies, who were hiding on either side of the door, burst in and trash her, trash her house, and steal anything that looks valuable."

"They're beating elderly women?"

"And elderly men. Real sick fucks. Laying the boots to helpless old people. Hard. One of them died."

"Jesus…"

"Yeah. Makes you want to get a shotgun and go hunting. And somebody's been hammering blacks and Asians lately, too. Probably the same bunch."

"Coppers'll get 'em eventually, but…"

"Exactly. They'll get a couple of years in the can, and probably not even serve that. Then they're out on the streets doing it all over again."

Bones refilled Mark's glass. "I'd lend you my shotgun, or take it out for a bit of hunting myself, but the problem with that is that the coppers'd get you in the end, too."

"Ahh, fuck it. Let's talk about something else."

"Suits me. I've actually got something on my mind that I could use an opinion on before you get too pissed."

Mark had the glass that Bones had poured for him halfway to his mouth, but he put it back down. "Okay, what's up."

"You know anything about the music scene down under?"

"You mean like Australia?"

"Right. And New Zealand."

"Not a lot."

"You ever hear of The Porkers? Or Skapa?"

"Of course. They're fuckin' great bands. They from down there?"

"That's right. They're thinking of joining up with a couple of lesser-known bands from England and doing a North American tour, and I was wondering how that'd go over. Four bands in a row that still aren't that well known up here."

"Who'd be coming from England?"

"Judge Dredd and Madness. You know 'em?"

"I'd be here for every one of them."

"And you reckon enough other people have heard of them?"

"Yeah, I think so. I think they'd draw pretty good crowds. Look at how well you've done so far this week with The Managers. They're from New Zealand, and they aren't all that well known. Besides, why are you asking me? You've been in the business a long time, you know who's hot and who's not a lot better than I do."

"Five years ago, maybe. Not now. Sometimes I feel like I'm losing touch with what's going on."

"Hey, those are all good bands. I think you should go for it. Advertise 'Down Under Month' or something. Put some Australian beer on special. Serve kangaroo steaks."

"You're probably right. Sometimes I think I'm getting too old for this business though."

That night, with a good meal and several drinks under his belt, Mark got down and dirty on the dance floor to the sound of The Managers. Just before the first break, he felt someone tap him on the shoulder.

"Heather!" He had to yell over the music.

The woman who'd tapped him pointed to the guy she was skanking with. "Jason! Hey man, how's it going?"

"Great."

Heather leaned in, speaking in his ear so he could hear, "Join us at the break?"

He gave her two thumbs up, and got back to dancing.

"We're sorry about your dad, Mark. Every one of us loved the man." Heather Strangway and Jason Takahashi had been regulars at the defendo classes. "We're gonna try to keep it going. No one can replace your old man, but Shanda and Big John have sort of taken over. The spirit will live on."

Mark thought about how close he'd come to dying on the street a couple of weeks previously. "Got room for one more? I'm moving back, and I think I'd better start training again." If what had happened in the ambulance service so far was any indication, he thought to himself, he'd better start training *hard*.

"Yeah, it'd be great to get you down there and kick your ass up around your ears. Although…" Jason took a long look at him, "it kinda looks to me like you've stayed in shape."

"I tried to train wherever I was stationed. It was good to do different styles, but defendo is where my heart is."

"So get down to the club on Tuesday. We'll kick you around for a while then head up to Sailor Hagar's and listen to you tell us lies about all the brave things you did in the army."

He hit the dance floor with them after the break and was working up a great sweat when he saw something through the crowd, something that reminded him of the first night the Juice Monkeys played this venue. It was just a brief glimpse of a lean, hard, female body in a tight black leather vest and black leather pants.

He yelled, "Later" to Jason and Heather, and began skanking his way gradually through the crowd, trying to get a better look. He finally got a good back view. It had been six years, but the memory of that particular body was so strong that he no longer had any doubt—in either of his heads.

Mark kept behind her till he was close enough to touch her shoulder. She turned slowly, keeping the beat, and looked up at him. Her eyes were slightly glazed, but after looking him up and down she rested one of her long red fingernails at the base of his throat and drew it down till it stopped at the first button that was done up.

The song ended, and she was able to speak in a normal voice. "Hello, soldier boy."

"How are ya doing, Helen?"

"Better than I was thirty seconds ago." She glanced down at his crotch. "Looks like you're doing okay, too." Her voice changed to the tone of command that he remembered so well. "Dance with us." She was skanking with a full-bodied blonde girl of twenty or so, and Mark was more than willing to obey. When the set ended, two songs later, she led him to their table, in the darkness at the very back of the room.

"So who's your friend?"

"Nicole. If you're a good boy, I might let you get to know her better. Would you like that, soldier boy?"

Mark peered down into major cleavage, and thought that getting to know Nicole would be just fine. He felt the wood growing in his pants, and decided that the sooner he got to know her the happier he'd be.

"Give Mike a kiss, baby."

"Mark."

"Whatever."

Nicole pressed herself against him, and pulled his mouth down to hers. "That's enough."

Mark didn't think it was enough, and from the way Nicole had been squirming against his crotch he was pretty sure she didn't think it was enough either, but Helen was clearly her master and she pulled away immediately.

Helen sat and pointed to the chairs on either side of her. "Just what I like," she said as they sat, "one of each." Her words were slurred, and the glaze in her eyes was obvious. "I'm trying to decide whether I need a drink, or whether I need something else even more." One of her hands was massaging Mark's dick, and he could see that the other one was busy under Nicole's short skirt. "Mmm. Maybe something else." She pushed her chair back slightly and reached up, pulling Mark's head down, across her own body, and into Nicole's crotch. "Give Mark an appetizer, baby."

Nicole spread her legs, then reached down with her own hands and pulled her pussy lips apart. No underwear. Mark's tongue flicked out automatically, but then recoiled before it touched flesh.

What the fuck was he doing? That was the kind of thing that a pig, like Shackrat Sheila would do. The kind of thing he might have done a couple of years ago when he'd been on the edge of going the pig route himself. He sat up as fast as he could, almost banging his head on the table edge.

"Not here. Let's go someplace private. You still got that place on Lakewood?"

Helen made him drive. She sat in the passenger seat, pushed it all the way back, and motioned Nicole to the floor in front of her. The buttons on her leather pants were rigged so the whole crotch could be exposed, and Nicole undid them and went to work while Mark drove.

He got them safely to Helen's house, and as soon as they were in the door, he was ready. This time, Helen didn't play any games. She was high on something, probably Ecstasy if the speed with which she hustled them up the stairs and started ripping off her clothes was any clue, but Mark didn't mind. He was more than willing to skip the games and get down to some serious sex himself.

He and Nicole peeled off each other's clothing, groping and kissing as they did, and then piled onto the bed and into a thrashing, moaning threesome that soon had Nicole eating Helen while Mark rode her from behind.

They all came quickly, and collapsed into a heap. Helen, as usual, soon had her hands busy, fondling Nicole's ass. Nicole seemed less in a hurry for more stimulation and rolled so that her arms were around Mark.

It had been months since he'd had a woman's arms around him. No wonder he'd come so fast. How long *had* it been? He tried to remember. The whore in Budapest? She was just the last of a five-year string of whores and shackrats, and the only one in all that time that had actually put her arms around him like it really meant anything was the woman in Edmonton. Kendra. The one he'd lied to and then run away from.

In fact, he couldn't remember any woman ever putting her arms around him like it actually meant something.

Wrong.

Memory flooded back. A month ago. The night his father had died. Terri Battle had put her arms around him and held him in his grief.

He pushed himself to a sitting position and looked at the women sprawled on the bed beside him. Helen with her hands kneading Nicole's ass. Nicole, turning, pulling Helen's head down toward her crotch.

It was every guy's wet dream, and yet...

He couldn't get the thought of Terri out of his mind. When she'd held him in her arms, it had been him, Mark Heaney, that she was holding. But for these two, he was just another body. Any other guy they'd picked up would have done just as well. Probably any other woman, for that matter.

They were locked in full 69 now, slurping and moaning. Helen's body started to go rigid with the first waves of an orgasm, but there was no thrill in it for him. No desire to jump back into the pile and start fucking and sucking. He stood, peeled the condom off his limp dick, dropped it onto the floor, picked up his clothes and walked out of the room, not bothering to answer when Helen called out after him.

He walked aimlessly at first, then with purpose. The autumn air was cool, but there was no wind, and he walked fast enough to stay warm, finally arriving at Skavoovee, just as the last customers were being eased out the door.

He went downstairs and was pushing the BMW out the door when Bones' voice came from the darkness behind him.

"So lad, did you get lucky?"

"I don't know, Bones. I really don't know."

CHAPTER 27

As well as they could, the Heaney family settled into a routine, and for the most part, Mark felt comfortable with their progress. His mother was not well, but her parents had agreed to stay an extra month and were helping her when she couldn't help herself.

Glen had changed, but at least he wasn't causing problems for anyone else. He was withdrawn, quiet, and spent most of his time in his room. He'd always been close to his mother, and Mark felt that as she came around, so would Glen. He decided not to push things, to give his little brother some breathing room. If he hadn't come out of his shell by the time Mark finished his EMA-1 course, well, there would be more time for companionship and advice then.

Sarah, on the other hand, seemed to be doing well. She still cried sometimes at the thought of her father's death, but she was strong and full of life, and he knew that she would recover fully. She'd been helped immensely by her new friendship with Terri. "She's terrific, Mark. It's like I've suddenly got a big brother *and* a big sister."

When Terri's shift allowed, she'd often pick Sarah up after school, and together they'd take old Sassy for a walk. If it was a Thursday or Friday, they'd walk to Skavoovee, and pull Mark away from his books long enough to go out somewhere for coffee and a donut.

At first Mark had worried. "I don't know, Terri. This part of town isn't really a great place for a thirteen-year-old."

"Oh, come on, Mark. I wouldn't bring her down here at night, but it's the middle of the afternoon, and we've got Sassy with us. Besides, she really does get a lift out of seeing you."

"I know. And I enjoy seeing you guys." He relaxed. "What do you think, little sister? Can you and Sassy keep Terri safe and out of trouble?"

"No problem," Sarah spoke around a mouth full of donut. "I just line her up with whatever man we can find and then Sassy and I can do what we want."

"Well, okay, as long as you don't tell her boyfriend." Mark knew that Terri had been dating the same man for several years now, and he sometimes wondered why she didn't either marry the guy or dump him.

"Oh, it's okay, as long as she buys me donuts, I won't tell."

The following Thursday, Terri and Sassy showed up without Sarah. "Your mom is actually doing some cooking, and I thought it would be nice if Sarah helped her in the kitchen. Sassy wanted her walk though, so I came down anyway."

They went for coffee at the usual spot. Without Sarah there, conversation drifted to work. They were both dealing with a side of society that not many people saw, and they both found that it was hard to talk to their friends and family about what really happened in the streets and in the ER.

"Rob is a good man. I like him, and we're mostly comfortable when we're together, but…" Terri shrugged, "… but it's really hard to be with him sometimes when he wants to talk about his latest sale, or about what's on TV, or whatever, and I've just come home from having somebody bleed to death all over me."

"Your dad understands."

"Yes, he does, and I'm thankful for that. But he's got his hands full with the Tavern, and well, he's my dad, not my friend or my lover."

When they got back to Skavoovee, Terri said, "Would you mind if Sassy hung out downstairs with you for an hour or so? Dad phoned last night and asked if I could fill in for one of the girls who can't make it in on time today. It'll just be till five-thirty or six. I'm just going to help Kyla and Brandy get things ready for the supper crowd."

"No problem. C'mon dog, let's hit the books."

But half an hour later, Terri was banging on the door, yelling, "Mark! Mark! We've got trouble upstairs."

He was beside her in an instant.

"There's some crazy bastards upstairs, they're hassling Brandy and I think they're going to beat up on somebody."

He took the stairs three at a time, shouting, "Call 911!" as he passed her.

He burst into the bar, scanning the room in full emergency response mode. A couple of customers were edging toward the door, obviously frightened of something. One waitress running up the stairs, ducking under the rope and onto the dance floor. Two broad-shouldered guys with their backs to him, one of them pinning an East Indian guy to the wall, laughing and spitting in his face. Another muscle-bound guy lounging with his back to the bar, drinking thirstily from a pint mug, and a fourth leaned over the other waitress, pinning her into a chair, pushing his hand down inside her shirt.

His first thought was 'freaks'. All four of them were hugely muscled. Body-builder muscled. And all four were shaven-headed, but wearing weird clothes. Not like any skinheads he had ever met.

That scan had taken him less than a second, and he hadn't even slowed down. He raced past the one that was molesting the waitress, delivering a karate chop to the side of his neck, paralyzing the arm that was doing the fondling, and carried straight on, grabbing the backs of the shirts of the pair who were tormenting the Indian and heaving with all his strength.

Sucking oxygen in and out as fast as he could, he turned his back to the wall and yelled, "Alright, break it up. Out the door, *right fucking now*!" With the usual trouble-makers that stumbled into the tavern, it probably would have worked. Most of them were too drunk to do much damage, and most of them could be intimidated easily enough.

But these guys were different. Mark knew that the steroids that had built up their bodies would also have fried their emotional controls. He'd run into a couple of steroid freaks in the army, and dealing with them was like dealing with unstable explosives.

The one at the bar turned his mug upside down, pouring beer on the floor, and smiled. "You telling me what to do, nigger?" He turned and threw the heavy mug into the bottle shelves, breaking glass, spilling liquor.

The two that he'd heaved off the Indian guy had untangled themselves and one of them came at him with a straight right. Not the wild swing of a drunk, but a real punch. It left Mark with no alternative. If these guys actually knew how to fight, there was no room for anything but full-scale damage. He parried with his left forearm, pushing the punch to the side, and hammered the guy with a straight right of his own, directly to the heart.

It was a punch that could kill, and Mark was counting on the huge mass of pectoral muscle to save the asshole's life. It was also one of the most painful shots you could hang on anybody and would have the guy out of the fight for a minute or two at least. He wanted to follow it up with a left to the solar plexus, and a knee to the face as the guy doubled over, but the other one was moving in fast, winding up for a swing that would send Mark into the next dimension.

Mark was on him even before his fist started to come forward. A quick palm strike pushed him backwards, then a knee into the thigh followed with a foot stomp and a chop to the throat. He'd never have tried anything like that on the first attacker, but this one clearly didn't have the same fighting skills, and the impact on the man's throat put him on the floor permanently.

Which left three heavily muscled freaks, at least one of whom knew how to fight. He hoped that Terri had got through to the cops because if they *all* knew how to fight, he was in serious trouble.

The one he'd nailed with the heart shot and the one he'd chopped on his way across the room were advancing on him, with the third one, the guy who seemed to be their leader, following right behind.

Mark pretended to start running for the door, then whirled, grabbed a full glass of beer that one of the fleeing customers had left behind, and let it fly at the one who'd been on the waitress, hoping to either blind him with the beer temporarily or at least distract him long enough to let Mark deal with his partner.

It didn't work. The guy ducked and kept on coming with the look of death coming from his eyes, with his fists up like a trained boxer. Mark was starting to think that maybe running for the door would be his only option when Sassy burst into the room, barking and snarlng, lunging for the one who was closest to Mark.

She didn't make it. She wasn't really old, but at ten, she didn't have the speed and strength she'd had six years ago, and the one in the rear managed to kick her as she went by, landing his boot hard enough to knock her down. "This your dog, Sambo?" He laughed crazily and booted her again as she struggled to rise to her feet, then stomped on one of her legs.

Chad, the one who'd kicked Sassy, turned fast and blocked the beer bottle that Terri was swinging, then stepped back and kicked her in the stomach. Mark went into a rage.

The one Mark had hit in the chest lost his concentration, and turned to see what was going on. It was the moment Mark needed. He stepped left and forward, drilled the guy in the kidney with the heaviest right hook he could manage, then stepped around him and flew at the one called Chad.

Chad turned to meet him, his guard coming up, but it was too late. Mark's first right was a feint, but the left hammerfist came down hard smashing teeth and breaking facial bones above the man's mouth. The boot that followed broke a rib, and before the man could retreat, or strike back, Mark hit him with a double ear slap, rupturing an eardrum, and putting him so far into the hurt locker that he was completely incapable of defending himself. But Mark didn't stop there. A chokehold put the bastard down.

If there hadn't still been one of them uninjured, Mark might have killed the man. The pain of Chad's ruptured eardrum was so blinding that he was a helpless target, and the rage that was flowing through Mark was almost uncontrollable, but he could hear the other one thundering toward him and he whirled, partially blocking the first blow, but unable to do anything about the shot to the ribs that followed it.

It was like being kicked by a horse, and it sent Mark flying backwards, crashing into a table, and tripping. He let himself keep on rolling, and came up ten feet from his attacker, with a table between them. He looked around frantically for a weapon, but the sound of a siren in the distance sent the four scrambling and limping for the door.

There were no windows in Skavoovee—no windows in any building in that part of town—and Mark was too concerned with Terri and Sassy to follow the savages out the door to see where they went. He hoped the police would see something, but the siren was still far enough away that he doubted it.

Sassy was whimpering, and twitching, blood dripping from one ear as she tried unsuccessfully to drag herself to her feet. Terri was curled in a tight ball, not moving. She was sucking air though, and a fast check of her vitals was reassuring.

He was still bent over her when the first cop came through the door. "Back away from her and raise your hands." The voice sounded like it was coming from behind a gun, so Mark rose slowly and spread his arms.

"I work here. She's been kicked but I think she's okay. I'd like to call an ambulance though. And my dog's in bad shape."

"It's okay Bryce. I recognize him." A second cop had come in. "He's the guy that wasted Kondrashin."

The first cop gave the room a fast scan then lowered his pistol. He didn't put it away though, and he got his back out of line with the door. 'Dad would approve' Mark thought to himself.

"Call in an ambulance." He was speaking to his partner, but his eyes never stopped sweeping the room. "Anybody else hurt?"

"No. Can I check my dog now?"

"As long as you talk to me while you do it."

Mark dropped down to where Sassy was now lying still. She'd given up trying to move, but she was whimpering in pain, and the blood was still oozing from her ear. Stroking her gently, he looked up. "Four guys trying to look like skinheads were assaulting a customer," he pointed to where the Indian man was slowly crawling out from the table he'd been hiding under, "and one of our waitresses." He gestured to Brandy, now sobbing in a booth.

"I was downstairs when it started and came up to break it up, but they wanted to party." He moved over to where Terri was now trying to sit up and lifted her gently into a chair. "This is Terri Battle. Her dad owns the place." He kept an arm around her shoulder. "I don't think she's seriously injured, but she took a kick to the gut and needs to get to the hospital for a checkup."

He leaned down to her. "You're gonna be okay, Terri, but I want you to go in anyway. There'll probably be some bruising, but they've got to check for internal bleeding…"

"Trying to teach granny to suck eggs?" she croaked. "I've been at this longer than you, Mark. I'm okay, but I'll go in just to keep you happy." She reached up and took his hand where it rested on her shoulder. "What about you?"

"I think I've got a cracked rib and my nuts really hurt. I'll go for a checkup, too, as soon as I get Sassy to the vet."

The second cop, the one that had called for the ambulance, stepped up. "Can you give me a description of the guys that did this? You said they were skinheads or bikers?"

Mark ran a hand over his own close-cropped head. "It was weird. They had shaved heads all right, but they weren't like any skins I ever saw. It was almost as if they were trying to disguise themselves as skins, but didn't really know how." He played the scene back in his mind. "They were all solid looking. They were wearing were really weird. Lumberjack shirts, for one thing. And they had hightop boots, but they were work boots, not Doc Martens or Rangers." He thought as carefully as he could. "One of them was named Chad, or at least that's what they called him."

"Height? Weight? Accents? Anything else you can tell me?"

He thought carefully. "One of them was over six feet, maybe six-two, the others were all a little less than that. Maybe just a bit taller than medium height, and like I said, they were all roid freaks. Bodybuilders, but way too stacked up to be natural." He paused. *What else?* "Oh, yeah, three of them were boxers. They knew how to fight. I mean, *really* knew. They've done a lot of training in a gym somewhere."

"Accents?"

"American. I only heard two of them talk, but they sounded American. They looked bikers to me but I don't know for sure. When they were beating on this guy," he pointed to the Indian, "I think I heard one of them calling him something like 'Paki bastard', and another one called me 'nigger' and 'Sambo'"

The two cops, and Mark all got the same idea at the same time. "Yeah, it fits, doesn't it?" said the one called Bryce.

"It sure does. I'm in the Ambulance service, out of 248, and we've been getting a lot of racially motivated beatings in the last three weeks. You've probably seen more of them than I have. I think there may be a club forming in the local area. Maybe they're trying to shake this place down."

"No shit. All those home invasions started about then too, and the muscle-bound descriptions match." The two cops looked at each other. "You're the first one who can identify them, though. They always wear masks."

More cops came through the door, followed by a couple of paramedics.

Mark recognized one of them. "Duncan, over here."

"Mark. What's happening." He saw who was in the chair. "Terri, what are you doing out of the hospital?"

"Waiting for you, Dunc."

"You're our casualty?"

"She got booted in the abdomen. Looks like it's okay, but…"

"Yeah, no worries. We'll run her over to the ER and let her see what it's like from the other side." He looked down at her. "Can you walk, Terri?"

"I don't know." She started to stand up, but grimaced and sat back down. "It hurts."

"I'll carry her." Mark scooped her up gently, grunting with the pain in his side, and followed Duncan and his partner out to the waiting unit. They brought the stretcher down and he laid her on it, then stood up. "Be good to her, guys. She saved my life in there."

"What?"

"No shit. If it wasn't for her, it'd be me on that stretcher, and in a lot worse shape."

He was about to go back in when Terri spoke. "Mark?"

He turned to her, and bent close when she crooked a finger at him. He was expecting her to speak but she put a hand behind his head and pulled his face down and kissed him on the side of his face that wasn't bleeding.

When she let him go she said, "Call dad and tell him what happened and that he needs to get down and deal with the staff. Tell him to bring the van, not his stupid little car, because you're going to need it to get Sassy to the vet. And then come to the hospital and get your rib looked at. If I'm still there, come and see me. Otherwise, phone me at home, okay? You can get my number from dad."

She pushed him away, and turned to the crew. "Okay, guys, show me how it's done."

Back inside, Mark got on the phone to Bones, then finished giving his statement to the cops.

At the end of it, the one called Bryce, the hard one that had reminded him a bit of his father, said, "Bontrager and I have to finish taking statements from everybody else here, but these two," he hooked a thumb over his shoulder at the pair of cops who had arrived with the ambulance crew, "they aren't needed. They can get your dog to a vet a lot faster than you can."

He stood up and motioned one of the other two over. "Alex, this is Mark Heaney, the guy that nailed Kondrashin. I need him here, but his dog got stomped in a fight. I want you and your partner to get the dog to the closest vet. String the door on your way out and call in for somebody else to come and keep the tourists away. We don't need any customers in here for a while."

Alex looked surprised at being ordered to do ambulance duty for a dog, but then shrugged his shoulders and said, "Sure," to Mark. "Glad to help. I've got a dog myself, so don't worry. We'll call in with the vet's address." He knelt down beside Sassy, scratched her gently under the chin, and looked up. "You got a blanket here?"

Ten minutes later the police were finished with him. They found the beer mug that Chad had thrown against the bottle shelf and bagged it, as well as all the mugs that were sitting at the table the fake skins had been sitting at. They told Mark he could clean up behind the bar, but no-where else, then began to take statements from the waitresses, and the customer who'd been roughed up.

Mark was down behind the bar, soaking up spilled booze with a cloth when a familiar voice sounded from the front door.

"I don't give a flying fuck if you're the High Constable of Hell. This is my tavern, so get out of the fucking way." There was a brief scuffling sound, then, "You want to start training your rookies better, Bryce." Bones walked in with a very young cop in front of him. "This one couldn't stop a cripple from climbing a ladder." He released the thumb lock he was using to keep the rookie under control. "Sorry, lad, but not even Bryce here would try to keep me out of this place."

"Jesus, Bones, take it easy. He's just doing his job."

"Aye, and I'm doing mine, which is to find out what the fuck has gone on here. You want a beer?" He turned to the red-faced young rookie. "What about you, lad? Will a pint make it up to you?"

"Bones, for Chrissake, we're not in England. You know we can't drink on duty." He turned to the kid that had been guarding the door.

"It's true, not even I would try to stop him from doing whatever he wanted to do. Go back to the door, and when this is over we'll bring you back here and Bones will apologize." He shot a meaningful glance at Bones, who was pouring a shot of whiskey and handing it to the waitress who'd been molested. "Right, Ian? You *will* apologize, won't you?"

"And open my beer taps for you." He turned to Mark. "Where's your dog? I've got the van out front."

"The police already took her in. But once we're done here, you can give me a ride to the hospital. I think the fuckers might have cracked a rib."

"Then stop making like Molly Maid and sit down. Where's Kyla?"

"Here, boss." It was the waitress who had run upstairs to hide.

"You okay?"

"A bit scared, but they didn't touch me. I'll be okay."

"The coppers finished with you?"

"I think so."

"Then get to work on this mess. Best thing to take your mind off what happened. That and the fact that I'll be paying you double time for this shift." He started to turn away, but then added, "And phone a couple of the other girls, whoever you think can make it in. Brandy probably won't want to work tonight, so you're going to need some help. Jurgen is on his way in, and I won't take Mark to the hospital till he gets here. The coppers'll have a couple of people here tonight, too, I expect." He found the cognac bottle and poured Mark a shot. "Bryce?"

"Yeah, we'll have a couple of guys here for sure."

"Make sure Jurgen knows who they are. He tends to break heads first and worry about affiliation afterwards. Now, how long are you going take with this crime-scene bullshit? I've got an empty cash register here and people out on the street are thirsty."

"Gonna be a couple of hours, Bones, I'm sorry. We've got all the beer mugs that they might have touched, and I've got statements, but I'm gonna have to get Ident down here."

"Why the fuck would your crime-scene nerds come to check out a bar fight? Bastards got nasty, and Mark taught 'em a lesson. End of story."

"Not that simple, Bones. There's about a one-hundred-percent chance that these are the guys that have been doing the home invasions and the racial beatings. We want 'em for murder, not just for busting up your bar."

"Ah." He decided to pour himself a drink. "You spilled some blood then, Mark?"

"Some. I broke a nose."

"That what you're after, Bryce?"

"Yup. Fraid we're going to be chopping bloodstains out of your carpet over there where I've got tape up. I told Mark he could clean up behind the bar, but that's it for now."

The X-ray techs couldn't find any cracks in Mark's ribs. "But it doesn't make all that much difference. Bruised can hurt just as bad as broken, so take it easy for a few days."

He put his shirt back on—carefully, because moving his left arm hurt—and went back to reception. Bones was waiting.

"They didn't find anything wrong with her, but she's in a lot of pain so they're keeping her in overnight. I'm going to go up and see her. D'you want to come along?"

The memory of her taking his hand, and of her kiss, flooded back over him. "Yeah. I want to come along."

Terri was out of hospital the next day, with no damage other than soreness. Sassy was another story.

"There's nothing we can do about the leg. I know you don't want to hear this Mr. Heaney, but it's not going to heal. If we don't remove it, she'll just get one infection after another and be dead in a month."

The vet was sympathetic, but straightforward. "I'm sorry, but you're going to have to choose between a three-legged dog or no dog at all."

"What kind of life will she have with three legs?" Mark had seen the odd three-legged dog, but Sassy wasn't young anymore. "And what about the blow to her head?"

"There's no obvious brain damage. I think she'll lose her hearing on that side, but it's too early to tell. As for the quality of life, well, that's up to you. If she's got a quiet home, and plenty of care, then she'll probably be okay. It'll take her a month or so to heal, but after that she should be able to learn to walk again without any problem."

For his mother, it was just one more blow from a cruel universe. She took to her bed for several days, losing much of the ground she'd gained.

Sarah took it fairly well. "Terri told me about the fight Mark, and how Sassy tried to defend you. I hope that one day you'll catch those assholes one at a time where they can't gang up on you."

For Glen, it was another non-issue, and Mark began to worry. The kid was fourteen years old, he should be more resilient than this. And he hadn't been all that close to their father in the first place. Why was this affecting him so strongly?

He had one week left till his final EMA-1 exam. He decided that he'd wait till after the exam, till he'd been out in the ambulance on his own for a week or two. If Glen hadn't come round by then, he'd have to do something about it.

CHAPTER 28

"Hey Sis." It was Friday night; he'd been a full-fledged Ambulance Service paramedic for two whole weeks, and he felt it was time to deal with Glen, who still hadn't returned to normal. But Glen wasn't around.

"Oh hi, Mark. Watch this." She held out a doggie biscuit, and Sassy got up out of the bed they'd made for her near the fireplace, and hobbled over, wagging her tail.

"Wow. She's really coming along. You've been wonderful for her, Sarah." The dog moved back to the bed, and Mark continued. "That's kind of what I wanted to talk to you about. Got a minute?"

"Sure."

They sat on the couch where Mark could reach down and scratch Sassy's ears as they talked. "Some ugly things have happened. Dad's accident, then his death, and now this. Mom's not doing too well, but she and dad had been close for almost thirty years, so maybe that's not surprising. Poor Sassy here took a beating, but she's pulling through with the old Heaney spirit, just like you and me, but I'm worried about Glen."

Sarah's face closed, as if this was a subject she really didn't want to deal with, and her silence made the answer jump out and bite Mark on the nose. "You promised him you wouldn't tell, right? You caught him shooting up and he told you he'd get clean if only you didn't tell dad."

It was as plain as could be, and the only reason he hadn't seen it from the beginning was his concentration on his father. Glen wasn't mourning anything. He was stoned on smack. Fourteen years old and doing heroin. Fuck. "How long has he been doing it?"

"I think he just started. I don't think he was doing it much until daddy's accident, when mom, well, you know."

"Shit. And I've been paying attention to you and mom, and to my work, and he's down in the fucking basement thinking 'They don't really care about me' and doing smack to forget everything." Mark was thinking furiously. "Where does he get it?"

"I don't know. He hangs around with some really creepy kids, older kids that don't go to the school."

"Do you know any of their names?"

"Mark, I promised..."

"And if you keep your promise, you'll kill him. It's not pot or acid or X, Sarah. It's not the kind of thing that we all did, the kind of thing that you're probably doing. Heroin's not like that. There's no good side to it, little sister, only death. Not even a fast death, like cocaine, but an ugly one that could go on for years."

She bit her lip. "I don't know their names, but I think they hang out at this place on Union Street a lot. I was walking by there once and I saw some of the guys he meets after school sometimes. There were a lot of Goths hanging around, like in the yard and on the steps, but the guys that Glen's been hanging with aren't Goths."

"Where on Union?"

"Um, you know where the train tracks go through there?"

"More or less. I can find them."

"About a block from there. On the opposite side of the street from this creepy little corner store. But Mark..." He'd started to stand, but she was tugging him back down. "What are you going to do?"

"First thing I'm going to do is find that house. If Glen's there, I'm gonna drag his ass home and chain it to the bed. Then, I'm gonna talk to some cops that I know, so that they can take down whoever is supplying smack to fourteen-year-olds. And then, on Wednesday, I'm gonna take Glen for a ride he'll never forget."

The house was easy to find from Sarah's description. It was a run-down, neglected, dirty old two-story. Windows were boarded over, but light leaked out, and so did loud music. A strange mixture of mods and bikers were hanging out on the steps, and as he shut down the bike, he saw a van pull up and four Goths piled out.

The only thing that could make bikers, mods, and Goths come within a mile of each other was access to drugs. He knew he'd found the right place. Nobody hassled him as he walked up the steps, just looked at him without much interest, except for one of the bikers who offered him a toke on a joint as he walked by.

"No thanks. Lookin' for something else tonight."

Inside was more of the same strange mixture of subcultures. More men than women, most with beers in hand, and most looking pretty stoned. He headed up the stairs and looked into every room. In one room two guys were playing chess, and in the bathroom a couple of women were smoking meth. Mostly though, it was people on beds, fucking. None of his business. The main floor was the party floor, but he'd already seen that, and a bunch of stoners shouting to each other over the house-jazz mix that was playing on the stereo... this wasn't what he was looking for, either.

That left the basement. It was quieter, and there were only two rooms, both with closed doors. He tried the knobs. Both locked, but he could hear murmurs of conversation, and among those murmurs was his brother's voice.

As rage mounted in him, he booted the door open and stomped in. "Hey, dude wha..."

He dropped the speaker with a straight shot to the mouth, and kicked the guy coming up off the couch in the chest, sending him flying. Glen was sitting on the edge of a bed, rubber tubing tying off his bicep, spike poised over a vein.

Mark slapped the syringe out of his hand and grabbed him by the hair, lifting him bodily off the bed.

"Ow, ow, ow. You're hurting me. Leave me be."

Footsteps behind him alerted him to danger. He bounced Glen off the closest wall and turned to see two bikers moving through the door, one pulling a gun as he came.

He never got the gun out of his belt. An elbow to the throat dropped him to the floor, thrashing.

The second one had a short club, but it didn't do him any more good than the gun had done his partner. He lifted it to bring it down on Mark's head, giving Mark an easy shot at his gut. When he folded over, his face met Mark's knee coming up. His nose broke, and teeth went through his lip then snapped off. The force of the blow stood him more or less upright, and the last thing he remembered of that night was the indescribable pain of his rupturing testicles.

Mark scooped the pistol out of the first guy's waistband, cocked it and flicked off the safety, then grabbed Glen's hair again and dragged him to his feet.

"Walk."

"Leave me…"

Whack!

Mark had let go of his hair and backhanded him across the face, grabbing his hair again as he bounced off the wall. "Walk."

Glen walked.

They walked up the stairs, through the kitchen and living room, and out the door.

Nobody spoke to them or tried to stop them. Nobody acted like they'd even noticed them.

"Get on the bike."

"But I…"

"Get on the fucking bike or I'll break one of your fingers." Glen got on the bike.

"Keep your hands around my waist, and don't say a fucking word, you understand?"

Glen nodded.

The fight chemicals burned out of his body as they rode home, but he was still not all the way down when they arrived. "We're going in, and I'm taking you downstairs. You are going in my room, and you're going to lie on my bed till I've searched your room. You can save us both a lot of grief if you tell me what you've got stashed there right now."

"Did you kill those guys?"

"I don't know. Maybe the one who pulled the gun." Glen wavered, put his hand on the wall for support.

"Gun? Someone had a gun?"

Mark unzipped his jacket and pulled the pistol from his waistband. He yanked the clip and ejected the round from the chamber, then tossed the weapon onto the workbench. "In places like that, someone *always* has a gun. Now tell me what you've got stashed in your room."

"I…" His face was pale, and he was having trouble speaking. "I'll show you." Downstairs, he pulled open a drawer, reached past some socks, and pulled out a baggy of weed.

"Nothing else? No down?"

"What?"

"Heroin. Smack.Crystal Meth? Where is it?"

"No. Just that. It's pot."

"Okay, here's the deal. You go into my room, and you lie on my bed. You get up only to use the bathroom. Understand?" Mark was calmer, but the menace in his voice was still real.

"Okay."

"I'm going to search this room. In the army I learned how to hide things where nothing could be hidden, if there's anything here, I'll find it, so I'm giving you a last chance. Is there anything more here?"

Glen just shook his head.

An hour later Mark walked in o his own room. "Okay. You were telling the truth. Get up, clean up the mess I've made of your room, then go to bed. We'll talk tomorrow."

"Are you working today Mark?" Sarah was stretched on the living room floor, reading a book.

"I work everyday, kid."

"No, silly, I mean at Skavoovee."

"Not today. I've got night shift this week and I'm really tired. I think I'll try to catch a nap this afternoon. It's Saturday night in the skids, and I'm going to need to be on top of of my game. Besides, I'm going to take Glen out and show him where he's headed if doesn't get the spike out of his arm."

"Sort of like *Scared Straight?*"

"Pretty much."

"What about Terri?"

"What about her?"

"Is she working at Skavoovee today?"

Mark thought about it. He saw her at the hospital fairly often, and practically every day for the past month he'd been meaning to ask her if she'd like to got out to a movie, or for supper, or... But he wasn't sure whether the kiss had really meant anything. She obviously wasn't ecstatic about her relationship with her boyfriend, but she hadn't said anything about breaking up with him either.

"Mark?"

"Huh?"

"Wake up, dumbhead. Is Terri at Skavoovee?"

"I think so. I saw her last night and I think she said something about helping out there this afternoon before she went on shift at St. Paul's. You could phone her and ask."

"No, I want to surprise her."

"Surprise her?"

"With Sassy. We used to take Sassy for walks all the time remember? Well, Sassy can walk again."

It was true. She'd healed well, and could get around on three legs quite well. "You're sure she's okay to walk that far?"

"It's only half an hour. And we can rest after we get there, before we walk back. Maybe we'll go out for a hamburger if she doesn't have to go to work till later."

"Sounds like a plan. I'll sleep, you walk the dog. And maybe I'll take Glen out for a hamburger, too."

Mark's alarm woke him at five. He collected Glen and headed upstairs. "I'm taking Glen out for supper, Mom, and then he's going to go out in the ambulance with me. Sarah's off visiting Terri, and might stay out for supper with her."

"Okay, Mark."

She did not look like the mother he knew. She wasn't even fifty-five yet, but she looked older than her own mother. Wasted. He wondered if she'd recover her enthusiasm for life, or if she'd just gradually slide downhill.

He hit the road with Glen. Their first visit was to the police station, where John Bontrager had agreed to give Glen a guided tour of the cells. "The problem with heroin is that once you're on it, you gotta pay for it. It's going to cost you a couple hundred a day, and there's no place you can get that much money working, cuz junkies can't work. So you steal, and we catch you, cuz you're too stoned to do it right, and this is where you wind up." He held up the pistol that Mark had given him. "Or in the morgue because you got on the wrong end of one of these."

The next stop was the needle exchange van. It was early, but it was also Saturday, and business was starting to roll. "Alex, this is my little brother, Glen."

"Howdy Glen, watcha doin' down here? Mark showing you the parts of Vancouver that the tourists don't get to see?"

"Um, sort of. I guess."

"Glen got the idea that smack would solve his problems. I figured you might have something to say about that."

Like everybody else who worked in the needle exchange program, Alex Klein was a recovering addict. He looked at Glen and the smile was gone from his face. "How old are you?"

"Fourteen."

"Jesus. Fourteen." He didn't say anything for a while. "You sit over here and keep quiet, there's something I want you to see." He pointed to the driver's seat, and Glen climbed in. Mark got in the other side and watched Glen's face as a pair of junkies came up and turned in their old rigs for new ones. They were miserable, skinny, decrepit human beings, and Mark was pleased to see the disgust on his little brother's face.

When they'd retreated back into whatever alley they'd emerged from, Alex said, "Pretty ugly, weren't they?"

Glen could only nod.

"Well, understand something kid, those were the best looking junkies you're likely to see. The ones that come to my van are the ones that still have their shit together. Most of 'em just don't care. They sit in alleys and shoot up with dirty rigs. They could walk half a block to my van, but they don't. They know that they're gonna get AIDS if they share their needles, and they just don't fucking care."

At seven, they hit the Maritime Cafe. "Eat up, Glen. Whatever you want to order."

Glen looked like he was going to throw up, not eat up. "This place is filthy."

"Yeah, well, look at those guys." Mark pointed to the filthy people that were sitting in the filthy cafe. "They don't seem to mind." Vacant-eyed people staring stupidly into space, others holding conversations with empty air, a few drooling in the corners. "These are the people that you'll be hanging with, and this is where you'll be eating if you stay on the needle. That is, if," he paused, "if you've managed to score some good money. Otherwise, you'll be eating what you can scrounge out of dumpsters."

The last stop was MacDonald's, but Glen couldn't bring himself to eat the burger Mark had ordered for him.

At the station, Mark introduced Glen to his partner; an EMA-2 named Tim Bryson, and gave him firm instructions. "You ride in the passenger seat, and you stay in the unit unless Tim specifically tells you to come out with us, okay?" By this time Glen was beyond words and could only nod.

Mark and Tim had asked dispatch to give them as many drug-related calls as possible that night, and since drug calls are among the least popular, everyone else on the shift was more than willing to cooperate.

They hit the jackpot on the very first one. It wasn't lights and sirens. It wasn't even a med. It was a body removal. A junkie who'd overdosed in an abandoned house and not been found for three days. He was lying in a mess of stinking piss and shit, his body covered in a cloud of flies, his belt still around his arm, and his rig lying on the floor beside him.

Mark was careful to point out the maggots crawling out of the corpse's mouth and what was left of his eyes. And the chunks of meat missing from the arms and face, where the rats had been feasting.

Glen vomited.

The next one was a Code 3 to an MVA. No drugs, but plenty of blood. "Could you smell the booze on her?" Tim asked Glen once they'd cleared the hospital and were out on the road again.

"Yes, sir."

Then came an assault. It was a hooker who'd taken a beating and was going to need a lot of stitches. En route to the hospital, Tim pointed out the track marks on her arms.

"She pays for her habit with her body. You're young enough and cute enough that you could probably make it as streetmeat, too. Think it'd be fun?"

Mark thought that Glen had probably seen enough and was going to suggest taking him home, when the radio came to life again.

"48 Bravo?"

"48 Bravo."

"Code 3 assault. In the alley between Carroll and Hastings."

"We're on it." Mark hit the gas. He knew the location well. It was the alley behind Skavoovee.

The cops were already there, and as Mark parked the unit, one of them raced up yelling, "Hurry, hurry, we're losing her!"

With a quick, "Stay in your seat" to Glen, Mark and Tim hit pavement with their jump kit and O2. They raced to where another cop was bent over the body of a naked girl, his gloved hands holding a towel hard against her upper abdomen. The towel was soaked with blood, and blood had covered the bare skin and was running over the pavement.

Tim had the jump kit open and Mark took over from the cop, giving the girl only a fast scan, letting Tim do the primary. He had an impression of a savage assault. The face had been an unrecognizable pulp, the head almost hairless but covered with cuts as if someone had cut her hair off with a knife. Cigarette burns and shallow cuts in the shape of swastikas were all over her body, and he could tell without a second glance that one of her arms was broken.

While Tim got an airway in, Mark concentrated on the wound, keeping the pressure on, trying desperately to stem the flow of blood, trying not to think about what kind of animals would do this to a kid who didn't look like she was much over fourteen.

"Get the stretcher for us," Tim yelled to the cops. "We haven't got any time, Mark. We gotta get her in now, I've got her breathing, but she's hardly got any pulse left. What have you got down there?"

"Deep transverse slash wound. Someone went in with a long knife and did some sawing. There's gotta be organ damage."

The cops came on the run with the stretcher and helped Tim place the kid onto it, while Mark stayed with the wound. Once they had her in the unit and strapped down, Tim got an IV in, slapped the oxygen mask on her face, then took over the major wound while Mark piled into the driver's seat, and headed for the ER under full lights and siren.

He could hear Tim's voice in the back, "Don't die on me, kid, don't fucking die on me now. We're gonna get you in, okay? Just hang on for one more minute. One more fucking minute, okay? Now breathe. *Breathe.*"

Talking like that to a casualty was totally against procedure, but Mark knew that he'd be saying the same things. He concentrated on his driving and was soon screaming into the Ambulance bay, where the ER trauma crew was already waiting.

He hit the brakes, shut down the engine, unbuckled, and was about to step into the back when he saw Glen's ashen face and followed his pointing finger to the arm that was strapped down on the stretcher. On the wrist, where he would have seen it earlier if he hadn't been so totally focused on the stab wound, was a bracelet.

Why they'd left it on her, when they'd stripped her of her clothes and hair, he didn't know. But he knew what was inscribed on the oddly shaped metal coin that hung from the bracelet, because he'd had to write it out himself for the old Hungarian jeweler in Budapest.

On one side would be the words, "13 yr olds rule" and on the other, "Happy birthday Sis."

Glen started to wail, and Mark screamed a long, mindless howl of anguish and rage, then hit the back of the driver's seat so hard that it came unhinged. With pain flooding through his wrist, he whirled on Tim and yelled, "C'mon, c'mon, c'mon, Get her out. Get her out."

For a fraction of a second Tim hesitated. Then said, "I've gotta keep compression on, Mark. You understand? If you want her to live, get a grip on yourself." Over his shoulder he called down, "Two of you, up here, *now*!"

The trauma crew jumped to it, and within seconds they were rolling Sarah Heaney into an operating theater where the doctors and nurses took over.

When Tim Bryson went to the admitting desk to deal with the paperwork he saw Mark carrying Glen in through the door.

"He's in shock. Tell them to keep him in here. No matter what he says, they're to keep him here. Under sedation if he gets hysterical." Mark pulled a pad and a pen off the counter and wrote a telephone number. "This is the number for Ian Battle. Phone him and tell him what happened. Tell him to get his wife over to my mother's place."

"Mark, what the fuck is going on?"

Mark broke down, sobbing. "Sarah... My sister... We just brought in my little sister. Oh god, they've killed Sarah." A sudden spasm of rage overcame him, and he whirled, punched the glass out of the admitting desk partition, and ran from the hospital into the night.

CHAPTER 29

For seven hours the surgeons worked on Sarah Heaney, never knowing from one minute to the next if she was going to live or die; and when they put away their instruments, having done everything they could, and the nurses wheeled her into an ICU recovery room, they still didn't know. By the next morning they were fairly sure she'd survive at least another day, and by that night, they felt that she was probably going to make it all the way.

Mark knew none of this. He'd seen the wounds, seen the breath and the pulse disappearing, seen the buckets of blood lost, and he knew that no one in that condition could survive.

For over forty hours he wandered. He knew it had been that long, because there had been darkness, then sun, then darkness again, and now it was late afternoon. He must have slept at some point, but he had no memory of sleeping. He felt no hunger, so perhaps he'd eaten. He didn't know. Certainly he must have drank, because he was not dehydrated. He looked down at his chest and arms. He was wearing a Levi's jacket. It was too big for him, and there was blood all down the right sleeve. He had never owned a denim jacket. Where had it come from?

His boots and his pant legs were filthy with mud and grease. Had it rained? Had he been in a garage or machine shop? And where was he now?

He looked around and registered houses and low-rise apartments. A residential district near downtown, by the look of it. For a few minutes, he simply stood, absorbing the sunshine, trying not to think. But not thinking was impossible, and the vision of his little sister's battered and tortured body rose again in his mind, forcing him to his knees, moaning, digging his fingers into the lawn he had fallen on, tearing out fistfuls of grass, then wiping his dirty hands on his face.

He might have stayed in the no-man's-land of grief for another forty hours, or perhaps even ended his own life in a jump from a bridge, but voices from the sidewalk brought him back to reality.

"Look at him, Barry. Just look. He's digging up grass and rubbing it on his face. Have you ever seen anything like it?"

"Crazy, homeless derelict. What's he doing around here?"

"What do people like that do anywhere? Have you got your cell phone? Maybe we should call the police."

"Yeah, it'll be our good deed for the ... Whoa, easy buddy, we're not going to hurt you. You just go back to eating that grass and we'll call some folks who'll come and take care of you."

The two men backed away, one of them dialing on his cell.

Mark ran around the side of the nearest apartment and kept running, not really knowing where he was or where he was going, just running to put as much distance between himself and the place the patrol car was going to show up. He ran down alleys, climbed fences, squeezed through narrow gaps, stopping only when he was in the relative darkness of a parkade stairwell.

It was there, sitting, hugging his knees on a landing in that dirty stairwell, surrounded by graffiti and the stench of vomit and urine, that he finally came to his senses.

There was no need to run. Nothing was chasing him except his own pain and there was no escape from that, no matter how far or how fast he ran. He stood, descended slowly to street level, pushed open the exit door, and realized immediately where he was.

Spread in front of him was half a block of asphalt, and towering up into the dusk at the far end of that was the twelve-story back wall of St. Paul's. He suspected that he'd been subconsciously heading this way from wherever he'd been, to confront the source of his pain.

His last memory was of late afternoon, so he must have been in the parkade for several hours. What to do? He started forward, with the vague idea of going around to the other side, and into the ER. He knew most of the staff there now, and perhaps they'd let him use a phone. He'd call Bones, ask for help. Maybe find out if Sarah had been buried yet and either visit her grave or sit by the body in the funeral home.

He raised his wrist to check the time, and the sight of his bloody sleeve was enough to stop him in his tracks. He looked down at himself. Filthy. He remembered noticing the bloodstain on his sleeve earlier, and the mud and grease on his pants and shoes, but now everything else was just as bad. Dirt and grass stains covered the jacket and the skin of his hands. Probably his face, too, for he remembered digging out clumps of grass and mashing them into his face in his grief.

He couldn't go in looking like this, but the thought of walking home and confronting his mother was almost enough to send him over the edge again. He sat, leaning against a car, unable to decide what to do. He was no longer insane, as he had been for the last two days, but he felt as if his will had been paralysed.

He forced himself to stand. Whatever he did, the first step would have to be to get off his ass and stop sitting in the middle of a public parking lot in the semi-darkness.

And the second was to get clean. There were a thousand washrooms in the hospital, and if he could find a little-used door on this dark back-side, he could probably skulk around in the basement till he found one. He opened the jacket to look at his shirt. Grubby, but not filthy. Once he was in the building, he could take off the jacket and with a little luck no one would hassle him.

He crossed the remainder of the lot, trying to stay in the shadows. When he was at the last row of cars, he studied the building. The main door from the parking area was on his right. It was well lit, and there was steady traffic in and out, but there were plenty of other doors, and off to the left, where a tall hedge blocked the light from the lot, he could prob-ably get in without raising a fuss.

Staying out of the pools of light cast by the parking lot lights, he edged left, but stopped beside a dumpster when a cigarette end glowed suddenly in the darkness at the end of the hedge.

Some member of the hospital staff out for a smoke?

He waited, wondering whether he should just walk past and try the door, but decided that that was asking for trouble. Whoever it was would probably either try to stop him or run for the main door and call security to come and take away the derelict that was trying to sneak into the hospital.

He was in the shadow himself, so he just stayed still and waited, concentrating on not moving, and letting his eyes become accustomed to the low light.

Soon he could distinguish the outline of a man. He was partially hidden by the hedge, and Mark couldn't get a good look, but when the butt glowed again, he could see the gleam of a bald head and the outline of broad shoulders and a thick chest.

It was vaguely familiar. Someone he'd seen in the bar or on the dance floor? An orderly who was a regular at Skavoovee? He was glad he'd waited. Bad enough to be seen in this condition by a stranger, but to be seen by someone who would recognize him… recognize him and spread the story…

The sudden arc of the butt being flicked away startled him, but he held his place, and waited for the smoker to go back in to work. But the man didn't move. He stayed in the shadow, and it gradually dawned on Mark that this stranger in the shadow of the hedge was doing the same thing that he was doing—skulking in the dark.

The man wasn't much good at skulking though. Mark's father's words came back to him from some long-ago conversation. "It's not hard to understand, son. Shit, even a moron could understand the concept. You want to be invisible in the darkness, all you gotta do is stay still. But *doing* it, well, that's a whole other story. Almost nobody can keep still. They fidget, they shuffle from one spot to another, they scratch their butts, they slap a mosquito. And then they die, because some other guy could force himself *not* to fidget."

They'd been talking about how to take out a sentry, but this was the same idea. Mark was staying still, the other guy was constantly making little moves. And smoking. That was just unbelievable. How could anyone who wanted to stay hidden do that?

Maybe it was a crystal meth junkie, just hanging out in the dark and thinking about getting inside and stealing something. Junkies could never stay still. But they were usually emaciated, half-starved weaklings, not muscled up like this guy.

More motion caught his eye and ear, and he knew even before he heard the scratch oft of a wooden match being struck that the idiot was going to light another smoke.

What he saw when the match came up, though, was not the face of a regular from Skavoovee, or someone he'd met on the skinhead scene. It was a face he'd only ever seen once, but that once was enough to ensure that he'd never forget it as long as he lived. A face that had been visible behind the upraised fists of a trained boxer. The face of a fake skinhead. A steroid freak. A dog beater. A biker. A home-invader. A murderer.

All thought of his own misery vanished, replaced by the flow of fight chemicals, and the sharpening of his focus as he went into hunting mode, analyzing angles and distance, light and shadow. He had no weapons, and there was nothing in the immediate area that could become a weapon.

Again, his father's words sounded in his mind. "There is *always* a weapon. Maybe if you're chained to a wall, naked, in a cell, you don't have a weapon, but any other time, there will be something."

The whole point of that conversation had been that you had to forget your definition of 'weapon' and start over. You might not have anything that could hit or stab, but a handful of pennies thrown into an opponent's face could be the difference between living and dying. Darkness could be a weapon. Light could be a weapon. "But the ultimate weapon is surprise." His father had been adamant about that. "If they don't see you coming, they can't defend themselves against you."

When the butt glowed again, he stepped sideways as quietly as he could, knowing that the asshole would see nothing but the glow of the cigarette an inch from his eyeballs.

Keeping the dumpster between them, he backed off, then circled a bit to the right, then moved directly out into the light. He hunched. He shuffled. He picked his nose. He kept up a steady stream of mindless mumbling, stopping only to tear at his flesh as if insects were crawling on it. He'd seen it a hundred times in the skids. Anybody who lived in the city saw it all the time and tuned it out. One more homeless crazy, mumbling curses at phantoms.

He stumbled toward the end of the hedge, timing huge indrawings of breath to sound like part of his craziness, keeping his eyes down, not looking at the man he knew was standing in the shadows, until he was right beside him.

"Birds." He said, and pointed up into the darkness. When the man's eyes followed his pointing hand, as he knew they would, he spun, putting everything in his body into the motion. Arms, shoulders, hips, every limb and muscle joined in the single task of accelerating his heel around into the asshole's right quadricep.

Sammy Sosa swinging a baseball bat couldn't have done much more damage. With no warning, with no fight chemicals in his body to mask the pain, with no aggression to keep him going no matter what, the man simply disappeared into a sea of pain so intense that he couldn't have stopped a Girl Guide from stealing his wallet. Even if Mark had not landed another blow, the fight would have been over. But he did land another blow, because sometime between the start of the spinning heel kick, and the end, when it crushed the goon's thigh muscle, he realized why the man was there.

Rage at what this freak and his buddies had done to his sister burned inside of him like venom. A venom that would eat him alive unless he transferred it to the monster that was crumpling to the ground in slow motion in front of him. It was a cold rage though, and he was careful. He put the toe of his boot into a bicep as the man fell, and then with the monster on the ground he put a boot into the short ribs, another into an armpit, dislocating a shoulder; then stepped around to the other side to repeat the process.

With one leg and both arms effectively useless, and so much pain radiating up from the broken ribs that he couldn't scream, the meth-head biker freak simply lay, twitching as muscles spasmed, gasping for breath. Mark squatted beside him and checked his pockets. A switch-blade came out of one, a wallet out of another, car keys out of a third. He hit the button on the knife and let the blade snap out in front of his victim's eyes, then grasped an earlobe and sliced. Just enough to separate lobe from head at the point where they joined.

"What kind of car is it, and where is it parked?"

"Fuck you." Between gasps.

Mark tugged on the earlobe, ripping the cut fully half an inch, convulsing the man in pain.

"We've got all night, asshole."

"Van. Arrrgghhh. Red van."

"What kind of van?" Mark tweaked the ear a little.

"Aahhh. Ford. Ford van." The man was actually sobbing with the pain.

"Where?"

"Behind. Around the corner." Talking like a three-year-old.

He choked the guy out enough to keep him still three or four minutes, stood up, and walked between the hedge and the back of the hospital till he could see the street. Sure enough, there was a red Ford van, with Oregon plates to match the accents he'd heard that afternoon in Skavoovee.

He moved quickly back, dragged the fake skinhead up so that it looked like he was helping a drunk, and got him to the van before he started coming around.

Into the van, another choke, and then a pause. He'd run on fight chemicals and oxygen to this point, but the fight was over. Now what?

He flicked on the overhead, and opened the wallet. Robert Deasdolish was the name on the DL.

"Well, Robert, what are we going to do with you?" He looked at the man slumped in the passenger seat. Even through the sweatshirt, he could see the muscles. Muscles growing on muscles. Circus freak muscles. "How much can you bench press with two dislocated shoulders? Do you want to tell me about your club?"

Deasdolish groaned, and Mark decided that with muscles like that holding them together, it was possible that at least one of the shoulders might not have dislocated.

He stepped out, opened the side door and searched the back of the van. There was a fairly complete tool kit, and, better yet, a ten- or twelve-foot length of yellow polypro rope. He quickly fashioned a noose, slipped it around Deasdolish's neck, ran the rope back through the headrest, and secured it to the inside back door handle. If the man got antagonistic, a tap on the brake pedal would set things straight quickly enough.

With that done, he examined the van more closely. Most of the floor was covered by a filthy mattress, and the mattress was covered with dried blood. How much of it was Sarah's he didn't know, but it was Deasdolish's death warrant. That the man was hanging around the hospital probably meant she was still alive, but Mark had seen what they'd done to her and knew she wouldn't survive. He passed a sentence of death on the man beside him.

He dug around in the toolbox and found enough wire to secure the unconscious man's right hand to the armrest. He might still be able to flail a bit with his left, but he wasn't leaving the seat until Mark had taken him for a ride to the cemetery.

There was a certain justice in that, thought Mark as he drove away from the hospital, through Vancouver's west end, and then across the Lion's Gate bridge to the North Shore. When the decision about his father's final resting place had to be made, Mark had felt that it would be fitting if he could be buried somewhere close to Grouse Mountain, his favorite place in this, his adopted country. He'd investigated, and yes, there was a cemetery at the north edge of the city, practically on the foot of the mountain itself.

He'd visited the grave many times in the last month, and often hiked into the forest at its north end, wanting solitude for his tears. There was an old, boarded-up shack there that he'd looked at several times, wondering what trapper or pioneer had built it. It would do for what he had in mind, and if Deasdolish screamed a lot, perhaps it would be music for his father's ghost.

"Party time, Robert." There had been several cases of beer in the car, and Mark shook one up and sprayed it in Deasdolish's face.

The eyes opened, and Mark could see the hate burning in them. He lashed out with the tire iron, striking the crushed thigh muscle, and the fire of hate went out, replaced by tears of pain.

He'd found more wire in the van, and, after prying the door of the shack open with the tire iron, had wired the man securely to the top of the ancient woodstove he found inside, after stripping his clothes off.

"It's a cold night, Robert. Would you like me to build a fire to warm us up?"

"Who are you... AAARRRGHHHH." Fresh blood ran out of the torn ear as Mark pulled it.

"Ask me another question and I'll tear the fucking thing right off. I ask, you answer. Understand?"

Deasdolish only moaned, but at the touch of Mark's finger on the ear, managed to mumble, "Yes," as he spat out bloody phlem.

"Good. Now, like I said, it's a cold night. I think I'll go out and get us some firewood." He didn't need the wood. The walls and floorboards were rotten enough that he could break off all the firewood he needed without stepping outside, but giving Deasdolish a couple of minutes to think about being wired down on top of a stove as the heat built inside it would have him so terrified that he'd give up all thought of holding out.

Two minutes later he returned with an armload of twigs and branches, and began stuffing them into the stove.

"Looks good, Rob. Now all we need is a match." As Mark dug into the man's pockets again, finding the matches he'd used to light his cigarettes, soulless eyes followed every move.

There had been several packs of smokes in the van, too. Mark pulled one out of his shirt pocket, removed a cigarette and lit it. "How about a little fire before the big fire?" He took a drag so that the end was glowing, then pressed it against the base of Deasdolish's throat.

The smell of burning flesh was revolting, and the scream was amazingly loud, but the wire did its job and kept the man from moving.

"Why were you at the hospital?"

"Visiting. Just visiting one of the members of our club. He's sick."

Mark picked up the sidecutters he'd found in the toolbox and severed the little toe from Deasdolish's right foot.

"Wrong answer. Lie to me again and another toe comes off. Now, why were you at the hospital?"

It took a while—Deasdolish was actually fairly tough—but Mark had no mercy and no compassion, and soon the story was pouring out. The fight at Skavoovee had left Chad Donovan with a broken nose, a broken rib, and a ruptured eardrum. He'd demanded revenge on the nigger that had done it to him; and his buddies, Robert Deasdolish, Vitt Fonda, and Kent Anchower were only too willing to help.

They'd befriended some local white power believers who had gone to Skavoovee for them to learn what they could about the black guy that had hung the licking on them. Robert, Vitt, and Kent couldn't go into the tavern, but they'd hung around outside, learning that Mark's little sister and his girlfriend often came for visits. They'd followed both of them home. They'd scouted the neighborhood. And they'd waited for their leader to heal, so that he could enjoy the revenge, too.

They'd taken to cruising the area around Skavoovee in either a van or on their bikes just about every afternoon, and two days ago they'd finally seen what they wanted to see—Sarah walking toward the tavern with her dog, and no one within half a block. They pulled up alongside her and Chad had jumped out, nailing her with a fist to the face, and killing the dog with a baseball bat.

If Mark hadn't needed more information, he'd have killed Deasdolish right then, but he held himself in check and extended the torture session. He promised himself that Chad would pay for what he'd done to Sassy and to Sarah, but right now, he had to concentrate on asking more questions, and getting more answers, including one that gave him at least a little peace.

"The bitch never really woke up."

They'd hauled her back to their squat and beat her and raped her, but the first punch had scrambled her brains and Chad had gone nearly crazy with anger when it didn't seem like she was really there to suffer the abuse he was giving her. In the end, they threw her back in the van, drove to the alley behind Skavoovee, and then dumped her on the ground after Chad slit her open and carved up her insides.

"But she didn't die. Fuckin' ambulance got there in time to save her."

When they found out on the TV news that she was still alive, they'd panicked. She'd only been semi-conscious throughout her ordeal, but what if she heard enough to remember them? Seen enough to know where they'd taken her?

They'd decided to scout the hospital and see if it was possible to finish the job there.

With every word that he'd forced out of the man's mouth, Mark had had to resist the impulse to kill. To raise the tire iron and smash it straight down on the shaven skull over and over until there was nothing left but spattered brain and shattered bone. But Deasdolish was only one, and he wanted all four. Plus the five local freaks that had joined in the destruction of his little sister.

"Where are the others?"

"Huh? Others what?"

Deasdolish was fading in and out of consciousness now, and Mark had to be careful. Too much pain and the man's mind would snap. Too little, and he'd simply stop talking and retreat inward.

"Where's Chad?"

"Waiting."

"What is he waiting for?"

"Girlfriend."

"Chad has a girlfriend?"

"Waiting for that nigger's girlfriend."

Ice formed in Mark's chest.

"Where is he waiting?"

"Hospital. Bitch is a nurse."

Terri! Oh god. Terri. He fought to calm himself.

"What's the plan?" He forced his voice to be friendly, like he was part of the conspiracy.

"Four. She gets out at four. They're gonna get her when she comes out. I gotta do the kid, but then I'll meet 'em."

"Where?"

Deasdolish tried not to tell. Mark couldn't believe that there was any resistance left, but it didn't really matter. He stretched the man's remaining earlobe, sliced carefully, then began to pull.

"*Aaiieeeeeee.*"

Too hard. Deasdolish had passed out again. Mark slapped him, but got no response. "C'mon, asshole, wake up." Another slap. "*Wake up fuckhead!*"

It did no good. The man just lay there, limp, with his tongue lolling out of his mouth, and his breath coming in uneven gasps. Mark slammed the wall in frustration, then got himself at least partly under control.

"Calm. Stay calm." *Air.* "Get some air." Fresh air would help. He opened the door and walked out for some cool air, and straight into the arms of two men.

If he'd had any warning, any at all, he'd have got at least one of them, but they must have been listening at the door, because they were on him instantly, immobilizing him and taking him to the ground.

But even as he prepared to die, regretting only that he could not take them with him to hell, he realized that they were not hurting him. That they were yelling his name.

"Mark. C'mon, man, stop the fucking thrashing. It's us, man, we're on your side."

His mind was split in two. Half still trying to make his body throw off the attack, half trying to come to terms with what he was hearing.

"Take it easy, bro, take it easy."

"Sandy?" He went limp, and when he did, they relaxed their hold on him. "Dean?"

"Right here, bro"

"What the fuck?" He sat up, and when he did, a third set of hands came from behind and helped him to his feet.

"Don't you look like a bag of shit."

"Bones!"

"Aye. I've been looking for you for two days, and now that I've found you, I'm not sure I should have looked. What's going on? Who have you got in there, and why are you torturing him?"

"I…" It was too much. He couldn't talk. He wanted to be unconscious. To be dead. He felt his legs beginning to tremble. Then he remembered Terri. They were coming for Terri.

He drew in several deep breaths, stood tall, pulled his shoulders back. "Give me thirty seconds."

He calmed his breathing, marshaled his thoughts, and began.

"His name is Robert Deasdolish. He's one of the fake skins that I tangled with in the bar a month or so ago. They're the ones who have been doing the home invasions and the racial beatings. They're the ones who…" He started to shake, fought for control, then continued. "They're the ones who raped and murdered Sarah. They're planning to do the same thing to Terri."

The shaking began again, and this time it was harder to control. "They're going to grab her when she goes off shift, and take her somewhere to do the same thing they did to Sarah. I'm trying to find out where they're going to take her, but he keeps passing out."

Bones said nothing for ten long seconds. In the light that was spilling from the lantern in the shack, Mark could see the concentration on his face. Finally he spoke. "She'll be safe, Mark. She was feeling shitty this afternoon and called in sick. They can wait there as long as they want, they won't find her."

He looked over Mark's shoulder at Dean and Sandy. "Take him down to the creek and clean him up. I'll look at what he's got inside."

"Yes, sir."

"Wait. How did you…"

"They'll tell you while you wash up."

The cold water was like a slap to his mind. He'd stripped off all his clothes and waded in, rinsing off dirt, mud, and blood by the light of

Dean's flashlight. He splashed his way back to shore and as he squee-geed the water off his body with his hands, his friends explained.

"It was Bones. He was worried about you and called us figuring that maybe we might have heard from you. He knows that you've been calling us pretty regularly since we got back from Croatia."

"Yeah, and when he told us what had happened to your sister, we were on the first plane out."

"How'd you get leave?"

"Leave? Well I guess yesterday and today are gonna be okay, but we're going to have to make up something good to cover tomorrow."

"We're sorry about her, bro, and about your dad. But at least she's going to recover."

"She is? But..."

"Yeah, Bones was saying that his daughter's been keeping pretty close tabs on her. I guess she's a nurse at that same hospital. She says they had her on the table for eight hours or something and managed to get everything repaired."

"She lost a ton of blood, but you guys got to her fast enough that it didn't kill her. She's gonna be okay, Mark."

Mark was overwhelmed with relief. He'd known from what Deasdolish said that Sarah was still alive, but he'd assumed that it was only barely, that she would soon be gone.

"And it sounds like Bones' daughter's gonna be okay, too." Sandy handed him his clothes. "All we gotta do is alert the police that the perps are hanging round the hospital somewhere, and they'll collar the whole lot of them. They're on bikes and there's a few vehicles as well that we need to watch out for."

Mark finished dressing. "Better get on to that pretty soon. It's gotta be past midnight already."

Dean's flashlight illuminated his wrist. "Midnight? Where you been, soldier? It's fuckin' near three-thirty. What time would she have got off work?"

"Four."

"Well then we better get on the phone pretty soon. They'll hang around for a while after four, in case she's havin' coffee after her shift, but eventually they'll bug out. You got your cell, Sandy?"

"In the car, but I think we oughta talk to Bones before we go calling 911. I mean, they're gonna want to know how we know, and I don't think we should tell them about Mark and that guy in the shack."

"Right. Let's go. You got your shoes on, Mark?"

"Yeah."

The flashlight illuminated the forest and they tried to avoid tripping as they made their way back to the shack.

"Bear left, man. We'll never hit it dead on in the fucking darkness. Let's just stay left a bit and we'll pick up the trail from the graveyard."

Dean angled about ten degrees left, and within a minute, they were on the trail. As they walked toward the shack he said, "So, is she your girlfriend? Is that why they were looking to get her, too?"

"Well, I…"

"Ah, you don't have to tell. We're just your best buds."

"And anyway, she's safe. They don't know where she lives, right?"

"They… Oh, fuck! They *do* know."

Mark hauled ass to the shack, calling, "Bones! Bones!"

Bones came to the door. "Where's Terri, Bones? You said she called in sick. Is she at your place or at her place?"

"Hers. What is it?"

"They know where she lives, Bones. He told me they followed both her and Sarah around. They'll know where her house is. We gotta get there. Right now."

Bones took over. He'd been out of the regiment for over twenty years, but his training had been a lot deeper than any of theirs.

"You come in that van we saw in the graveyard?"

"Yes."

"Stephens? Publicover?"

"Here, sir."

"Hang on a minute." He pulled his own cell phone off his belt, dialed, listened for a minute, then said, "Terri, it's your father. This is important. If you're listening, pick up the phone." He paused a moment, then continued. "Okay, when you get this, call me immediately on my cell. Immediately. It's the guys who attacked Sarah. We think they may have you on their list."

He turned to Mark and the two soldiers. "You okay to drive, Mark?"

"Yes."

"Okay, take these two and head for Terri's house. You know where it is?"

"Yes."

"Good. Now listen. Stop at the first payphone you see and call 911. Give them Terri's address, tell them she's going to be murdered, and hang up. Then…"

"I can call them as soon as we get to the car."

"Yeah, and when they track you down from your number, you'll tell them that you knew because Mark kidnapped and tortured this guy?"

"Ah. Right."

"Okay. Stop at the first payphone. Call 911. Then motor for Terri's place. Stop a few blocks away and scope it out. If the police are there, then stay the fuck out of their sight. And for Christ's sake remember that cops *always* back each other up. There's going to be another car or two cruising that area, and if you act the least bit suspicious they'll collar you." He stared at them, one after the other. "You guys got that?"

"Yes, sir."

"What about you, Bones?"

"I'm going to stay here and talk to the guy inside. You did okay, Mark, but I'm a professional. I'm not going to let him pass out and he won't hold anything back. Not from me."

Bones' voice was so savage that Mark felt the muscles up his spine shiver. "As soon as he tells me where they're hiding out, where they'll have taken Terri if they get to her before the cops do, then I'll phone you and you can start heading that way."

"We need your phone number, sir." That was Dean. Calm as if it was an afternoon walk they were going on. "And do you remember Sandy's?"

"Yeah, I do. 413 802 3544. Right?" He pulled out a business card and handed it to Dean. "Mine's on there." He reached into his pocket and pulled out a key ring and removed one of the keys. "Mark, this is the back door key to Skavoovee. There's a sawed-off shotgun in a bracket under my desk. You'll be going within a few blocks on your way to Terri's, so stop off and get it. Shells should be in the lower-left drawer. Now go."

Five minutes later they were at an all-night 7-11. The call took less than thirty seconds and they were on the road again, across the Second

Narrows Bridge, and barreling in along McGill toward the center of the city.

"Keep the speed down, man. We get pulled over and we won't be helping anybody."

Mark fought to keep his foot lighter on the gas, then just about jerked the van off the road when Sandy's phone rang.

"Yeah... Okay, hang on a sec." He passed the phone to Mark. "It's Bones." Mark took the phone and spoke into it. "Yeah?"

"You know the big sugar refinery on Powell?" Mark could hear the sound of an engine. Bones must be on the road himself.

"Yeah, we're going to be passing it in a minute."

"That's where they've been squatting."

"Three blocks and I'm there."

"Don't stop. The tavern's only another five minutes and we need the shotgun." Bones's voice was steady, but Mark knew the man well enough to hear the tension in it. "There may be as many as ten or twelve of them in there, Mark, and that's just too many to deal with unarmed."

"But what if..."

"Mark, listen to me. Even if they've got her in there, they'll have only just arrived. They'll be keeping her alive for as long as they can, and we've got a hell of a lot better chance of saving her if I've got that gun."

"But..."

"I'm her father, Mark. I've loved her for a lot longer than you have. Do as I say."

"Yes, sir. What about the police? They've got SWAT teams trained for this sort of thing."

"I've been trained for it, too, Mark, and so have Stephens and Publicover. Now drive on, get the gun, and meet me at the main gate. I'll probably get there about the same time you do. Now, let me talk to Stephens."

Mark handed the phone to Sandy and concentrated on his driving. He could hear only one side of the conversation, but he knew what was happening.

"Stephens, sir." Then, after almost a minute of silence, "We could, but we're not going to. He's our best friend. He's saved both of our asses... no way we're walking out on him now." He paused for a moment, then added, "Besides, if we walk, then you're going to *have* to let the police handle it, and that means that some of the fuckers will live."

Dean, who'd figured out what was going on, took the phone and said, "You going commando on this, sir?" Then, "Not as easy as that, sir. It's true that a SWAT team could do it, but there's no way they're going to run an operation like that just because you phone and tell them to. It'll take them way too long to set it up. They'll have had her for a couple of hours by then." He listened for a while. "No, no firearms. Nothing. What have you got in the tavern?"

When he hung up, he turned to Mark. "We're going in with you, bro." Mark reached behind him and threw his arm around Dean's shoulders.

"Thanks, man. But you better think about this twice. It's not the kind of war where you get medals. If anything goes wrong, you're in jail for the rest of your life."

"Shut up. When you crawled into that ditch and dragged me out, you wouldn't have gone to jail if something went wrong, you'd have been fucking dead. Besides, if these are the same guys that you told us about after that fight, then they murder helpless old people and kids. So don't talk about it anymore. Just drive."

"What was that about firearms?" asked Sandy.

"I told Bones we didn't have any. He's got the one shotgun, with two or three rounds in it. There *might* be a box of shells in the drawer but he says he thinks he took it to the range a few weeks ago. There'll be plenty of knives in the kitchen. They won't be combat knives, but the cooks use them and they'll be real sharp. He said we should bust up a couple of chairs too, use the legs for clubs."

"What about the bad guys?"

"The ones that Mark fought don't have any firearms, but apparently one of the guys they've hooked up with has a pistol."

"We're here. Let's go." Mark hit the brakes in the alley behind Skavoovee and jumped out, fishing the door key out of his pocket. "You guys been here before?"

"Yeah, we were here for supper."

"Okay, go upstairs, bust up a chair or two. I'll find the shotgun and grab whatever knives I can find in the kitchen."

A couple of minutes later, they were back in the van, headed for the sugar refinery. Mark was explaining the layout as he drove.

"It's on the waterfront. There's train tracks everywhere, so you'll have to watch where you're running. It's huge, and deserted, and there's tons of smaller warehouses around it. Better call Bones and find out where he wants us to meet him."

Sandy dialed, then handed the phone to Mark. "Bones, we're on our way back. Where do we go?"

"Straight along Powell till you cross the tracks, then turn left onto the main access road, the one the trucks use. Go past the sign that says you're not supposed to be there, then take another left and drive along the front of the main building till you come to the end, then turn right. You'll be heading down toward the docks, but turn left again just before you cross another set of tracks. You'll be beside a small machine shop. I'm there now."

"Two minutes. Three at the outside."

He handed the phone back and drove, watching his mirrors and the road ahead for police cars. The refinery loomed ahead, huge and dark. Broken windows high up, gaping like blind eyes. He turned and followed Bones's directions into an industrial slum that was almost completely unlit.

When his headlights lit up Bones's van, he pulled up, killed his lights, and opened his door, but left the engine running. Bones materialized out of the darkness.

"Move over."

Mark moved into the back beside Dean, and Bones climbed into the driver's seat, turned the van so it was facing back the way they'd come in, and killed the engine. "Their squat is in the refinery. It's huge, but they only use one section, on the third floor. They go in and out through a broken door on the waterside, and that's the way we're going to have to go in and out as well."

Bones reached up, found the overhead light, and switched it on. Mark almost gasped. His face and his sandy hair were black

"You guys know what to do with this?" Bones held out a small pail of black grease. "It's not as good as charcoal, but it'll have to do, it's all that I could find in the machine shop. I've stirred some dirt into it."

Dean took the pail and began smearing his face. Sandy followed suit. "You too, Mark."

"I'm so dark I'm almost black already."

"Doesn't matter." Sandy spoke as he was greasing his face. "It's not so much for camouflage as it is for effect. We bust in there looking like a bunch of commandos, and half of 'em are going to piss their pants in fright before the fighting even starts."

"Okay." Mark dipped into the pail.

"Now, everybody better understand right up front that if Terri's not in there, we fade out as silently as we came in, and tip off the police." Bones stared directly at Mark as he spoke. "That means you, too, Mark. I know you want revenge, but there's a good chance that we'll be killed or injured, and the only thing that makes that a risk worth taking is saving Terri. You understand?"

"Yes."

"I need your word on this, Mark. Sarah is going to live, and she's going to need you."

Fury bubbled through Mark's blood, but he understood. If it had been only his own life, he'd have thrown it away carelessly for a chance at revenge, but to get his friends killed... "You have my word."

"That's good. Now, what did you find for weapons?"

Mark handed him the shotgun. "No extra shells. But we did find these." He unrolled a towel to show half a dozen chef's knives. "And these." He reached down to the floor and picked up four heavy chair legs.

"Won't need 'em." Bones pulled an eighteen-inch length of one-and-a-half-inch steel pipe from his waistband. "There's a stack of these in the machine shop." He opened the shotgun's magazine and tipped it to let the contents fall into his hand. "Shit!"

"What?"

"Only one in the magazine." He checked the chamber to make sure there was a round there, then dropped the shell back into the magazine. "I get two shots, and then I'm down to using it as a club."

"Better than nothing, sir. And these guys aren't trained. We could probably take 'em out without the gun."

"At least two of them know how to fight, Sandy." Mark was starting to get worried. "And we don't know how many asshole friends they've made since they got to town. We could be walking into something ugly."

"Yeah, but we've got surprise," said Dean. "Don't forget that. They ain't gonna be expecting us. We're gonna have speed, aggression, and surprise." His voice had turned into a chant, "Think that, and…"

Sandy and Bones joined in, "*it will keep you alive.*"

Bones turned to Mark. "One on one, you can take any of us, Mark. But I know what I'm doing here and you don't, so you're going to have to take orders. Can you do that?"

"Yes, sir."

"Okay. Into the machine shop, get a pipe each."

They all returned a minute later with weapons. "Mark, you take a knife as well. You two," he turned to Sandy and Dean, "you know anything about knives?"

Mark spoke for them. "They'll think they do, but they don't. Better if they just use the pipes."

"But…"

"He's right. Mark, take a knife and a pipe; you two, pipes only. One of you," he sized them up, "Publicover, you take two pipes, be ready to give one to me once I've emptied the gun."

"Yes, sir."

"I'll take point. Publicover, you follow, a bit to my right. Mark, you tuck in behind him, slightly to my left. Stephens, you got tail-end Charlie."

"Yes sir."

Mark understood. Dean was big and tough, but Sandy was more careful, and Bones had picked that up. Mark was the best fighter, he would be better with his left hand, so he got the left side, while Dean would be able to use the hand he was best with. If they got into serious hand-to-hand, that would all go out the window, but on patrol it was the best arrangement.

"Okay, let's go. Walk softly and stay about three meters apart. If I stop, you stop. Any sentries, I'll deal with them."

They filed into the darkness, following the older man back toward the refinery, staying in the shadows, making good time and no noise.

When they had reached the back wall of the huge building, they re-grouped. Bones spoke: "The door is near this end. You wait here, I'll find it and check it."

He was back two minutes later. "It's clear. Once we're inside, pause for thirty seconds to let your eyes adjust. It's pretty dark, but not black; we'll be able to see if we move carefully. There's a short hall, then a door to some stairs on the right. We go up two flights, to the third floor, where they are. The guy I interrogated told me that it's a huge room, gymnasium size, and there's a lot of old machinery in it. They tend to hang out at the far end. They've blacked out as many windows as they could, but there are some they couldn't reach so they tend to use as little light as possible. Clear?"

"Clear."

"Yes, sir."

"Yeah."

"Okay, there'll be a door at the top of the stairs, but it opens directly into the room, and he didn't think there was a window in it. That means we're not going to know what we're up against until we're actually in, which is fucked, but it's what we're going to have to deal with. When we get to the door, I want you three to back away from me about two me-ters, and let me ease the door open. Clear?"

"Yes sir," they repeated.

It went pretty much as Bones had said it would, and they were soon on a landing, facing a big steel fire door, in darkness, that was about one degree less than absolute. Bones worked on the door, a millimeter at a time until he could glimpse the room on the other side through the crack. The thump of drums and bass oozed through to their side, but not much light.

With it open further, the music got louder and they could make out the outline of an enormous vat, as big as a small house, with huge pipes leading up from it to the darkness above, and beyond that something else. Some kind of huge machine.

Bones went down on one knee and stuck his head through the gap, swiveled it, and hauled it back. He stood again, motioned them close and whispered, "I'm going in. If I come back through the door at speed, take off back down and to the vehicles as fast as you can. If I stay in, and nothing happens for a while, just wait, I'll be doing a recce. If you hear the gun go off, come and save my ass. Fan out, Stephens to the left, Mark up the middle, Publicover to the right, and race for the front of the room. The vats'll give you plenty of cover at first, so make speed. Got it?"

"Yes sir," all three echoed.

He gave the three a thumbs-up and slid sideways through the door. Mark and his two friends held their breaths for a moment, tense with anticipation, then gradually relaxed enough to breathe again.

A full minute passed, and each of them was imagining Bones, slipping from behind one big vat or machine to the next, getting nearer and nearer to ... *blam*!

The sound of the shot hadn't died before all three of them were through the door, fanning out. Sandy went left, Dean went right, and Mark raced between them. It was a huge space, and it was full enough of the big vats and whatever the big square machines were, that at first they couldn't see the far end.

Blam! Bones' last shot.

Mark cranked his speed and when he rounded the last of the vats with the pipe in his right hand and the knife in his left, he saw pretty much what he'd expected. Ten young men, running in every direction, shouting, confused, terrified, angry. In the center of the open space, lying on a mattress, naked and bloody, lay Terri. Bones was standing over her, and behind him, half off the mat and even bloodier, was the body of a man with no pants, and half his chest shot away.

Between Mark and the mat was another corpse.

Even as he took the scene in, it changed. From his right came the blast of a pistol and Bones dropped. Mark's impulse was to charge toward the gun, take out whoever had used it on his friend, but that was Dean's side of the room, and Mark kept his discipline. He didn't slow down, but charged the figure closest to him, bringing the steel pipe down with all his strength, feeling the skull shatter.

There were screams now. Shouts of confusion, then of anger as the men in the room realized that they were under attack and then realized that they outnumbered the attackers.

Another blow with the pipe dropped a kid who was reaching for something under his jacket. Dropped him but didn't kill him.

Fuck. Were they all armed?

Mark dived on top of the kid, plunging the knife into his throat, then reached into the jacket, and pulled out a short-barreled revolver. It was a popgun, a .22 stubby, but it was all there was, and gunfire from his right told him he'd better use it.

He rolled to his feet, parried a kick, leaped back behind one of the big vats, then sprinted to where he figured the shooter must be. He rounded the corner in a long shallow dive, tucked his head and rolled, coming up with the gun in front of him. The shooter was ten meters away. Standing over Dean, aiming down, about to give him the executioner's bullet.

It was too far for accuracy, but Mark fired anyway, one-handed, not with any hope of nailing the guy, but needing to stop him from killing Dean.

It worked, and now Mark dropped the pipe, lined up in classic two-handed posture, and started aimed fire as the guy turned, bringing his own pistol up. He had no idea where his shots were going, though, and was about to dive for cover when Dean grabbed the shooter's ankle and tipped him over. There was a deafening racket of a full clip being hosed as the guy went down, but the shots weren't aimed at anything, and Mark had closed the gap between them before the guy hit the ground, diving the last ten feet, and smacking the pistol away. The little revolver had one shot left, and from two inches, Mark didn't miss.

He had no time to check Dean. Either he would bleed to death, or he wouldn't, but if Mark tried to do anything, they'd probably all die. He grabbed a pipe from where Dean had dropped it and went back to work.

There had been twelve of them originally. Less than thirty seconds after the first shot had been fired; there were only three left. Bones had taken out two with the shotgun, Mark had taken three, counting the one he'd just shot. Dean had nailed one before he was shot, and Sandy, with no guns to deal with, had also taken out three.

That left three. One of them was the bald biker that had landed the shot to Mark's ribs in the brawl at Skavoovee. He was faced off against Sandy Stephens, arms up, ready to use any weapon he could find against him. The other two were coming for Mark, one of them with a knife, the other swinging a length of chain.

They were coming fast, and the guy with the knife looked like he knew how to use it. Mark stooped, grabbed the pistol from the ground, aimed at the chain swinger's chest, and pulled the trigger.

Nothing happened, but Mark was prepared for that and his attacker wasn't. He dived to his left to avoid the shot, exposing his entire side. Mark nailed him across the back of the head with the pipe and turned to face the knifeman.

Not fast enough. The knife that was coming for his upper back sliced his right shoulder as he turned, and his hand went dead. He heard the pipe hit the ground but didn't dare stoop to pick it up.

His attacker backed up a couple of steps. Smart. The more time Mark had to bleed, the weaker and slower he'd become. But by backing away he also gave Mark the chance to pick up the pipe.

Mark bent slowly, but halfway down clasped his shoulder and began to topple forward. A slow smile spread across his attacker's face, and the knife came up in preparation for the final stab.

He never got the chance. Mark turned the fall into a forward roll, and came out of it with a foot sweep that took the guy down like he'd had the earth ripped out from under him. The leg that had swept forward now came back and Mark's heel took the guy square in the face.

He didn't let go of the knife, though, and if Mark hadn't made it to his feet first, he'd have been in serious trouble. He continued with his feet, booting the knifeman in the center of the chest as he started to rise, toppling him onto his back. Then in the exposed crotch, then in the temple.

The temple shot was usually a killer, but Mark took no chances. He scooped the pipe from where it had fallen, and used it to spatter brains over concrete.

The sound of running feet brought him upright, but it was Sandy, coming to his aid.

"You okay?"

"Don't know. He sliced my shoulder pretty bad, but check Pubs before you worry about me. I'll check Bones."

He started toward the mat, but stopped when Terri called, "He's okay, Mark, I can take care of him. You help Dean."

He turned back to where Sandy was kneeling over his friend. "He's unconscious, but he's breathing okay."

Mark knelt and checked Dean's vitals. He *was* breathing okay, and his pulse regular. Weak though. "He's probably losing blood. Find out where."

He turned to Terri, said, "I think we're going to…" and collapsed slowly to the ground.

Returning to consciousness after a general anesthetic is a strange process. Mark came fully awake all at once. Awake, but disoriented. He started to speak, but realized he didn't know what he wanted to say. Then realized that there was no one to say it to.

Strange room, but somehow very familiar. Hospital. That was it. He was in a hospital. With an IV drip plugged into his left arm.

His arm! He turned his head and looked at a mass of bandages on his right shoulder. Something had happened to his arm. He knew that, but he didn't know how or what. Something about a metal pipe was important, too. What? What about the pipe?

Holding it. That was it, his shoulder was cut and he couldn't hold on to the pipe.

Very carefully, and fearing the worst, he tried to curl the fingers of his right hand.

They worked. They didn't work perfectly, but they did work.

What about his arm? He started to move it, but the pain in his shoulder shut him down instantly.

He lay back and tried to calm himself.

"Breathe." He said it aloud. In. Out. In. Out. Slowly, gradually deepening the breaths.

When he was centered, he just lay there. Anesthetic recovery can include panic. He was a paramedic. He knew that. So he didn't try to think or reconstruct the events that had put him in this bed, he just concentrated on the fact that he was alive and in hospital. Someone would be along soon enough to explain the why of it.

Someone did come along, but it was a nurse, and when Mark nodded "yes" to her question about pain, she hit a plunger on the IV, and pretty soon he was floating out on Demerol.

When he returned to awareness, Bones was there. So were his memories.

"You're alive."

Bones looked up from the newspaper he'd been reading. "So it seems."

"Dean?"

"Dean, too. He lost blood, but he'll be fine."

"No tissue damage?"

"Tissue… Oh, I see. No, lad, he didn't get shot. He got sliced, same as you. He lost a lot more blood, but there's no muscle or nerve damage. We didn't even bring him to the hospital.

"What about Terri?"

"She's okay. They'd slapped her around some, and cut her a couple of times, but we got there before the raping or the real beating started."

"Not by much, we didn't," Mark remembered a corpse with no pants. "And Sandy? Is he okay?"

"He's fine. He didn't have to face any guns or knives luckily for him."

Mark thought for a while. "Why are you here, and not the cops?"

"They'll be here soon enough, which is why you and I have to have a little chat."

"You sure we shouldn't just tell the truth?"

"If it was just you and me, that's what I'd do. After what they did to Sarah, there's not a court in the world that would sentence either of us, but with your friends involved, it's going to look different. They helped us kill twelve people, Mark, and their sisters and daughters weren't involved."

Mark wasn't happy, but he understood. "I'd like to tell the whole world that we got rid of a bunch of rapists and murderers, but I suppose you're right. But…" he shook his head, "how are we going to explain away twelve bodies?"

"We aren't. And you aren't going to have to explain anything at all. You were in shock after what happened to Sarah. Your ambulance partner and your little brother and half the staff in this hospital can vouch for that. So all you've got to say is that you don't remember a thing. You brought Sarah in, and that's the last thing you remember till right now."

"What about my shoulder?"

"Nothing. You have no idea."

"Bones, it's obvious that I got knifed."

"No shit. And I was right there when it happened. Saved your life, I did. I'll tell the coppers all about it. Maybe even get a medal."

"What about..."

Bones held up his hand. "I don't know how much time we've got, so shut up and listen. You brought Sarah in, in the ambulance, you woke up here. No matter what they ask you, or how they ask it, you don't remember anything in between. Period. End of story. You understand?"

"Yes."

"Say it."

"I remember bringing Sarah in, but then nothing more till I woke up here. But wait, what about this visit? Won't they ask me about what you told me?"

"Probably not. If they do, just say you don't really remember. Stick to that, and don't waver. You can... Whoops, here we go."

Bones stood as two men entered the room.

"Mr. Heaney, I'm Doctor Richards. How's the shoulder?"

"It hurts. What happened to me?"

"You were slashed with a knife." Richards poked and prodded a bit, asked Mark to move various fingers, and then said, "I suspect you'll heal just fine. We'll want you in here for at least another day, but you'll probably do just as well at home after that." He straightened and backed up a step. "This is Detective Hofstadter. He'd like to talk to you about what happened. You feel up to that?"

"I guess so, I..." He let his voice trail off, then, "My sister. Oh my god. How's my sister?"

Dr. Richards looked confused, but the cop stepped forward and said, "She's fine, Mark. She's going to be fine. She would have died if you hadn't got her in as fast as you did, but you got her here in time, and she's going to be okay."

Hofstadter was a heavyset man of about fifty, with dark eyes, dark hair, and thick, dark eyebrows. "I know how you must feel, given that it was the same scum that attacked your sister, but I need to ask you some questions about the fight and..."

"What fight?"

"Last night, when they attacked you."

"I was attacked? After I brought Sarah in?"

"You don't remember?"

He did as Bones had told him to do. He felt stupid, but Hofstadter didn't appear to have any problem with it. So he said, "I don't really remember" about ten times, and then asked if he could get something for the pain in his shoulder.

Hofstadter said, "I'll find a nurse for you on my way out. And once you're feeling a bit better, ask Bones here to tell you what happened. I think you're in for a bit of a surprise."

No shit, thought Mark, and when the detective was gone, he said, "Well? What the fuck have you told them that explains away twelve corpses? And why the fuck are you here with me in the first place? I thought you got shot."

"I did." He turned sideways and bent so that Mark could see the shaved and bandaged area on the back of his head. "Just touched the back of my skull. Knocked me cold, but no real damage."

He stopped while the nurse came in and gave him a couple of codeine tablets. When she was gone, Mark turned back to Bones. "So?"

"Right. Your bedtime story. It seems that after bringing your sister in, you wandered around town, out of your mind with grief, and last night, just about closing time, you showed up at my Tavern. I let you in, and we talked for a long time, till sunrise. When I let you out the back door, you were jumped by a couple of the guys you'd rumbled with a month ago, the same ones who had attacked your sister. One of them managed to slice your shoulder, but I leaped from the dark doorway and saved you by cracking both their skulls with a piece of pipe that I keep by the back door for just such occasions."

Mark let that sink in. "Okay, what about Sandy and Pubs?"

"What about them? They were at my daughter's place, sound asleep."

"Which she, of course can swear to."

"Absolutely, but she'll never have to because they're simply not part of this."

"And the guys who supposedly jumped me? The guys you supposedly bashed with your pipe?"

"Lying dead in the alley, with their brains spattered on the pavement."

422

"What about the other bodies?"

"What about them?"

"They're going to be discovered eventually, aren't they?"

"Maybe, but it's not our problem. We have a perfect alibi. We were busy killing some other guys. Now go to sleep."

When he awoke next, Terri was in the room. Holding his hand, even though he'd been asleep.

"Hi Terri."

She shifted in her chair, but kept his hand. "Hello Mark."

"Can you help me sit up?"

"Sure. I'm a nurse, remember?"

Once he was sitting, he put his hand out and she took it again. "You're okay?"

She didn't answer immediately, but eventually said, "I've asked myself that question a lot, and I think I'm being honest with myself when I say, 'Yes, I'm okay.'" She squeezed his hand.

"I was scared… I knew they were going to rape me, torture me, and then kill me. So yeah, I was terrified. But they hadn't really done much other than rip my clothes off and slap me around a lot when you guys arrived." Tears started down her cheeks. "Honest Mark, I was more scared about what had happened to my dad than about myself."

Mark didn't want to ask the next question, but he knew he had to. "How's Sarah? Everybody says 'she's doing just fine', but that sounds like bullshit to me."

"It is and it isn't." Once again Terri thought carefully about what she was going to say. "Physically, she's in rough shape, but she's going to heal. She'll be in hospital a lot longer than you, but eventually, she'll be fine. Emotionally, there's bound to be permanent damage. Anybody who says otherwise is insane. But I've talked to her quite a bit now, and I think that there's hope that it won't turn out as bad as you're worried it will. You see, when they jumped her, the first thing that happened was that one of them leaped out of the van and hit her right in the face with his fist."

"This is good? Those guys are trained boxers. It must have…" He thought about what Terri had said, "She was unconscious for most of it, wasn't she?"

"She was. She's going to be told what happened to her, but she won't really remember it. She'll need lots of support, but maybe, just maybe, she'll come through without too much damage."

She stood up from her chair and sat beside him on the bed. "Does it hurt if we sort of lean against each other?"

"No." He put his good arm around her. "No it doesn't hurt at all."

HELP US

If you'd like to help us out please go back to where you ordered the book from online and put up your review with your comments. Let us know if you'd like to see this expanded into a series or not. We'd appreciate this massively and we look forward to reading your review. Thank you!

SUBCULTURE

Ska music for those that don't know, originated from Jamaica long ago. Most of the bands that you will see in this section played it. The pictures within cover the late 80's to 90's mostly. Vancouver subculture during the 1990's wasn't a stand-alone thing. There were many groups of people that intermingled. At gigs and also at pubs like the Rose & Thorne, which was on Richards Street in Vancouver. At a punk show you could expect to see skinheads, punks, gothics and scooterists' all under the same roof. You could even expect to see skaters and even the odd surfer too. These photo's cover a span of several commonwealth countries and show faces of people who enjoyed going out and seeing a live show of non-mainstream music. It was varied and it was a lot of fun. Sadly Vancouver has changed dramatically since that time with a population and real estate surge, which has erased much of what once was. Many of the local music venues are now gone. So here's to all of you who lived the rebellious life back then.

All pictures except for one have come from a book previously published in 2001 called Skavoovee. It went out of print. It's the same story rebranded. Less Pictures this time around though.

Heather, Kari-Anne, and Marie at a local show in Vancouver, 2000

Lise Wessling, vocalist for the Managers, a Ska band in NZ

A gray day in New Zealand, 1991

A long time ago. Whiterock, B.C. 1989

Victoria's ska festival 2001

Being on the sound team is usually a thankless job, but not here!
Thanks very much for a really fun Ska Festival guys.

Jeannette and Scotty

The female Ratpack (Faye, Heather, and Marie) Vancouver, B.C. 1991

Ricky takes a smoke break in Victoria, B.C.

No longer in Business unfortunately

Marie's ska night.

The punk rocker guy and his lady friend.

On the streets in Gastown, Vancouver

Having fun at Ska Fest in Victoria, British Columbia

Andrew enjoying a beer

CFUV Radio's Skanksters Paradise
Dave & Chris

Fed, Daver (of Skankster's Paradise) and his girlfriend in Victoria, BC

Brandon the nomadic traveller. He's travelled to over thirty countries with nobody's support but his own and has worked in every one of them. He's only 27! We can learn a lot from this lad.

What would life be without one's dog?

Pete and Marnie in Australia, Gary's behind them.

Marie's friends in Poland, having a few laughs on public transport.

Jay on his chopper in Vancouver, B.C.

Gary and Kelly (left), Elizabeth and Pete Porker (right).

Heather in Vancouver, B.C.

Heather, Faye, and karri-Anne in the background

The Allentons

The Hoodwinks. Tyler, Mike, Jesse, and Mick

At a local gig in Vancouver, BC.

If we were there we'd be smiling too brother!

Vancouver, B.C. in the early 90's

Buster Bloodvessel of Bad Manners and the Revrend Raph from The Seen

Dave Wakeling of The English Beat and Lorraine Kingpin
of Montreal's infamous band – The Kingpins

Here's one of Chris Murray's releases, which fans can purchase at
either Asian Man records on the net, or through Chris' own web site
at www.chrismurray.net.

Here's Monkey Bone, trombonist of the Arizona band Warsaw Poland Brothers. He's addicted to working out as you can see – nothing wrong with being healthy and strong.

The Seen's guitarist. What a beauty of a guitar!

Behind the scenes – breakfast on the road with The Kingpins.

A couple of Australia's typical hotties at the Bad Manners show in Melbourne

Aaron and Chris, two of the three Poland Brothers,
doing their thing. Great bunch of guys

Mike hanging out with Buster Bloodvessel after a wicked show
at the Evelyn Hotel in Melbourne, Australia

One of the three Poland Brothers, on stage.
They're traveling like no other ska band – 300 shows a year!

The Porkers, as of late 2002.

Faye in Vancouver, B.C.

The Kingpins. One of Canada's best Kept secrets til now.
Check them out at www.thekingpins.com.

Warsaw Poland Brothers (Ska Band) singing the night away!

Victoria, B.C. Scooter Rally in 1991. Picture taken by Simone Gore.

Marie and Kari-Anne

Happy Couple in Vancouver

Oi!

Vancouver, B.C. early 1990's

Great ink jobs!

More of the same.

Greg and Lorna

The dog farts were really bad!

Dennis and Heather with Chris Murray in Vancouver, B.C.

Mike Williams at PBS in Melbourne,
Australia doing his ska-reggae radio show.

1989, Vancouver, B.C.

Legendary front man – Chris Murray of King Apparatus (ska band) with a local trombone player named Andy.

Pete Porker in Australia getting ready to go on next.

Chris and a buddy. Vancouver, B.C.

Buster Bloodvessel on the right from Bad Manners

Riding on the hard sand beaches of
the North Island, New Zealand, 1991

Johnny (Left) and Jarrod (Center),
at the English Beat, 2001, Vancouver, B.C.

Pete Porker (left) with Buster Bloodvessel on the beach in Australia

The Porkers – A legendary band from NSW, Australia

Jay, Early 1990's in Vancouver, B.C.

Having a great time at Ska Fest in Victoria, B.C.

Vancouver, B.C. Year 2000

Pete at Greasy Joes in St. Kilda. Melbourne, Australia